A Vampire for Christmas

Laurie London

Michele Hauf

Caridad Piñeiro

Alexis Morgan

A Vampire for Christmas

**LAURIE
LONDON**

**MICHELE
HAUF**

**CARIDAD
PIÑEIRO**

**ALEXIS
MORGAN**

HQN™

ISBN-13: 978-0-373-77644-3

A VAMPIRE FOR CHRISTMAS

Copyright © 2011 by Harlequin Books S.A.

The publisher acknowledges the copyright holders of the individual works as follows:

ENCHANTED BY BLOOD
Copyright © 2011 by Laurie Thompson

MONSTERS DON'T DO CHRISTMAS
Copyright © 2011 by Michele Hauf

WHEN HERALD ANGELS SING
Copyright © 2011 by Caridad Piñeiro

ALL I WANT FOR CHRISTMAS
Copyright © 2011 by Alexis Morgan

This edition published by arrangement with Harlequin Books S.A.

For questions and comments about the quality of this book please contact us at Customer_eCare@Harlequin.ca.

® and TM are trademarks of the publisher. Trademarks indicated with ® are registered in the United States Patent and Trademark Office, the Canadian Trade Marks Office and in other countries.

www.Harlequin.com

Printed in U.S.A.

CONTENTS

ENCHANTED BY BLOOD

For Kandis, who shares with me a love for horses
and books, as well as a birthday.

Acknowledgments

Thank you to my sister, Becky,
who happens to be my critique partner,
for pointing out the bad stuff without making me
feel...well, bad. Janna, Mandy and Kandis,
my beta readers, were willing to drop everything
on a moment's notice. I seriously love you ladies.
Thank you to my editor, Margo Lipschultz, because
without her, this story wouldn't have existed, and
thanks to the team at Harlequin Books for their
incredible support. My husband and two children
totally get the blue ribbon cool family award. And to
Alexis, Caridad and Michele, I am truly humbled.

CHAPTER ONE

"So who are you planning to kill?"

Trace Westfalen didn't glance over at the sound of his friend's voice. Instead, he shoved his phone into an inner pocket of his suit, strode to the wet bar in the corner of the conference room and poured himself a straight shot of Jack. Without waiting for his fangs to fully retract, he drained it in one swallow.

"I wish," he said, wiping his mouth with the back of his hand. "That would improve my mood substantially."

Dominic Serrano shut the double doors and approached the bar, his boots thudding heavily on the hardwood floor. From his leather pants, black leather jacket and the *brindmal* coiled at his hip, Trace knew he must be heading out soon. As the leader of the Seattle field team of Guardians—vampires tasked with keeping the peace among their own kind and the existence of vampires a secret from humans—he wasn't one to sit back and send others on duty out to take care of Darkblood scum. He led by action, not rhetoric. Trace really respected the guy for that.

Dom raised an eyebrow. "Council bullshit?"

"Yeah, you could say so."

Normally a fairly patient man, Trace rarely lost his temper—necessary traits for a member of the Governing Council. Only that was the problem. He hadn't been sworn in yet and the vote, scheduled for next week, had been postponed again. His family had held a seat on the Council almost from its inception centuries ago and the transfer from parent to child was usually just a formality. He gripped the edge of the counter, fighting to control his growing impatience.

"Pour me one," Dom said, holding out a glass. "Not too much, though. I'm on the clock tonight." After Trace filled it, Dom sat in one of the high-backed chairs and took a sip. "I feel for you, man, I really do. I've had my share of run-ins with them. No offense, but they often have their heads up their asses."

Trace laughed bitterly. "No offense taken."

"Want to hit the streets as a Guardian tonight, for old times' sake? Take your mind off what you're dealing with? Might do you some good to work off some of that excess energy." Dom crossed his legs and the leather creaked. "Believe me, wailing on DBs or other vampire riffraff can be very therapeutic."

"Yeah, don't I know it." After his father had passed away last year, Trace had resigned as a Guardian with the Agency, the Council's enforcement division, and moved to the Seattle area to take over his father's seat. He'd been in limbo ever since, doing mundane tasks but having no real power. Tonight's update to the Council using the field office's secure video feed basically amounted to busywork. They'd been dicking with him, dragging their feet, coming up with one excuse after another for why they couldn't take the vote. Although he knew they were slow to make changes, he was starting to get a really bad feeling about this.

"And it's very tempting, but—" Trace pointed to his Ferragamo loafers and Armani suit "—do I look like a guy who's ready to kick some Darkblood ass tonight?"

"That can be easily remedied. We've got whatever

you might need. We've even got things you didn't know you needed." Dom leaned back in his chair and clasped his hands behind his head, clearly unaffected by Trace's foul mood.

He couldn't believe how calm and easygoing his friend seemed. When the two of them had worked as Guardians out of the Southeast's Perdido Bay Region, Dom's temper had been of Richter scale proportions. In fact, he'd gotten kicked out of the region and sent to the Seattle field office to chill out, which was where he'd ended up meeting a woman and falling in love. Guess it was true that everything happened for a reason, because marriage and fatherhood seemed to agree with the guy.

"Boots, leathers, weapons, guns," Dom continued. "In thirty minutes, we'll have you outfitted and ready to go. What do you say?"

Looking at Dom's *brindmal*, a bullwhiplike rope entwined with silver threads designed to weaken their enemies, Trace flexed his fingers. God, he'd totally love to grab his favorite weapon, a dual-tipped scorpion knife designed to slash multiple attackers, and put it to good use tonight.

It had been a long time since he'd charcoaled a DB. Pierced the heart muscle with a blade of silver and watched the body curl in on itself and turn to ash. It was pretty satisfying knowing you'd eliminated a threat to the vampire race's peaceful, yet secret existence alongside humans. Unfortunately, Guardians hadn't yet succeeded in eliminating the threat completely—if they ever would. The Darkblood Alliance believed they belonged at the top of the food chain, feeding from and killing humans, not comingling with them. To profit from their depravity and expand their influence, they harvested human blood and sold it on the vampire black market to fringe elements of their society. Sweet, the rarest of all blood types, was extremely addictive and went for the highest price. Trace had to admit, frying one of these bastards tonight would be very therapeutic.

As he reached for the bottle again, a vague unease skimmed along his nerve endings. He tried to take a deep breath but it felt like something was coiled around his lungs, slowly choking him. He loosened his tie but that didn't help. Glancing around the conference room, he was struck anew by the fact that the field offices were located far beneath the city streets with no exterior windows. The walls seemed to be closing in, pressing against his chest, making him wish he was anywhere but here.

Fresh air. That's what I need.

"Thanks, but I've got a long drive back to the estate." He rapped his knuckles on the back of Dom's chair as he passed. "I'll catch you later."

Now that his job here was done, he couldn't get out of the field office fast enough. Within minutes, he'd climbed into the black BMW X4 and roared out of the garage. But instead of jumping onto the freeway and beginning his drive home, he found himself heading to a part of town he hadn't visited in a long time. Despite the winter chill, he rolled down the windows and inhaled deeply.

Finally, he was able to breathe again.

CHARLOTTE GRANT had made a serious mistake by not inviting another friend along tonight, but there wasn't much she could do about that now.

She stood outside the Wonder Bar and watched as Kari hung on the arm of a guy she'd met less than an hour ago and disappeared around the corner without so much as a wave back.

"Live and learn," Charlotte muttered to herself as

she dug out her car keys, automatically sticking a finger through the loop on her pepper spray. No doubt she'd let the location of the club sway her decision to go with Kari.

She'd always loved this part of the city, with its eclectic mix of shops and galleries situated on one of the hills overlooking Elliott Bay. Especially at this time of the year, when the air had a bite to it and held the promise of snow. Her breath fogged in front of her face. She imagined how nice it would be to stroll along the sidewalk with someone special as they looked at all of the holiday window displays. His hand would be warm, or maybe his arm would be around her shoulders. His laugh would be infectious. If she tried really hard, she could almost smell his cologne. Sandalwood maybe? No, an evergreen smell, she decided. Like a Christmas tree.

She sighed and shook her head to get rid of those silly thoughts. As if she'd expected to meet someone like that at the club tonight.

"Want me to call you a cab?" A bouncer the size of a refrigerator held the door open for a large group of people leaving the noisy club. "Looks like your friend ditched you."

"Yeah, she pretty much did," Charlotte agreed.

Kari wasn't known for giving a crap about anyone but herself. And Charlotte should've known better. Especially when a hot guy was involved. Although this particular guy's hotness was debatable. He was much older and had the physique of someone who spent all his time behind a computer. The only way he'd have a six-pack was if he'd added it on Photoshop.

The bouncer cleared his throat, yanking Charlotte from her thoughts.

"I'm fine, though, thanks. My car's not far away." She

pointed down the street. "I can just about see it from here."

A large group of women exited the club, laughing and hanging on to each other's arms. Charlotte stepped aside to avoid getting jostled.

"Hey," the bouncer said to the group in general, "which way are you ladies going?"

That way and down there, were several of the replies. Same direction as Charlotte's car.

The bouncer held his hand out with a flourish. "I give you your escorts."

At least someone cared about her welfare tonight. Charlotte flashed him a grateful smile. "Thanks."

"No problemo."

The seven women moved like a swarm of bees down the sidewalk, constantly buzzing with mindless chatter. Every few feet, they'd stop and laugh at something else. It wasn't hard to keep up with them, just frustrating. Charlotte was tired, cranky, and kept thinking how good a long soak in her tub would feel.

"He's great, isn't he?" Kari had gushed in the ladies' room right before she told Charlotte she was going home with that guy. "I just love his sense of humor." Code for *I know the guy isn't hot but I need an excuse to sleep with him.*

"Yeah, if you like older men who don't know your eyes are above your cleavage." Charlotte knew the real reason her friend was attracted to the guy—his company's fat wallet. In sales, the client was king and quota was everything, and Kari was one of those people who'd do anything to meet hers.

Charlotte didn't care how desperate or at the end of her rope she was. She had scruples and self-respect. Even though she and Kari worked in different industries, she'd never sleep with a client. If she couldn't land a design job on her own merits, then it wasn't meant to be.

The beehive stopped again—this time to take off someone's shoes. Charlotte sighed. She'd had enough. The parking lot was on the next block and, from where she stood, she could see the red car she'd parked next to. She bypassed the group, dancing out of the way as a woman flung her arm out dramatically, and continued down the sidewalk.

Served her right for going out on a weeknight anyway. She reviewed tomorrow's busy schedule in her head. A few client meetings and she couldn't forget to check on a delivery. Mrs. Wilson would be really upset if her new dining table didn't arrive as scheduled. Charlotte had redecorated the woman's home, convincing her that the dated old table had to go. With the holidays right around the corner, Charlotte was afraid Mrs. Wilson would have kittens if the new one didn't come in soon.

As she stepped off the curb, something flashed in the corner of her eye. She glimpsed a pale blue Volkswagen Beetle parked in front of a Dumpster in the alleyway. Peering into the shadows beyond it, she saw nothing but darkness. She moved to the far edge of the sidewalk anyway and picked up her pace.

A breeze blew past her, its icy blast ruffling her hair. She shivered. Taking a bath in a tub filled with hot soapy water up to her earlobes was sounding like the best idea she'd had all day.

As she pulled her coat up around her neck, her heel caught in one of the cracks of the cobblestones. She tried to catch herself, but she lost her balance and hit the ground fast. A jolt of pain shot through her wrist.

Something sounded behind her. Laughter, maybe?

God, how embarrassing. Could this evening get any worse?

She winced at the pain as she pushed herself up. Had the women seen her? She glanced around, but the bee-hive had crossed the street and were on the next block over, just as oblivious as ever.

Only the wind, she decided. She brushed tiny bits of gravel from the heel of her hand and wondered whether it was bad enough to warrant being iced when she got home. Her ankle, too. Damn. The next time she talked to Kari, she'd—

There was a whisper, then a shuffle of feet.

She whipped her head around and surveyed her surroundings. Nothing but an empty sidewalk lined with colorful awnings, large potted plants and—

A shadow on the ground outside the vintage clothing store she'd just passed looked a little odd. She narrowed her eyes. It definitely didn't match those cast by the plants in a nearby pot. It seemed thicker. Like…a person.

Was someone hiding behind one of the trees? Was… was someone following her? A cold lick of fear snaked down her spine, threatening to morph into panic.

She walked away as fast as she could without running, her heels clicking efficiently. It was nothing, she told herself. These buildings were filled with apartments and condos above the ground floor. Probably just a tenant. At night, spooky things were easy to imagine. Besides, if she screamed right now, a zillion people would run to her aid.

Thank God her car was near—she could see the bumper now.

When she glanced back over her shoulder to reassure herself that it was just her crazy imagination, she almost choked. Two dark figures, less than twenty feet away, were coming straight toward her. Something dangled from one guy's hand. A rope?

Dread settled over her like a wet blanket.

Ignoring the pain in her wrist, she turned and ran. She pressed the remote on her key ring. The taillights on her car blinked, the *chirp chirp* a friendly hello. She'd jump in and quickly lock her doors. Should she use the button on the door handle to lock it behind her or use the remote? Remote, she decided, as she sprinted into the parking lot.

Wait. The panic button on her car alarm. She could hit that and—

A large man stepped from the shadows between two cars and jerked at the tie around his neck.

Arms flailing, she slid to a halt on the loose gravel.

As he stormed straight at her, a roaring, rushing sound rang loudly in her ears. Oh, God, he was going to use it to tie her up. This had to be a setup.

Before she could scramble and change direction, he strode up and steadied her with a large hand. She wanted to shrink away from him, but he held her upright. Thanks to the overhead streetlight, much of his face was in shadow. All she could make out was the hard set of his jaw and a steely glint in his eyes as he surveyed the darkness behind her.

Just as she smelled the faint evergreen scent of his cologne, the white of his dress shirt drew her attention. A hoodlum in a suit? The image didn't make sense. Was it possible that this man didn't belong with the two chasing her? That he was here to help her?

He leaned in close. "Get into your car, lock the doors and wait for me."

The concern in his voice was unmistakable. Maybe he

was in law enforcement and knew a bad situation when he saw it.

Without waiting for her response, he dropped his hands and was gone.

CHAPTER TWO

TRACE WAS GOOD at getting people to follow orders, but for once, he wished he wasn't.

As he rounded the corner of the building and found the tan Volvo parked in the exact same spot it had been twenty minutes ago, he felt a strange mix of satisfaction and anger.

He flexed the fist that had just made contact with someone's jaw. He'd easily caught up to those two parasites who'd been after Charlotte and taken care of them. They weren't Darkbloods, but they weren't model citizens of the city's secret vampire population, either. As soon as they realized that Trace was one of them but wasn't carousing around on the hunt for the same thing they were—a vulnerable human host—they'd taken off. He'd hauled their asses to the ground in a nearby alley and called one of the Agency's capture teams for a pickup.

Good God, what kind of a woman would listen to a complete stranger? A sane, reasonable one would've gotten the hell out of Dodge the minute she climbed into the car.

And the Charlotte Grant he knew had always been sane and reasonable.

How the hell had all this happened tonight? Why had he been drawn here when she'd needed him the most? It wasn't like this was an area he'd frequented much. In fact, the last time he was here, he'd been with Charlotte.

He kicked a small stone, watched it bounce off the edge of the sidewalk. He recalled the claustrophobic sensations that had forced him to abruptly leave the field office, as if his subconscious knew something he didn't.

His stomach clenched at the thought of what those two would've done to her. Being a former Guardian, he knew only too well the horrors his kind could inflict upon humans.

And Charlotte was—

Jesus, why hadn't he insisted she take a self-defense class? Taught her how to use a gun? Given her a blade of silver and shown her how to wield it? He thought about her canister of pepper spray. Sure, it was effective against human lowlifes, and for that, he was glad she carried it. But it was hardly a deterrent to a revert, a vampire who gave in to the bloodlust of their ancestors. The urge for blood was a powerful one and once activated, it was not easily controlled. No, he decided, self-defense techniques wouldn't have worked on those two.

Over the past year, there'd been many times when he'd ached to see her, wanted to drive past her house to see the light on in her kitchen window. The thought had even crossed his mind to "casually" bump into her from time to time. In line at her favorite Starbucks. At the bakery where she bought her bread. At the pet store where she bought Augustus's special cat food. He could've easily inserted himself back into her life, but he hadn't. He'd remained true to his promise, his pledge to stay away.

Until now.

He recalled the way she'd looked at him under the streetlights. She'd been leery at first, frightened. Yet there she was in her car. Waiting for him.

Doubt nagged at the back of his mind. Maybe the memory wipe hadn't been deep enough. Could she have remembered him on some level, enough to know that he wasn't a threat?

Impossible, he decided as he tugged at his already-loosened tie and headed across the lot. He'd been thorough and very careful. Others he'd worked with over the years in the Agency may have been reckless and foolhardy, but not him.

As he approached Charlotte's car, he tried not to think about how long it'd been since he'd last seen her. Tonight, she was simply a stranger he'd helped, not someone with whom he'd once had a passionate affair.

Yes, just a stranger.

He knocked on the driver's side window.

Charlotte jumped, her eyes widening before she rolled it down halfway. Holy hell, she looked good. Twin spots of color formed on her cheeks, her skin just as smooth and touchable as he remembered.

"Did you—"

"What the hell are you still doing here?"

Her jaw dropped as if he had slapped her. "You told me to wait, didn't you?"

"And you always do what a stranger tells you?" Things would've been so much easier if she had left. He didn't want to deal with her. He just wanted to forget her.

Why did I ask her to wait then?

Irritated with himself, he wanted to pound on something again. Split-second decisions for a vampire among humans, especially a Council member, had to be the correct ones. Slipups and mistakes could be costly. Why did he always forget who he was and what his responsibilities were when he was around this woman?

Her chin jutted out indignantly. "I couldn't just leave. Not without knowing what happened."

"Why? You don't know me."

"Well...I..." For a moment she looked flustered, unsure of herself. Then, just as quickly, her expression darkened. "If I think the stranger is a cop, then yeah, I listen. I might need to give a statement or something. I don't know how these things work. It's not like I've ever been the victim of an almost-mugging before."

More like an almost-murder, he thought bitterly. "A cop would identify himself. I didn't."

"Yeah, I get that now." With a shaky hand, she tucked her chin-length raven hair behind an ear.

"You're way too trusting," he growled.

"Gee, thanks for the insight." She grabbed the keys, sucking a hissing breath through her teeth as she tried to turn the ignition.

"What's wrong? Did they hurt you? I thought—" If he knew those two bastards had touched her, he wouldn't have arranged for a pickup. He'd have staked them then and there and watched their bodies turn to ash.

"I'm fine," she said curtly. "Thanks for coming to my aid."

No, she wasn't. "Let me see your hand." He opened the door and leaned in.

She gasped.

Damn. He was being too forward with her, forgetting that he needed to act as if she were a stranger to him. To make himself less intimidating, he knelt so that he had to look up at her face.

The faintly vanilla scent of her skin filled his nostrils, bringing back all sorts of memories. Talking. Laughing. Long walks through the city. Burying his nose in her hair as he made love to her.

He ground his teeth together and forced those thoughts from his head. Relationships with humans were frowned upon, especially for a Councilperson who was supposed to set an example for others to follow. Although matings between vampires didn't always produce offspring, those with a human never would. Maintaining their population, especially given that its numbers were so low, had always been one of their prime objectives.

His relationship with Charlotte last year had progressed quickly. What he'd intended to be just an indulgence had turned out to be so much more. Although she hadn't known the truth about him, he had begun having real feelings for her. Then there was that horrible business with his cousin, which, coupled with the deathbed promise he'd made to his father several months before, had been the catalyst that had forced him to do the right thing. Over and over he'd told himself it was a blessing in disguise when he had to wipe her memory. She could never know the truth about him. Not only did she deserve much more than a relationship built on lies, but if he wanted the Council to vote him in, things between them had to end.

"I told you, I'm fine. I don't need your help. You can leave now." Her voice was strained and she still looked frightened from her ordeal. He'd been too short with her.

This would be the perfect opportunity to step away and close the car door, let her leave, he told himself. But his feet felt cemented to the spot. "Please."

She hesitated, but still didn't give him her hand.

"Those two were bad news. I figured you'd just drive away." He ran a finger inside his suddenly too-tight collar.

She looked appalled. "Without knowing what happened? What if you had needed help? It was two against one, you know."

Touched by her concern, he resisted the urge to reach out to her, run a finger along her jaw. Nothing had changed about her. She was still more concerned for someone else's well-being than her own. Hell, if he'd thought things through, he'd have known she wouldn't leave without finding out what had happened to him.

He'd count to three, he told himself, and if she still refused his help, he'd go.

One. Two.

She held out her hand and he took it before he said three.

The instant he touched her, a jolt of electricity shot up his arm and she gave a gasp of surprise. Just as quickly, he put up a mental barrier to stop the sensation.

He'd forgotten how easily her energies transferred to him. Or how easily his body accepted them. Most humans couldn't feel when a vampire was absorbing their energies like this; they'd simply be more lethargic than normal. But Charlotte sure did.

"Sorry about the static electricity. Happens to me sometimes." Gently, he turned her hand over, trying to ignore the residual warmth flowing through his system.

There were some minor abrasions on the skin, he noted as he brushed off the dirt. Had she broken a bone? Torn a ligament? As gently as he could, he felt the joint. "Does this hurt?"

"A little, but it's nothing. If it's bad tomorrow, I'll go have it checked."

A knot twisted in his gut as he thought about watching her drive off again the way he'd done last year.

"Hold on," he said, stalling. "Let me buy you a cup of coffee and we'll get you some ice. There's a late-night diner on the next corner. It'll give you a chance to catch your breath before you leave."

She seemed to be examining his hands as he held hers.

Her wrists were tiny and he could easily encircle them with his fingers.

"I don't even know your name," she said quietly.

"It's Trace." He purposefully didn't give his last name. She shouldn't recognize it, and yet…

"Well, it's nice to meet you, Trace. I'm Charlotte." She lifted her lashes, the turquoise blue of her eyes meeting his.

And after a moment between heartbeats that seemed to stretch forever, she agreed to have coffee with him.

Ten minutes later, they were sitting in a booth, staring at a plate of stale cake doughnuts they hadn't ordered.

"I'll bring you that ice in a minute, hon," their waitress said, heading back to the counter.

Charlotte looked at the doughnuts then raised her eyebrows quizzically.

Trace shrugged. "When you come in late like this, they bring out any extras to get rid of them. They're not bad if you dunk them."

"I don't eat carbs at night."

That was right. He'd forgotten. "Suit yourself."

He added cream to his coffee and stirred it around with his finger. Then he broke a doughnut in half, dipped it and took a bite.

When he glanced up, Charlotte was looking at him, a mixture of amusement and disgust on her face. "What?"

"Ever heard of a spoon before? It's an eating utensil first used by ancient Egyptians, originally made from ivory, bone and wood."

He leaned back against the red vinyl and laughed. Yes, his dunking was rather uncivilized. Being a Guardian hadn't done much for his manners. He often slipped back into old habits when he wasn't thinking about it. "Thank you for that trivia lesson."

"My pleasure."

He rubbed a hand over his stubble as he studied her. She lifted the white coffee mug to her lips, blew off the steam and took a sip. Evidently not finding it too hot, she took another one.

That raven hair of hers swung playfully against her delicate jawbone as she moved. Earrings with ruby and amber crystals dangled like pendulums. Her cheeks were still flushed from the cold, and she kept her lips parted slightly, even after setting down her cup, as if she were catching her breath.

Or as if they'd just made love.

Intimate memories immediately flooded his thoughts. He was as powerless now to resist her charms as he'd been when they first met.

Last year, his grandmother had hired her to decorate the family estate for the holidays. Despite trying to remain aloof, he'd found various excuses to be with her. Not only was she one of the most beautiful women he'd ever met, but he loved her funny stories, her sharp wit, her passion for making things beautiful. He could walk into one of the many rooms in the mansion and know that Charlotte had done something to it, even if he couldn't put his finger on what had changed. All he knew was that the room had a better feel.

The fact that she cared about the smallest detail fascinated him. Things he'd never deemed important—the placement of a decoration, the way the lights needed to hang just so, the perfect pleat in a pillow—began to have meaning to him because they had meaning to her. Hell, he'd even gotten into the habit of doing the karate-chop thing to fancy pillows, because it was something she'd done.

Everything about her was unexpected, including the

first time they'd made love. He'd been helping her decorate one of a dozen holiday trees inside the mansion—each one with a different theme. As he recalled, this particular tree had a forest animal motif or something. She'd been on the ladder, reaching forward to hang a wooden squirrel ornament, when she lost her balance. He'd caught her before she hit the floor. He still remembered how she'd smelled that day. Like vanilla with a touch of evergreen tree. She'd even had pitch on her fingertips.

Before he'd known what he was doing, he'd kissed her. And she'd kissed him right back. The next moment, one hand was sliding under her red cashmere sweater and the other went to her tight little bottom. When she responded by curving her hips against his and wrapping her arms around his neck, it was all over.

Thank God they'd been in the library. He'd kicked the door closed, locked it and set her down roughly on the edge of the desk. Before he'd even unzipped his trousers, she'd lifted her skirt and removed her panties. He could still remember her fingers digging into his backside and the beautiful sound she'd made when he—

"Hello. Anyone in there?"

He blinked to find Charlotte looking at him, an ice pack on her wrist. The waitress was looking at him, too, her order pad out, her pencil poised above it.

And he had one monster hard-on beneath the paper napkin in his lap. Shit.

"What was the question?" He crossed his legs, put a hand casually over his knee.

"It's a complicated one," Charlotte said. "It goes something like this—'Can I take your order'?"

Smart-ass. He laughed, balled up his napkin and tossed it at her. "What are you having?"

"I'm fine with just coffee."

To the waitress he said, "I'll have two eggs, over easy, with a side of bacon and an orange juice." Ordering a meal would stretch the time he had with her. He waited until the waitress left to address Charlotte again. "So tell me, what you were doing walking alone on the streets at night?"

"I wasn't. Not really."

"Well, it sure looked that way when I saw you." What the hell had she been thinking anyway? He knew precisely the kind of filth that roamed the streets at night and Charlotte had no business leaving herself vulnerable to it.

She told him about her friend leaving her stranded at the night club and about following a group of women almost to her car.

"Almost?" he asked her. "Almost only counts in horseshoes and hand grenades."

"Isn't it supposed to be *close?*" She lifted an eyebrow as if to taunt him, her eyes sparkling with mischief over the rim of her coffee mug.

"Excuse me?"

"The expression is, 'close only counts in horseshoes and hand grenades.' Not *almost.*"

He'd forgotten how she'd loved being right and pointing out how he was wrong about things that didn't matter. Just like his grandmother, she was a trivia hound and a member of the grammar police. Which was probably why the two had gotten along so well. His grandmother had been sorely disappointed when he'd told her about wiping Charlotte's memory—she hadn't spoken to him for weeks afterward. But she knew the rules just as well as he did. If humans found out about the existence of vampires, their memories had to be erased.

There'd been too many instances in the past when this hadn't been done and rumors of vampire attacks panicked whole villages. Those had been dark days for their kind, caused by a few careless individuals. The Council was formed to establish a rule of law for his kind to live by in order to keep their existence secret.

Charlotte was looking at him expectantly. He almost argued with her about the horseshoe thing—he was pretty sure she was wrong—but he didn't. He couldn't let her affect him that way. The playful teasing. The easy back-and-forth. He couldn't let her work her way into his heart again. For his sake and hers, he needed to remain detached. He'd stay long enough to make sure she was okay to drive and that would be it.

When the waitress returned with their order, his stomach growled. He'd had no idea how hungry he was. The meeting tonight at the field office had involved dinner, but he hadn't felt like eating then.

"How is your wrist feeling?" he asked, lifting the eggs onto the toast with a fork. "Is the ice helping? Think you'll be ready to drive in a few minutes?"

A shadow passed across her features. She nodded and turned slightly away from him, rattling her coffee mug as she set it in the saucer. "Yeah, I'm fine."

She was not fine. She was clearly still shaken up. Frazzled. Hell, knowing what those guys had been planning still had him freaked-out, too.

While Charlotte had another cup of coffee, he finished eating. He couldn't let her drive home like this, he decided. No way, no matter how unwise it was to prolong his time with her.

"I'll give you a lift and you can come back for your car tomorrow."

"No, I couldn't ask you to do that."

"You didn't. I offered."

She sucked in her lower lip, chewed on it a moment as she played with the balled-up napkin he'd thrown at her.

He tried again. "I won't be able to relax until I see that you're home safe and sound."

If she said no, he could always follow her. Or he could check up on her later, assuming she lived in that same little house east of Lake Washington. Yeah, he could make sure she was safe, but she'd still be freaked-out. The overwhelming urge to comfort her and take away her fear was too much for him to ignore.

She narrowed her eyes, tilted her head just slightly. "Are you sure you don't mind?"

"Not at all." He could've sworn he saw a hint of relief in her expression. He quickly paid the bill and ushered her out of the restaurant.

CHAPTER THREE

WHAT HAD POSSESSED HER to let this man drive her home? In her car?

With one hand on the steering wheel and the other resting on the console between them, he sat comfortably in the driver's seat of the Volvo, as if he'd been driving strange women home all his life.

She studied him out of the corner of her eye. He appeared to be in his early to mid-thirties, the lines in his face apparent only when he frowned or smiled. His light brown hair was fairly short, yet long enough to look messy. Bed-head messy. He had large, capable hands, with slender fingers and short, neat nails. She'd always felt you could tell a lot from a man's hands. His were fairly smooth, but there was a rugged quality to them that suggested they hadn't always been that way. If those hands were anything to go by, she'd guess he had brains and brawn.

One of the most attractive men she'd ever seen, he had an intense magnetism about him that was undeniable. If he'd kissed her back in the restaurant, she was pretty certain she wouldn't have refused him. But letting him drive her home? God, what was she thinking?

Rather than taking his car, he'd insisted they take hers, then he'd call a cab to bring him back. At first she'd protested. He'd done enough to help her out. But when she remembered her busy day tomorrow, she had second thoughts. The meeting with Mrs. Wilson was first thing in the morning. If she had to come back beforehand to pick up her car, it'd put her way behind schedule. She just couldn't do that to the woman. Her client was keyed up enough as it was.

Readjusting the bag of ice on her wrist, she stared out the window at the twinkle lights on the trees lining this city block. It wasn't like she was pulling a Kari, going home with anyone who suited her fancy. She was simply taking up a Good Samaritan on his offer, that was all.

She watched, mesmerized, as he tapped his pointer finger on the steering wheel to some unknown beat. Her heart seemed to synchronize itself to the rhythm. One… two…three…four.

What would it feel like to have that hand sliding over her flesh? Her face heated at the thought. Would he be gentle or commanding? Were his fingers dexterous and skilled, able to find all the right places and know what to do when they got there? She was certain that this man knew his way around a female's body. He was too gorgeous not to have been with many women.

Okay, she seriously had to stop thinking this way. She shifted awkwardly in her seat, trying to eliminate the sudden twinge in her lower belly. It was as if she could feel the beat of her heart there. Calling to him. Needing him.

Char, come on, girl. You're not Kari.

Reaching into her handbag, she pulled out a tube of lip balm and smeared some on her lips.

It wasn't just his hands that captivated her. His eyes did, as well. Inside the restaurant, she'd found herself staring at them, wondering if they were blue or gray. With just a rim of color around the edges, his pupils were unusually large, like twin tunnels leading straight to his soul. She could totally get lost in those eyes if she weren't careful, agree to things that she'd normally never consider.

At this time of night, traffic over the floating bridge was light. Less than a half hour after leaving the diner, they were pulling up to her house. She started to reach for the door handle and winced as pain shot through her wrist.

"I'll get it." In a flash, he was out of the car and opening her door.

She stared at the long, narrow walkway through the trees and cursed herself for not having replaced a few of the burned-out landscaping lights. The house was set back from the road and these patches of darkness would've really freaked her out if Trace hadn't been with her. She couldn't imagine walking here on her own after what she'd experienced tonight. "I can't thank you enough."

She glanced at him as they strode toward her front door. She couldn't help but notice that he carried himself with a casual elegance and didn't look at all like someone who had just beaten up a couple of hoodlums in a dark Seattle alleyway. "It was nothing."

"So, what do you do for a living?" she asked as she stuck the key in the lock. "You really did seem like a law enforcement officer of some sort back there in the parking lot. Once I got over thinking you were one of the bad guys, that is."

One side of his mouth curved up and when he rubbed a hand over his jaw, she heard the faint rasp of his stubble. Her face heated at how intimate it sounded. It was the familiar sound, not of a stranger, but of a lover first thing in the morning before he'd shaved. The heaviness again gathered low in her belly at the thought of waking up next to Trace.

"As a matter of fact, I am in private security. It's a family-owned business. So I guess you could say that people's safety and well-being is a concern of mine."

Ah, that explained a lot. She swung the door open and stepped inside. "Can I get you something to drink before the cab gets here?"

He looked at her again with those fathomless eyes. "A glass of water would be great."

She put her things down and entered the kitchen. "I take it you work downtown?" Now that she was back home and feeling a little more centered, she had a million questions for him.

"The company has offices all over the world," he called from the other room, "but right now, I'm here."

When she returned a moment later with his water, he was thumbing through her design portfolio, which she'd left on the coffee table, and absently petting her cat.

"Wow, Augustus doesn't normally like strangers. I'm impressed."

A shadow passed over his face, but just as quickly it was gone. "You're an interior designer." It was a statement, not a question. "With your own business?" He sounded surprised. Did he not like her work?

"Yes," she said, her tone guarded. "I broke out on my own a few months ago."

He scratched behind Augustus's ears, nodding thoughtfully as if he were analyzing a business decision. "And what is the name of your company?"

"Charlotte Grant Designs. I do a lot of home decorating, also staging homes for sale."

He looked confused as he flipped through more pages. "What are these party photos?"

For some reason, it pleased her that he'd actually looked at the pictures closely enough to notice that. "I've done some event planning, too. Small corporate affairs, mostly. Christmas, New Year's, product launch celebrations, that sort of thing."

When she sat down next to him on the sofa, her hand accidentally brushed his. In an instant, a snap of static electricity tickled the tiny hairs on her arms before she jerked it away. She laughed nervously. "That was, um… weird again. It doesn't usually happen unless I'm walking around the carpet wearing my fuzzy socks."

"Not a problem." His tone, a tad deeper now, sent tiny chills along her arms. "How's your wrist feeling?"

"Much better. Thanks."

She glanced up to find him staring at her, as if he were looking at her for the first time. Her cheeks heated under his scrutiny.

"You…ah…sure you're okay?"

She was touched by his lingering concern. Most men wouldn't bother to ask, let alone notice that she might still be shaken up even if she seemed fine on the outside.

"Yes, I'm much better now." *Because of you,* she wanted to add.

She was suddenly aware that her knee was almost touching his thigh. Less than a finger's width separated them. If she relaxed her leg slightly, it would fall against his. Holding it very still so as not to brush him, she reached for the portfolio and turned the pages. "Here… ah…let me show you the pictures of one of the last events I did."

As he examined the three pages she'd devoted to it, a tiny muscle in his jaw flexed and his nostrils flared slightly. Was he pissed off? she wondered, tensing her shoulders. Her dad used to do the same thing prior to one of his tirades, like he was holding back his anger for a moment before it all exploded.

"Does Xtark regularly employ you?" he asked icily.

Surprised he recognized the company from the event photos, she was confused by his reaction. "Xtark Software? How did you know? Are you a gamer?" Although they designed other software, Xtark was known mainly for its games, and Trace didn't strike her as someone who played them.

"I'm familiar with their corporate logo." He pointed to a picture. "It's on this banner."

Still, that was very perceptive. "It was the first time I worked with them." She chewed on her lower lip, wondering whether to leave it at that. But she had to know what was bothering him. "Why?"

He hesitated as if he were considering his words carefully. "Let's just say that I've heard about some less than positive things they may or may not have been involved in."

Talk about a qualifying statement. He sounded like someone who didn't want to commit one way or another. Aware that their knees were now touching, she didn't want to move for fear she'd only draw attention to the fact that she'd noticed. "They seemed fine to me. Very supportive of my ideas. They paid well and they paid on time. I'd gladly do more work for them."

He grabbed her hands, startling her, his expression ice-cold. "Promise me you won't work with them again."

"Um…" It was the biggest check she'd received all year. How could she say no if the job came up again? "I don't understand. Why does it matter?"

"Because…I don't trust them and…" He stared at her mouth. Her lips felt hot, almost swollen, under his gaze. Sparks of excitement shot down her spine. Was he going to kiss her? Her breathing grew shallow and she saw just the tip of his tongue before he spoke again, though this time it was more of a whisper. "And you matter to me." He leaned in close and captured her mouth with his, stealing whatever it was she was going to say.

SHE WAS MUCH TOO VULNERABLE. He couldn't believe she'd done work for Xtark. Guardians had become suspicious that it was a front for Darkblood activities and were planning an investigation. No matter how much they paid her, it wasn't a place for a human—particularly not a beautiful woman like Charlotte.

Her lips were soft, her breath minty from the gum she'd chewed earlier. She leaned into him and he pushed his tongue inside before he could think about where that action would lead them. With a tiny moan that made him ache, she wrapped her arms around his neck, opened her mouth to his.

He leaned into her, pushing her back onto the sofa, and slid a hand roughly up her shirt. His residual anger about Xtark morphed into a driving need to care for and protect Charlotte.

Did she still wear the bras with the closure in the front?

He reached up, caressed the soft flesh spilling out the top of the lacy cup. Yes, she did. His fingers easily unfastened the clasp and her breasts sprang free.

"Oh, my God," she whispered against his lips, as his thumb brushed over her nipple. Her fingernails scraped across his scalp, grabbing a handful of his hair possessively. "Yes."

That was all the invitation he needed. With one hand, he unfastened his jeans, eager to feel her from the inside for the first time in almost a year.

Although he'd slept with other women since they'd been apart, it had been mindless, meaningless sex, meant only to keep his aggressive tendencies in check. Most vampires were very sexually active because of this, Trace included. But with Charlotte, things had always been different. Sex with her hadn't been to simply satisfy a need. Sure, that was how it started, but they had connected on so many other levels, as well.

"The bed," she mumbled against his lips. It was a command.

Not one to ignore an order like that, he pulled her from the sofa and led her down the hallway. He didn't bother to ask directions; he knew the way.

By the time they reached the bed, his erection was straining painfully behind his zipper. Without a word, he pulled off her boots and tossed them behind him. When he reached under her skirt to pull off her tights, she gasped, her eyes widening.

Had he somehow read her wrong? Was this too much? Had he gone too far? Too fast? He hesitated, his fingers curled under the waistband of the tights, not moving. After all, he was a stranger to her and he was acting as if he'd done this with her before. Which he had. Only she didn't know it. "You don't want this?"

A laugh bubbled from her lips. "Um, quite the opposite. It's just that I don't normally do this sort of thing with men I've just met."

Relieved, he flashed her a smile. The last thing he wanted to do was freak her out in any way.

Without looking, he opened her nightstand drawer, found the condoms she kept there—he resisted the urge to count how many in the box were gone from the last time he was here or see if it was a new box entirely—and he quickly sheathed himself. Although a vampire couldn't get a human woman pregnant, he needed to keep up the illusion that he was human. A twinge of guilt nagged at him, but he shrugged it away.

She'd found out about the existence of vampires once and he'd suffered the consequences of losing her to a memory wipe. He wasn't about to arouse any suspicions that he was anything but a normal human male. A man she'd never seen before. He was simply a one-night stand.

"Oh, my God, you're…you're… It's really big." Her eyes widened as she stared at him.

Masculine pride surged in his chest. Having her think that this was the first time they'd made love definitely had its advantages. He pushed open her legs and settled above her. Her inner thighs were warm and smooth, just the right amount of softness under his fingers.

"Will it fit? I mean, well, of course it will, but…" Her nails dug into his forearms, her hair splaying out on the pillow beneath her like a dark, wild halo.

"I'll go slow, Char. I promise." He kissed her mouth, her neck, the tender spot right behind her ear where her pulse beat frantically beneath his lips. All the while, he kept his fangs carefully in check.

He reached between them, slipping a finger inside her. She was warm and silky soft. She moved against him, encouraging him to continue. Easing in a second one, he pressed his thumb against the little ball of flesh at her opening. She moaned against his lips and his fingers slipped in deeper.

He chuckled. "It'll fit now."

Her heart was pounding so loudly that he heard it in his head, like a drumbeat calling a warrior to battle. Thank God he'd taken blood not long ago and it was only desire that called to him now.

Her fingertips were cool as they tracked up and down his back. He knew from experience that he'd be feeling her nails in a minute. "Good, because I really want you."

He grabbed the base of his erection and positioned

himself carefully. As he slipped the tip between her folds, he stared at her heart-shaped face to gauge her reaction. Her lashes were thick against her cheek, her tongue darting out to wet her lips as she waited for him to continue. Slowly, he pushed into her warmth.

Holy mother of God. His fingers curled around the sheets beneath her and balled into fists. Her body was tight—so damned tight around him. Every fiber of his being urged him on, demanding he claim this woman as his own. Deeper, harder, all the way to the hilt.

But he couldn't. He needed to go slow.

She hissed in a breath.

"Are you okay?" he asked, hesitating.

"Oh, my God. Yes." Her short nails dug into his back, urging him to continue.

Inch by inch, he continued to ease himself in, pausing several times to give her a chance to adjust to his girth. It was a lesson in patience, but he didn't want to hurt her. Finally, when she arched her hips a little more, he slid the rest of the way in. Out of habit, he reached for the small decorative pillow beside her head and tucked it beneath her bottom to keep her hips tilted up. She giggled.

"What?" he asked, but then he remembered. She's always found it funny that he used her pink polka dot pillow this way.

"Nothing," she answered. "It's…this is…incredible."

Yes, yes it was. "Char," he managed to say into her hair. "You feel amazing. I'd forgotten—" Man, he needed to seriously slap some sense into himself. He'd almost screwed up and told her this wasn't the first time he'd made love to her.

When they'd been together, they could hardly keep their hands off each other. It was as if their bodies were calling to each other on a totally different plane, demanding more than each of them expected. Then, in the car tonight, he'd tuned in to the beating of her heart.

Want me. Take me. Love me, it seemed to be saying.

And he couldn't get that rhythm out of his head.

Oh, God, how he'd missed this. Forgotten how it felt to have this woman beneath him. He kissed her and slid his fingers into her hair. There was that tiny moan again, vibrating against his lips. Rocking his hips back, he began to move inside her. A voice in his head said maybe it had been foolish to take her home, because it would be harder to stay away now, but he told it to shut up. He'd worry about that tomorrow.

"So...so do you," she said.

He had to have her this one last time. The Fates had put him on the street tonight when she needed him the most. Yes, he'd indulge himself in her sweetness, then he'd never be back again.

He pushed himself up and glanced down. He was now completely hidden within the walls of her body, liquid heat surrounding him. Like this, they were one entity with one goal, joined intimately for each other's pleasure. He sensed the rapid beat of her heart as if it were his own.

Slowly, carefully, he eased himself almost all the way out. Moisture glistened on his shaft, a visual indication of how her body was reacting to his.

"Don't stop," she said breathlessly, her nails digging into his arms.

He laughed. "Believe me, I'm not. I'm just very visual." Although he could tell she was ready for more, seeing it with his own eyes, rather than just feeling it, totally turned him on. Her lips were parted, her chest rising and falling. If he hadn't been in such a hurry, he'd have undressed her properly so that he'd be gazing at her breasts right now.

He grasped her hips and thrust back inside. Harder this time.

With a half gasp, half moan, she arched her head into the pillow, exposing her graceful neck. "Oh, my God," she groaned, grabbing the headboard behind her.

He almost laughed again from the sheer joy of it all. This felt so right, so perfect. Just what he'd been missing. The hole in his heart, present since last Christmas when he'd watched her drive away, suddenly seemed less empty.

Her muscles tightened in successive waves around him, signaling her approaching climax. He sped up his rhythm then, pushing deeper into her warmth each time. The added friction incited every nerve ending along his shaft. In his body. Hell, even his toes tingled. Her body was coaxing, compelling him to let go, as well. "Jesus, you're incredible, Char."

He considered holding back in order to fully experience her pleasure, but it was too much. The whimpering sounds she made were driving him mad with desire.

One last mighty thrust was all it took to send him over the edge with her. She dug her nails in as he came, stilling his hips, locking him deep inside her. A million tiny lights sparked behind his eyelids, his release so intense, it almost hurt. Even though he wore a condom and even though he couldn't get her pregnant, he still imagined his seed shooting out and traveling to all the corners of her body. Leaving a part of him with her when he left.

CHAPTER FOUR

WHEN TRACE ROLLED OVER, it took him a moment to realize the sheets against his skin weren't his own. He cracked open one eye and looked around.

Oh, yeah, he was in the field office. And then, a heartbeat later, memories of last night crashed around him.

He'd stayed at Charlotte's place too long, ignoring the taxi's horn at first, then running out wearing only a towel to throw the guy a fifty.

It was well after dawn by the time he'd left, the sun of the living already cresting the mountains. Without a daysuit or any other protective covering, he struggled to make it out to the waiting cab, the energy leaching out of him with each moment spent under the ultraviolet rays. He wouldn't be able to make the long drive back home, so he'd had the cab drop him off at the Seattle field office. They kept extra rooms available, and he'd slept here several times when he was up from Florida on Guardian business.

He grabbed his phone, half hoping he'd see a missed call from Charlotte before he realized he hadn't left his number with her. She'd looked so beautiful when he stole out of her bed this morning. He'd leaned over, brushed a strand of hair from her sleeping face and kissed her goodbye.

Thinking about their intense connection yet knowing they'd never share a future gnawed at his heart like a freshly opened wound.

He could still hear her laughter ringing in his ears. Taste her on his lips. Smell her scent on his skin. He reached down and gripped the base of his erection. As he recalled every detail about last night, he imagined he was making love to her again and he climaxed quickly.

"Ah, Charlotte, what have you done to me?" he said aloud to himself. He got up and took a quick shower in the adjoining bathroom.

When he re-entered the bedroom, he checked the time on his phone. Six in the evening already? Great. He'd slept most of the day. Everyone in the field office had been up and working for hours. Yawning again, he knew he'd need to get some human energy—maybe blood, as well—to make up for what he'd lost in the sun.

Christ, he hadn't been this unmindful of the hour since he went through his Time of Change centuries ago. As a youthling, getting accustomed to your body's new cravings and staying out of the sunlight didn't happen overnight. Without thinking, you'd step into the sun, then suffer the consequences. But he hadn't done that in ages. However, Charlotte had always had a way of messing with his head.

What was she doing right now? he wondered. He missed her already. Not only had the sex been amazing—hell, one thought of her tight little body was enough to get him rock hard—but he'd loved her insanely funny stories about one of her clients, and the enchanting sound of her heartbeat when she was nearby. He wished he could call her to see how her day went. Had that table arrived for her neurotic client yet?

For the millionth time, he wondered if he'd made a mistake when he wiped her memories last Christmas.

Would she have accepted him as a vampire after witnessing what she had? Sebastian could be a sadistic bastard sometimes, and although Trace hadn't been present when Charlotte had walked in on him feeding from a human host, it had to have been graphic. The shock on her face had said it all.

He sat down heavily on the bed again.

Had Trace's father been alive last Christmas, he'd have been furious at what happened, but he'd died a few months earlier. In his gruff tone, he'd have told Sebastian to be more discreet in his feeding habits, and to Trace he'd have said to quit screwing around with that human woman and act like a Councilperson. He would've chastised both of them into doing the right thing for the Westfalen family. Although technically Sebastian was from the Taft side of the family tree.

Staring at the blank phone screen now, he knew that he didn't have a choice. Not then and certainly not now. It was his duty to take over his father's position on the Council, and at some point, mate with a vampire female. He'd been preparing for this all his life. If he were lucky, the union would produce a child. Given that vampire fertility rates weren't nearly what humans' were, many of the old families had not been able to produce heirs over the years and their lines had died off. His father was adamant that this not happen to their branch of the family.

A sour taste formed in his mouth. After being with Charlotte last night, he couldn't imagine having sex with another female for the purposes of starting a family. Somehow, it didn't seem…right.

Just as he was getting up, the door banged open. Jackson Foss sauntered into the room wearing black sweats, flip-flops and a graphic T-shirt with the name of some gym plastered across his chest. The Guardian had changed the streaks in his hair to crimson since the last time Trace had seen him.

"You look confused." Jackson gestured at Trace's phone with the sandwich he held. "Trying to decide if you're going to click some naked pictures on the internet or what?"

"Don't you knock?"

Jackson ignored the question, took a bite and continued talking. "Oh, wait. I forgot. You're on the Council now. Gotta behave yourself."

"It's not official yet," Trace said, sitting back down on the edge of the bed. "The elders are voting on it next month, right after the first of the year."

"Yeah, but that's just a formality."

"I don't know about that," Trace admitted. He wouldn't have said this to just anyone, but he counted Jackson as a friend. "I'm starting to think something more is going on behind the scenes, like someone doesn't want me to take over. Maybe the incident that happened with my great-uncle is to blame. Our name isn't exactly untarnished."

George Westfalen had been found to be keeping a blood slave on his property to feed his Sweet habit, an act forbidden by Council law. Although the old man had been manipulated by an unscrupulous business manager who got him addicted to the rare human blood in order to gain control over his vast finances, the fallout had reflected poorly on the whole family.

"Any word on how the guy's doing?" Trace asked. "The...ah...blood slave. You keeping tabs on him?"

Most of the field offices kept a list of known sweet-bloods in the area—people who usually came to their attention as the result of an attack. When time permitted, they did drive-by status checks of these humans most vulnerable to unscrupulous vampires. In accordance with

Council law, their memories had to be wiped, but the Agency felt it was their duty to watch over them as best they could.

"The sweetblood guy? Finn? He's cool. Doing work for the field office as a helicopter pilot. And he's got something pretty serious going on with one of our medics, Brenna Stewart. Don't know if she was here when you were, but she's working at one of the clinics now."

How interesting. Most of the field offices did have a few humans working within their midst who knew about the existence of the vampire race, but a sweetblood? He recalled that Dom's wife had been a sweetblood before becoming a changeling. Maybe that had something to do with it. "Her name does sound familiar."

Jackson stuffed the rest of the sandwich in his mouth. "Since you're on your best behavior, I take it, no hanging at the Pink Salon for you? A couple of us are heading there later."

The downtown club had always been one of Jackson's favorite places to pick up women. Actually, he did more than just pick them up there. An entire relationship consummation occurred. "They name one of the private rooms in the back after you yet?"

"No, but I'm working on it."

Trace laughed. "I'll bet." A part of him yearned to be that carefree again. No policies, traditions or family obligations hanging over his head, dictating his every decision, where the only concern was where you were going to go after work with your buddies to get drunk and get laid.

"Then come with us," Jackson urged.

He scrubbed his face, not sure why he was suddenly feeling this way. When he left Florida, he'd been eager to leave the life of a Guardian behind him.

"Best behavior, remember?" He told Jackson about the two guys he'd pounded on last night. "God, it felt good to beat the living crap out of a couple of losers. I do miss that the only conflict you deal with is between your fist and a DB's face. Now, all the sparring and conflict in my world is verbal."

"You're so full of shit. Come on, you're a natural at this stuff—schmoozing with the suits, getting them to agree with you. Besides, you've got it all. A job where everyone knows and respects you. A beautiful home. You've probably got women throwing themselves at you. I mean, you were a decent-looking sonofabitch before, but now that you've got power and money, you're the man. I'm sure all the single ladies want a piece of that. And some of the married ones, too."

"I've been too busy with Council affairs to chase women." He sighed. There was only one woman he wanted to find him irresistible and she was off-limits. He'd need to be satisfied with the memory of last night.

"Speaking of carousing," Jackson said, "are you going to throw that big holiday party again this year? Last year's was the bomb. People are still talking about it— the party atmosphere, the food, the dancing, the sexy times. I hooked up with a couple of lovelies who did me right and I wouldn't mind a repeat performance. Who says that under the mistletoe is just for kissing?"

"No party. Not with everything that went down with Uncle George. The family is lying low."

"Aw, man, that's the very reason you should throw a party. Everyone had such a good goddamn time."

Trace shook his head. "I don't think so."

"If you're worried about the vote, what better way to spread goodwill than by throwing a party for everyone to enjoy themselves? A celebration of epic proportions will trump what happened with your uncle. Push it into the past."

He hadn't thought about it that way. Last year's party had been great. He propped the pillow up behind his head. "Yeah, but it's already late in the year. I'm not sure I could pull everything together in time. Besides, people probably have plans already."

"Some will, some won't. Why don't you just hire that cute little gal who handled everything for you before? She seemed pretty capable."

His gut lurched as if Jackson had just punched him. "Charlotte?" The Guardian's most notorious playboy remembered her?

"Yeah," Jackson answered. "Is she the one with the—" he gestured pointedly "—and the—?" another gesture.

Trace could feel his pupils dilating with anger. He wanted to grab his friend by the throat and shove him against the wall. Sure, he liked knowing that other men thought his woman was hot, but he didn't want to hear it put quite so crudely. And he sure as hell didn't appreciate knowing they were ogling her. Through narrowed eyes, he scrutinized Jackson. If the guy was thinking about her sexually, so help him, the shit was going to hit the fan in a very big way.

Charlotte was off-limits. She was his, and his only.

He rose from the bed and paced to the other side of the room, his heavy footsteps rattling a bunch of crap on one of the tables.

Wait. Why was he thinking so possessively about Charlotte? What was he thinking? Despite their hookup last night, she was definitely not his woman. He rubbed a hand over his stubble and listened to the rasp. What he needed was to be more like Jackson. After having sex, chicks became a distant memory. His friend was in it for one thing and one thing only.

"Since she handled the party once," Jackson continued, apparently clueless that he'd pissed Trace off, "this year should be a snap."

"It would be if she remembered she'd done it."

"What are you talking about?" Jackson stared at him for a moment before he narrowed his eyes at the realization and laughed. "You dog. You boned her and accidentally pronged her, didn't you?"

Trace's fingers curled into fists at the vulgar way he made it sound. If he had ever taken Charlotte's blood, he'd have discussed it with her first and he'd have been gentle, so as not to frighten her. "No, I didn't."

"So what happened then?"

"During the party, she walked into one of Sebastian's little sexcapades."

Jackson whistled. "I'm assuming she saw more than a little horizontal action?"

"Yep. Apparently, she saw him in all his glory. Fangs, blood, sex. All of it."

Jackson's brow furrowed. "You wiped her memory of just what she'd witnessed, though, right?"

"No." He grabbed his suit jacket, which had been hanging over the back of a chair, and pulled out his folded scorpion knife. Opening and closing the dual blades a few times, he nodded, satisfied, at the clicking sound it made. "I wiped her memory of the whole time we were together."

Jackson spread his hands, palms up. "Dude, why?"

Trace shrugged. He recalled the deathbed promise he'd made to his father about duty and honor and family. "I realized things had to change."

Sure, he could've wiped her memory of the incident

and continued on as normal. In fact, he'd automatically touched a hand to her forehead to begin the simple process of sifting through her memories. But as he looked into her eyes, he'd realized how unfair and selfish he was being. He had lied to her and would need to continue to lie in order to maintain their relationship. For his sake, and his sake only. In the end, he'd respected her too much to do that, so he'd done what he thought was best, even though it was one of the hardest decisions he'd ever made.

"It was best to just clear her memory of the whole thing."

"That's intense. Was it hard? I mean, you guys seemed pretty close."

What was it with the goddamn questions? "Yeah, and what does a guy like you mean by that? You get close to every woman you meet. It can't be that difficult to break things off with them. Why are you flipping me crap?"

"Whoa. You need to chill out." If Jackson's eyes were daggers, Trace would have been sliced in two. "My definition of *close* is obviously very different from yours." The guy patted his pockets, searching for something. Not finding it, he walked over to the other set of bunk beds and spent a good minute smoothing a hand over the pillow.

When he spoke again, his voice was uncharacteristically quiet. "I'm talking close. You know, talking and shit, really getting to know each other? Not just rolling around in the sack. Hell, that needs no communicating. When you play poke in the dark as much as I do, it's obvious what fits where."

He flicked the red-streaked hair out of his face with an angry toss of his head and turned back to Trace. "In case you didn't realize it, my friend, there's a very big difference."

His friend's words hit Trace like a punch to the kidneys. He'd had that kind of relationship with Charlotte, but he'd thrown it away.

CHAPTER FIVE

"THE ESTATE IS DIFFICULT to find," Trace had said on the phone. "I'll send my driver to pick you up."

Charlotte forced herself to sit back against the leather seats as the limousine slowed and turned into a long, winding driveway. She'd been in the car for over an hour and was anxious to see the place. Although she strained to see through the tinted windows, she could only make out a few landscape lights marking their way in the darkness.

It had been more than a week since he'd left her house at dawn without saying goodbye. If she'd had his number or a way to contact him, she might have considered calling him herself, thanking him again for coming to her rescue, but she couldn't. But then, the more she thought about it, even if she had his number, she probably wouldn't have called him anyway. He was the one who left her, not the other way around.

At first, she had to admit she'd been a little disappointed when he hadn't called the next day. And it wasn't like he couldn't get *her* number. He knew the name of her company and could easily search the internet for her website. But she, on the other hand, knew nothing concrete about him. Not his cell number, his place of business, the city or suburb he lived in. Hell, she didn't even know his last name.

They'd talked about many things that night—their mutual love of travel, sushi, old horror flicks, watching golf on TV though neither of them played, early Aerosmith tunes. He made her laugh and seemed truly interested in her. And then there was Augustus. God, that cat loved him, which was really saying something. Augustus hated everyone.

But whenever she delved into topics about Trace's work or family, he'd deftly changed the subject. She hadn't realized what he was doing until she thought about it later. Like a politician, he presented only what he wanted her to know about him. Even though she'd had what was probably the best sex of her life, the man was a mystery.

And yet, there was something so familiar about him, too. Something that she couldn't quite place. Like a well-worn groove in the road, she seemed to fit comfortably with him without really thinking about it. She'd resigned herself, however, that it had just been a one-night stand and decided to forget about him.

Then, yesterday, he'd called, wanting to hire her to decorate his home for a big party he was throwing.

At first, she'd considered telling him no. Despite Kari's code of ethics, having had sex with someone wasn't a good way to start a new client relationship. But when Trace told her again how impressed he'd been with her portfolio, she caved. His flattery had totally stroked her ego. Besides, decorating an estate in Rainier Falls, an exclusive, gated community in the foothills of the Cascade Mountains, would look great in her portfolio. She'd be a fool to turn down the opportunity.

She crossed her legs and retied her wool coat, straightening the ends of the fabric belt. Had she remembered to remove the sales tag? A quick check of the sleeves and back collar confirmed that she had. After making the appointment and thinking about what she'd wear, her old coat had seemed a little dated, so she'd splurged on a new one. Surprising what a stylish coat, heels and a good haircut did for one's image, she thought as the car finally came to a stop.

She was merely concerned with her business image, because the last time Trace had seen her, she'd been naked. Her face heated at the memory, even as her heart quickened at the knowledge that she was about to see him again. Not a very professional image by a long shot, so she had quite a big deficit to overcome.

The door opened and the gloved hand of the driver reached in. She exited the vehicle to see a huge mansion looming in front of her. She took a deep breath, hardly believing she was going to be in charge of decorating such a place. It looked more like an English countryside manor with its ivy-covered stone exterior, gabled roofline and massive wooden door. An unexpected architectural style here in the Pacific Northwest, it was much larger than she had imagined. Not knowing how many floors and wings it had, she estimated the footprint to be at least ten to twelve thousand square feet.

She turned to thank the driver, but he'd already climbed back into the limo.

A flutter of movement drew her attention as she strode toward the door. Glancing up, she saw a darkened second-story window, its draperies settling back together in the middle, as if someone had parted them to look out on her a moment ago. Despite the wool scarf around her neck, a shiver of cold whispered down her spine.

She shook the sensation off as she focused again on the house. She couldn't wait to see the inside. Did it have a single, grand staircase leading up or two on either side of the foyer, meeting at a second-story landing? An impressive chandelier? An entry table with fresh flowers?

Marble flooring or travertine? What kind of artwork was on the walls? Postmodern? Impressionist?

Tucking her hair behind one ear, she took a deep breath and raised the heavy brass knocker. But before it could make a sound, the door swung open with a mighty creak of hinges, and Trace stood in the doorway.

Although he wore jeans, a white T-shirt and boots, he could've been heading into a corporate board meeting given his confident and commanding presence. He filled the whole space. She tried not to notice how broad his shoulders were or remember the feel of his muscular back and tight ass flexing under her fingertips.

"Hello, Trace," she said, keeping her tone business-like.

"Charlotte." He nodded, hesitating for a moment before he grasped her outstretched hand, then quickly releasing it.

His warmth lingered on her skin like ripples on the surface of a pond long after the skipping stone hit the bottom. She absently rubbed her thumbs along her fingertips as he closed the door behind her.

"Look, Charlotte, before we get started, I just want to make sure you know that whatever happened between us back at—"

Cringing, she held up her hand, interrupting him. He didn't need to voice all that. "Don't worry. What happened is in the past. This is business only."

A strange expression crossed his face. Relief probably. Most likely he'd expected her to react differently.

"Good," he said, confirming her assessment.

A tiny part of her wished she hadn't been correct. That he saw her as something more. A woman he wanted to get to know on a deeper level, and not just someone he'd spent one night with and now viewed only as an employee. She quickly shoved that futile longing out of her mind and considered the task before her.

The place was just as she envisioned. A grand staircase led to a landing and branched off into twin sets of stairs that curved around to the second story. A massive chandelier with thousands of crystals sparkling overhead cast an array of colors against the walls. The effect was almost magical. She made note to capitalize on that somehow with the decorating. Marble flooring, not travertine, stretched in every direction. And straight ahead on a Louis XIV center table, Christmas lilies were arranged in a blown-glass vase.

She exhaled slowly. "Your home is absolutely stunning."

He smiled, his eyes suddenly more blue than gray. A glint of something she couldn't identify lurked behind them. "Thank you. The estate has been in the family for many years."

"Is it just you here?" She couldn't believe she hadn't brought that up on the phone. At her place, she'd casually asked if he'd ever been married, to which he'd answered no. Sure, he could've been lying, but she was almost positive he wasn't. And yet now that she was here, she felt a little…uneasy.

"Except for my grandmother, who arrived yesterday for the holidays, yes."

"Your grandmother?" A rush of relief eased her tension.

"Yes, I'll introduce you in a few minutes. You'll love her." An undefinable expression crossed his face for a moment. Resignation? Defeat? Was she reading him correctly? If so, for some strange reason, it made her feel… happy.

She took a few steps farther in the foyer until she was almost directly under the chandelier.

This place, these things seemed oddly familiar. As if she'd been here before, which was impossible and yet… She imagined hearing Christmas music playing in the background, silverware clinking against china, the sounds of laughter.

Something else was there, too. Something she couldn't quite put her finger on. Her skin prickled as if brushed by another lick of cold air and she rubbed the back of her neck.

Something frightening. She shivered and fingered the tiny beaded tassels on her wool scarf.

For goodness' sake, she chastised herself as she unbuttoned her coat and slid her purse from her arm. There was nothing frightening about Christmas.

Halloween—yes. Christmas—no.

Like any designer who could visualize things before they became reality, she simply had a vivid imagination. And this was a huge, if not Gothic, old mansion.

"Okay," she said, shaking off those ridiculous sensations. "Let's get started."

WHAT THE HELL had he agreed to? Trace asked himself as he led Charlotte into the sitting room. He was a weak man. That's all there was to it. That, and a damn liar.

As the limousine pulled up the long driveway and stopped at the base of the stone entry steps, he'd watched from the upstairs hallway. The door opened and it had been those legs of hers he saw first as she climbed out. Her skirt had ridden up high on her thighs. A few more inches and he imagined he'd have seen her panties. She did a cute little shake of her ass as she pulled down the skirt then closed the gap in her coat. Heaven help him, that move had gone straight to his groin. He'd absently reached down to rearrange himself, then had taken the stairs two at a time down to the first level.

If he had any hopes of keeping things platonic between them, he had to stop letting Charlotte affect him that way. He couldn't make the same mistake he made last year.

"Ah, there you two are," his grandmother said, setting down her daily crossword puzzle and smiling like a Cheshire cat.

Trace shot her a reproachful glance, still not believing she'd talked him into having Charlotte decorate the house.

After the conversation with Jackson about throwing another party this year, he had to admit the prospect did have its merits. So he'd consulted with his grandmother, whose counsel he'd always valued. Of course, she thought it was a wonderful idea.

"Will Charlotte Grant be handling the decorations again, too?" she'd asked.

He wasn't fooled by her cloying tone. "Absolutely not." He'd planned to hire another firm to handle the party.

Little good that had done. His grandmother had almost made the call to Charlotte herself.

Now she rose hesitantly, pushing herself up from the sofa.

"Grandmother, please." He rushed to help her, steadying her frail body. "This is the woman I was telling you about," he said pointedly. Although she'd lived a long time and had plenty of experience dealing with a human's memory being altered, he felt the need to remind her that she was to act as if she'd never met Charlotte. He tried his best to ignore the stab of guilt at the charade.

"Don't fuss over me," she said to him. "I'm fine. And you must be Charlotte. How do you do, my dear?"

Charlotte extended her hand. "Very well, thank you."

"I'm Victoria Westfalen, but please, call me Vik." An impish look crossed her face and he felt the beginnings of a headache. Although she was in the twilight of her life, having lived through many centuries, she was as sharp as a tack and had a wicked sense of humor. "It really is lovely to see you…" Her voice trailed off and she hesitated. Trace held his breath. She wasn't about to say *again,* was she? "No wonder Trace is so enamored," she continued, spinning a gnarled finger in the air. "Turn around, dear. Let me look at you."

"This isn't a fashion runway," he growled, his mood darkening. "Miss Grant is here to do the decorating, not to be a decoration herself. That is, if she'll even take the job."

"Oh, for heaven's sake, Trace. I just wanted to get a better look at her, that's all. When you get to be my age, looking in the mirror doesn't have the same appeal it once did. Seeing a cute young thing like her brings back an old lady's fond memories from a long time ago." There was that sparkle in her eye again, no doubt caused by the knowledge that Charlotte had no idea his grandmother wasn't referring to a point in time approximately eighty years ago. More like quadruple that.

Charlotte laughed. "I don't mind. My grandmother used to do the same thing. Though she also corrected my posture, told me to enunciate and examined my hands to make sure I was using the miracle cream she ordered from TV. I…I miss it, actually."

"I'm terribly sorry. How long ago did she pass?"

"Several years ago now," Charlotte answered. To Trace she said, "You're a lucky man to still have yours."

"Well, you come sit next to me, my dear." She patted the sofa next to her.

Trace ran a hand over his jaw. She might as well have said, "Come into my lair where we will plot against the sensibilities of my grandson." Last year, she'd made no bones about how much she liked Charlotte. Unlike the old cronies on the Council, his grandmother had always been progressive in her thinking.

"Trace," she continued, "will you have Marcel prepare a pot of tea and a few finger sandwiches? And the cream scones, too. Charlotte had a long drive out here and I'm sure she's hungry."

"Oh, I'm fine, ma'am. Thank you. I ate a little something before I came."

"Nonsense. You haven't truly lived until you've tried Marcel's pastries." His grandmother cupped a hand to her mouth as if she were letting Charlotte in on a secret. "They're to die for."

Trace left them in the sitting room discussing various brands of hand cream. The holidays couldn't come and go fast enough.

CHARLOTTE HAD TO CRANE her neck to see the ceiling in the formal living room and mentally calculated the height. Although the room was large enough to accommodate a very tall tree, she didn't want to go much more than about sixteen feet, purely from a logistical standpoint. "Real or fake?"

"Excuse me?" Trace asked from the arched entryway.

"Are you thinking of a fresh tree or an artificial one?"

He looked up from his phone for a moment, one eyebrow raised as if he hadn't heard the question. "Just do whatever you think is necessary."

Some help he was going to be. She talked through a few of her ideas. A large tree near the window, greenery on the fireplace mantel, Christmas-themed ornamentation, naturally.

"Sounds good to me." He didn't look up from his phone, just kept punching away.

She narrowed her eyes, suddenly needing to test him. *Let's just see how much he's paying attention.* "And then I'll bring in a moose head and nail it to the wall over there. It'll have giant antlers and I'll stuff a bunch of mistletoe in its mouth." She glanced over to him and saw him nodding, so she continued. "I've got a life-size blow-up Santa that we'll set on the sofa and we'll also dress a blow-up doll in a Mrs. Claus outfit. We'll put red and green lights, the large ones, everywhere. From the ceiling, around the doorways, in all the potted plants."

Still he nodded, concentrating only on that damn phone. If he was playing Angry Birds or some other game, she was going to be seriously pissed.

"Then we'll crochet some red and green pillow cushions for the sofas and I'll get a holiday sweater for you to wear at the party. You know how everyone loves wearing Christmas sweaters. You'll have a light-up tie that twinkles when you turn it on. You'll be the envy of all your guests. What do you think?"

"I think it sounds great."

She groaned loudly. "You're hopeless, you know that?" Impossibly gorgeous, but hopeless nonetheless.

"Pardon?" He dragged his attention from the phone and looked up. "I'm sorry. I've got a lot of work-related issues hitting the fan right now."

"I see." Why had he even bothered asking her to run her ideas past him if he wasn't going to listen to a word she was saying? He should've just turned her loose in the house and told her to go for it.

"And, no," he said with a chuckle. "I nix the moose head idea, but the blow up dolls could be interesting."

The laugh that burst from her throat came out more like a snort. Embarrassed, she clamped a hand over her mouth and almost dropped her notebook. He grinned and her face heated up. Great, she'd totally misread him. He had been listening after all. She made a mental note not to underestimate him the next time.

"Are you always that creative?" His eyes sparkled with amusement.

What did he expect, she thought, lifting her chin slightly. He'd been glued to that phone the whole time. "I didn't think you were paying attention."

"You didn't?" He advanced toward her. She wanted to step backward, but knowing the sofa table was behind her, she stood firm. "So you were testing me." He leaned in close, his breath ruffling her hair. The smell of his cologne was warm, but subtle.

Her heart raced as she imagined running her hands over his chest, feeling the muscles beneath his shirt. She would press her nose to his skin, breathe him in, and—Good God, what was she thinking? She grabbed the edge of the table behind her in an effort to regain some control. "I suppose I was."

With his lips parted slightly, he examined her face slowly. Her earrings, her hair, her forehead, her chin. When he stretched out his arm to her, she stilled. But instead of touching her, drawing her close, he reached past her to fish a piece of candy from a crystal bowl on the table. As he unwrapped it, she saw the faintest hint of a smile. Like he knew precisely the effect he was having on her and was enjoying every minute.

"Rest assured," he said. "I couldn't not pay attention

to you even if I tried." Then he turned and she had no choice but to follow him out of the room.

He took her down a wide, window-filled gallery, and Charlotte tried to focus on what she was hired to do, rather than on her hot tour guide. Curiously, all the windows were outfitted with retractable shutters. If she hadn't been examining all the details, she may not have noticed them because the windows were unshuttered now, the blackness outside pressing against the panes.

When they entered the library, her heart rate jumped. The walls were lined with floor-to-ceiling bookshelves. A ladder on a track reached to the second set of shelves above them. Everywhere she looked, there were books. Probably more than some small-town libraries could boast.

The atmosphere seemed charged, almost electric. Like the room was filled with possibilities. Which, she supposed, was accurate.

Needing a distraction, she examined the large antique desk set at an angle near the window. The top was well polished, the scrollwork on the front exquisite. It had to be several hundred years old. She ran her hands over the wood and for some ungodly reason, she found herself wondering if any of its owners had ever had sex on it. It would've been unplanned, of course. Sex on a hard surface wasn't something one set out to do. It would've happened spontaneously.

Her belly tightened, heat concentrating between her legs.

What was wrong with her? Her imagination. These sensations. Clearly, her night with Trace had addled her brain, had left her completely out of sorts.

Despite her efforts to control them, images from the other night kept appearing in her head. She and Trace had made love several times. At first, she'd been fully clothed with only her panties gone. He'd paused only long enough to drop his trousers before he was on top of her. The whole experience had been deliciously naughty. But instead of leaving afterward, as she half expected him to do, he'd undressed her and made love to her again.

This time, with her on top.

Had she really told him she didn't think he'd fit? She tried not to smile at how silly that sounded now. Chewing at her lip, she walked around to the far side of the desk. Every man must dream of a woman saying that to him. Although she'd have to imagine she probably wasn't the first woman to say it to Trace. He hadn't acted all that surprised, just pleased.

Goose bumps sprang up on her arms at the memory of him. He'd been slow and surprisingly gentle at first. One thing she was sure of: it was a night she wouldn't soon forget.

"So how do you envision decorating this room?" he asked.

She gathered her wits about her, took a deep breath, and turned to face him. With his arms crossed, he'd been watching her, a dark expression on his face. Anger? Irritation? Boredom? He seemed so emotionally closed off now, like he'd suddenly erected a wall between them. What was going on with him? She could've sworn he'd been warming up to her. Or maybe it was just her wishful imagination. She stifled her disappointment and had to remind herself that a relationship with a client wasn't a good idea anyway.

"Given that your event is right around the corner, there won't be time to place any orders," she said to Trace as she chewed on her pencil. "I'll have to make do with what we have. Where do you keep your holiday decorations?"

"We've got a storage room downstairs, but I'm not sure what's in it."

"A storage room?" She shivered. Normally, she enjoyed taking inventory of what a client had that she could use, but for some reason, the mention of a downstairs storage room gave her chills.

As if sensing her discomfort, he added, "I'll have one of the staff bring all the holiday boxes upstairs."

She relaxed and opened up her planner. "Perfect. I'll go through the boxes when I come back tomorrow and make a list of things we need. Don't worry. I'm very re-sourceful. Then the following day, I'll hit a few places in town before the Xtark Software holiday party, and if I can't find what we need, I'll—"

His head jerked up, his eyebrows two dark slashes above his eyes. "Xtark Software?"

"Yeah. I didn't handle their party—they'd already had it contracted—but they did invite me."

"And who are you going with? Do you have a date?"

The strain in his voice pleased her for some reason. Was it a tinge of jealousy? "I'm meeting up with a couple of girlfriends there."

"Including the one who left you at the club?" he asked.

"Kari? Yes. She works for Xtark."

"Well, there's been a slight change in plans." A deter-mined light shone in his eyes, as if he automatically ex-pected her to agree with whatever he was about to tell her.

"What do you mean?"

"You'll be going to the party with me."

CHAPTER SIX

BY THE TIME CHARLOTTE and Trace had arrived at the Edgemont Hotel, the event was in full swing.

He hadn't told her any details about his concerns with Xtark, citing confidentiality issues, only that he didn't trust them. What did he suspect they were doing? Selling body parts? Shanghaiing partygoers? Even though she wanted to be ticked off at the forceful way he'd invited himself, it thrilled her to know he cared. She was pretty sure if someone else had spoken to her in the same manner, she'd have told him where he could stick it, but then Trace had a knack for getting away with things other men couldn't.

The ballroom was brimming with activity. Twinkle lights hung from the ceiling, illuminating the dance floor, and the band was playing a rock version of a holiday classic. Columns of gold and silver balloons were positioned randomly between the fifty or so linen-covered tables. She liked the simplicity of the centerpieces: large crystal bowls filled with silver ornaments and small gold-wrapped boxes. Probably takeaway favors for guests at the end of the evening.

Too bad she wasn't as pleased with her outfit as she was with the decor. Why was it that some people had a natural knack for knowing what to wear while others didn't? She looked down at her black cocktail dress, then glanced at Trace's jeans and sport coat. Everyone else wore jeans, as well, making her feel self-conscious and overdressed. She should've guessed that "cocktail attire" for a software company meant a button-up shirt and a clean pair of sneakers.

"You look very beautiful, by the way," Trace said softly, sending tingles down her spine.

She looked into his face to find his eyes dark, yet sincere. The pulse at the base of his throat flickered, drawing her attention. And as she exhaled, she found herself wondering how it would feel to have her lips pressed there.

"Thank you," she managed to say, marveling again at how perceptive he was. The fact that he'd picked up on these subtle cues of hers that no other man would've noticed made her feel relevant and important to him. And she rather liked it.

She paused to talk to a few people she knew while Trace went to get them drinks.

"Whoa, girl, he's really hot," Kari said, scrutinizing him as if he were a piece of meat in a butcher's display case. "Where on earth did you find him?"

"I didn't. He found me." She quickly explained how she'd almost been mugged.

"That's sooo chivalrous." Rose Marie covered her heart with one hand.

"I agree," said Deb.

Kari twirled the swizzle stick in her drink. "Damn. I obviously went home with the wrong man."

"Thank God you did," said Rose Marie. "I don't want to think what could've happened to Char if he hadn't been there."

"The dude I did go home with turned out to be a total bust, too," Kari continued, ignoring Rose Marie's comment. "He keeps giving me one excuse after another why

I can't meet with their vendor manager about selling into their company."

"I thought he was the one making the decisions," Charlotte said.

"Yeah, I did, too." Kari rolled her eyes. "So, speaking of good hookups, your man looks loaded."

Charlotte glanced over at Trace, who was still in line at the bar. "I don't know about that."

She purposefully angled herself so that Kari would have to turn her back on Trace in order to continue the conversation. His family might be wealthy, but he seemed pretty unaffected by it. He was more down-to-earth and relatable than many of the guys she'd dated.

"Bull. I saw the car you guys drove up in. That had to set him back over eighty K."

"I don't pay much attention to cars, so I wouldn't know. It was nice, I guess."

Kari let out an exasperated sigh. "How could you not know that?"

"Not everyone's a gold digger like you, Kari," said Rose Marie.

"Humph," Kari replied. "Maybe he's overcompensating for something."

Deb laughed. "You can be such a bitch sometimes."

Charlotte had to agree, though she didn't find it funny.

"Who's the chick your hottie is talking to?" Kari asked, taking a sip of her pink-colored cocktail.

Charlotte glanced up but Trace was no longer in line. She followed Kari's stare to the other side of the dance floor. Trace was talking to two people—a woman in skinny jeans and a man with a cane.

Trace angled close to the blonde, said something in her ear before ushering her through the crowd toward a side exit. When they got to the door, she spun around to face him. From the looks of it, she was arguing with him. Given his stiff posture and the stern set of his jaw, he was pissed. Clearly, they had some sort of history together.

A twinge of jealousy shot down Charlotte's spine. Was she an ex-girlfriend? He hadn't mentioned that he knew anyone who worked here, but then again, maybe the man was an Xtark employee, not the woman.

"Beats me," Charlotte said breezily, though she was curious, too.

Rose Marie and Deb turned around to look just as the blonde put her hand on Trace's arm and took a half step closer. Charlotte's cheeks heated, the twinges of jealously turning into full-fledged barbs. She wished she could read his expression, but he was turned slightly away from where the four women stood.

"Looks like he's trying to get her to leave," Kari said, "but she doesn't want to. Do you think he's doing that because he doesn't want the two of you to meet? Maybe she's his not-so-distant ex and he thinks he can still can control her."

"Jesus, Kari," said Rose Marie. "Sometimes you go a little too far."

Charlotte set down her plate and decided to scratch Kari from her list of friends. There had to be a reasonable explanation. The bar had no line now, so she headed over and was soon sipping on a glass of the house cabernet.

Could there be any truth to what Kari had said? Was the woman a former girlfriend of Trace's? It certainly wasn't outside the realm of possibility. Was that why he'd insisted on coming tonight, hoping he'd run into her? Staring into her wineglass, she considered that a moment. A man like him playing games? No, it wasn't possible. If he wanted to see someone, he'd just do it. He wouldn't make up some elaborate story just so he could come with Charlotte.

Someone jostled her arm, almost spilling her wine, and a conga line weaved past her. She quickly moved out of their way before one of the dancers grabbed her to join in. She took her wine and headed out to the lobby. The window display of a high-end furniture store had caught her eye when they arrived. With the crowds thinner there, she'd check it out, give herself a chance to collect her thoughts, then she'd head back in a few minutes.

She really needed to get a grip on her runaway feelings for a man she hadn't known for long. First of all, she and Trace weren't a couple. He'd made that abundantly clear when she'd arrived at the mansion. Business only. Which was fine, right? If he ran into an ex-girlfriend, big deal. Given his impressive physical attributes and his prowess in the bedroom, celibacy clearly wasn't something he practiced. And second, even though there was something utterly magnetic about him—something she couldn't quite put her finger on that was both exciting and comfortable—it meant nothing. She'd always been one to overanalyze things.

Sure, she felt at home with him and had really connected with his grandmother, but that shouldn't surprise her. He was confident and seemed truly interested in her as a person, while Vik reminded her so much of her own grandmother. It didn't mean that she had any claim to him or that she should harbor any expectations. No, she really wasn't falling for him. Especially since he was now a client.

"So, who do we have here?" Charlotte spun around to find the woman Trace had been talking to towering over her. With pouty red lips and blond hair framing her face, she was beautiful, but her eyes were dark, cruel. "Are you already planning on what furniture to buy when you move in together?"

Damn. Kari was right. She had to be an ex-girlfriend.

Charlotte took a half step back. "I'm sorry. Have we met?"

"I know what's going on. Are you hoping that he'll change you, too? That you'll need some well-made furniture built to last a lifetime?" The woman flashed a BOTOX smile, showing a row of perfect white teeth, but it didn't reach her eyes. They stayed dark, unanimated, with just a rim of color around the pupils.

Alarm bells rang in Charlotte's head, her skin suddenly cold. Oddly enough, Trace's eyes would darken like this, as well, but with him, she'd never felt uncomfortable. Now, it was as if Charlotte were a rabbit looking into the muzzle of a hungry wolf.

"Get the hell away from her, Leona," Trace growled, stepping between the two of them.

A sigh of relief escaped Charlotte's lips. Where had he come from? Unlike when the woman had come up behind her, Charlotte was now facing the main lobby area and hadn't noticed him approaching. Without looking, he reached back and clasped her hand, warming her icy fingers.

Leona rubbed a fingernail below her lower lip as if to wipe off excess lipstick. "Don't worry. I wasn't going to *hurt* her. But she does look delicious. We were just talking, weren't we?"

Hurt? What was she talking about?

"I said go away." Trace's tone, though quiet, was sharp enough to cut paper.

"You're such a goddamn hypocrite," Leona said. "Sitting on the Governing Council, telling the rest of us to stay away from humans when you've got a human girl-friend yourself."

"That's enough."

"Is she petitioning you to become a changeling, too? 'I'll do anything,'" Leona said in a fake vibrato. "'My body…my blood…if you'll just turn me.'" She smiled again, broader this time, and Charlotte's blood ran cold.

Two small fangs hung from Leona's mouth, making indentations on her lower lip. "I want to be a vampire just like you," she mocked.

"Expect to be summoned," Trace said curtly. Turning to Charlotte, he added, "Let's go."

ONCE OUTSIDE, CHARLOTTE grabbed Trace's coat sleeve, forcing him to stop. Before he exited the hotel lobby how-ever, he'd sent a quick text to the field office. Guardians would soon be here to take care of Leona, as well as find out just what her human friend knew.

"What the hell was…*that?*" Charlotte whispered. "I know what I saw, but—vampires?"

"We'll talk about it in the car." Maybe he could con-vince her it was nothing. Was that even possible after what she'd seen and heard? If not, he knew what he had to do.

"No, I want to talk about it now."

He glanced around. There were too many people to risk it here.

"Come on," Charlotte said, as if sensing his reluctance. "Let's take a walk." Incredibly, she tucked her hand into the crook of his elbow.

"A walk?"

"Yes. I love this part of town. Besides, we'll both think more clearly if we're walking, and I have a feeling this is going to take more than a simple explanation."

He gave a short laugh. "You got that right." Why did it feel so natural, so comfortable to be with her? he thought bitterly as he automatically matched his stride to hers.

They passed a liquor store, making him wish he had a pint of something right now. Maybe it'd loosen up the knots of apprehension twisting in his gut. He wasn't ready to say goodbye to Charlotte again. Hell, he'd barely said hello.

"Listen, Charlotte. You weren't meant to see what you did back there. That's why I insisted on going to the party with you in the first place…so something like that *wouldn't* happen."

"So what did happen?" Charlotte asked, her breath fogging in front of her face. "Leona kept referring to *humans,* not *people.* The fangs. The Council. Changelings." She gave a nervous laugh but still hadn't let go of him. "You can't possibly be a…a… Can you?"

"First of all, no matter what you saw or what you think I am, I care about you. A lot."

He cursed himself for thinking he could hide his true nature from her. Especially when he'd let himself get close to her again. Since hiring her, he'd spent time poring through the storage room boxes with her, taken her shopping for holiday décor, sitting down for afternoon tea with her and his grandmother. God, he loved spending time with her. It didn't matter what they were doing.

What a fool he'd been to think he could keep his distance this time, underestimating how powerful his feelings for her would be. The first instant when he'd laid eyes on her in the parking lot, he'd desperately wanted her back in his life, whether he'd been ready to admit it then or not. And now this? He cursed Leona and he cursed Xtark Software.

"Yes…yes, I know you do. And I…well, maybe it's crazy, but I feel the same way. About you."

She cared about him? Even now? Confused, he glanced down. Her chin was lifted, her expression relaxed, and she was leaning slightly against him as they walked. Not exactly normal reactions when a human woman suspects that the guy she's been with is a vampire. But she'd clearly put two and two together. A spike of hope jabbed at his insides, trying to find a place to settle in and take hold. But he wouldn't let it. He couldn't.

A group of clubgoers approached. They were within earshot, so he hesitated and waited for them to pass.

"I love this little store," Charlotte remarked, dragging his attention to the lighted display window. "Notice how all the elements are different and yet they work so well, grouped together like this."

He saw an eclectic mix of knit caps and scarves, hand-painted nutcrackers, driftwood picture frames, and antique toy trains. He would never have thought to lump such different items together, but she did have a point.

They continued walking and with each step he took, his heart grew heavier and heavier. He wasn't ready to say goodbye. A few minutes later, they reached a small city park overlooking the water, empty at this time of night.

"Listen, Charlotte." He reached for her hand, pulling her down to the park bench with him. "Before I tell you what's going on, you need to know one thing. I would never do anything to hurt or harm you."

"You said that already."

No matter how much he wanted to, he wouldn't tell her that he loved her or admit to knowing her last year. Because that would make his logic sound even more self-centered than it already was.

It's the holidays and I didn't want to be alone, so I lied to you again. Jesus, what an asshole.

He'd tell her a limited version of the truth, because she at least deserved that. Then he'd do what he needed to do and never see her again. For real, this time.

"I have a feeling this is going to be complicated," Charlotte said when he didn't start talking right away. "Tell me about your freaky ex-girlfriend. What's that all about?"

He laughed at her frankness. "First of all, she's not my ex."

Charlotte narrowed her eyes. "You certainly seemed to know each other."

"She knows who I am, but I've never seen or met her before tonight. Because of my position, I am known among people who are…like me."

"Which is?"

His heart thudded heavily in his chest with the anticipation of what he was about to tell her. He had never breathed a word about who he was to any human before—he'd never come close. Lying about himself when he was with them was almost second nature. To keep their existence secret was written in the old edicts—he'd read them with his own eyes. He exhaled loudly and ran a hand through his hair. "Leona and I are what used to be called Night Brethren—now, we're simply referred to as…as vampires."

There, he'd said it. He watched as Charlotte's eyes widened. He couldn't tell if she was going to laugh or cry. "You're serious? You…you really are a vampire?"

"Yes."

"You mean blood drinking and all that?"

"We do need small amounts of human blood to survive, as well as human energies."

Sitting on the edge of the bench, her back rigid, she

stared out, lights from the city mirrored in her eyes. "This is just so unreal, Trace. I mean, I saw her fangs and all, but…" She snapped her head around. "You're not messing with me, are you?"

"I wish it were a joke. But, no."

She studied his face as if trying to decide whether or not to believe him. Finally, when she spoke again, her voice was quiet, yet firm. "When's the last time you had blood? Have you…done that to me? Would I have known if you had?"

"We have the ability to take away a human's memory when that happens. However, I've not taken blood from a human host in years, only from a vial. So no, I've never taken yours."

She visibly relaxed. "And Leona?"

"Probably. Most of our kind do, but because of my position with our Council, I don't. We believe that our kind can live peacefully among yours. Or I should say, because of my potential position with the Council."

"Leona seems to think you're on this Council."

He briefly explained the situation, including what had gone on with his uncle. Then he told her about Sweet blood addictions and Darkbloods, leaving out as much of the gore as he could.

"I can't believe it," she said, shaking her head.

He braced himself. All of this had to be a hell of a shock and—

"So they're going to hold the actions of someone else against you? Someone who wasn't guilty of a crime in the first place? Your great-uncle was an old man, for God's sake. And someone took advantage of him."

He snapped his head up. That wasn't the reaction he'd been expecting. "I'm afraid so."

She angled her body to face his. "Why would you

want to be a part of an organization that judges you not by your actions, but by someone else's?"

"It is my duty." It was all he knew, what he was destined to become.

She made an exasperated sound. "How is it that humans haven't found all this out by now? Plastered it all over the internet?"

"From time to time, they have. For instance, the man with Leona was a human who'd been petitioning her to change him."

"So that's why she thought I was wanting you to turn me into…someone like you? To become immortal?"

"Technically, we're not immortal. We just live much longer than humans. And it takes the blood of two vampires, not one, to turn a human to a changeling. But, yes, that's what she'd assumed about you."

"If I believe you, which I haven't decided yet because it's so…far-fetched, then why are you able to go out into the sun? You left my house at dawn when you…ah…stayed over."

"Not all the myths perpetuated about our people are true." He explained to her how the UV light affected their kind.

"So have you ever taken my energies? Or wiped my memories?" she asked cautiously.

"I have taken your energies at times," he admitted, pointedly ignoring her second question. He wasn't ready to confess that yet. "I try not to, but it flows so easily into me that I really have to concentrate. But sometimes when I'm with you, my thoughts are focused…elsewhere and I let down my guard."

She rubbed her arms. "So why are you telling me all this? Why not lie?"

He stared out at the bay before he replied. Lights from

the city and the far shore danced in warped patterns on the water. A marine horn echoed in the distance, a mournful, melancholy sound in the night air. "Because it makes me feel good to finally tell you the truth."

Neither of them said anything for a full minute. Then she turned to face him again.

"What do you mean by *finally?*"

He let go of her and rubbed his eyes with the heels of his hands, but the dread in his heart remained. "Because we didn't just meet two weeks ago in the parking lot. We met last Christmas, when you decorated the house for the party."

CHAPTER SEVEN

"TAKE ME HOME."

Those three words pointed one way, and one way only. It had sounded like a death sentence at the park. She'd not said anything more.

Trace parked the car in front of Charlotte's house and started to get out, but her hand on his wrist stopped him.

"I was in love with you, wasn't I?"

He sat back against the leather seat and stared out the windshield. "You never told me if you were or not."

"But I was. I can feel it in my bones. That night when we met again…when you took care of those two guys… part of me knew that I'd loved you. I don't think I'd have ever let you take me home and…well…do what we did together otherwise. Instinctively, I knew I could trust you. Like it was hardwired into my system. I just didn't remember that I did."

Trust him? Shit. He was the last person she should trust. "Charlotte, please."

"Were you afraid that I'd tell about you and your people? Is that it?"

"Of course not, but it's written in the old edicts that a human cannot know about the existence of our kind. Once you found out, I had a duty to uphold."

"So what exactly did I see last year?"

Trace remembered it as clearly as if it were yesterday. The party guests had left, and he'd insisted that Charlotte spend the night rather than drive home. "You were clearing up stray dishes and I was upstairs checking on one of the houseguests. Somehow you ended up downstairs near—"

"The storage room?"

"How did you—? Yes, the storage room just past the wine cellar."

"I knew it. The other day when you were on the phone, I ran down there to check for a missing box. I got such an uncomfortable feeling that I came back upstairs without going inside. I didn't know why." She closed her eyes and rubbed her temples. "I don't remember anything, though. What happened?"

"I'm glad you don't, because—" He silently cursed Sebastian. "You walked in on my cousin and one of his lady friends."

"And he was…drinking her blood?"

Trace nodded.

"Then what happened?"

"I remember pausing in the upper hallway, an extra pillow in my hands, sensing that something wasn't quite right. By the time I got downstairs, you were in the foyer with Sebastian."

Charlotte had looked terrified that night, confused, and yet somehow she held herself together. When she spotted Trace, she'd started to go to him but Sebastian had laughed. "Run away, little human. You're right to be afraid. But if I were you, I'd think twice about running to Trace. He's one of us, too."

The look on her face had nearly killed him. Because he'd brought Charlotte into his world without telling her the truth about what he was, she was suffering. Then he'd remembered his promise to his father and his duty to his family. The Council would never accept him if he was in love with a human. A fling, maybe, because it could easily be ended. But Charlotte had been much more than that. And so, for her sake as well as his own, he'd made the only choice he could.

"I took you to your car and—" He'd blocked it out of his mind—the pleading look, the disbelief as he put a hand to her face. "And then I watched you drive away."

The atmosphere inside the car now was charged as Charlotte took it all in. "You took away my memories. Not just of what I'd seen your cousin do, but of you. Your family. What we had together. And you did that without giving me any input into the matter."

"Yes," he said flatly.

The slap across his face happened quickly. He welcomed the sting.

"Bastard." Charlotte's eyes blazed with anger.

Yeah, he sure as hell deserved that, and a lot more.

"I don't care about your rules or your duties or your promises to your father. Were you in love with me?"

He didn't want to admit it to himself, let alone Charlotte. Regardless of his feelings, she didn't fit into his carefully crafted world. "I can't love you."

"I didn't ask you if you could or couldn't. I asked if you did."

Jesus, why did she always have to be so damned precise? He sighed loudly. "Charlotte, I'm poised to take over my family's seat on the Council. I cannot be with a human no matter what my feelings are. They are…immaterial."

"So you do care about me," she mumbled under her breath. "Well then, take me back to your place. I've got a house to decorate and an event to finish planning. Plus, I'd like to see your grandmother again. Then, when the holiday party is over, you can do whatever it is you feel you need to do."

With a determined lift to her chin, she crossed her arms over her chest and waited expectantly for him to start up the car again.

Was he understanding her correctly? "You mean you want to stay there until the party is over? You're okay with what I am? You're not frightened or repulsed?"

"Those are two words I'd never use to describe you, Trace. Angry with you? Yes. But I…I care about you… very much. The truth about who you are doesn't change that." She straightened the ends of her coat belt, which lay in her lap. "You know, I had an interesting conversation with one of my girlfriends back there at the party. She had noticed the car we drove up in and remarked that you must be really wealthy. The truth is, Trace, I don't pay attention to things like that. Just as I don't care that you're a…a vampire. As odd as that may sound. Who you are inside, which is all I care about, isn't synonymous with any of that."

He scrubbed his face. Would it hurt to extend the time they had together? It wouldn't change anything in the long run, just make the holidays a little better. The secrets would be gone between them. They both knew they couldn't be together long-term and that he'd still need to clear her memory, but it'd be postponed for a while. Hell, his grandmother would be ecstatic.

"If you're going to spend the next two weeks with me, don't you think you'll need to pack a few things? Including your cat?"

CHARLOTTE ARRANGED the greenery on the fireplace mantel and glanced over at Vik, who sat on the sofa working on a crossword puzzle and petting Augustus.

She'd had a lot to think about since Trace had come clean with her last night. The least of which was the fact that he was a vampire. And so was his grandmother. Given that she'd never felt threatened around either of them, she realized that they weren't all the fearsome monsters that books and movies made them out to be. Some of them were, Trace had admitted, like those guys in the parking lot, but most of them peacefully existed alongside humans.

"So do you, like, bite people, too?" Charlotte couldn't picture this kindly old woman doing anything remotely violent or vicious. In fact, the thought was mildly amusing.

Vik looked at her over the top of her glasses. "Honey, I haven't fed from a live donor in years. Too much work. Besides, our blood and energy needs decrease as we get older. I take what I need from vials. But it's the reason I like to shop so much. A pat on a salesperson's hand gives me just the right amount of energy."

Charlotte smiled and made a mental note to take the woman shopping soon. Who wouldn't want to shake this kindly old woman's hand? "Well, you can take energy from me any time, Vik."

"That's sweet of you, but I think you need to keep your energy for whatshisname." The sparkle in Vik's eyes made Charlotte blush.

"Had he always intended to take over for his father?" she asked, changing the subject.

"Yes, the eldest usually does. But his father—my son—was really tough on him. Took after my husband, the sonovabitch. God rest his soul. Believed in stern discipline and duty first, above all else. Including matters of the heart." Vik reached for the silver teapot and refilled her cup. "Would you like some more tea, dear?"

"Maybe in a minute," Charlotte answered as she tucked in a few strands of red berries. "Let me finish this section and then I'll take a break. What do you mean by matters of the heart?"

"Because our race doesn't produce many children, love is not considered a good enough reason to marry. A union between our people is to produce offspring, first and foremost. Love is a nonessential element. Or so the Council professes."

"You don't sound convinced of that philosophy."

The china clinked as Vik set down her cup. "I just want Trace to be happy, and when I see him following in his father's footsteps, I worry about him. Being on the Council requires political savvy. Good speaking skills. Thinking on your feet. Being able to find commonality between two opposing viewpoints and determine a compromise both sides can live with. And sometimes it requires the ability to make difficult decisions."

"Trace is very good at all those things."

"Yes, he is, but deep down, I believe that he still doubts himself. That doubt is at the core of who he is. He doesn't want to go back on the promise he made to his father. But I'm afraid he's honoring that promise at the expense of his own happiness."

That explained a lot.

"If I were his father, I'd be very proud of him." Charlotte hesitated, her hand on one of the pillar candles. "You didn't marry for love?"

"No, I didn't. But it was a good union. We had three children."

A heaviness hung in the space around her heart as she stepped back to examine the mantel.

That was it then. She lacked the DNA that would make their union an acceptable one. If only her stubborn emotions would give up the fight so she could simply enjoy what she had today, rather than worry about tomorrow. The fact that she was falling for Trace a second time just wasn't enough.

CHAPTER EIGHT

"WEATHERMAN SAYS SNOW this evening," Mrs. Wilson said, as Charlotte gathered her things to leave. "I can feel it in the air."

Earlier in the day, back at the mansion, Charlotte had received the woman's panicked voice mail. Good thing she'd thought to check it from Trace's home line, because her cell coverage out at Rainier Falls was sketchy at best. The table and chairs had been delivered to Mrs. Wilson's home, but the fabric on the seats wasn't what the woman had been expecting.

Gearing up for disaster, Charlotte drove to the woman's home, but it turned out that everything was fine. She figured Mrs. Wilson had just wanted confirmation from Charlotte that it looked all right…in addition to helping her arrange the centerpiece and table settings for the dinner party she was hosting that night.

Charlotte was soon back in the Volvo, heading to Rainier Falls. Would Trace be around now? she wondered as she stared at the late-afternoon sky. A few light snowflakes hit the windshield. Given the short daylight hours and the low UV light, he'd told her that this was a favorite time of year for his people. They could come and go a little more freely.

In the week since she'd arrived at the mansion, every night she'd stared at the door adjoining their rooms and wished Trace would knock. But he hadn't. She'd even tiptoed over to put her ear against the door, like a naughty schoolgirl doing something she shouldn't, but all she'd heard was the tap-tap-tapping of his keyboard. Early in the morning, when she'd gotten up to get a drink of water, she'd still heard it. She'd known he was dedicated to his work, but did he ever sleep?

She knew he was giving her the time and space to sort out this new reality, but she'd sorted it out enough in her mind. She cared about him. Maybe even— Well, she wanted to spend the rest of the time they had with him, not apart. Tonight, she made up her mind to go into his room. Invitation or not.

By the time she got close to Rainier Falls, it was snowing hard. The flakes were wet and heavy, making it difficult for the wipers to keep the windshield clear. With both hands on the wheel, she slowed down and concentrated on the road in front of her. As she came around a bend, two giant headlights showed up in her rearview mirror, barreling straight for her.

Crap. He was right there. Inches from her back bumper. What an ass.

She hugged the side, giving the driver room to pass. But before she knew what was happening, her outside tire went off the edge of the road and the car started sliding. She gripped the wheel, holding the vehicle steady, and eased up on the gas. The rig behind her zoomed past just as her car came to a halt. She caught a glimpse of large tires and chrome wheels before the snow it threw off sprayed her windshield. She revved the Volvo's engine, but there was no forward movement. The tire was stuck. A quick check of her cell phone confirmed she had no coverage, either.

That's just great.

Thank goodness she'd worn boots today and had on

her heavy coat. The mansion wasn't more than a mile or two away. She'd make the trek and have Trace come help her with the car so it wouldn't sit stranded on the side of the road all night.

As she was grabbing her things, a loud rap made her jump. She jerked her head up to find a man standing outside the driver's window.

Holy shit. Her heart did a flip-flop in her chest.

With dark eyes and his collar turned up against the weather, he looked almost like a—

"Come on," he said through the window, indicating for her to roll it down.

Had he come from the rig that passed her? Through the windshield, she could just make out red taillights in front of her that she hadn't noticed before. Evidently, he had. She opened it just a crack.

"Jesus," he said. "You practically ran me off the road."

Given that he was the one driving what amounted to a street-legal Sherman tank, she highly doubted it, but then again, she hadn't been able to see the center line, either. It was very possible that she had been driving in the middle of the road. "Sorry. I couldn't see much."

"Well, who do we have here?" Something flickered behind his eyes as he smiled and his expression softened somewhat. A few snowflakes dusted his dark hair. With a cruel set to his jaw and a soul patch under his lower lip, he was good-looking, devilishly so.

She chose not to answer him. He gave her the creeps. "Would you be able to give me a little push?" she asked. "If I can just get that tire back onto the road again, I think I'll be fine."

"Sorry. I'd like to help, but I'm afraid I'm not dressed for it. This snow is ruining my shoes as it is and I'm freezing my ass off standing here." He glanced in her back-seat. "Can I...give you a lift?"

Like hell was she going to get into a car with him. That night in the parking lot with Trace was the only time she'd gotten into the car with a stranger, and he'd turned out not to be a stranger after all. "No, I'm fine."

"Let me guess. You're heading to the Westfalen place."

She scrutinized his face. He didn't look familiar and yet— "Yes, I am. How did you know?"

"Call me clairvoyant." He laughed, but she didn't find it comforting. "We're heading there, too."

How convenient. "We?"

"Yes, my girlfriend and me. I'm Trace's cousin and we're here for the holidays."

His cousin? *The* cousin? She swallowed and clutched her coat tighter around the collar. Although she couldn't remember anything about what she'd seen last Christmas, she definitely didn't trust this guy.

"If you don't believe me..." He pulled out his wallet and showed her his driver's license. Sebastian Westfalen-Taft. Yes, he definitely was *the* cousin. "What do you say? Do you want a ride up to the house or do you want to walk? Your choice."

She considered her options. A long, cold trek in the snow or a quick five-minute ride.

A woman's voice called from Sebastian's vehicle. "Come on, baby. I'm getting cold."

Okay. He had his girlfriend with him. How dangerous could he be?

TRACE LED CHARLOTTE into his bedroom suite. "You're staying with me now."

A delicious thrill skittered along her nerve endings. "What are you talking about?"

"In my bed. My cousin isn't stupid enough to try anything, but now that he's here, under this roof, you'll be safer with me."

Guess she wouldn't need to force herself on him after all. "I'm surprised you invited him here after what happened last year."

"Believe me, I didn't. But he's family, so I can't throw him out."

She looked around the room, a mirror image of her own in terms of size and layout, and yet very different. Heavy midnight-blue tapestries, extending from the ornately carved moldings, covered all the walls. Although the room was spacious, it felt intimate because it absorbed the sound so well.

Her heart beat loudly in her head as she stared at the massive Louis XIV bed taking up a huge portion of one side. Its brocade panels were tied back, revealing luxurious pillows of various sizes. She had to imagine that when those panels were shut, it would feel very intimate inside, as well. The tender skin of her inner thighs heated at the thought of lying there with Trace.

She turned to find him staring at her, his eyes dark, his lips parted slightly, as if he were out of breath. God, she wanted him, and she wanted him bad.

Ever since that night at her house when he'd rocked her world, she had wanted more. And now that she knew the truth about him and that she had once loved him, things felt even more natural.

Shutting the door, she reached up on her tiptoes and kissed him roughly. His mouth moved against hers and she slipped her tongue inside.

He chuckled, the sound rumbling against her lips. "My God, Char, what are you doing?"

"What does it look like I'm doing?" She pushed him

to the bed, where he fell back onto the mattress, pulling her with him.

"You are my responsibility now," he said. "And I'm not one to take responsibilities lightly."

"I'm glad. Neither am I. Now, take off your clothes."

He laughed. "God, are you always this bossy?"

"I can be."

When they'd pulled up in Sebastian's SUV, Trace had stormed out of the house and swept her from the vehicle. It had surprised her at first, but then she saw the relief in his face. The way he'd glared at his cousin made him look like he could rip his head off. She found his intense concern for her incredibly attractive.

It took only a moment for their clothes to be piled on the floor. Charlotte leaned over him, caging his body under hers. She held his arms above his head, her nipples brushing his muscular chest.

"You know, I'm used to being the one in charge." His eyes were dark as he looked hungrily at her breasts.

His short hair was bed-head messy, just the way she liked it, the pulse just under his jaw flickering madly. The muscles of his shoulders were bulky, his chest smooth and well-defined. Everything about this powerful man turned her on.

"And I like that." She released his hands, but before he could take control, she slipped down between his legs. His thick erection lay against his belly, a teardrop of liquid glistening at the tip. She flicked it off slowly with her tongue and he groaned. "But are you saying you want me to stop? Because I will if you want me to."

He said nothing. Just waited. And watched.

His balls were heavy and loose in her hand as she took him into her mouth. He arched his back and hissed loudly.

She was pretty certain that was her answer.

"So tell me about this Council," Charlotte said, running her hand over his chest. "Who is on it and what do you do?"

"There are twelve North American regions, each with its own small Council. At the local level, we function like a court, deciding cases among our people and interpreting laws. Several times a year, the regions meet to make necessary policy changes and to carry out execution orders. We also meet periodically with our European counterparts."

Charlotte shivered. "Does that happen a lot? The executions?"

"Given our aggressive tendencies, my people are more prone to violence and that requires a certain brand of justice. These laws have held our people together, kept our existence a secret from humans for many, many centuries. And although they might seem archaic at times, even barbaric, they've served us well."

Charlotte was quiet for a while before she spoke again. "So, what does it feel like? You know…when a vampire takes a human's blood?"

Trace stared at the draped fabric above their heads. It felt good to be talking so openly and honestly. Surprisingly good. He caressed the back of her hand. "My understanding is that it's a sharp, stinging sensation as the fangs pierce the skin, but that the pain quickly subsides."

"Is it clinical, where the person holds out their wrist, or is there something more?"

"It can be fairly clinical, yes. A quick sip at the wrist and the whole thing is over. But it isn't always. Why are you asking? Being around us, are you worried that something might happen?"

Her hand stopped moving, resting directly over his heart. "Because I want to experience that with you."

His pulse thundered in his ears. Surely, he hadn't heard her correctly. "I don't understand."

"If my memories need to be taken, I want to leave something of me with you, even if it's temporary."

Stunned at this revelation, he considered it for a moment. Her lifeblood in his system, feeding him, nourishing him, giving him strength. Just thinking about it made him hard again, despite the fact that they'd just made love. "But I haven't taken blood from a human host for a long time."

"Good. Then it'll be extra special for both of us."

He rubbed the tip of his tongue behind his teeth, where his fangs were threatening to emerge. She wanted him this badly?

She reached between his legs and stroked him. He moved against her hand.

What would her blood taste like? Although she wasn't a sweetblood, he knew it would taste sinfully sweet to him.

"If you don't want to," she continued, "that's okay, too. I mean, if it's against your beliefs and all that."

"You mean now?"

"Yes," she answered.

He almost laughed as he pushed on her hip. It wasn't that he didn't believe in it—there was a reason his kind had the ability to wipe a human's memory—but he had never wanted to be distracted by it. Taking blood from vials had always served his purpose. Until now.

She lay back for him against the bed, her eyes dancing with excitement. Would she find the experience as thrilling as he knew he would? Many found it pleasurable, which was why the lure of a vampire's kiss could be so seductive.

"Are you sure about this?" As he tuned in to the beat

of her heart, his fangs broke through his gums and he turned away slightly. "Don't look, Char. It may frighten you."

She held his face between her palms and stared at his mouth. "Trace, I find everything about you beautiful. Your body, your mind, your dedication, your passion. And yes, even this."

And in that moment, he knew that he loved her. His aspirations of sitting on the Council suddenly didn't seem as important as this amazing woman who thought this about him in spite of everything he was. Instead of his father's admonishments ringing in his head, he remembered instead all of his grandmother's talks as she gave him permission to be happy.

And being with Charlotte made him happier than he'd ever been in his life. She accepted him for what he was now, not what he could be or should be in the future.

With his tongue, he found the precise spot on her neck where his fangs would penetrate. Her pulse beat madly under his lips as it waited for him, her skin slightly salty. "Are you sure you're okay?"

She ran her hand up his arm, encouraging him to continue. "Yes, Trace, I am." She spoke those words with soft conviction.

He wanted this, too. More than he'd ever thought possible. His teeth grazed her neck and she shivered. Then, without waiting a moment longer, he locked onto her vein and bit.

"Oh," she gasped, as his teeth sank into her flesh. He hesitated and she stroked his hair. "I'm fine, Trace. It's… it's really kind of nice." When she spoke, her voice was more like a purr, a vibration against his lips.

Sealing his lips over her vein, he closed his eyes and let her blood fill his mouth. Oh, God, it was indeed sweet on the back of his tongue, sweeter than any he'd tasted before. He could hardly believe that this beautiful woman so freely gave herself to him. Even after all he'd done. When he swallowed, her warmth traveled down his throat and he felt it rejuvenating his body.

There had to be another way, he thought as his mouth filled again. And if there wasn't…if the Council balked… well… He just wouldn't give her up, he decided. He loved her too much to let that happen. Instantly, it felt as if a million pounds had been lifted from his heart. The dilemma he'd grappled with the past few weeks—the past year—gone. She meant more to him than the seat on the Council.

CHAPTER NINE

CHARLOTTE SLIPPED HER FEET into the strappy heels and took one last look in the mirror. She certainly wasn't used to seeing herself like this. With her hair up, her makeup done professionally and this beautiful dress, she felt as if she were ready to walk down the red carpet at a movie premiere. All she needed was a handsome man to escort her. She had just such a man in mind.

She'd put the finishing touches on the last few decorations this morning and the caterers had arrived at noon. The party was now someone else's responsibility until it was time to dismantle everything again. She thought about Trace—how he respected her, cared about her ideas, really listened to her, laughed with her—and she realized it wasn't the tangible stuff that she'd miss. It was Trace. She could be in a cabin in the middle of nowhere—far from the city lights, the gourmet meals, the elegant trappings—but if Trace were with her, she'd have everything she needed. That is, if she could remember him.

The past few nights with him had been amazing. After he'd first taken her blood, he'd done so every time they'd made love since. She loved the anticipation of his warm lips at her neck. The sharp sting followed by the endorphins flooding her system. She'd teased him that at this rate, she'd have to start taking iron supplements. But he only took a few sips each time before he withdrew and sealed the marks. She touched her neck now. A little tender, but it was the good kind of hurt.

She didn't want to think that soon this would all be over.

Earlier, Vik had brought in her hairdresser and nail person and the two of them spent all afternoon getting ready. The estate had a small salon on the lower level, complete with shampoo bowls, massage chairs and several nail stations.

Vik had said it was much more fun having a lady friend to get ready with. Hearing that had warmed Charlotte's heart and made it hard to refuse. It was something her own grandmother would've said to her. Charlotte sensed that it had been a long time since Vik had had much female company.

After her hair and nails were done, Charlotte had returned to their quarters to finish getting dressed. Expecting to slip into the cocktail dress she'd brought from home, she was stunned to find a new outfit laid out on the bed. She skimmed her hand over the sequined fabric that clung to her hips and twirled a circle in front of the full-length mirror.

How in the world had he guessed her size correctly? The dress hugged her curves as if it were custom-made. It was simple in the front, with long sleeves that came down over the tops of her hands and a hemline kissing her toes, and the back had a beautiful drape to it. She had to admit, Trace had excellent taste in haute couture.

The shoes were perfect, too, even though her feet were probably going to be killing her in about an hour. Four-inch heels, and they showed off her new pedicure, including the tiny crystals on her toes.

She was so focused on not stepping on the hem of her dress as she exited the room that she didn't notice Trace until she heard his low whistle. He'd been sitting on a wood bench in the hallway alcove and rose to greet her.

Her heart forgot how to beat for a moment as her eyes drank him in. A nice-looking man in a tuxedo was always eye-catching, but Trace took it to a whole different level. The cut of the jacket emphasized his broad shoulders and didn't hide how his muscular torso tapered down to lean hips.

God, how she'd love to undress him right now. Inch by inch and button by button, she'd deconstruct him carefully in order to savor the experience.

Trace definitely wore the suit. The suit didn't wear him.

As she approached him, she grazed her fingertips along the top of the occasional table to steady herself. His hair was just the right amount of messy, his skin smooth and freshly shaven. The sandalwood and pine scent of his aftershave was subtle yet distinct. Clean, pure, unadulterated male.

His lips were slightly parted and she could just see the tip of his tongue. But those eyes of his were what really captured her attention. She wouldn't have been able to look away from him if she'd tried.

They were dark, intense, hungry.

All because of her.

And she loved it.

He sauntered toward her like a lion approached his mate—powerful, in control and confident. If it struck his fancy right now to lift her skirts and make love to her, she had no doubt she'd comply willingly. Despite the guests starting to arrive two floors below them, one word from him would be all it would take. She'd slip her hand into his and lead him back to the bedroom.

His gaze wandered lazily down to her toes, then back

up again, as if he had all the time in the world. A know-ing smiled curved his lips, making her skin tingle with delight. "Are you wearing them?" His voice was deeper than normal, making her acutely aware of that sensitive spot where her inner thighs touched.

"Yes," she answered.

He exhaled slowly, ruffling her hair. "I knew you would."

Then, gently, he drew the back of his finger down along her neck and leaned in close. She arched her head back, wanting to feel his lips against her.

Alongside the gown on the bed had sat a gold box. In-side, beneath the tissue, was a gorgeous black lace cor-set, panties and stockings. The printing on the card was bold. "The gown is for you. These are for me."

She'd never worn a corset before, so it took a few min-utes to figure it out. It felt strangely, yet wonderfully, restrictive. The lace wasn't all that soft and the boning pushed her breasts up, making her cleavage much more substantial than she was used to. But when she slipped the gown over her head and covered it all up, she felt very naughty. Like she was harboring a delicious secret. To-night, everyone would see the gown, but they'd have no idea what she had on underneath.

Except for Trace.

Even now, she could feel the slight scratchiness of the lace rubbing against skin that wasn't used to the texture. No matter where she was tonight or what she was doing, the sensation would always bring her thoughts back to the corset and him. He'd done that on purpose, she real-ized.

"Good God. What have I done?" He practically growled as he pressed her against the wall.

She laughed, pleased by his over-the-top reaction. "Why? What seems to be the problem?"

"You, Charlotte, are the problem. I'm not used to feeling this way. I've got a hundred guests arriving, and I should be down to greet them, but all I can think about is you."

"Me?" she asked innocently.

"Yes. You are absolutely stunning. Without a doubt, you're the most beautiful woman I have ever laid eyes on. And it makes me want you all the more knowing that underneath this gown, you're wearing the items I selected for you." He rubbed his hip against hers as if to prove his point.

Damn. He wasn't kidding, she thought, a delicious shiver racing down her spine. He laughed softly then. The thin triangle of her panties suddenly felt hot as she imagined him pushing inside her.

"Later, after the party is over and most of the guests have left or retired to their rooms, I plan to see what you look like."

She could hardly breathe. "You do?"

"Yes. And did you happen to notice that the panties had tiny snaps at the hips?"

"They do?" She'd been so focused on getting everything on that she hadn't even noticed.

"That's so I can remove them without you taking off the corset or garter."

Remove just her panties while leaving on everything else? The ligaments in her knees threatened to give way as she visualized what he planned to do to her.

"I want you to keep those shoes on. And the corset. Did you have any difficulty getting it laced up on your own? I'd have offered to help, but I'm afraid it would've made us much too late."

"I managed it fine." Actually, it had been a royal pain in the ass, but she wasn't about to complain.

He tilted her chin up and for a split second, she thought he was going to kiss her. His lips parted and he dipped his head to hers. Then, far below them, the doorbell sounded, and he hesitated.

Probably a good thing, she realized and she took that opportunity to duck under his arm. He needed to be downstairs greeting his guests, not up here with her. No matter how much fun this was.

"If I thought I was having a hard time keeping my hands off you before," he growled, "tonight is going to be an utter nightmare."

She liked the swooshing sound the gown made as she walked. "Then don't even try."

TRACE STOOD NEAR the large Christmas tree in the main living room, listening to the hushed whispers of a few Council members about what was going on with Darkbloods in a small village near Prague. Evidently, there'd been a few vampire sightings—otherwise known as vampires behaving badly—and the locals were scared. Events like this happened periodically before Guardians were sent in to take care of things.

"Shall we continue this conversation in the library where things are more private?" Trace asked.

As he navigated the small group through the crowd and past one of the buffet tables, he looked for Char but didn't see her anywhere. Focusing on her heartbeat, he could feel her presence nearby, a side effect of having taken so much of her blood recently, and he couldn't help smiling to himself. He loved that she gave it to him freely, but he really should learn to pace himself. For both their sakes. But when he thought about the corset she wore right now, he rather doubted his pledge for self-restraint would start tonight.

"And that's not all," Rodderick Tjorval said once they were in the library, the door safely shut behind him. "One of the old European families is suspected of having ties with the Darkblood Alliance."

"Oh, for God's sake," someone said.

"No kidding?" asked someone else.

"Yes," Tjorval continued. "There's an ongoing investigation into their activities over the past several decades and things aren't looking good."

Trace opened the humidor and offered his guests cigars.

"What will happen if those suspicions turn out to be true?" Nicklaus Mercada asked.

"They'll lose their seat on the Council." Tjorval chose one of the Cohiba cigars and held it to his nose. "And if the charges are serious, they'll go before the court to plead their case and await judgment."

Trace had never heard of such a thing happening before. "What constitutes serious?" He handed the man a cutter. He snipped off the end and held the cigar out for Trace to light.

"Any number of things. One of the foremost would be if they participated in or funded activities which led to the killing of humans for blood sport."

Trace suddenly got uncomfortable. These people did not need to be reminded of this a few weeks before they voted on his fate. Then again, it might not matter at all when they found out about Charlotte. However, he'd prefer to have his future decided by actions he took himself, rather than by the actions of a family member that had nothing to do with him.

"That's not necessarily true." He hadn't heard Sebastian

come in. Without waiting to be offered a cigar, his cousin grabbed a Montecristo from the humidor and snipped off the end. "Another branch of the family can petition the Council for the seat, make the case why they should have it instead, right, cuz?"

Trace stiffened. He wasn't sure he liked where this was going.

"Didn't that happen to your family, Trace?" Henry DeGraff asked.

The lingering taste of the cigar suddenly turned bitter on the back of his tongue. "Yes, that's my understanding. Something happened all those years ago and the seat changed hands."

Sebastian laughed, smoke streaming out of his mouth like a dragon. "My great-grandfather fell in love with a human woman—that's what happened. It didn't seem to matter that they had plans for her to become a changeling. At that time, relationships with humans simply weren't done. Lucky for Trace here, those rules have loosened considerably."

With a wine bottle in each hand, Charlotte returned to the main floor and headed into the kitchen. The catering staff had needed more white wine, and given that Marcel was already frazzled, she'd offered to run down to the cellar. Once there, she'd eyed the storage room door at the end of the long hallway. Not allowing herself to dwell on what she must've seen last year, she quickly grabbed the bottles and headed back upstairs.

After dropping them off in the kitchen, she headed to the ballroom to look for Vik. The quartet was playing a melodic tango and a few people were dancing, but she didn't see the woman anywhere. Maybe she was in the—

A hand came around her waist, and she bristled. She knew instantly it wasn't Trace.

"Looking for a dance partner?" With his dark hair lightly slicked back and those perfectly white teeth, Sebastian was seductively charming. Like a cobra. Before she could answer or protest, he swept her onto the dance floor.

Since Sebastian and his girlfriend had been here, she hadn't seen them at all. Thank God the mansion was huge. They took all their meals in their quarters in the guest wing. It was as if they were living in a hotel. She'd wondered if Trace had talked to him, told him to stay away.

He held her much too close now, his hand spanning her rib cage. It dawned on her that he could probably feel the boning of her corset, which was disconcerting. That should be a secret for Trace only.

"So it seems the two of you have reached some sort of agreement with this tenuous relationship of yours."

"I wouldn't call it tenuous."

He twirled her around then pulled her close again, his mouth against her ear. All she could think about were his fangs, hidden now, but inches from her jugular. A barely there memory hung just out of reach.

"Then what would you call a relationship between a vampire and a human?" His voice was saccharine smooth.

"We are simply a man and a woman. In love."

He laughed softly and a forgotten dream tugged at her thoughts. Faint recollections and hardly perceptible sensations. Dreadful sensations.

Drops of something dark on a white dress. Blood? The curve of a woman's neck and shoulders. Lifeless eyes. Razor-sharp fangs.

Oh, God, the woman from last year. Panic knotted

around her gut as the images became less murky. He hadn't just fed from her, as Trace had thought. He'd killed her. That was what Charlotte had seen.

She tried to pull away from Sebastian, but he held her tightly against him. Although the room was stifling hot, her fingers and toes went numb.

"Ah, and you are so naive. Like most humans. Trace is a man—yes—but with very inhuman needs."

With a sudden detached curiosity, she looked at her hand in his, aware of a strange prickly feeling moving down her arm. Out of her body and into his.

"Those inhuman needs might one day become too powerful to control. And if anything were to happen to you, he'd be the first to be blamed. Charlotte, did you know that most murders are perpetrated by a loved one? That is why they are called crimes of passion."

His voice was soft. Lulling.

"And with the Council rules being what they are, his seat would revert back to me and my family."

She held back a yawn. Her eyelids felt heavy. So tired. She needed to tell…to tell…someone about something. Trouble was, she couldn't quite remember who or what.

CHAPTER TEN

THE DRUMBEAT INSIDE Trace's head became almost unbearable. He really should stay and listen to these Council members discuss policies and politics, but he just couldn't take it any longer. The walls felt as if they were closing in on him.

"Excuse me, gentlemen. I should circulate, make sure my other guests are comfortable." He quickly exited the room.

The last time he'd felt this way was when Charlotte had been in danger outside that club. Where the hell was she?

He strode through the main rooms, looking for the telltale silver sparkle of that dress. Groups of people were laughing and eating, but no Charlotte. A few guests tried to strike up a conversation with him, but he didn't pay any attention. A quick check of the kitchen showed she wasn't there, either.

He sprinted through the gallery and into the ballroom. The string quartet was playing a holiday classic and dozens of couples were dancing. Above the music, the sound in his head became an incessant roar.

Find me. Find me. Find me.

Jackson, who'd been flirting with a different woman every time Trace had seen him this evening, suddenly appeared right in front of him. "Dude, are you all right?"

"It's Charlotte. Something's happened. I can feel it."

His friend wasted no time going into full Guardian mode. He unbuttoned his jacket to make his weapons more accessible and punched a code into his phone. "When did you last see her? Is she on the premises?"

"It's been more than an hour." Trace reached inside, centered himself. "She's not far away, but I can't tell if she's inside or not."

"Dom's gonna be pissed he left early. He'd be all over this."

"Yeah, I know he would," Trace answered. "But if there is something going on, maybe it's best that Mackenzie and the baby aren't here." If only Charlotte was also somewhere safe....

"We'll find her, man. Don't worry." Jackson headed for the stairs. "I'll check up here. You take downstairs. Meet you back in five."

Trace wrenched open the double doors and took the steps two at a time. Although it was faint, he could almost smell the vanilla scent of her skin. She'd been down here at some point recently.

If something happened to her, he didn't know what he would do. Whether it was the seat on the Council or his status among his peers...none of that mattered if he didn't have Charlotte in his life.

It had taken losing her, then finding her again for him to come to that realization. He wasn't about to lose her again.

The wine cellar was empty. He was about to head back upstairs when his gaze landed on the storage room door. When he wrenched it open, all he saw was were a few empty boxes of Christmas decorations.

No Charlotte.

And yet...

His cousin's face flashed in his mind. The hungry, wolfish grin. His disregard for the rule of law.

Trace got the distinct feeling that Sebastian was behind this somehow. He'd left the library soon after dropping the bombshell about his family and Trace hadn't seen him since.

By the time Trace got to the foyer again, Jackson was coming down one of the twin staircases.

"She's not up there," Jackson said. "And I checked all the rooms. Including the occupied ones. Do we search the exterior premises or could she have left by vehicle? Can you tell?"

Trace focused inward, but heard nothing from her. He shook his head.

"Come on," Jackson said. "Let's go out and see if you pick up anything there."

"I'll be right there." A moment later Trace was in his bedchamber, where he pocketed his scorpion blade and a few other weapons. He was not going to lose Charlotte without a fight.

Back downstairs, just as he was about to head outside, the wrought-iron door to the elevator opened. His grandmother was sitting on the small bench inside.

"Have you found her yet? When your friend burst in on me and said—"

"No, Grandmother." He didn't have time for—

"I last saw her dancing with Sebastian. About twenty minutes ago. I remember thinking it seemed a little odd, but didn't think more about it until that young man, the Guardian with the red-streaked hair, came into my room, looking for her."

Sebastian. He'd been right to suspect his cousin's involvement.

He bolted outside and quickly located Jackson. "My cousin—he's driving a black Escalade. He took her."

The valet he'd hired stepped out from his station. "Sir, a black Escalade left the party about fifteen minutes ago."

Jackson palmed his keys. "Then let's go."

They climbed into the Guardian's jacked-up truck and careened down the long driveway. But just as they were about to turn onto the main road, a strange feeling came over Trace. The mental pull seemed to be lessening. He was almost certain Charlotte hadn't come this way. She… she…was behind him somewhere.

"Let me out," he demanded.

"But—"

Trace opened the door and Jackson slammed on the brakes, spinning the truck in a one-eighty.

"Follow up on the Escalade, but it could be Sebastian's girlfriend leading us on a wild-goose chase. I'll be in touch." Before the car came to a complete halt, Trace was on the ground, running.

DRIFTS OF SNOW had blown in under the trees, blanketing the forest in silence. All Trace could hear was the muffled sound of his footsteps and his own even breathing.

He'd forgotten about the guesthouse on the back of the property. It had been a favorite hangout of Sebastian's when he'd visited as a kid. If he had Charlotte, he may have taken her there.

The lights from the main house didn't extend to where the cottage stood at the edge of the forest, dark and forgotten. Years ago, his mother had used it as a potting shed, but now, it was rarely occupied. The mansion was more than big enough to accommodate any guests.

The closer he got, the more certain he was that Charlotte was somewhere inside. He could feel the pull of her blood. Whipping out his phone, he sent a quick text to Jackson then stuffed the thing back into his pocket just as he reached the white picket fence.

He knew he should circle the cottage to assess the situation and wait for backup, but fury clouded his judgment. He couldn't stand to have Charlotte spend another moment inside.

In three strides he was on the porch. Then with one mighty kick, he brought the front door down.

Charlotte was slumped in a wooden chair in the center of the room with Sebastian leaning over her. He snapped his head up when Trace crashed into the room, surprise registering on his face. Fangs hung from his mouth and blood—Charlotte's blood—trickled down his chin.

A burning rage shot through Trace's system, ringing in his ears.

"Motherfucker!" Trace launched himself at his cousin.

His right hook made contact with the side of the guy's head, while his left hook got him in the belly. Sebastian doubled over, but he didn't go down.

"A relationship…with a human…can't work, Trace. You of all people should know that." Sebastian groaned as he straightened up and flashed a weak-assed smile. "In fact, did you know…those were the exact words…your grandfather said to mine…the day he stole the Council seat…from us?"

"But why would you go after Charlotte? She's innocent."

"I was thirsty, what can I say?" Sebastian touched the corner of his mouth where Trace had hit him.

"That's bullshit. You're a coward, that's what you are. I'm the one you should've come after, not her."

"Who says I didn't? I kill Charlotte, but you take the blame because they assume you fucked up and took too much of her blood. You lose your seat on the Council, and it shifts back to the Tafts, where it rightfully belongs."

The next punch knocked his cousin all the way down and Trace jumped to Charlotte's side. "Are you okay? Did he hurt you?" But she didn't answer. Gently, his cradled her face in his hands. Her normally rosy lips were tinged blue and her skin was cold. Sebastian had taken too much from her.

Without thinking, Trace pulled out his scorpion blade and drew it across his wrist. As the blood welled up, he held it to her mouth.

"Drink," he commanded her.

But she remained still, lifeless in his arms.

Clutching her body to his, he yelled to the heavens. The only time in his life he'd ignored his duty, forgotten his promise to his father and dared to love the forbidden had resulted in this unspeakable tragedy.

The woman he loved was gone.

HUSHED VOICES CAME from somewhere faraway. Charlotte knew she should open her eyes but the effort was just too much. She was so tired. So cold. All she wanted to do was sleep.

Strong arms lifted her up and her face pressed into the hard, warm plane of someone's chest. He smelled of sandalwood and Christmas trees. Trace.

If only she could hold him one more time. Tell him how much she loved him before she had to go. As her life force ebbed out, faint memories flashed before her, including the first time she and Trace had been together.

Just as she'd suspected, she'd loved him then, as well.

More jostling, more voices, then something warm touched her lips.

If only she could tell him just one more time....

CHAPTER ELEVEN

"JUST BE PATIENT," his grandmother said. "These things can take time."

It had been twenty-four hours since he'd first found Charlotte in the cottage with Sebastian, her body nearly drained of blood.

As Guardians took care of Sebastian, he ministered to Charlotte.

Desperately, he'd given her some of his own blood, but she was too far gone for it to do any good. It was only when he rushed her back to the house that his grandmother suggested her one hope was to become a changeling.

He knew these things required approval by the Council after a lengthy waiting period. But Charlotte didn't have that kind of time.

His grandmother hadn't hesitated. She'd grabbed the scorpion blade from Trace and drawn it across her wrist, then held it to Charlotte's lips.

"Hush," she'd told him, though he wasn't about to protest. "I'm not ready to let this girl go, either."

And now, a full day later, Charlotte's body finally stirred. Her eyelids fluttered, the color returned to her cheeks.

"Char, can you hear me? If you can, know that I love you. Very much."

For an endless moment, there was no response. He held

his breath, marking the passage of time with each heart-beat. Then, slowly, her fingers reached out and curled around his.

One month later

CHARLOTTE STOOD AT THE BACK of the cavern with Trace and adjusted the collar of his silk cape, part of the ceremonial dress his people had been wearing for centuries.

Two nights ago, they'd arrived in Madrid, the original headquarters of the Night Brethren, where important Council ceremonies were still conducted. At first, Trace had argued with her, said she wasn't strong enough yet to travel. However, with the help of Trace's friend Dom and a few other well-respected officials, she'd been granted an audience before the Council yesterday. She wasn't about to pass up the opportunity to speak to them.

Other than being a little tired as her body adjusted to its new way of acquiring and processing energy, she felt great. Her muscles were strong, her vision was better than before, her mind was sharp and her bond with Trace was even more powerful. She hadn't wanted to say anything to him yet, but she felt certain that their union—as his people, now her people, liked to call it—would someday produce a child. A Westfalen heir. The prospect thrilled her.

When she awoke after the transformation to change-ling was complete, Trace had fallen to his knees, an emotional wreck. She'd learned that he hadn't left her bedside since he rescued her from Sebastian. If she'd ever had any doubts how he felt about her, she needn't have worried. Again he apologized for wiping her memories last year and for what she'd gone through because of him. She'd laughed, stroked his hair and told him how much she loved him.

Yesterday, everyone present had remained quiet and reverent throughout the various proceedings. When it was her turn, however, she'd boldly walked to the stone podium, her hair covered by the hood of her robe, its hem trailing out behind her. In a clear voice that echoed throughout the chamber, she'd read the speech she'd written with Vik's help. It outlined all the reasons Trace should be sworn in to the North American Council.

One of the elders had brought up concerns about the Westfalen family's commitment to Council philosophy because of the business with Trace's uncle and now, his cousin.

"What's contained in a man's heart speaks more to his character than his lineage," Charlotte had replied. "Trace has demonstrated time and again that he believes in what the Governing Council stands for and isn't afraid to fight for his beliefs." She held out her arms. "I'm living proof of that."

In the end, Trace was voted in. Today marked the day he took his oaths.

"How do I look?" he asked now.

He towered over her, his shoulders proud and strong. The red lining of his cape, which signified his family's lineage, brought out the blue in his eyes, she noted, even in the dim light of all these candles. His muscular bare chest begged for her to run her hands over it, but she restrained herself. There'd be time for that later. Lots more time, she thought with a smile, considering her extended lifespan.

"Just about perfect," she whispered. "You look very vampirish. And very sexy."

A guard dressed in full military regalia stepped out of the shadows. It was time.

Trace pulled the hood of her robe to cover her hair, his fingertips brushing her jawline. "And I can say the same about you."

The guard cleared his throat.

"Ready?" Trace asked her.

"As long as you are, I am."

The ceremonial chambers were packed, with rows of people lining the walls, making the space feel even smaller. A human had never witnessed the swearing in of a Council member before, although technically Charlotte wasn't human any longer.

Trace's voice boomed out strong and confident, sending shivers of pride skating down her back. This was her man, she thought. The man she was spending the rest of her life with. His grandmother would be proud of him, as well. Charlotte was sad Vik hadn't been able to make the trip over to witness this.

After reciting his allegiance to the Governing Council, Trace picked up the large pillar candle in front of him and approached the eternal flame burning from a pit behind the altar. He lit his candle, then carried it to a wall, where he placed it alongside dozens of others. When he turned around, everyone clapped and cheers rang out around them.

It was official then. Trace was now a member of the Governing Council. She couldn't wait to show him how proud she was of him.

"THE SHOES. They stay on for now."

He chuckled when he noticed Charlotte's hand pausing on the strap of her heels. Trace had asked her to wear the lingerie he'd bought her for the Christmas party since he hadn't been able to fully appreciate it back then. And he'd bought her a new dress—red, this time—which she'd worn under the ceremonial black robe today.

"But—"

"Don't worry, you're not going to be doing any more walking."

He swept her into his arms and carried her into the hotel suite. His footsteps pounded on the hardwood floor of the hallway, echoing the tempo of her heart. When they entered the bedroom, he kicked the door closed and set her next to the bed.

She reached around to unzip the dress, but he stopped her. "I'll do it."

Her lips were soft but demanding against his as he eased the zipper down himself. They hadn't made love since her transformation—not only had he worried about controlling the urge to take her blood, but he'd wanted her to get accustomed to all the changes first, despite her attempts to convince him otherwise. But after witnessing her performance in front of the Council yesterday and today, his needs could wait no longer. Hooking his thumbs under the neckline of the dress, he slid the bloodred fabric from her shoulders and let it drop at her feet.

His erection throbbed as he stared at the creamy mounds spilling over the top of her corset. He touched her soft flesh, warm and yielding under his fingertips, and her breath hitched. God, she was so perfect. Curling his fingers inside, he brushed the tips of her nipples, barely concealed by the lace.

"I've wanted this so badly, Trace. You, this, everything. Promise me you will never make me wait this long again."

That'd be an easy promise to keep. "You have my word."

As he debated whether or not to unlace her corset, Charlotte unsnapped her panties and did that little shimmy thing until the scrap of lace fell from her hips. Then she reached under his drawstring waistband and her cool fingers wrapped around his shaft.

"Good God, Char." He rolled his hips forward and felt the glorious friction of her hand.

She gripped him tighter. "I love the easy access of your ceremonial garb. You should wear clothes like this more often."

A groan that sounded more like a growl burst from his throat. Nope, he decided. He didn't want her to undress further. He'd take her just like this.

He nudged her onto the bed, but before he joined her, he hesitated.

"What are you doing?" she asked, propping herself up on her elbows.

"You'll see." He strode to the walk-in closet and retrieved the large antique mirror he'd spotted earlier. Thankfully, it had castors on the bottom and slid easily over the carpet toward the bed.

Charlotte laughed. "No way."

"I told you," he said as he adjusted the mirror. "I'm a very visual person."

He sat on the bed next to her and ran his hands over her thighs, still encased in the silk hose. Pushing her knees wider, he exposed her sex. It would be hot inside…slick… and very, very tight. God, dressed like this, she was sin, personified. There wasn't much he wouldn't do for this woman. Including breaking every law known to man and vampire. Hell, he'd broken many of them already.

Kneeling between her legs, he spread one hand on her flat lower belly and slid two fingers of his other hand into her warm folds. Her muscles gripped him tight as he moved in and out. He placed the pad of his thumb on her swollen nub of flesh, pressing it gently at first.

"Oh, God," she said, digging the heels of her shoes into the sheets on either side of him. Her muscles tightened, so he pressed his thumb a little harder. "Oh, God," she said, over and over this time, her voice raspy and raw.

He glanced at the mirror and his eyes locked onto hers. How long had she been watching him pleasuring her?

She came quickly against his fingers. When she was finished, he withdrew and planned to bury another part of himself deep inside.

"Hold on," she said, rolling over. "Let me adjust the mirror. I want to be able to see all of you as you're making love to me."

Heaven help him, he thought as he stared at her. Positioned like she was, on all fours, it'd be easy for him to take her this way. His balls ached, suddenly feeling even heavier between his legs. Again, their eyes met in the reflection.

"Yes," she answered his unspoken question, arching her back slightly.

Gripping himself, he slid just the tip against her swollen opening and it easily slipped inside. She tried to rock back on him, but he held her steady for a moment. He turned his attention to the mirror to find that her breasts had spilled out over the top of the black lace. Good. He'd be able to watch them bounce and move. Her bottom was round, gorgeous, her daggerlike heels pointed out behind him. From this angle, he could see a few inches of his erection. But if he moved over, he might be able to…

Shifting slightly, he— Christ, he could see every-thing now.

"My God, Char. You're so hot, you should be illegal." Curving his fingers around her corset-covered waist, he thrust his hips forward. And in one amazing instant, he watched as he slid into her body.

"Oh, my God, Trace. This is…is…"

She wasn't going to say *big* again, was she? Not that he would've minded.

He molded his chest to her back, rested his hands beside hers, then began to move inside her. The friction of each stroke ignited all his nerve endings to the point where he didn't think he could hold out much longer. His fangs were already fully extended.

"You're so beautiful, Char," he whispered into her hair. "And I love you so incredibly much."

"And I love you, too."

With his tongue, he easily located the pounding pulse of her vein. In one swift movement, his fangs clamped down and plunged into her flesh. She stiffened momentarily, let out a soft hiss. And as he swallowed that first sip of sweetness and felt her muscles spasm around him, he came hard, releasing his seed in an explosion of white-hot pleasure.

"Honestly, Char," he said as they lay in each other's arms a few minutes later. "I don't know what I did to deserve a woman like you."

All his life, he'd tried to live up to his birthright, holding duty and honor above all else. But in the end, although those things were still important to him, it was the love of this woman that had truly completed him, making it possible for him to fulfill his destiny. Oddly enough, were his father still alive today, Trace was pretty certain he'd have been proud of him and the choices he had made.

"Simple," she said. "You were true to yourself and followed your heart, which made you the man of my dreams."

* * * * *

Don't miss Jackson's story,
TEMPTED BY BLOOD,
coming soon from Laurie London
and HQN Books!

And be sure to check out
the other sizzling Sweetblood novels:
BONDED BY BLOOD,
EMBRACED BY BLOOD
and the e-novella, HIDDEN BY BLOOD,
available now!

MONSTERS
DON'T DO CHRISTMAS

CHAPTER ONE

THE WEREWOLF'S FIST packed a remarkable wallop. Daniel Harrison had developed some kind of funky, supernatural strength since he'd transformed into a vampire a year ago, but he'd quickly learned that strength was nothing when matched against a werewolf.

Why did these guys hate him so much?

There were two of them, and the biggest, with no discernible neck, served a pummel of blows to Daniel's gut. He wasn't in position to latch on to either with his fangs, and the idea of clamping down on their nasty flesh didn't suit his preference for a clean bite.

A Christmas storm battered New York City. Snowflakes stung them with an icy scrape and at times hindered Daniel from seeing the oncoming punches.

He knew why the dogs had been following him on his nightly hunt for sustenance. They sought an unaligned vampire who had no ties to the local tribes to bring home to the pack and turn into a chew toy. Wolves did nasty things with vampires, like lock them up, force them to endure UV light torture, then after the vamps were starving and raging for blood, the wolves pitted them against one another in a battle to the death. This vampire wasn't down for the count yet.

With renewed vigor, Daniel swung and landed a forceful punch in a werewolf's kidney. The bruiser grunted and toppled backward, landing in his cohort's arms. Bouncing on his feet like a boxer, Daniel had to smile at the swift move.

"Hey!"

At sound of the female voice, all three—vampire and werewolves—twisted to spy a woman tromping down the snow-packed alleyway with a grocery bag in hand. Furry boots rose to her knees and were tied with laces capped in thick fur balls that bounced with each step. A fur-rimmed hood covered her head and her face was bundled against the winter storm with a scarf that protected her mouth and nose. Bright green eyes sought each of them with chastising force.

"You think you made your point?" she said to one of the werewolves, who punched a fist into his palm. "I don't want trouble. But you do know the police station is around the corner."

Both wolves exchanged nervous glances. One shook his head and sneered at Daniel.

Daniel could feel the pansy accusation from the werewolves waver through the air at him and strike him smartly in the testicles. Defended by a woman? Not cool. He smacked a fist in his palm.

"We're out of here," the wolf with the steel fist announced, and they shoved roughly past the woman and tromped off.

Nice. Like he needed one more thing to make the wolves laugh at him, the unaligned vampire who was this close to cashing in all his chips, be it as a werewolf's bitch or by the stake.

"Had 'em right where I wanted them," Daniel said, his anger rising at the humiliation of having a woman defend him. "And I didn't need you to interfere."

"Uh-huh." She stepped through the flurry of snowflakes, her path obviously aimed toward the iron stairway hugging the brownstone. "You were eating that brick wall, buddy."

Furious at her catty comment, he grasped her by the furry coat lapels and swung her around, slamming her against the wall. The bag of groceries crushed against her stomach. The werewolves had caught him tonight before he'd satisfied his hunger, and she looked warm, mortal and appetizing.

"Oh, yeah? That's not what I have in mind to eat." He willed his fangs down and worked his best scary snarl on her.

The woman tilted her head, eyeing his canines, but he didn't feel so much as a shiver when he leaned against her body. What was wrong with mortals nowadays? Their scare factor had dropped off the scale.

"Aren't you afraid?" he demanded, feeling his own fears rise from that awful night a year ago when the vampires had attacked him in the subway. Yes, he'd been fearful. He hadn't believed in monsters, hadn't time for that fantasy bullshit. Now he couldn't get away from it.

"I'm not afraid," she offered boldly.

Daniel laughed inside, but on the outside he remained serious. Sweet little thing didn't know what she was dealing with. She probably thought the fangs were fake. Or…

"I get it. You're one of those chicks who gets off on men with fangs. You put posters on your walls and swoon over the movie star vampires with the stupid hair. Like to tail around behind us, and beg to get bitten."

"Not particularly." She reached for his face, which made him flinch, but the soft yarn mitten managed to stroke his aching chin. "I bruise easily, and I can't abide stupid hair."

She was not processing the enormity of her danger. Must be in shock.

Daniel tightened his jaw, but when he met her eyes, the anger that had built inside him for a year dissipated like a faulty snowball dispersing midair. It felt wrong to play the big bad to brave Miss Bright Eyes. Why hadn't he been capable of standing up to his attackers like she had? He wasn't a pansy, and he used to go a few rounds in the boxing ring every weekend with a buddy. It was just that werewolves were so strong.

"I live at the top of the stairs," she said, thick snowflakes dusting her lacy dark lashes. "Why don't you come up and let me tend that bruise. Who beats up a vampire and actually wins?"

"Werewolves," he said sharply, and then waited for her to panic.

But she didn't. Instead, she nodded, accepting. Something was seriously wrong with this woman.

"They didn't win," he corrected. "You arrived just when I—"

"I know. You had them right where you wanted them." She slid out of his grasp and started up the stairs that hugged the side of the brick brownstone, her boots clunking on the iron steps. "Coming?"

Daniel couldn't figure what had just happened. Maybe the woman was a witch or demon or—hell, someone in the know. Mortals didn't accept him so calmly. Screaming was the usual response. The occasional stake was to be expected.

Shoving a hand over his hair, which was wet with snowflakes and probably some of his own blood, he licked his lips. The bruises and wounds the werewolves had inflicted would be gone in minutes. But resist an invite into a pretty woman's home?

He looked around, shuffled his feet, and shoved his hands into his front jeans pockets.

He was a monster, and a hungry one at that. The pretty lady had best beware.

OLIVIA ADORATA SHRUGGED off her winter coat, wool mittens and hat, and tossed them over the back of the worn leather easy chair in the tiny apartment she rented throughout the year, but only got to visit about five out of the fifty-two weeks. Her hair was a mess and she wore yoga pants and a bleach-stained shirt. She hadn't expected to encounter a handsome man on her way home, or to so boldly invite him in—make that a handsome *vampire*.

Behind her, the vampire stood in the open doorway, snowflakes whipping in around his tall, lean frame and onto the carpet.

A vampire.

She'd met plenty of actors who played vampires and even a nonactor who had completely believed himself a denizen of the dark. But she'd never met a real vampire. Thanks to her mother's penchant for all things spiritual and otherworldly, Olivia believed they existed, or at least, wouldn't discount them just because she hadn't met one before.

She prided herself on being open-minded, but hadn't expected to ever come face-to-face with one—and come so close to his fangs. That had freaked her, but she possessed the incredible ability to remain calm on the outside while inside she was screaming. Attribute that to her profession. Never let them see you sweat.

And how to be frightened by a man who looked like he belonged in a men's fitness magazine? The muscles were apparent through his thin leather jacket, and that solid jaw and sharply buzzed dark hair added to his appeal. Freckles on his nose granted him a bit of a boy-next-door look — with fangs. She loved freckles.

Too intrigued not to invite him in, Olivia hoped she wasn't doing the last thing she'd ever do. On the other hand, the horned devil sitting on her shoulder prodded her with its pitchfork and whispered, "Risk," and she jumped at the opportunity.

"Come in," she coaxed, and offered the man a warm smile. She tugged down her shirt, hoping to hide the bleach stain at her hip. "It's nothing fancy, but it's home. Wish I had time to get a tree, but I'd never be able to lug it up the outside stairs. Maybe a small one." Oh, how she tended to babble when she was nervous. *Deep breath, Olivia. Chill.* "Come in."

As if released from an invisible barrier, the vampire stepped inside and closed the door behind him. He stomped his boots on the mat.

"So you really need an invite to enter a place? That's so cool."

"Personal property, yes. Not so much on the public property. What are you?"

"I don't understand the question." She strode toward the bathroom. "I'm going to get some medical supplies."

"What I mean is," he called after her, "what kind of monster are you that you know what I am, and don't seem the least bit frightened by me?"

She glanced in the bathroom mirror. Monster? If he only knew she was an even bigger monster. *Did* he know? He hadn't said anything to clue her that he was aware who she was. Interesting.

On the other hand, she wasn't exactly playing up the glamorous mode right now. She reached for the medical supplies and forced herself not to dash on some blush and eyeliner. That would look too obvious.

Returning to the living room with alcohol, cotton balls and Band-Aids, she set them on the glass coffee table and gestured for him to sit on the leather couch. "Do you want me to be frightened of you?"

He shrugged, which only drew attention to his broad shoulders. The man was not shockingly pretty, but a good, solid stretch of sex appeal and confidence—mercy, those melting snowflakes in his hair twinkled under the lights. Olivia was so tired of models and hangers-on. This guy was a bright gift of normality, aside from the fact he sported fangs, which added an irresistibly dangerous twist to this encounter. He was everything she should avoid—hell, run from and never look back.

"Sit down," she said, with another gesture to the couch. "What's your name?"

"What's yours?" He stalked to the couch and made himself at home, slamming his wet boots up on the coffee table.

Olivia shoved his feet off and then pulled off his boots and tossed them to the rug by the door.

"Hey!"

"The carpet is beige and a bitch to clean."

And he—damn, he smelled delicious. A mix of winter snow, leather and aggressive male. While all her caution alarms sounded, Olivia decided this was an opportunity she couldn't let pass. If she could do this, she could do anything. And what she really needed in her life right now was a burst of confidence.

"I'm Olivia…." She paused, waiting for his reaction, but sensed if he hadn't already said something, that he likely wasn't aware who she really was.

"I'm a common mortal," she offered, avoiding all the sensational details that half the population knew better than she, "who is not a monster—although, there are times I can be very monstrous—and happens to believe that the world is populated by all sorts. Though I've never met one of those, uh…*sorts* until now. At least, not a real one. Those fangs are real, right?"

He nodded and she kneeled before him and unscrewed the cap from the alcohol bottle. "So what's your name, and why were werewolves beating you up?"

As she said the *W* word it got stuck at the back of her throat, and a scream almost slipped by, but her stage training rescued her nerves from becoming all-out fear.

He leaned forward, meeting her gaze. Deep brown eyes flecked with dark spots to match the freckles on his nose held her mesmerized. How often did a man look a girl directly in the eyes? Didn't seem to happen enough in her life. Wow. How long did it take before a look moved from stranger to friendship to so much more? Only a matter of seconds, she knew that. Wow, again. Holding his gaze, she realized he looked a little…lost.

Fighting the urge to touch his mouth, to feel him—was he different than a mortal man?—Olivia fended off the foolish move.

"Name's Daniel," he said, leaning back and stretching an arm across the leather couch. His shirt tugged over tight abs and a rip down the side gaped to expose the rigid structure of his awesome physique. "And the damned dogs don't like vampires. Not really in the holiday spirit, is it? Goodwill toward others and all that Christmas bullshit. It's a vamp-werewolf thing, as far as I understand. They normally get along, but you'll find racists among any breed."

"Interesting." Her mother would have loved this moment. She gestured with an alcohol-laden cotton ball that he lean forward so she could dab at the cut she'd seen on his lip when he'd had her slammed against the wall outside. "It's going to sting."

"You don't need to do that."

Running her tongue along her lower lip, she slipped into a fantasy about the mouth inches from her eyes. Those firm lips would feel warm against hers, and he'd take from her exactly as he wished as he ran his hands over her body and pulled her against all his hard planes. And she'd like to give him whatever he desired.

Oh, Olivia, sounds like the lyrics to some stupid pop song. He's not going to ravish you, no matter how much your silly heart wants him to. The guy just escaped werewolves. Why are you not freaking?

She looked for the cut. His lips were thick and inviting—would a kiss taste like blood?—but…no cut.

"What's wrong?" he asked in a smooth baritone that hummed in her chest and made her want to perform a duet with him, one composed not of singing, but of lusty kisses and explorative touches. "Finally realize you've invited a monster into your home?"

"No. Well, yes, there is that, but it's—the wound is gone."

"I heal fast. Don't need medical attention, that's for sure."

"Then why did you come up?"

"Because I got an invite from a sexy woman. Not a man alive who could resist that. Even though I suspect you're a little crazy for not freaking over a vampire and two werewolves. Why did you invite me up here? You like to play with fire, Olivia, who is just a common mortal?"

"You think you're fire?" She strolled her eyes down his face and to the tear in his shirt. The cusp of rock-hard pectorals teased. She could feel his invisible flames licking at her inhibitions. "Maybe I asked you in so I could…"

Should she be so bold? The risks were high. For both of them. But she needed this foray into danger.

Hell, a girl only lived once. "Kiss you."

Daniel gripped her by the neck and when she thought the vampire would lunge and rip out her carotid, he smirked, cluing her that she'd reacted with the fearful response he'd been hoping for.

Releasing her breath, her heart thundered and her skin grew clammy. Could she really do this? She wouldn't even look over her shoulder in an attempt to find that approving nod she'd once always required.

This time you're on your own. Can you make a decision without the approval you've grown to expect?

"You want to kiss the vampire?" His tone was teasing. "I knew you were one of those fang junkies."

"I'm not. I already told you I bruise easily. My wanting a kiss has nothing to do with you being a vampire. In fact, the whole Dracula part does unsettle me. Fangs are not sexy. And sure, werewolves freak the crap out of me, but I didn't know that's what they were until after they'd left and you told me."

"Yeah, don't call me Dracula. I don't do capes."

Now she did dare touch his mouth because she noticed a few freckles on his top lip and couldn't not touch. "It's you, Daniel. You're…hell, you're sexy and something about you appeals to a part of me that needs danger in her life. What's wrong with a girl wanting to kiss a handsome man?"

He quirked a brow. That simple motion started a fast burn from her neck down to her breasts, where her nipples perked and her whole body sighed in anticipation. His husky voice melted through her skin and made her want to grab him, touch him, the threat of fangs be damned.

Could the girl, even when clad in the most unsexy outfit ever, do the ravishing? She didn't see why not.

Olivia stood and pushed the vampire's shoulder against the couch. "I'm going to kiss you, Daniel, but if I see a flash of fang, then you're out of here. Deal?"

"You're pretty bossy, you know that?"

"Does that mean there is no deal?"

He pondered it a moment, his now-we've-gone-beyond-friendship stare locked to hers for long seconds. "I'll behave. For now."

Disregarding his inability to fully commit to the deal, she straddled his legs and, kneeling on the couch, kissed him. His mouth was warm, firm and tinted with winter's cool tang. They fit perfectly, and that was saying a lot for a first kiss. Nothing felt awkward about kissing Daniel, and everything felt right. And he wasn't about to let her control the kiss because his hand went around her thigh, claiming her with a squeeze and pulling her closer.

She danced her tongue across his and surprised herself that she didn't feel the sharp prick of fang. He tasted wonderful. Not like blood, but rather, coffee and caramel and maybe a dash of cream. The idea of a vampire drinking coffee was silly, yet so mysteriously sexy, she clasped his head with both hands and deepened the fierce kiss. A sense of success giddied through her system. She'd done it; mastered her fear of being unable to take risks.

She'd experienced an excess of lackadaisical lovers of late. Pretty boys who merely wanted to be seen with her, but when it came to pleasing her? They hadn't studied Woman 101. Daniel the vampire was no slacker. He knew his curriculum, and oh, but he knew how to kiss.

A giddy thrill swirled in her core, a reward for stepping up and taking a chance.

"Hell, you taste incredible," he murmured, and then pressed kisses along her jaw that alternated between nips with his front teeth and lush, licking strokes that curled her toes.

When he neared her neck, Olivia pulled back and pressed a palm to his iron-hard chest. Thundering heart-beats warned her not to get cocky. She hadn't mastered this one, after all.

"This could get hot and heavy, Daniel."

"I thought it already was. You willing to take it to the next level?"

"I never sleep with strangers. That's not my thing."

"So why'd you invite me up? You were the one who kissed me. If you're a tease—"

"Because I was curious, and…I want you," the danger-seeker inside her confessed. "But in order for me to know if I can trust you—"

"You can't trust me." He opened his mouth to reveal a fang.

"Pretty. But still not scared."

He was right; she was crazy if pin-sharp fangs did not frighten her. But that was what this little embrace was all about: risk and conquering the debilitating need for approval.

"What I mean is, there's a deeper kind of trust involved when a man wants to get busy with me. And seriously, I'm as much a monster as you are. It's hard to explain. You have to see it to understand."

"That makes no sense whatsoever."

Standing, she grabbed his hand, and led him toward the door. "Put your boots on, sexy. I've a gig tomorrow night at the Wollman Rink in Central Park. Stop by around 9:00 p.m. if you want to see me again, and get another kiss."

He pressed his hand to the door frame over her shoulder, pinning her against the door. Olivia's heartbeats rocketed to her throat. Did her rapid pulse attract the vampire?

"Just a kiss?" he asked.

Oh, she hoped not. "The kiss will be a start."

Considering, he nodded. Daniel shoved his feet into his boots, then swept a kiss onto her mouth before she even saw it coming. Glee sparkled in his freckled eyes at the stolen morsel. "You know, there's nothing to stop me from creeping back into your place in the middle of the night now that you've invited me in."

"You won't, if you are the man I think you are."

"Oh, sweetie, you are sadly mistaken. I'm a monster. And monsters don't ask permission."

"Still." She opened the door and shoved him outside into a brisk flutter of snowflakes. "If you keep the date, I'm all yours. Beyond kisses, I promise."

CHAPTER TWO

WHAT KIND OF GIG took place at the Wollman ice rink? Was Olivia a figure skater? An athletic woman appealed to Daniel's sensual cravings.

The area was packed with an audience that made him wonder if an Olympic gold medalist were skating. Teen girls jumped up and down and screamed and wielded banners that read We ♥ Olivia. Even the guys were getting into it as they waited for someone to take the stage.

The stage? It had been set up at the end of the ice rink and while some skaters glided and twirled across the span, it appeared the focus was not going to be on the ice.

What was all the fuss about?

Walking a wide circle around the crowd, Daniel got near to the backstage area and heard the loudspeaker introduce Olivia. Just Olivia. No last name. The crowd went wild, cheering and pumping their fists.

Lights flashed in Daniel's face and swept around to focus on the woman who took center stage in a long red gown. Black fur rimmed her wrists and circled her neck, caressing her porcelain face. She began to sing a Christmas song.

"A singer?" And a popular one at that, to judge from the cheers.

He leaned in next to a man who listened raptly. "Is this chick pretty famous?"

"Dude, she's going to be the next Celine Dion. Where have you been?"

"Working eighty-hour weeks as an investment broker?" he tried, but didn't add, *lately, stalking humans for their blood at night.*

The man ignored him and went back to adoring the singer on stage. The crowd had joined in on the chorus of the popular Christmas carol, and cigarette lighters flickered a constellation around the rink. The skaters now performed a routine to the song.

Daniel whistled softly and shook his head. This was an interesting development. How often did famous singers walk around with their own groceries and defend vampires against werewolves?

Not that she'd defended him by any means.

But seriously? The last thing he needed was to get involved with someone famous. He didn't need the media carnival that must surround her. But they weren't involved. They weren't even together, though he'd thought when she'd asked him to meet her here, they'd hook up and head back to her place for a roll between the sheets. No strings, no expectations beyond sex and a bite.

But this? This was lights, camera, attention! All focus on her—and probably anyone she chose to associate with. That was the kicker. Much as Olivia's kiss still lingered on his mouth, Daniel didn't need the headache, or the media following his every footstep as he stalked mortals for blood.

Good thing she had invited him here. He would have really hated to start liking the woman only to later discover what he'd gotten into.

You already like her for her fearlessness around you, and that sexy smile.

Yeah, but fortunately, it wasn't too late to jump that sinking ship.

Shoving his hands in his coat pockets, Daniel turned and wandered out of the park as Olivia's song ended and the crowd roared ecstatically. Christmas carols, of all things. Scrooge was more his speed this time of year. He'd never been into the holiday, and had always worked through it. Hell, days off had been myth in Daniel Harrison's life story. A man never got anywhere sitting on his ass, waiting for others to make things happen. He'd established his career, had bought a few expensive toys and had a fine Manhattan apartment to show for his hard work.

Those had been good times.

Hell, the abrupt switch from corporate raider to vampire hadn't really sparkled up his attitude or outlook. Happiness was for mortals and anyone but him. All this Christmas cheer? They could shove it. He'd find a sexy looker to wrap his arms around and sink his teeth into somewhere else, and in a much quieter setting.

Fifteen minutes later, he stepped onto the street and didn't slow his stride as a taxicab cruised up alongside him. The back window rolled down and a tuft of black fur slid along the door.

"Hey!"

Daniel kept walking, but his libido reacted to the familiar voice by tensing his muscles and speeding up his heart. She'd followed him? Didn't famous people hook up with other famous people? She must be desperate. Or else mentally unsound. That was it. She hadn't freaked over his fangs, and now, as he'd suspected, she had developed an obsession. She wanted to get bitten.

Well, he wasn't going to fulfill that twisted fantasy.

"Why didn't you come backstage and talk to me?" she called out.

"You were busy entertaining the masses. A singer?"

He swung a look to her. Bad idea. Wide green eyes framed by silky black lashes had never looked so lush. Captivating. A soft cloud of black fur surrounded her face. He could almost feel his fingers running through the fur and landing on her hot skin that glistened with some kind of sparkly stuff. To kiss her pale, parted mouth, and—

Daniel paused, shaking his head at how quickly the horny thought had risen. So he had his fantasies. He turned to the cab. "I get it now. You wanted me to see that you're some big freakin' star. Is that what the trust thing was all about?"

"That, and I wanted you to see that I'm as much a monster as you claim to be."

He chuckled. The woman was far from monstrous. And far too naive to be fooling around with his sort.

"I don't need your kind of trouble," he said.

"I see. So you're frightened of me?"

She teased him with the same question he'd asked her. Sly chick. Nothing scared him. Not even werewolves—though he should get smart and learn to avoid the dogs like the plague.

Olivia slicked her tongue along her upper lip, and—mercy—her dress was cut so low amidst the black fur the tempting rise of her breasts drew his eyes like a target.

He could imagine touching that soft, sexy skin, warming his chilled flesh against her angelic paleness. There had been a time when he'd but to wink at a woman and she'd follow him home and into his bed. But he'd never follow with a second date. Too much commitment. And those women had only been attracted to his money and power.

Lately, his romance mojo had been broken due to the fact that his bite usually accompanied a roll between the sheets. Sure, the fangs fascinated some chicks, but they thought them fake, and when they realized they were the real thing? Daniel hadn't known some women could scream so piercingly. Way to make a man feel like a leper.

What could it hurt to have a quickie with the pretty girl, then disappear before the sun rose? And before the media set up their cameras.

Nothing. Wouldn't hurt a single soul. And she was asking for it, so it wasn't like his using her—and biting her—would be a surprise.

"Slide over," he said and opened the taxi door.

"Why no limo?" Daniel asked as the cab rolled down the street. He spread his legs and sat back, hands between his thighs. Olivia loved that he got comfortable and wasn't worried about sitting just so and having dark sunglasses on in case a camera flashed. She was through with celebrities and their egos. She hoped she'd never succumb to a blasé attitude, but doubted she'd avoid it completely.

She didn't move her leg away from his and the heat of their connection tickled higher. Desire curled between her legs and she licked her lips in anticipation of another masterful kiss like he'd given her last night.

"It's easier to make an escape from all the fanfare in a cab. Usually I slip out of my gown and into something less glamorous—you've seen my unglamorous look—but the guy I was looking for took off so fast, I had to move quickly."

"You want me that bad, eh?" he said, a smirk curving his lips so appealingly, Olivia tilted against his body as if she were a magnet snapping to steel, bringing their faces close.

"Anything wrong with that?"

"Not that I can figure out. So you're someone famous?"

She had needed for it to be out there—her monstrosity. Yet she hoped it would be the least important thing between the two of them. Because right now the only thing important was getting as close to Daniel's skin as she possibly could. "That I am."

"I've never heard of you."

"That kills me. Though I will grant that I am a rising star. I've been on the scene two years. My last single hit the top ten *Billboard* chart. You haven't heard 'Daydream' on the radio?"

"Sorry. Don't do much daydreaming lately, though I do listen to the radio."

"You're probably into heavy metal and don't listen to light pop stuff."

"Actually, I'm more of an oldies—Frank Sinatra and Sammy Davis Jr.—fan. Christmas carols, eh?"

"It is the holiday season. I'm officially on a month vacation, but I agreed to a couple quick appearances during the week leading up to and Christmas Eve. I love holiday songs. What about you?"

He shrugged, then offered as if an afterthought. "'Little Drummer Boy' used to be my favorite."

"Oh, I love that one! *Ba rum pa pum pum.* But why did it *used* to be your fave? Do you have a different one now?"

"No, I've never done all that Christmas stuff. Celebrating Christmas implies you believe in all that religious ballyhoo. And monsters don't do that belief."

"I see." She tapped a finger on his mouth. "Just because you keep saying it, doesn't make it so. I don't see a monster sitting next to me."

With a glance in the rearview mirror to verify the cabbie was humming to the tunes streaming through his earbuds, Daniel then flashed her some fang.

They were pretty and sharp, but— "It's going to take more than a little fang to scare me off."

"Yeah, why is that? What do you see in me that you can't find in anyone else? So much so that you're willing to risk the bite? Convince me you're not a fang junkie."

Fang junkie? Not her. But what did she see in him beyond his obvious physical appeal? Freckles and a sexy smile did not make for the ultimate boyfriend. Though the fact he'd not ripped into her throat last night, and had coyly played along with her *and* had come to see her tonight earned him major points in the romance department.

"I'm not interested in you biting me." But certainly the risk had been what initially attracted her. "I'm interested in the man who had no idea who I was last night, and who wanted to kiss me and make some skin-on-skin contact. Someone who doesn't care if my next record tops the charts or if I can walk on stage in a sheer dress with strategically placed rhinestones."

"You have a dress like that?" He waggled his eyebrows.

"I might."

She studied his mouth, which was slightly parted, and she could feel the heat of his breath kiss her cheek. So close, yet she didn't want to kiss him with the cabbie three feet away. She wasn't stupid. Even the most unsuspecting carried a camera, waiting for opportunity to make a cool bundle on the pictures they could snap of her.

"What say we monsters discuss it further at my place?"

The cab rolled to a stop and Daniel glanced up and down the street. "This neighborhood doesn't fit with my idea of where a star would live. It's old money and old ladies walking old dogs."

"Exactly. No one ever thinks to look for me here. And New Yorkers are famous for ignoring celebrities, no matter where they see them, which makes for a perfect vacation getaway." She reached over him and opened the door. "When I take off this gown, I shed Olivia Adorata, the star, and become plain ole me. A girl who wants to help you shed your monster, too. You want to give it a go?"

Having already gotten used to Daniel's apparent need for long stares, she loved the intensity of the connection. It burned into her and read something in her that even she didn't know about. Was it a vampire gaze that could seduce her to his will? She didn't feel as if he were trying to overtake her mind, perhaps only wrestling with his own confused sense of right and wrong.

"Are *you* willing to take the risk?" he finally asked.

She nodded. Probably a wiser response would have been "What are the risks?" but right now all she desired was to slide her hands up Daniel's rock-hard abs and push him down on her bed.

Risks, be damned.

How was that for a girl who normally had trouble making decisions without her mother's approval?

OLIVIA LED DANIEL INSIDE the cozy second-floor apartment and flicked on the stove burner to boil water for tea. She couldn't come down from a performance without chamomile tea. Though other things she had in mind to do—sexy, lustful, naughty things—might have the same effect, by no means would those things calm her.

She'd forgo calm for that option in a heartbeat.

The vampire stood by the door on the rug, looking around, hands shoved in his pockets. He looked too normal. Perhaps that was his most dangerous attribute. Must be easy for him to lure in an unsuspecting woman for a bite.

"Having second thoughts?" she asked. Should she be asking herself the same question?

No, she was far from unsuspecting. She was charging into this affair with eyes wide-open and a heart that wanted to learn, love and experience. And this time, she was dressed properly and had makeup on, thanks to a professional stylist.

"I'm just trying to figure you out."

She ran her fingers along the rabbit fur edging the dress's neckline. "That's probably dangerous."

"So no strings, no callbacks? Is that how tonight is going to work?"

"If that's what you want." She didn't want to be pushy, but it did disappoint her he wasn't planning for a repeat performance.

Hell, one step at a time, Olivia. You may regret this soon enough.

She strode through the living room, lifting her long, wavy hair to splay it out across the fur. Admittedly, she worked the dress because she sensed Daniel's eyes take in her figure. Let the seduction begin. She knew what she wanted.

Yet he had become oddly reluctant since crossing her threshold, and that baffled her.

"Daniel, you should be right here." She slid a palm up her stomach, her fingertips stroking the fur that topped her breasts with a soft come-on. She tried her best come-hither look. "What's the problem?"

He stood before her in a blink, and she wasn't sure if

it had been vampire speed, or just a hungry man being given permission to take as he desired. He pressed a cool hand over her breast and leaned in. "No problem. Just want to be sure we had the rules down before diving in."

"I hate rules."

"I do, too. No man ever made his fortune by following the rules."

"True, but now that you mention it, I do have one. No biting."

"Impossible." He ducked to nuzzle his nose against her neck, which pricked up her defenses, but also sent a surprising shock of desire skittering across the surface of her skin. "You don't get to tell a vampire not to bite."

"It's not that I'm afraid of being bitten."

"Then what?" He licked her neck, chasing those skitters with liquid, warm shivers through her entire body.

Olivia sighed and grabbed the front of his shirt, pulling him closer so she could feel the hard length of his erection against her hip. Oh, baby, she wanted some of that. But she was anything but reckless. Caution must be weaved into this delicious fantasy or it could become a nightmare.

Then why did you jump in the first place? For this to work you have to sink in all the way.

"I don't want to…die. Or end up a vampire. Could you imagine the media frenzy over that?"

"Not going to happen." He licked a trail along her jaw and to the lobe of her ear. "I wouldn't make another monster if I was forced. And despite my former nickname of Killer when I was an investor on Wall Street, I'm not a real killer."

She believed him. The conviction in his tone spoke of integrity and honor. Wall Street? Everything about Daniel felt right, and not at all monstrous.

Or maybe she was already lost in the fantasy of sur-rendering to this man's dark and dangerous allure. It was a delicious fall, and she deserved the plunge.

She pulled open his shirt and melded her body against his, fitting her breasts to his warmth and measuring the steely tension in his abs with an inhale.

"Man, that feels so wrong in all the right ways," he murmured.

His hands slid around her back and down to cup her derriere through the body-clinging red silk. The hardness of him crushed against her hip, pleading her surrender, and she tilted her head, allowing him to kiss from her neck down to her breasts.

In the kitchen the teapot whistled.

"Tea's ready," he whispered on a gasp.

"Screw the tea. I need to feel your body against mine, skin to skin."

"You don't have to tell me twice. But first." Daniel rushed into the kitchen and turned off the burner below the whistling teakettle.

She crooked a finger and led him into her bedroom where the almost-full moon glowed through the sheers and fashioned the purple-and-white room more glamor-ously than a Hollywood movie set.

Daniel walked in, noticed the stereo on the vanity and flicked it on. "Let's find some mood music." He played with the controls until a soft Rat Pack beat crooned into the room. "Ah, Michael Bublé. I like this one." He tugged the shirt over his head. Hard muscles strapped his body like steel. His outstretched hand pleaded to Olivia. "Come sway with me, Olivia."

She took his hand and he did a few steps, hips shift-ing in the subtle cha-cha rhythm she was familiar with, having incorporated it into one of her songs last year.

"You dance," she said. "That's impressive."

"I do have a few moves that I intend to unleash upon your unsuspecting soul tonight."

"Sounds exciting."

"It could be. Ready for this?"

She nodded and he spun and then dipped her, bringing her up smoothly. The rush of the elegant move chattered out in a gleeful laugh. Olivia spread her arms over his bare shoulders and matched his moves. They managed a pretty respectable cha-cha in the aisle between the bed and the vanity.

"I've never danced with a guy before. You're spoiling me, Daniel. And look, you've freckles on your shoulder. That's so sexy."

"I've noticed you tend to chatter when you're nervous. Are you nervous?"

"No. Yes. No." She nuzzled against his cheek and let out another giggle. "Yes."

He whispered the words next to her ear, "Sway me more."

And Olivia fell hard. He could sway her all he liked.

The song segued into another smooth dance number from the past, and Daniel caught her about the waist and found the zipper down the center back of her gown. Both still swaying to the music, his fingers moved down her spine, and she loosened in his embrace and snuggled her revealed breasts against the rough texture of his shirt and the hot hardness of his chest.

"Still nervous?"

"Aren't you?"

"A little," he whispered against her mouth, and then kissed her. "Makes touch more exciting, don't you think? Being unsure, tentative, but eager."

"Very." The gown dropped at her feet. Olivia stood in

tiny red panties and a matching strapless bra. She slid up a foot and crooked it along his leg. When she unzipped his jeans, he sucked in a gasp.

"Mercy." He slipped his fingers through her hair. "You're moving fast, Olivia. Let me catch up."

Shrugging down his jeans revealed he believed in going commando. His erection sprang up proudly. The man was fashioned of sin and dark danger. The idea of him standing in her humble little apartment, getting naked before her, was almost too much to fathom. For once, she was not the one being admired or draped across an arm as an accessory. It felt great to be on the adoring end. Powerful.

He lifted her in a sweep and laid her on the bed and crawled over her legs. "I love these sweet little nothings you're wearing." Dancing kisses along the inside of her knee, one, then the other, shimmered delicious chills up her body and peaked her nipples tightly. His tongue traced a love letter along her thigh.

"You smell like sugar," he breathed.

"I baked cookies all day. It's my vacation tradition. I get very domestic when I'm not working."

"Here I thought it was because you're so sweet." He lashed his tongue higher, seeking the humming core of her. Snagging the delicate lace with his tooth, he tugged her panties down. "But I know better, because only bad girls invite monsters into their beds. Nothing sweet about that."

"Well, you didn't jump out from under my bed, so I think I can handle any dark scaries you have in mind."

His tongue speared her folds and the heat of him tangled her thoughts and she lost interest in chatting. Clutching the sheets, Olivia closed her eyes and surrendered to the heady sensations the man's touch stirred within her, a wicked witch's brew of sensation. And when his tongue trailed up her stomach, she sighed at the lost connection to her core, but the humming only increased as he kissed one nipple and then the other through the lace bra.

She slid her hand over his and moved it between her legs.

"You do like to order me around," he murmured against her neck as his kisses giddied her closer to the edge.

"I know what I like. Anything wrong with that?"

"Nope."

A flick of his finger across her wet heat worked like a tightened string, pulling her back to a curve. Daniel's erection nudged her entrance and she moaned, hoping he'd understand her invitation. They needn't pause because she was on the pill. And he needed to cross her threshold now because she was so close to losing it.

Skimming her fingers through his hair, she cried out as the swollen head of him entered her. Unreal heat radiated through her and her body bucked wildly as the orgasm took hold. At her breast, his lashing tongue was replaced by a certain sharpness, but she had surfed into the climax and took the sensation as another erotic foray toward the edge. He had entered her with bold assurance. No permission needed as she surrendered, sinking into the flight of pleasure.

A satisfied warmth loosened her muscles. The hiss of sheets sliding off the bed accompanied the hiss of Daniel's breath as it moved down her stomach.

Olivia surfaced from the orgasmic high gasping, and her fingers fluttered down his hot back. She skimmed a finger over her breast. Two tender wounds sat upon the rise. "You bit me. Daniel. I didn't want you to—"

He kissed the wounds and suckled at her probing fingers. "Never promised that, lover. That's what you get when you crawl between the sheets with a vampire."

She twisted a look over the side of the bed. "The sheets are on the floor."

He chuckled. "So they are." He dashed his tongue over the bite mark and licked it. "Don't worry, saliva seals the wound. You're not going to change into a monster like me."

That relieved her, but she hated that he labeled himself a monster when he'd just shown her the real man he was. "You're not so bad. It's what's inside that matters. I suspect the monster runs only as deep as your fangs."

He nudged against her neck and the sharp prick of fangs alerted her. "Want to take a chance on that theory?" he asked in a surprisingly taunting tone.

"No. I'm deliciously exhausted, yet I'm already considering round two."

"There she goes again, bossing me around."

"Sorry, I tend to say what I feel. Got a problem with that?"

"Nope." He sat on the edge of the bed and reached for his shirt. "Olivia, you are a goddess."

"I try. But only when I'm not doing the big star thing, you understand. Goddessing takes so much out of me."

He leaned in and kissed her deeply, and she felt as though she were entering him and getting lost, affixed to his being. And she never wanted it to end.

Daniel tugged on his shirt.

"You're leaving? We're just getting started." She glanced at the LED clock on the nightstand—3:00 a.m. The bite on her breast ached tenderly. "Do you have to leave before the sun rises?"

"I can handle the sun in small doses. And winter sun is too weak, so I can be outdoors much longer."

"Don't go." She trailed her fingers along his powerful thigh, higher and into the nest of curls clinging to his erection, which was still firm and possibly ready for round two. "I want to wake up lying next to you."

With a heavy exhalation he looked her over. Was it so difficult to stay? The vampire had gotten what he'd wanted—her blood—and now he was off?

The last time she'd woken next to someone it had been on a tour bus next to a smelly drummer, and they hadn't had sex; it was only because sleeping arrangements were so spare when on the road.

"How can I resist those pretty green eyes?" Daniel nodded and pulled off his shirt. "I'm going to pull the curtains, though. Just in case the sun decides to blast out a few powerful beams."

CHAPTER THREE

OLIVIA WOKE WITH A SMILE. Her cheek nuzzled against a heat that felt like the sun, but it smelled better than any summer day. Masculine and freckled down his shoulders, Daniel's flesh drew her in to sniff and then lick the tiny jewel of nipple beading his hard pectoral. She spread her hands over his abdomen and pressed her hips against his, blending their subtle heat differences in a cool-hot crush of soft and hard.

She lay next to a vampire. Who had bitten her. She could feel a subtle tingle at the place on her breast where his teeth had invaded her in a surprisingly sensual way. Lost in orgasm, she hadn't noticed the bite until it was too late, but sensed it was what had increased her pleasure and sent her reeling.

A part of her flowed through him now. Strange to consider, but still, she hadn't the sense to be frightened, only intrigued at her bold step into the unknown. And nervous, but dancing with him had quickly allayed that jittery tension and made her like him even more. She was going to have to download that Bublé song to her iPod later.

The room was dark, yet a pale illumination behind the curtains proved it was morning. Her lover roused with a satisfied groan, and his hand slid along her back, stirring her to instant arousal. She playfully nipped his nose.

"You think so?" he murmured in a sleepy voice.

"I do think so." Sliding her hand down his rigid abs, she grasped his semihard shaft, and it reacted by thickening and growing harder. "And parts of you do, as well."

Burrowing under the covers, she kissed down his taut abdomen and to the head of his erection, licking the smooth helmet of flesh and deciding he could return to sleep if he wanted to; she didn't need his participation to do what she had in mind. Pushing down the sheets and straddling him, she glided her mons over the steely length of vampire hardness.

"You're a little pushy in the mornings, you know that?"

"Let me guess. You're not a morning person?"

"Not exactly," he said with a wince. He blocked his eyes with a hand. "Those curtains don't shut out much light."

"Don't worry." She pulled the bedspread over her shoulders and tented it over the two of them, returning darkness to her vampire lover's eyes. "How's this?"

He grabbed her hips and nudged his way inside her. "Good morning, lover."

IT WAS DIFFICULT to rise and get dressed, but Daniel wasn't going to stick around for coffee and chatter. He didn't do the lingering thing. Despite being compelled to lean in and kiss Olivia after putting on his shirt, and after pulling up his jeans, now he paced the room looking for his socks, but he wasn't sure if returning to bed for a snuggle would be such a bad idea after all.

On the other hand, he'd missed an appointment last night. It had completely slipped his mind. His body had been eager to leave, but his mind and his skin had been lured back to Olivia's side. He'd get hell for that. Or rather, hell may have emerged because he'd been too focused getting busy with the pretty singer. He had to get out of here and go make amends.

Nestled in the wrinkled purple sheets, Olivia asked, "Do you have a soul?"

Now she wanted to talk deep stuff? Best to nip this conversation in the bud, and fast. "Yes, but it's dark as hell."

He snagged a sock and pulled it on, but had to sit on the bed to do so. Claiming arms snaked around his waist and her cheek nuzzled against his back. He closed his eyes, taking in the sweetness of the touch. She hadn't screamed last night when he'd bitten her. She could never know how much that meant to him.

"I don't believe that," she said.

"That I have a soul? I do, far as I know. Never got the course on Vampires 101, but I've learned a few things over the past year. Vampire souls are not bright and shiny. We do evil things to…"

"To survive. But you said you don't kill."

"Couldn't fathom the act."

"And you don't create other vampires?"

His jaw tightened to think of the appointment he'd missed. A life was at stake. And he had let that life—and two others—down.

"Creating another bloodsucker would be worse than death."

"Then your soul is as bright as I think it is."

The woman had an optimistic streak that he didn't want to get caught up in. It was like a sunbeam flashing across a dusty room. They'd known each other but a day, and now was no time for a deep conversation about life and whether or not vampire souls were dark or bright.

Bright? Hell. Olivia was naive, and he intended to

walk out the door and never return. She didn't deserve the corruption he could give her.

"You think you can't have love," she said.

Daniel shook his head, smirking. "Love is the last thing I worry about."

"That's too bad. Everyone needs love."

He turned abruptly and grabbed her under the jaw. "You spent the night having sex with a vampire, Olivia. Not exactly a traditional way to spend the Christmas holiday. Think about that one, will you?"

He wandered out into the living room, but paused beside the couch, finding it difficult to move forward. He had to fist his fingers and think about bad things, dark things—*himself*—to resist the pull to return to her side. At Olivia's side it was warm and bright and soft, and like nothing he'd ever had before. And her blood had tasted so damn good. Bright, unlike him.

Daniel gritted his jaw and forced out, "I'll see you later!"

"Promise? Will you come back tonight?"

So hopeful. And for what? Another no-strings fuck? Fine with him. But if she expected love and a relationship and all the emotional baggage that accompanied it, she was going to get hurt.

Daniel palmed the front doorknob. It was probably best to hurt her sooner rather than later.

He didn't reply to her question. Because he wasn't sure if he could hurt her by not returning, or if he'd instead inflict that hurt on himself by returning for another kiss from the most intriguing thing that had ever happened to him.

THE GIRLS WERE ALL RIGHT, but upset he'd not shown last night, as promised. Daniel explained that he'd had something else to do and his apologies were taken with nods and heavy sighs. Their disappointment clawed at his heart. Deservedly so.

The Jones family was fine, if *fine* meant gritting teeth and clinging to an edge of oblivion that scared even Daniel.

He promised to show tonight, and it was imperative. The moon would be full on Christmas Eve, of all the bloody nights. The holiday wasn't going to be merry for the Jones family. But he'd do what he could to ensure another monster did not walk the earth. He left the girls with promises and with a smile as encouraging as he could manage.

Now, if he could clear his mind of the soft, sweet-smelling Olivia. Maybe he needed to scare up a couple werewolves to keep his mind from distractions of the heart?

He didn't have to walk far to find the dog he'd started to think of as Punch. His partner in crime was Judy— hey, the wolf wore pink tennis shoes—but he was no-where in sight. Daniel veered across the street to avoid meeting the oncoming wolf, who hadn't yet noticed him. Hands tucked in his jacket pockets, he doubled his pace, and only cringed when he heard the throaty chuckle and a fist smack into a palm.

Damn wolves could smell a vampire a mile away. Best thing to do? Run.

Daniel turned to face the werewolf lumbering toward him and planted his feet. A year ago his sorry-ass investment broker in crisp white shirt and gold cuff links would have run like a sissy from any threat larger than himself, despite his biweekly visits to the gym to work out. Now?

"Bring it," Daniel muttered, and nodded to the right

toward a narrow alley littered with cardboard boxes waiting garbage pickup.

The wolf veered and they strode down the alley side by side.

"You don't have your girlfriend with you today," Punch said. "But I can smell her on you. Tasty."

"She's not my girlfriend. And you lay one grimy paw on the woman and you'll pull back a nub."

The wolf shoved Daniel against a wall, and a garbage can clattered and rolled, spreading its packing peanut contents on the snowy tarmac. He reacted with a kick that landed on his opponent's hip and sent him stumbling backward. His best defense was to move quickly, and he did so, pummeling the wolf with a fist to the chin, nose and ears. The ear shot had to do it, because the wolf let out a groan and balled forward in on himself.

"I'm not going to let you use me for your twisted games," Daniel said. Hell, people depended on him. He wasn't about to let the Jones girls down again. He delivered another punch to the wolf's head, spinning the bruiser onto his back in a sprawl. "Haven't you anything better to do?"

Punch spat blood to the side and grinned. "I can think of twenty better things involving your woman."

"A nub, buddy. She's not your plaything."

A final punch to the temple succeeding in knocking the wolf out cold. Daniel eyed the perimeter and checked their tussle hadn't been witnessed. The neighborhood was rough, but the weather kept most tucked in their snug homes. He strode away quickly, a brief smile curving his mouth at having defeated the wolf. But now he worried that Olivia would never be safe unless he could take the wolf out permanently.

He'd insinuated himself in her life, and by doing so, had brought along all his scary baggage, including were-wolves.

WHEN THE DOORBELL RANG, Olivia set the hot pan of fresh-from-the-oven cookies on the stovetop and ran to answer it. It was early evening, and her manager had strict rules not to visit during her vacation, so it could only be one person.

Daniel leaned against the door frame, hands in his pockets and eyes set to smolder. Olivia's heart pittered and her pulse pattered. Her lover sniffed the air. "Cookies?"

"I've been baking all day."

"Smells great in here." He closed the door but didn't cross to the kitchen to follow her. "All day? That's a lot of cookies."

"Seven dozen so far." She slid a spatula under a cookie and transferred it to the cooling rack. "I love Christmas and cooking. This is the only time of the year I get to my-self so I try to do everything I used to do with my mother when I was younger. We used to make dozens of cookies and then take them around to the neighbors in brightly wrapped packages."

"Sounds like a lot of work."

"Sounds—" she slid another cookie off onto the rack "—normal, to me. This is what you're supposed to do at Christmastime. Not traverse the country on a tour bus eating Doritos and washing your clothes in the sink. Come in, Daniel. What's up? What are you hiding be-hind your back?"

The man's sexy smile curled up into his eyes and it beamed a teasing smile onto her mouth. He walked closer but she could see he was concealing something. "A present for you."

"Seriously? I love presents. It's not a Christmas present, is it? Because it's another few days until Christmas Eve. No presents until then."

"So you don't want it?"

"Are you kidding?" She tugged off the oven mitts and scampered over to him. Hands clasped behind her back, she closed her eyes. "Lay it on me."

"For a kiss?"

"Of course!" She leaned forward, puckering her lips.

A warm, dreamy connection, mouth to mouth, breath to breath, curled her up onto her tiptoes and she wrapped her arms around Daniel's shoulders. His jacket was cold, but his mouth was molten hot.

They'd known each other for such a short time, but she wanted this moment to go on forever, melting into his kiss. She could write a song about Daniel's kisses. It would be filled with words like *hot, demanding, magical, firm* and *wondrous good nummy.*

"Mmm," she murmured, eyes still closed. "That was the best present ever."

"That wasn't the actual present."

"Too bad, 'cause I'd like to open that one every day. Again and again."

He kissed her quickly and dashed his tongue along her lower lip, marking her, making her his own. After last night's performance, he could have her in any way he desired. And she did not think that was attributable to the bite—or she hoped not.

He said, "Open your eyes."

"Oh, Daniel!"

He held a miniature pine tree, potted in a bright red

basket. It was about a foot high and perfectly formed. "I love it!"

"You said you wanted a little Christmas tree."

"I did! This is perfect, especially for my tiny apartment. And I bet it was much easier getting it up the stairs." She took the tree and smelled the fragrant pine needles. Placing it on the coffee table, she knelt before it. "Now I need to find some miniature ornaments. It's so cute."

"Then maybe—" he knelt beside her and his warm breath tickled her ear so she tilted against him like a rose seeking the sun "—it's a good thing I bought this, too." He pulled something from his coat pocket and handed it to her.

The small silver star twinkled with rhinestones and had a tiny coil at the base to attach to a treetop. Olivia didn't know what to say. That he'd thought to do something like this for her was incredible. People gave her gifts all the time. Big, flashy gifts that were always hung with an invisible *expectations* tag. This felt too genuine, from the heart. "I love it. Thank you."

"It's just a silly tree."

"No. It's the fact that you were listening to me when I mentioned I wanted a tree, but something small for my place. No one has ever given me such a thoughtful gift. For that, I'm going to let you have two cookies." She pulled him into the kitchen and selected a warm candy cane cookie to hand him. "Can you eat food?"

"Yes, but I don't need it for survival." He took a bite and nodded his approval. "I think my mom used to make these. Did you have to twist the red dough with the white dough and then shape them like this?"

"Yes, making them always brings back memories of my mother."

"She not around anymore?"

With a brave lift of her shoulders, Olivia nodded. "Died two years ago from a brain tumor. She was my biggest supporter and never got to see me hit the big time."

It always strummed the broken chord in her heart to remember her mother's brave last weeks fighting the tumor. Olivia had been on her own since, and missed having someone to confide in who wasn't paid to listen and nod in agreement to everything she said.

"I always used to look to her for approval," she said.

Driven, even as a child and through her teens, she'd had her mother's unconditional support as she'd entered the world of professional singing. She had always asked her mother's opinion whenever trying something new. Until recently, when her manager and the record label had suggested she take a risk and pair up for a duet with a hip-hop singer with hopes it would increase her appeal to listeners and rocket her to superstardom. Olivia had looked over her shoulder—but her mother hadn't been there to nod approval. So she had shaken her head, and hadn't been able to commit to the project.

So that's why you invited the vampire in. He's the risk you don't dare take in your career.

Wow. Wonder what her mother would say about that? Likely she would have approved a vampire for her daughter's lover because Mom had been open-minded enough to be fascinated with the pairing. Yet she might have steered Olivia away from allowing the man to bite her. Especially on the first date.

Lifting her chin, Olivia pasted on a smile that quickly turned genuine.

"Will you help me package the cookies and then take

them around to the neighbors? It'll put you in the Christmas spirit," she added hopefully.

He slapped a hand across his jeans, wiping away cookie crumbs, but didn't respond.

"Come on," she said. "It won't take long. The old guy who lives below me is a codger, but I bet these cookies will make him smile. I've a Santa hat with a white fluff ball on it you could wear—"

"I can't do this." He tossed the half-eaten cookie onto the kitchen counter.

With that act Olivia felt as if he'd just snapped his fingers across her broken heart chord. "Fine. You don't have to come along, but if you could help me put some cookies on plates…?"

"Olivia, I…" He scrubbed a palm over his face then stated plainly, "I don't need to feel the Christmas spirit. I just…don't want to do this."

"I see." She tipped up his chin with a fingertip. His eyes didn't meet hers, and she suspected she'd touched a dark spot on that blurry soul of his. "Who put the coal in your Christmas stocking?"

He looked aside. His tension was tangible but she couldn't figure why.

"Daniel?"

With a heavy sigh, he clasped her hand in his and pressed it against his heart as he said, "You have your memories. I have mine. And mine are just as depressing."

"Memories of my mother aren't depressing. I remember the good times we shared together. What is it about Christmas that haunts you?"

He tilted back his head and shook it. "It would Scrooge you out."

"Come on, I can take it." The fact he hadn't moved away from her and still held her hand meant he wasn't ready to charge out of here, so Olivia tilted down her head and captured his gaze, pleading with him to share with her.

The vampire sighed. "Fine. Here's the details. A year ago, a few days before Christmas, I was a normal mortal guy, minding my own business, going about my life, despite the fact that normal life was as an investment broker for the biggest trading firm on Wall Street. I was known as Killer in person, but behind my back I know their favorite term for me was asshole."

She gaped. For some reason she'd thought he'd always been a vampire. A foolish assumption. Even if she knew little about the creatures, it seemed apparent they could become vampire at any time if all it involved was a bite.

"I always worked well into the night, and one night as I was strolling the subway to catch the train to the airport for a last-minute trip to Vegas, a gang of hungry-looking street punks corralled me into a corner—and bit me."

"Vampires," she said on a gasp.

"Vampires." He crossed his arms and turned to pace behind the couch, away from her. He put up a wall and Olivia was inclined to respect his need for distance. "I woke up in the E.R. My cot was shoved along a wall like I wasn't high enough on the triage list to warrant immediate care. And I knew what had happened. Vampires had bitten me. How to explain that to the doctors without earning a one-way ticket to the loony bin? So I snuck out while I had the chance.

"I didn't know where to go, what to do, who to tell. So I didn't tell anyone. I quickly lost my job to a hotshot upstart who'd used my difficulty with concentrating and fighting against the blood hunger to prove to the boss I was an addict. A ridiculous accusation, but I could hardly defend myself with the truth. A week later the hunger pangs grew so strong, I...attacked a guy. Beat him up and bit him. I transformed to vampire that night, fangs and all."

He stopped pacing before the window. She'd closed the curtains, expecting his visit, yet pale winter sun streamed around the edges, touching Daniel's face as if hope attempted to permeate his darkness.

Olivia felt the vulnerability in his silence. To be attacked and forced to change into a creature who must live on human blood to survive? No one would ask for that. Only a strong man could survive.

She respected him for the trust he'd given her. It wasn't an easy commodity to share.

"I'm sorry," she whispered. "I didn't know."

"Now you do. And now you know that it's probably better if I walk out that door and not come back."

When he stepped toward the door she made a move to block his path. "Daniel, you being a vampire has nothing to do with you never coming back. I'll deliver the cookies later. They can wait."

"I'm harshing your Christmas spirit," he said. "Vampire Scrooge doesn't play into your dreams of sugarplums and stockings hung by the chimney with care."

She had to smile at his attempt at lightening the mood. "Come here." She held out her arms. "You need a hug."

He shook his head in disbelief. "It's going to take more than a hug to get over what I've become."

"I know that, but I want to help."

"Don't worry about me, Olivia. I'll get this figured out."

"I know you will. But I still want to hug you."

Standing but an inch from his body, her eyes traced his, and he allowed the long stare, the intimate look into his soul. And what she found there was no monster, but a kind, smart and determined man who had been wronged.

"You know if I hug you," he said, "I'll want to touch your skin. And if I touch your skin, I'll want to kiss it. And if I kiss it…you'll never get your cookies delivered."

"The cookies can wait."

CHAPTER FOUR

DANIEL HAD NEVER honestly enjoyed a woman before. Hell, he took what he could during sex, and gave back, as well. He could bring a woman to orgasm more than a few times, and have her whispering devotion to his talents. But when he'd been a corporate drone, he'd always been on a schedule. Everything had a time limit, including sex. He hadn't time following sex to linger in bed and cuddle, or even draw his fingers along a woman's dewy flesh to watch the subtle rise and fall of her breath, the tug of her muscles, the sighs that set up tiny goose bumps here and there.

Lost in the discovery of Olivia's flesh, he trailed a fingertip down her ribs and above her belly button. There, he made a circle and delighted to see her skin prickle at the light touch, and then smooth out as her breathing increased.

Why had it taken so long for him to simply relax and be in the moment?

Touching the tip of his tongue to her belly, he drew a slow curve, painting his wants and needs onto her, and receiving a delicious moaning reply. This was a moment he had to remember. Imprint it like a video in his brain so he'd always have something awesome to behold. He'd never had it all.

Wait. Daniel's conscience gave him pause and he

kissed Olivia's skin, yet tilted his cheek against her stomach to think.

He *had* had it all. He'd been top of his game, making a fortune, highly respected. Yet he'd never taken the time to acknowledge that fortune and status. Nor had he taken time to revel in a woman's body. What a fool to have had life in his grasp and to have squandered it with endless hours of work.

And then a gang of vampires had taken it all away.

And the result? He'd been given the opportunity to step aside from that former self and take a different path. A path that had initially freaked him. He was only now getting accustomed to vampirism and the idea of using an innocent mortal to sustain his life. It still felt wrong. Monstrous.

Could he ever get over his new bad self and just accept?

"You tired, lover?" she whispered, nudging him with a hip.

Daniel glanced to the clock. Hell, it was after ten. Screw having it all. If he let down the Jones women again he wouldn't be worthy of having all this sweetness he'd suddenly gained.

"Not tired. Just thinking about all that I once had and lost."

"Your job. Your life as a mortal. You want it back?"

"I don't think so. I think the attack happened for a reason. Maybe to make me look at my life and all I still have. It's not so bad, I guess."

"Did the monster just say he wasn't so bad?"

He smiled and kissed her stomach, then glided up along her body to fit himself against her lush curves. "What do you want from me, Olivia? From this?"

"Truth? I want to take it slow."

"We haven't exactly been taking things slowly."

"I know, but what's happened so far was a reaction and there's nothing wrong with answering a mutual pining for connection. We were drawn to one another and neither of us overthought that attraction. I'm accustomed to tabloid relationships that aren't even real. The paparazzi snap a shot of me walking with a male celebrity—usually someone I'm not dating or even considering dating—then slap it on the front of some rag stating we're hot and heavy. A week later the headlines have us arguing, and a week after that we've broken up. I'm surprised I haven't had a secret baby yet. I want to have a relationship that hasn't been orchestrated by a tabloid. Something real."

"I can understand that."

"I know it's tough to date a person whose life involves cameras and complete loss of privacy."

"You do have a great little hideaway here."

"Which I am thankful for. But it won't last forever. Sooner or later the paparazzi will find me. Where do you live?"

"Here in Manhattan. Still got the thirtieth-floor bachelor pad. You'd get recognized in a heartbeat there."

"I suppose. I have my official place on the other side of the park. But this place is my only real home."

Daniel sat and arched his back as Olivia drew her fingers down it. It felt like home here, and he liked that fine. But he wouldn't jump into things, and he appreciated Olivia's honest confession that she wanted to take things slowly.

Had he the courage to begin something with her?

You've already begun.

The question was: Could he continue or would he wimp out and leave her high and dry? He'd never mastered the relationship thing. And slow? Had to be even harder to accomplish.

"Do you have to leave?" she asked.

He nodded, and assumed her silence meant she thought he was heading out to scam for blood. He wouldn't argue the point.

OLIVIA WANDERED INTO the bathroom and turned on the shower to warm the water. Daniel had left quickly after she'd mentioned her designs on a real relationship. Did he think their tryst was just a few nights between the sheets? Had mentioning taking it slow repelled him?

She should have asked him if he had left to go drink blood. The question had felt too weird even thinking it, though.

"I want more," she said to her reflection. "I need more of him. Can I have that?"

There were so many factors working against a positive answer to that question. And even if they managed to keep a tight lid on a relationship, there was always the fact Daniel couldn't do press with her, which naturally, her manager would insist upon. Couldn't keep the sexy man all to herself. Would he show in a photograph? And if he did, would the paparazzi catch him sneering at them one day, fangs bright and out there? What if they caught Daniel drinking someone's blood? They followed her everywhere; they'd follow him.

No, Daniel would never get that close to the fanfare that surrounded her. For as much as she loved her job, it was a curse to her private life.

"I wonder how often he has to drink blood?" She stroked her breast where the day-old bite mark had, interestingly, already begun to fade. He hadn't bitten her again. Because he hadn't needed blood or because he hadn't been interested in her blood? Did he not like the taste of her?

"Could he drink from me often without...killing me?"

A tilt of her head wondered at her brazen claiming of the vampire. Did she really know what she was getting into?

"I miss you, Mom. And I need your advice. There's this guy, who I know you'd like, but...well, he has issues."

She wanted Daniel to want her. As more than a Christmas liaison.

She'd give anything to make this work.

"Even blood?" she asked the mirror, and her reflection nodded.

A CALL FROM HER MANAGER was not unexpected, only not entirely appreciated during her vacation. Olivia set aside the pan of mulled wine as she wished Lisa a merry Christmas and asked the requisite questions about her children.

"They're drooling to open presents," Lisa replied in her rapid Jersey drawl that no six-shooter could outdraw. "I wanted to let you know I got a date for you tomorrow night."

"A date? I don't need—"

"I know, you never need anything. But you do need all the publicity you can get if you're going to hit it big. And the performance is going to be aired on a major network that will feature background bios of the performers, along with candid shots of them backstage. Don't you even want to know his name?"

Olivia's silence was only allowed a split second before Lisa replied, "Parker Troy. Dude is hot, sexy, has a number-one single on *Billboard* right now, and he's singing right after you tomorrow."

The singer with whom Olivia hadn't been able to commit to performing a duet. "Lisa, I—"

"It's spin, Olivia. You show up on his arm. The paparazzi goes wild. We get a few shots of the two of you holding hands backstage. Then when we ask his manager to do the duet you've been dying to do with him, they agree."

"I haven't been dying to do—"

"It's what your record label wants, Olivia, and that's how we'll spin it to Troy's manager. You need to take the next step, to be seen, and this is the only way to do it. Oh, and you let him kiss you, too."

Olivia gaped. She understood that putting two people together before the paparazzi was spin and that it could definitely help her career. But kiss the guy? He was handsome as all get-out, dated supermodels and actresses and was known to spend a fortune on them, but she had no interest in him romantically.

Lately, she preferred her men a little mysterious and sharper of tooth.

"Lisa, I don't think I can do this. In fact, I know I can't. I have—" A boyfriend? Not really. A lover, more like. But could she even claim that?

"No arguments, Olivia. And no avoiding this issue with indecision. It's your next step. Parker is looking forward to seeing you tomorrow night."

"It's just a clutch and a cheek kiss," Olivia said. "I'm not going home with the guy."

"Why? He's the most adorable thing you could put between two slices of bread."

Lisa and her weird analogies about handsome men. They were crushable, lickable, swimmable or sandwichworthy.

"We'll talk more tomorrow night," Lisa said. "I gotta go. The puppy is tearing a package open!"

The phone clicked off, and Olivia tossed her cell phone toward the couch. Every part of her being cringed and shuddered as if finally her fears over a vampire had arisen, except the only bloodsuckers involved were mortals with dollars signs in their eyes.

She poured a cup of the mulled wine and sat before the kitchen counter, but couldn't drink the spicy brew. Pressing her forehead to the counter, she kicked herself inwardly for not standing up to Lisa. Screw the duet. She didn't need that kind of press. Her mother would not have approved. Maybe. She didn't know anymore. When she looked over her shoulder there was no one standing there to offer a nod and confidence.

But what mattered even more: What would Daniel think?

And why did she care?

"You care because he means something to you."

She only wished she meant the same to him.

DANIEL WATCHED THE CLOUDS move over the moon, which looked full, but he knew tomorrow was the night. The woman who had fallen asleep in his arms had done so only because he smelled vodka on her breath and suspected the entire pint sloshed in her belly now. She was desperate, and he didn't blame her. But alcohol wasn't the answer.

Slipping away from her, he rubbed his head and then squeezed his temples, wishing he could make it all better with a snap of his fingers. But that wasn't the answer, either. Nothing was worth it without a fight and good hard work. Tomorrow night would try his skills in ways he couldn't imagine. What skills? Mortality retaining powers? Hell.

He pushed open the gate and spied the two girls sleeping on a wooden bench in front of the old apartment building beside which their mother had passed out. He'd once offered to put them up in the hotel down the street but the mother had refused, and the oldest girl had stood by her mother. They frequented a local shelter. The little one wouldn't have minded; he knew that.

"See you tomorrow night, girls," he said, and the oldest thanked him then nodded back to sleep.

What kind of world allowed things like that to happen? Hell, allowed vampires to walk the earth? It was just wrong. He was wrong.

But he'd be damned if he'd let the wrong continue.

His anger rising, he fought to keep it to a simmer. He didn't need to go around punching in heads or flashing his fangs because his world wasn't right. He needed grounding.

And he knew where to find that.

WITH A YAWN, Olivia opened the door and tugged Daniel across the threshold. It was two in the morning, but she hadn't been able to sleep. Now that he was here, she could.

"Missed you," he murmured as she snuggled into his cool embrace. Snowflakes sifted down her back and skimmed the slinky silk nightgown. "Shouldn't be here, but can't stay away."

"Here is the only place you should be," she said, and led him into the bedroom. "I figured you needed to go out to…"

"Yeah, I had to do that," he agreed.

Imagining Daniel leaning over a woman to sink his

fangs in her neck made her heart ache, so she quickly pushed the image away. "Let's not talk. Just touch me."

"Works for me."

They landed on the bed like lovers who had been together for years, finding each other's sensitive spots with ease and lingering until the heady climax bonded them in ways neither would ever unravel. And yet they were new lovers, so finding an unexplored sensitive spot behind Daniel's ear with her tongue gave Olivia a giggle. And he wanted to spend time searching for her G-spot, which she didn't mind at all, and—mercy, but he found it.

Skin flushed from exhaustion hugged and caressed. Lips tendered kisses to every inch of arm, leg, stomach and breasts. Fingers learned to speak a sign language shared by lovers with taps and tickles and strokes.

Hours later, Olivia rolled into Daniel's embrace. "Don't leave me tonight."

He kissed her forehead. "I won't. It's almost morning and the curtains are drawn. I can't think of anywhere else I'd rather be."

"Me, too. Daniel, I love you."

She felt his muscles tense and when he moved away from her, Olivia's world shattered.

"Sorry, sweetie, you can't love a monster. I don't deserve that." He winced and smoothed a hand over her hair. "My soul doesn't deserve you."

"You've a beautiful soul, Daniel." She kissed him in the darkness, two mouths, one making promises the other didn't want to speak, didn't know how to accept. "I wish your soul felt worthy of love."

"Yeah, well, it doesn't." He rolled to his back and allowed her to snuggle against his arm, but she sensed he'd shut down, no longer open to emotion.

"I'm not going to apologize, because I meant it," she said. "I don't need you to love me back. I wanted you to know how I feel. This past week has been amazing. You've distracted me from my world and—"

"And brought you into my world. That was stupid of me, Olivia. Hell, you said you wanted to go slow."

She had said that. But apparently her heart hadn't been listening. She wanted him to want her, to want to share his world with her. But she understood his reluctance.

Didn't make it any easier on her heart right now.

"I should leave," he said.

"No. Please. I know you probably don't need much sleep. Can I fall asleep in your arms? You can slip out when I'm snoring."

"Olivia."

"Please." She kissed his ear, the side of his eye where his lashes flicked faery kisses against her nose. "And I'd like you to bite me. I want to feel that intensity again."

It was as if their souls had bonded in that moment. And whether or not he could deal with that emotion, she needed it desperately. It was a sacrifice that didn't feel like a sacrifice. It felt like the next natural step to their relationship.

He nudged his nose against her neck. "You smell like sex and cookies. My favorite smell."

"Can I be your favorite taste? Can you bite me more often, without causing…you know?"

"I could do it a few times a month without changing you or making you weak. I thought you weren't interested in the bite?"

"That was before you bit me."

"The swoon is good to mortals. Makes you sway with me. I like that."

"It makes me feel so close to you and jealous of all the women you've bitten."

"No need to be jealous of a quick bite. It's just that. It feeds my need."

"Is that how it was when you bit me?"

"Never." He tilted his head and kissed her neck, tonguing it lazily, which brought her back to the delicious bliss she'd felt when they were making love. "Sway me more, lover."

The vampire's fangs glided into her vein and Olivia gasped and clutched his bicep. Her soul glittered and reached for the intrusion, pricking itself upon Daniel's darkness and drowning, sinking, but loving every wicked moment.

HE SLIPPED OUT OF her bedroom as soon as he guessed she was sleeping. Dressing on his way to the door, Daniel shoved his feet in his boots and then quietly left. Outside, he pressed his back to the door and closed his eyes.

He could still taste her on his tongue. The rich, thick treat glided through him, seeking to cling, to master him. To overtake his soul with her brightness.

She thought his soul was deserving of love?

He wanted to be worthy, he really did.

CHAPTER FIVE

OLIVIA ADORATA WAS a sensation. Daniel could feel the love radiate out from the Times Square crowd as her voice carried over their heads and segued into their hearts. Her face filled the Jumbo Tron and snowflakes fluttered about her head. She sang "O Holy Night," and he found himself staring in awe and mouthing the words he'd learned as a kid along with the audience.

Dressed all in white and sequins, she sparkled onstage, a brilliant star to lead wanderers to a promise of happiness. She wasn't a monster, not in his mind. But he could understand now how she felt, in her heart, that her stage persona had become monstrous and too huge for her normal self who liked to be tucked away in a tiny apartment and bake cookies.

The vampire he had become was too huge for the investment broker he'd once been. But standing here in Olivia's aura of sound and emotion, he knew he could stand forever—and he wanted to get a grasp on his monster so it didn't bring them both down. He'd bitten her again. He wasn't sure if that was good, bad or just plain evil.

He really liked her. Hell, he might even go so far as to—no, probably better not think it. Wouldn't get his heart broken that way.

She said she loved you last night. Way to spoil the moment by freezing up on her, dude. You haven't learned a thing about timing and women.

Yeah? What man did have a handle on the emotional stuff?

Scrubbing a hand over his head, he closed his eyes and concentrated on the words she sang. *Fall on your knees... O hear the angel voices... And the soul felt its worth.*

Lucky soul, that.

She wielded the voice of an angel who had touched his dark heart. And maybe, just maybe, a small portion of that heart, or even the edges, glowed brightly in the sound of her voice, responding to her touch in ways that brought him to his knees, wanting to worship her, not as a popular music idol, but as a gorgeous woman who needed love and understanding as much as he did.

His soul. Did it feel worthy of Olivia's love?

They were two struggling through the mire, and had stumbled upon one another. Why couldn't they make it work?

Hell, he wished it wasn't Christmas Eve. The moon was high in the sky, though he couldn't see it standing here in the middle of the city illuminated by unnatural lighting. But he felt the moon's ominous presence and knew he had better things to do than lament the love he could never deserve.

Just as he forced himself to turn and leave, the crowd burst into applause. The song was over. Daniel cheered along with everyone, shouting out a few whoops—until he saw a new singer walk on stage to renewed cheers, and the man put his arm around Olivia. She introduced him as Parker Troy and he agreed to sing a duet with her, "I Saw Mommy Kissing Santa Claus."

And then he kissed Olivia full on the mouth to uproarious applause.

Daniel slapped a hand over his heart and stumbled backward, his steps stuttering as rapidly as his heartbeat.

Knew it, his conscience whispered. *She was never yours. That soul of yours? Dark to the core and as unworthy as they come.*

Turning and pushing through the tangle of worshippers, he blindly escaped the roar that threatened to suck him down to the ground and stomp upon his tender heart.

Spying Olivia's driver as he passed, he avoided eye contact with the man, then kicked it in gear and headed north until he arrived at the same place he'd been every other night for the past ten days. The girls standing before the shoddy wood fence ran toward him. Charity, the quiet one, was eight, and Mary was twelve, the bossy one who looked after her little sister and mother.

"Where have you been?" Mary said, grabbing him by the wrist and tugging him along. "She's really bad. You said tonight was the night."

Daniel flinched when Charity tugged his jacket hem. Wide brown eyes sought his. Her hair was tangled, and he bet she hadn't eaten a wholesome meal in weeks.

"Is my mommy going to be a vampire?" the little girl asked.

"Charity, we said not to use that word," Mary admonished.

Daniel winced and considered what to say. To lie to them would be cruel, and their mother hadn't lied since she'd been bitten and had been struggling against the inevitable vampirism that could overtake her soul. Little girls shouldn't have to know such horrors as homelessness and vampirism. Yet Mary was so straightforward, she was like a forty-year-old in a twelve-year-old's body.

"Not if I can help it," he offered. A mournful moan echoed from behind the fence. It was where the mother had been living with her daughters for the past few months. "She had anything to drink?" he asked Mary.

"No money for vodka. But I did get her some Pepsi."

Since her mother had lost her job, the girl had been forced to grow up too quickly. Daniel could relate in a strange way; he'd been forced to view his life differently since vampirism had lost him his job. The body did what it had to do to survive. It was the minds of these sweet girls he worried about.

"I'm going to check on your mother."

Mary shoved him toward the makeshift gate, while Charity clung to him. He put a palm to her head. It was so cold. She needed a cap, though the mittens he'd brought them a week ago were on her hands. How could he have forgotten caps?

Kneeling to put himself at eye level with the misfortunate shivering thing, he asked Charity, "You know what tonight is?"

She nodded. "Santa comes and brings toys to the kids who have homes."

His heart shattered. He felt Mary's stern admonishment of her sister without having to look at her stoic little face.

"Santa is make-believe," he said and didn't regret the truth. These girls deserved his honesty. "Christmas is the celebration of a great man's birthday. Good things happen on Christmas Eve." He stopped himself from saying "I promise," and patted Charity's head before pushing through the gate.

Laura Jones sought his gaze, her pale eyes—circled not with black makeup but instead darkened from her struggles over the past week—were wide and manic. Her shoulders shook and her hands did, as well, as she rubbed them along her jeans as he approached. He prayed she hadn't succumbed to the madness.

Daniel had learned, only after he'd been bitten and

had answered the insane compulsion to drink blood, that there were a few ways a mortal could avoid transforming into a vampire. They could commit suicide. They could stake the vampire who had bit them—good luck finding the asshole. Or they could attempt to not drink blood before the next full moon, which would then allow the vampire's taint to pass through their system.

Only problem with that last one was sure madness overtook the mortal who fought the blood hunger. Or so he'd been told. He'd had two weeks to go before the full moon, but had succumbed to the insane craving within five days. If he had known better, he would have tried to wait for the moon. He hadn't known better.

But Laura would now benefit from his knowledge. With her daughters to occupy her during the day and his nightly visits, she was succeeding in beating the hunger. She had to make it through tonight, or actually past midnight when the moon was highest in the sky.

He kneeled before the woman and clapped his hands together in determination. "Let's do this."

"I can't." She beat against his chest with ineffectual fists. "I can't wait. I need it now. You said if the craving got too strong you'd let me drink your blood." She lunged for his neck but he gripped her wrists and pushed her against the fence.

"I also told you, tasting vampire blood is not going to work. You need mortal blood—hell, Laura, you can do this. It's just a few more hours. Don't you want to get through this for your girls?"

"Girls?" Her eyes flickered toward the gate. "Yes, bring one here. A nice warm drink of blood."

He swallowed and shook his head. He remembered the craving. It was relentless and would not cease. Much like the tug he'd felt on his heart upon seeing that bastard kiss Olivia.

Don't think about what you've lost. You need to be here one hundred percent for this family.

Laura struggled and pleaded that he was hurting her. He wasn't, but he knew if her daughters heard her cries, they'd rush back here, even though they had respected his ban and stayed outside.

He leaned in and pulled the woman onto his lap, and gently wrapped a palm about her mouth so her scream, which sounded right now, was muffled.

"We'll get through this together, Laura. I'm going to make sure those beautiful girls out there have a mortal mother to take them into the New Year. Let's think about anything but blood and vampires right now. Did you notice it's starting to snow?"

Heavy flakes fluttered from the sky, and the only thing he could think was the girls should be snuggled in warm beds with stuffed animals tucked under their arms. Laura had been laid off in the summer, and as a recent widow without life insurance or close family, she'd ended up on the streets months later. She hadn't asked for the vampire to attack her.

Only proved everyone was vulnerable. Even white-collar stockbrokers with attitudes a mile wide.

What had Laura Jones done to deserve this crappy deal?

"What about Christmas carols?" he asked, the gorgeous sound of Olivia's voice returning to him. The world felt right when he heard her voice. Until that bastard had kissed her in front of everyone. Who the hell was he—no. Didn't matter anymore. It was apparent Olivia had more than a vampire tucked in her Christmas stocking.

"Do you know any Christmas songs?" he asked Laura.

She shook her head negatively and tried to bite his fingers, but he held her firmly. He had the strength of ten men now—and one werewolf—so he had to be careful he didn't lose control.

"You want to know my favorite? It's that drummer boy song. I bet you remember that one. *Pa-rum-pa-pum-pum.*"

He sang a few verses, and was transported to the back-seat of the cab with Olivia—damn it, he had to get her out of his head!

Laura began to nod and hum. Wild eyes flickered at him, but he sensed it was safe to let go of her mouth.

She sniffed back tears and hummed along with the next verse.

Only a few hours, he told himself. If Christmas truly was a magical time, as he'd told the girls, he wished for a miracle tonight.

OLIVIA'S DRIVER HAD FOLLOWED Daniel, as she'd instructed him to do if he caught a glimpse of the elusive vampire. She hadn't told anyone she was seeing a vampire, of course. They drove down Broadway while she changed in the backseat. She'd mastered the art of tugging a bulky sweater over her evening gown and slipping up jeans without revealing skin to the driver.

Twenty minutes later, the car pulled over across the street from what looked like an abandoned house, sandwiched next to a vacant lot. A scrappy wood fence connected the plots, and two girls huddled on a broken bench that hadn't seen a bus stop for years.

"This is the place," the driver announced. "I don't think you should go out there, Miss Adorata. This neighborhood is not safe."

She glanced down the street. A neon café sign advertised beer and Irish rum. A golden glow from the street-light highlighted the heavy snowflakes. Looked like a scene that belonged inside a cracked snow globe.

"I'll be fine. Just give me a few minutes."

She got out and tugged up the parka hood to conceal her appearance because she was still in full makeup. No one was around but she could never let down her guard. None of that mattered because she was concerned the girls were outside alone with no caps.

The taller of the two approached Olivia as she neared and her posture emulated that of a tough prison guard with attitude. "Who are you?"

"I'm looking for a friend," Olivia said. "His name is Daniel."

The smaller girl began to say something, but the one Olivia guessed was her older sister pushed her back toward the fence. It was then she heard the soft singing on the other side of the fence. She approached and put her gloved hands to the wood and listened.

"You can't go back there," the girl warned. "Fancy lady like you could get in trouble in this neighborhood."

"Who is he with?" she asked.

"My mommy," the littler one offered. She dodged her sister's hand as she tried to grab her and managed to sidle up along Olivia. "He's saving her. We don't want her to turn into a vampire."

"Charity, you don't tell strangers stuff like that," the older one hissed.

A vampire? How could Daniel save a person from becoming a vampire? Had he bitten someone and now as a result, she was changing?

She pressed against the fence, but when the older girl insinuated herself before her, Olivia stepped back out of respect.

"I don't want to cause any trouble," Olivia offered. "If he's busy helping your mother I'll catch him later."

The younger of the two tugged on Olivia's sleeve and said, "Your eyelashes are really long."

Olivia blinked. The false eyelashes were also annoying, but much needed on stage. "They're not real."

"Like Santa? Daniel told us Santa isn't real."

"He did?" How dare he? Though she shouldn't judge. She had no idea the mood or context in which he'd said that to the girls. "Santa is real if you want him to be."

"But he still doesn't bring presents to girls who don't live in houses," the little one said and followed with a dramatic sigh.

She didn't know what to say to that. Hell, she could write a check and put the girls and their mother in a nice hotel for months. But that would never solve their problem if the mother had no stable form of income.

"Aren't you girls cold?" She placed her hand on the little one's head and felt little warmth. "How about I buy you some hot chocolate at the café down the block?"

The girls exchanged looks, but Olivia could read the warning flash in the elder's eyes to her sister.

"Right," she said. "I'm a stranger. You should never go places with strangers. You two are very smart."

The soft tones of "O Holy Night" echoed out from behind the fence. Daniel was singing with a woman. For what reason, she couldn't know. But it wasn't her place to intrude. She'd wanted him for herself tonight, but obviously, he had more important things to do.

He has a life away from your bed. Get that into your brain. You scared him off by confessing love. The risky move failed.

A life that obviously had much more meaning than she could ever see beyond his fangs and danger.

"Daniel's a good man," she said to the older girl. "You can trust him."

"I know that. He's been here almost every night since my mom was bitten. Except that one night. Don't know where the heck he was then."

Snuggled in Olivia's bed beside her. Hell.

"He'll save her," the oldest offered. "I know he will."

Olivia managed a weak smile. For the sake of the girls, she hoped Daniel could save their mother. Her heart warmed to know what he was doing. Truly, his soul was worthy.

"Merry Christmas," she offered, and wandered down the street. The driver followed at a slow creep.

In the café she ordered three cups of hot chocolate to go, and upon spying a lost and found box full of mittens and caps, asked if she could take two. The owner said they'd been in there for months, so she was welcome to them.

THE MIDNIGHT BELLS from a church down the block had chimed over an hour ago. Daniel eyed the moon, noting it had fallen in the sky. The bright disk reminded him of the Christmas tale of the wise men following the star. Pray, Laura's soul had followed the bright this night.

He held her tightly still, and she hadn't moved in a while. Maybe she had fallen asleep? It was the best option to fight the cravings.

Thinking about cravings… *She* had been here. He'd felt her presence outside the fence earlier. Had smelled her delicious sugar cookie scent. She'd come looking for him? He was glad she'd not interfered, but sad he'd missed her gorgeous smile.

Until he remembered that kiss onstage. She would have never let it happen if the man hadn't meant something to her. He couldn't accept it had been a sweet peck, either. He'd lost her, yet he'd never really had her.

How to possess a bright star when she belonged in the sky, shimmering for the masses to follow?

The smell of hot chocolate stirred his appetite. Giggles from outside the gate surprised him. That Charity and Mary could find some humor on this bleak night heartened him.

In his arms, Laura stirred and lifted her head. She stretched her mouth in a yawn and tugged out of his grasp to sit against the makeshift cardboard walls of her lean-to.

"How do you feel?" he asked on a raspy whisper.

"Oddly…not hungry for blood." She shifted her tongue in her mouth and tilted her head. "Do I smell hot chocolate?"

He nodded. It was too incredible to believe, but he couldn't prevent jumping into the excitement of what they may have accomplished tonight. "I think it worked," he said.

She nodded. "I think so, too. I mean, I feel that it did work. I made it." With new wonder, Laura looked to the gate. "My girls? Tell them to come here."

He called them in, and Mary allowed her sister to lunge into her mother's arms first.

"Did he save you, Mommy?"

All three women looked to him. Daniel could only shrug.

"He did," Laura said. "I know he did. Thank you, Daniel."

"Merry Christmas," he said, but regretted that it meant little.

He slipped out through the gate while the reunited family hugged and sniffled back tears. He wasn't much for

Hallmark moments. He'd saved one woman from a horrible life. But how many more had transformed because they'd not had someone to help them?

He shoved his hands into his pockets and strode down the street, but noticed the car parked across the way. The black Mercedes did not blend into this neighborhood. Seriously?

Hell, he didn't want to talk to her.

Yes, he did. It was going to hurt, but it was best to exorcise this wicked ache from his heart swiftly.

Daniel beelined toward the car. The back window rolled down to reveal an angel's face.

"What are you doing here?" he asked.

"Don't be angry. I had my driver follow you from the concert. I needed to see you tonight. To apologize for the things I said."

"Doesn't matter."

"It does matter. I'm sorry, Daniel."

"For what you said." She'd said she loved him. And now she was apologizing? He nodded and looked over the top of the car. His chest tightened and he couldn't bring himself to look at her again. "That it?"

"Y-yes. Come inside, and let's talk. What you did for that woman and her daughters was amazing."

"You must have bought the girls hot chocolate. I noticed they had caps."

"Is their mother going to be all right?"

"I think so. She made it to the full moon without drinking blood. I think she's going to be as fine as a homeless mother of two can be on a cold winter's night."

"I offered the girls money, but the older one only took a twenty. She's very proud."

"I offer their mother money every time I see her. Always refuses. She just needs to find a place to live and get a job."

"It'll happen," Olivia said. "Santa will find them."

Daniel smirked and shook his head. "Charity thinks Santa only comes to kids who live in houses."

"Then we'll have to change her mind, yes?"

"Olivia." He winced at the rush of emotions that welled in his chest, squeezing his broken heart, and wished he'd been smarter and had walked away, but now he was here, and he was no man to walk away without all the answers. "I saw him kiss you."

"Him? Oh." Her hands fluttered to her lap and twisted within one another. "Daniel, that wasn't—"

"No need for an explanation. I know where I fall on the scale of all things starstruck and famous. Dead bottom. It's expected. That's the way life treats me. Just swell."

"Daniel."

"Things never go my way. I thought me and you were going to be a one-night thing, or maybe a flash in your holiday vacation. I was cool with that. Until…"

He locked his jaws shut and beat the top of the car. *Out with it then, and then you can cleanse this star from your heart and toss it back into the sky where it belongs.*

"I fell in love with you, too. It's been nice knowing you, Olivia. Luck with your career."

And he pushed from the car and swung around, beating a path to the opposite side of the street and down the sidewalk. He heard her call after him, and started humming that damned drummer boy song to tune her out.

CHAPTER SIX

HE DIDN'T WANT TO GO to Olivia's Fifth Avenue sanctuary.

He did want to go there.

It had been two days without the smell of her sugar cookie skin brushing his cheek. The shimmer of her hair over his face. The hush of her voice tendering into his heart.

And he missed her so much it hurt worse than the blood hunger after he'd been bitten.

In an attempt to block out the soft call of her haunting spirit, Daniel stalked down the alley behind a nightclub booming with techno music. He wanted blood. He needed it coursing through his body, fulfilling and darkening his lighter desires. It was the only way to rip her cleanly from his soul.

He passed a gaggle of women in skirts too short for winter and makeup too gaudy for all seasons. A couple guys in suits and smoking clove cigarettes nodded at him. He didn't care for this scene, but it was the furthest from her he could get.

Until he walked right up to the tour bus with that bastard's face on it—Parker Troy. The man stood in the bus's open door, flashing his expensive fake teeth at the crush of screaming women who wanted to touch him, grope him, have his baby. Whatever.

Ramming a fist into his palm, Daniel wondered how easy it would be to circumvent the screaming fans to get inside that bus. Ripping out the guy's throat played through his brain, and then...

He turned and marched away from the bus.

"Idiot," he admonished. "You don't rough up a guy because he got the girl and you didn't."

He turned sharply and headed for the liquor store, which had become a weekly ritual for him over the past year. His life had changed from suits and business lunches to scamming for blood and late nights watching lovers in Central Park. But all in all? He wouldn't go back. Because it was the small things that mattered to him now. Like Charity and Mary and Sam.

As usual, Sam was sitting on the broken iron bench out front of the all-night liquor store. He nodded to Daniel.

"Saturday Night Sam." He acknowledged the old man. "How's life treating you?"

"Well enough." He was a man of few words and even fewer teeth.

"As it should. Give me a few minutes. I'll be right out."

He entered the store, crowded down the short aisles with doodads and snack foods and alcohol in every flavor, color and proof.

"Give me a pack of Marlboro," Daniel said as he selected a pint of vodka and set that on the counter.

The guy at the register reached for the cigarettes while managing to not take his attention from the TV sitting on the side of the checkout counter.

The service nowadays, Daniel started to think, but then his attention found the screen, as well. She glowed, her face all soft and delicate. She was wearing the white gown she'd worn nights earlier, so the interview must have been previously taped.

"Olivia is so hot," the clerk said as he leaned on an

elbow, pushing aside a display of silver snowflake ornaments.

"She is," Daniel agreed, but not with any conviction.

He fingered a snowflake, wondering if it was real silver. Couldn't be. But the shiny metal couldn't distract from the bright star shining on the television screen. His heart pounded as her voice burrowed through his flesh and into his soul. But seeing someone else swoon over her cemented for him how unattainable she was.

"So you and Parker Troy are an item now?" the television interviewer asked.

Olivia chuckled and looked aside, not answering. Her dark lashes flicked the air.

Daniel gritted his jaw. She used to dust those lashes across his bare skin. Of all the times to walk into this store, he had to pick this one?

And then Olivia straightened and looked directly into the camera. "No, we're not an item. That was staged on Christmas Eve. You know how the record companies are. Well, if you don't, they do things like that. It's a part of the job. Parker and I are going to sing a duet together but that's it. But…"

She sighed.

Daniel leaned forward, his heart pounding.

"I shouldn't have agreed to the kiss onstage. I hurt someone that I care for deeply. And it wasn't being honest to my fans. I'm so sorry."

Daniel whispered that he was sorry, too.

"What's that, dude?"

He swung a look to the clerk, who had put the vodka in a brown paper bag.

"Uh…nothing." He grabbed one of the snowflake ornaments and muttered he'd buy that, too, then shoved it in his pocket. Tossing some bills on the counter, he thanked the clerk. Walking outside, he pressed the bag and pack of grits to Sam's chest. "Here you go, man. Take it easy."

Sam called after him, "Merry Christmas, Daniel!"

"Yeah, that's what they tell me," he said, and for the first time in days, he smiled.

It had all been a performance.

THE RITUAL OF PACKING away everything in the kitchen until next Christmas vacation was never fun. Olivia went through the cupboards, aligning the pots and pans, made sure the dishwasher was empty, and scrubbed the counters and washed the tile floor. She went through the tiny apartment with a vacuum, even though Lisa always suggested she hire a maid to do it.

Maids were for sissies, she thought with a smirk. Getting a chance to do anything domestic was her kind of excitement. It reminded her that she was just like everyone else, somewhere, deep inside, where no camera or television recording could ever venture.

She wrapped up the vacuum cord and tucked the machine away, then wandered into the bedroom to straighten the closet where she kept clothing year-round, but only winter stuff.

When finally she sat on the bed and realized it would be only an hour before the limo arrived to pick her up and take her back to her celebrity life, tears spilled down her cheeks. The bed felt too big and awkward when she sat on it alone. It was missing Daniel's wide shoulders and strong, powerful muscles. And his intense kisses and even his sharp bites.

She stroked her neck. The bite ached a little. When she touched the small wounds it felt as if he were blowing softly upon her skin, marking her with his delicious darkness. Her blood stirred to think of the vampire who had stolen her heart with a kiss and a bite. And a dance.

That had been what made her fall in love with him, that dance in this very bedroom, swaying against him, learning there was more to the monster than just fangs.

You took the risk and it paid off. She'd gained confidence, and had made the decision to be seen with Parker on her own, no approval necessary. It hadn't been a good decision, but she was learning.

But it had been a risk Daniel could not accept.

It would probably never have worked out. But she wished she'd had the opportunity to learn that for herself.

"You did learn that," she said. "It didn't work out. End of story. The guy hates you because he thinks you're Parker Troy's woman. Ugh."

So what if she had been ready to figure out a way to make it work? Singers had relationships with regular people all the time, and they managed to keep their private lives private. Daniel didn't need to tour with her, and she could fly him in to major cities and meet him at hotels under an assumed name.

It would have been worth the trouble.

She'd gotten due karma after that stupid stage kiss.

So back to the crazy, monstrous life of a singer. She'd lose herself in her music and touring. It was the only way to keep thoughts of him away.

A flicker outside the window caught her attention. The streetlight beamed over fluffy, gently falling snowflakes. Olivia strolled to the window and before she could admire the sight, she noticed the man standing across the street, back against an iron fence fronting a walk-up brownstone, head bowed.

Willing him to look up, she pressed her palms to the

cold window and it fogged around her hands. She wiped away the condensation but that only smeared the glass.

Rushing for a coat, she pulled it on, stuck her bare feet into her boots by the door and clattered down the iron staircase. Running toward the street, she didn't pause to think that he might reject her. He had come to her. He wanted to see her.

They had a chance. They two—monsters—could really make this work.

Before she could cross the street, the familiar click of a camera and a blinking flash paused her at the curb. Daniel took one look at the photographer who'd been waiting around the corner and rushed him.

DANIEL HAD BEEN WATCHING the guy for fifteen minutes. He'd been lurking outside the front foyer of Olivia's building, trying to pass himself off as just another guy, perhaps waiting for a friend, but Daniel had seen the glint of a camera lens sticking out of his pocket.

He'd wanted to go up the side stairs to Olivia's apartment, but his suspicions about the lurker had been confirmed. Damned paparazzi. How had they found her?

This was not a situation he wanted to get into, but there was no way he was going to allow the guy to take photos of Olivia in a place she considered her sanctuary.

He dashed across the street and shoved the photographer against the wall. "Back off, buddy."

"You touched me!" the guy yelled.

Olivia tugged his sleeve "Let's go, Daniel."

"Of course I touched you." He jerked his arm from Olivia's grasp and approached the man, who had the audacity to act affronted. "You've no right following the woman all over the place and taking pictures without her permission."

"She's a public figure," the cameraman argued. "That means she belongs to the public, buddy. They—we—put her where she is today. The least she can do is repay that generosity with a few pictures."

"Your concept of public and private is whacked," Daniel argued.

"So is yours. I think I'm going to bruise." The cameraman touched his arm where Daniel had shoved him. "I'll sue."

"Yeah? And I'll—"

Before he could reveal fangs, Daniel felt Olivia tug his arm again. "It's not worth it."

"Is he your new boyfriend, Olivia? That was quick. You and Troy didn't work out?" The cameraman shot a few clicks of Daniel. "Much ruder than the last one. Who are you? What's your name? You a singer? An actor?"

His anger boiling, Daniel lunged toward the man. "Can't the woman have a day or two to herself? It's Christmas. Give her a break."

"Christmas with the new boyfriend," the cameraman recited as he continued to click pictures of Daniel. "This one will make the cover of the *Daily Tattle* for sure. Pop singer's angry boyfriend is a handful *and* wounds cameraman."

"Oh, bull crap." Daniel fisted the guy about the collar and held him up until his feet dangled.

"Think, Daniel," Olivia said behind him. "You're only giving him more ammunition."

"But he knows your secret hideaway now. You going to tell anyone where Olivia lives?"

"Hell, yes," the guy croaked. "And I'm suing your pants off. Let me down!"

Daniel glanced to Olivia, who stood with arms crossed over her chest and a frantic look pleading with him to stop. Right. He'd gone too far. He'd reacted. Exactly what these crazy reporters fed on. He'd failed her.

"Sorry." Daniel set the man down to stumble against the brick wall.

Without a word, Olivia walked around the corner.

"I'm sorry, Olivia!" he called.

No reply.

The cameraman sank to a crouch, scrambling in the snow to retrieve the dropped camera. "I got your picture, buddy. I will find out who you are. This story is going front page, I promise you that."

Daniel snatched the camera from the man's grasp, flicked open the card holder and broke the digital storage card in two. The man protested and when he pulled a punch, Daniel caught the fist with his palm. He narrowed his eyes on the man's gaze and peered into his soul. It was dark in there. The guy didn't care who he trampled to earn a buck. He made a living by tracking down celebrity dirt and plastering it all over the tabloid rags without a care for the lives he was damaging and the secrets he exposed.

Daniel spoke slowly and deeply. "You dropped your camera and when you try to remember what happened, you'll recall it was as you were crossing a busy intersection. You were not here. Yes?"

The man nodded, his gaze lost in Daniel's vampiric thrall.

"You have no desire to take a picture of Olivia Adorata again. You're going to get in your car and drive away, and forget you were ever in this neighborhood. And me? Just a friendly guy who pointed you in the right direction. Now go."

The cameraman blinked, and looked about as if he'd surfaced from a coma. He asked Daniel, "Which way?"

"North." Daniel pointed down the street.

"Thanks, man." He got in his Volkswagen and drove away.

Watching until the car was out of sight, Daniel decided the thrall was a handy tool that he didn't use often enough. But could he use it every time he and Olivia were caught out by the paparazzi? Those bastards swarmed in hoards. He could only work his thrall on one person at a time.

Not like it should matter. He'd proven how unworthy he was of a relationship with the gorgeous singer who depended on the public's interest to survive.

He hung his head. He'd come here to see if they stood a chance. The answer was all too obvious.

"Daniel," she whispered from the corner of the building.

He didn't look at her. Couldn't. Not when he'd shown her yet another dark side of the monster within him.

"Thank you," she said. "I don't know what you did, but I think it worked."

"Vampire tricks," he muttered. "I'm sorry."

She plunged against his body and nuzzled her face alongside his neck.

"Daniel, I need you. I love you. Parker means nothing to me. It was a stupid publicity stunt."

"I know that now. I made an assumption that was wrong. That's why I had to come here today. Hadn't expected to show you my inner asshole with the cameraman, though. Can you forgive me?"

She nodded and snuggled closer to him, and he opened his jacket and pulled her against his chest. God, that felt great. Like Christmas should feel. "There's nothing to forgive," she said. "We both have issues. Big ones."

"I'd argue my issues are bigger than yours," he said, "but we both know that's not necessarily true."

Nothing needed to be said. Everything needed to be spoken. He would always be this way, dark of soul and heart. He had to do things now to survive that mortals could never fathom, not the good ones, anyway.

"Can we work, Olivia? I don't do the media and camera flashes and television interviews. I don't even think I can follow you around on red carpets or stand in dressing rooms waiting for you to find me."

"I don't want you to do that. I want you to be my normal."

He smirked, and revealed a fang. "Normal?"

"You know what I mean. Music is my life. It is where my heart belongs. I won't ever stop doing what I'm doing. But you, Daniel, only you make my heart sing. I want to sway with you. I love you."

"I love you, too, God help us both."

"And remember I said I wanted a slow relationship? Well, we've plunged in and know what we're dealing with—a pop star and a vampire. Now let's learn about each other, inside. Take things slow."

"Like seeing each other only when you're on vacation?"

"Can you do that? I can't. I do have a private life away from the stage. But I can't promise we'll never run into another photographer together."

"He got me so angry the way he acted as if it was his right to invade your privacy."

"That was a strange situation. Normally they find me when I've got my monster on and expect the flashing bulbs. This was private. I don't know how he found this place, but they go to extreme measures sometimes."

"I can't promise the need to protect you won't make

me smash in another photographer's face, Olivia. It's too strong. You mean too much to me."

"We'll figure things out." She tapped his lip and kissed the corner of his mouth right over the fang. "Monsters get to love—you can't tell me otherwise."

"I won't try to."

"Let's go inside."

"You go up. I'm going to peek around the corner and make sure ole snap-happy didn't return."

The coast was clear. Daniel felt vindicated having used his thrall to protect his woman.

His woman.

Yes, he could get behind that one hundred percent. It wouldn't be easy, but like she'd said, they'd figure things out.

Turning the corner, his heart jumped to his throat. At the sight of the nasty werewolf holding his woman, he charged. The wolf backed down the alleyway, clutching Olivia in front of him, a knife to her neck.

"Let her go. It's me you want," Daniel tried cautiously. "You okay, Olivia?"

She nodded minutely, but the blade kept her from speaking.

"I think I want to play with this one awhile," the guy said on a growl. It was his favorite werewolf, Punch. "You had your chance, vampire."

"Seriously? Because I didn't leap into your twisted death ring, now you're going to punish me by hurting an innocent mortal?"

"That sounds about right."

"You're an idiot." Daniel approached but sensed the wolf would pull the blade across Olivia's neck out of spite, so he had to play this right. "You'll get more enjoyment out of starving me and feeding me to another hungry vampire."

Olivia's eyes widened. So his life was dark and fucked up. Did she really want him? Because if she did, he was ready, willing and able.

"Let her go." Daniel started backing down the sidewalk, hoping the wolf would see who was the better snatch. "And I swear you got me. Dude, you know you're stronger than me. Come on. Catch me if you can." He splayed out his arms in surrender.

With a hungry growl, the wolf shoved Olivia against the wall below the iron stairway and charged after him.

Daniel took off in a run, hoping to lure the wolf as far from Olivia as possible. "You don't follow!" he called to her. "Go inside and lock your doors!"

"Or the big bad wolf will eat you," his pursuer said as he leaped and landed on Daniel's back.

They went down in a snowbank plowed up at the edge of a small city garden lot. Daniel felt the icy scrape of the knife over his hand, but it didn't feel as if the wolf wielded it. Instead, it must have fallen from his grip. He grasped the handle and groaned as the impact of a fist pummeled his gut.

The knife slid down the snowbank and the werewolf began to choke Daniel. He couldn't go down now that he had the perfect reason to survive. An angel had looked into his soul and proclaimed it worthy of her love.

God, he loved her.

And then he remembered he had one weapon yet to hand, but it was a long shot. Reaching in his pocket, he palmed the snowflake ornament, then dragged it roughly across the wolf's neck. Blood spotted his chin and the wolf grabbed his throat.

Daniel scrambled to stand and step away as the wolf staggered and fell to his knees, gagging on its blood.

"You're lucky that wasn't real silver," he muttered. If

silver entered the wolf's bloodstream, it wouldn't take long for a grisly death. "I'll defend her to my death—or yours, if it comes to that."

The werewolf met his eyes with bright gold irises. "You're wasting your time on a mortal," he growled, then choked up blood. "Especially that one." The wolf collapsed upon the snowbank.

Wincing, Daniel stepped away. *Especially that one.* No, it wasn't a waste of time. Couldn't be. He wouldn't allow it to be. Any second he got to spend in Olivia's arms was one less second he stood alone.

Daniel clutched his chest and someone grabbed him from behind. Olivia's hopeful green eyes connected to his. "Come with me," she said, and he grabbed her hand and rushed down the street. A limo waited at the curb, and she opened the back door. "No questions asked from this moment forward. We leave our strange Christmas normal behind," she said. "If you want to be my monster lover, then come with me."

Every fiber in Daniel's soul felt Olivia's bright star touch it, and he dived into the back of the limo and drew her in beside him.

He kissed her deeply. "To monster love," he whispered. "We can do this."

"Of course we can. But can we make a stop before going to my other place?"

"Where?"

She tugged out a set of keys from her pocket. "I think I know a family who could use my apartment until their mother can find a job."

"Did I tell you I love you?"

"You did. Merry Christmas, my monster lover."

* * * * *

WHEN HERALD ANGELS SING

To my mother, Carmen Piñeiro,
who always believed that anything was possible
as long as you reached for it with all your heart.

CHAPTER ONE

Jersey Shore, December 23, 1931

THE GALE-DRIVEN SNOW lashed at his skin, tearing into his flesh like stinging nettles, but Damien did not budge from his position high atop the lighthouse tower. Even when the nor'easter threatened to rip him from the narrow ledge, Damien held his ground.

The force of the wind was such that each gust delivered a punishing body blow, but he relished the pain. He deserved it. The physical discomfort was nothing compared to the anguish in his heart.

Tomorrow was Christmas Eve. Tomorrow it would be a year that he'd lost Angelina. For the second time.

The first time he'd lost her, it had taken over a century for her to return to him.

The woman he had come to know as Angelina had looked slightly different each time they'd met, although there had been strong physical similarities with each of her apparitions. The raven hair and jewel-like green eyes. The voluptuous figure any man would want to touch. Full lips with a Cupid's bow meant to be kissed.

What hadn't changed was Angelina's spirit. Her inherent goodness brought light to his soul. Her kindness had called to him on two occasions over the past century and on two occasions he had failed her.

And his failure had killed her.

Damien raised his head into the wind and howled with the pain of her loss and his guilt, but the storm was such that his cry blended with the screeching winds. Only he heard his anguished voice.

How much longer will I have to wait for her? Will she ever return to me? Damien wondered, peering into an afternoon sky made so dark by the storm it seemed almost as if night had already descended. Perfect for a vampire like him, but not so good for any poor wretch who might be caught in the tempest.

He had battled such dangerous gales in his earlier life as a ship's captain. Dared the sea and Poseidon himself in those misspent hell-raising days before he'd lost his mortal life.

His father—the one who had not even deigned to claim the bastard son who had slipped from his lover's womb— had heard of those adventures and proclaimed Damien was not his, but rather the Devil's spawn. The old man had never had a kind word for him nor had he ever believed that Damien would make something of himself. With each and every overture Damien had made, his father had rebuked him.

So Damien had stopped trying to please the old man. Instead, he had pleased himself—in every conceivable way with any available woman in every port in which he had ever set foot.

Until he met Angelina…the first time.

His gut fisted into a knot once more as he thought of her. Acknowledged all that he had lost because of his own ego. He tightened his grip on the edge of the railing as a particularly powerful squall nearly cost him his precarious footing on the slim ledge around the beacon of the lighthouse. He was tempted to let the wind take him. On occasion lately he had thought about tossing himself over the side, down onto the rocks below. As a vampire, the fall would likely not kill him, but it would break his body and Lord knew he deserved to suffer. Maybe after, the kiss of the morning sun would finish him off and end his insufferable existence.

But Damien would not embrace death tonight.

Angelina had come to him just before Christmas Eve on both of the other occasions. In his heart, he prayed that she might somehow return to him again soon.

There had been a sense of anticipation building for days, warning him that something unexpected approached. Some would have said it was the excitement of the upcoming holiday, but Christmas had never had any special appeal for Damien. His mother had tried her best to make it special, but with their meager existence, that had been difficult. She always somehow managed to scrape together a little gift and roast a scrawny chicken to perfection.

Sadly, Damien had not realized that his mother's love had been what had made the holidays bearable. Much like it had been Angelina and her love that had first brought joy into his life.

If by some miracle she did return this Christmas, Damien vowed that he would not fail her again.

He was about to return to his home at the base of the lighthouse when the sweep of the beacon highlighted a dim shape on the water. He squinted and looked hard against the driving snow. With another turn of the light he noted the hazy outline on the surface of the ocean. Scrutinizing the horizon more intently, he confirmed that there was a ship at sea, battling the immense surges caused by the winds.

He wondered what would possess someone to be out

on a day like today, but as the vessel drew closer, the vague outline sharpened and he recognized its shape.

Fury rose up in him at the sight of the rumrunner manned by his nemesis, Captain Pedro Ramirez. No wonder the boat was out tonight. The vampire captain and his immortal crew would have little fear of death in the churning waters any mortal man would avoid.

As Damien watched, the crew struggled with something cumbersome along the schooner's deck. To his surprise, they raised a skiff over the lip of the starboard side and lowered the small vessel into the rough seas. The boat pushed away from the schooner, manned by two crewmen who furiously rowed through the surging waves. Time and time again the sea tossed the meager skiff up into the air before crashing it back down against the water's surface.

Still the vampire crew pushed ahead, unmindful of the dangerous ocean.

Damien wondered anew why they would be out in such weather and why they were headed directly toward his lighthouse. But Damien understood that Ramirez delighted in torturing him. In taking Angelina from him, time and time again. With Christmas Eve arriving tomorrow, maybe Ramirez wanted to remind Damien of what he had lost last year.

As the skiff hit the shore, the two crewmen jumped overboard into the pounding surf and hauled the vessel up onto the sand to beach it. Then they reached in and dragged out a long, lumpy roll of canvas clumsily bound with rope. They tossed the package onto the sand and then dragged it upward until it was well beyond the reach of the angry surf.

Then they pulled the skiff off the beach and back into the waves for a return trip to the rumrunner.

A present from Ramirez? Not likely, but Damien couldn't resist the temptation of the package. Curiosity might have killed the cat, but he was already dead, both physically and spiritually, so who cared what danger lurked within the bundle?

With a surge of vampire speed, he nearly flew down the spiral staircase and out the lighthouse door, racing over the sand and snow to the package not far from the water's edge. As he approached, he could see the brownish-red blotches along the outside of the canvas. Even with the wind, his vampire senses picked up the smell of blood and the hushed heartbeat pulsing beneath the fabric.

Damien dropped to his knees and swiftly undid the thick ropes wrapped tightly around the rough blood-stained canvas. His fingers shook as he wondered who was trapped within. As he both hoped and feared that it was Angelina.

The wind picked up one edge of the cloth, what he now saw had once been a sail, as he finished untying the rope. Freed, the sail flew upward into Damien's face, strong enough to open a gash along his cheek.

Ignoring the wound, which his vampire body would heal in the space of a few heartbeats, he ripped the canvas sheet away from his face and held it down with one knee. But before he could undo the rest of the bundle, a hand fell from beneath the other edge of the canvas.

Petite and bloodied. A woman's hand. Achingly familiar.

Angelina.

She lay naked in the center of the sail, her raven hair spilling out against a mosaic of bright red and rusty brown on the white canvas. There was no denying the scent of blood, but more powerful was her familiar aroma. Even with the storm swirling around him, her natural perfume filled his senses, making him think of bright summer days and fields of wildflowers.

Impossible. Wonderful. He reached for her, encircling her in his arms. The heat of her blood bathed his hands. Seeped through the thin wet fabric of his cotton shirt.

He drew her close and kissed her temple, detecting the thready pulse of life beneath his lips.

She was alive, he thought with joy. As her eyelids fluttered open, recognition came alive in their emerald depths.

"Damien? Is it really you?" she said in the voice that had been haunting his dreams for nearly a year. He realized then that her voice had not changed during any of her visits. Each word she spoke was like music, strumming elation and desire to life deep in his gut. Her voice wrought peace in his soul, as it had every time she had come into his life.

"It's really me, Angelina. This time nothing will take you from me."

CHAPTER TWO

THE PITCH AND ROLL of the ship made it nearly impossible for Pedro Ramirez to see what was happening onshore, but the vampire captain was not to be deterred. Nothing would keep him from savoring Damien's reaction to his special gift.

Going aloft on the rigging to the highest point on the schooner's mast, Pedro trained the spyglass on the couple, watching the tender reunion. One which would be short-lived, if his plans were successful.

Plus, if Pedro succeeded, Angelina would be his for all eternity. A rare gift for him to savor, time and time again.

Even now, the softness of her skin was vivid on his lips. The taste of her blood lingered on his tongue as he recalled feeding from her as she lay unconscious. Her blood had filled the emptiness inside of him with life. How much sweeter it would be when she was his, as his Master had promised. Only then could he spend an eternity sipping from her whenever he wanted.

Only then could he finally say that the last shreds of decency within Damien's soul had been lost. That the goodness that challenged Pedro each time they met and which so far had not been driven from Damien had finally been vanquished.

This time Pedro would claim Damien's eternal soul and in so doing, own Damien's true love Angelina, as well.

It had been a long time in coming, but Satan, who understood best the demonic power of anger, wanted his due. Pedro would be the instrument of that payment.

When Damien lifted Angelina into his arms and disappeared from sight in a blast of vampire speed, Pedro likewise retreated down the rigging to the warmth of his captain's chambers to savor a spot of fine Cuban rum like that he had off-loaded the day before. Several more kegs would be delivered tonight and by Christmas Eve his ship would be docked in the Manasquan Inlet. While his crew enjoyed the spoils of their work, Pedro would go to Damien and Angelina just as he had during their other two meetings. Satan had led Pedro to Damien because Satan found Damien's pain and anger powerful and wanted to make the hell-raiser one of his own minions. But so far that goal had proved elusive.

This time Pedro had something he knew Damien would kill to safeguard: Angelina's immortal soul.

Pedro had no doubt that the threat to Damien's beloved would goad the vampire into that final violent act. Satan had been right. Damien was filled with delightful anger. Pedro had come so close before only to have sanity, or maybe that damn meddler Angelina, prevent Damien from taking a life and sealing his eternal Fate.

But if all went as planned on this Christmas Eve night, Damien would lose his immortal soul by killing Pedro.

Not that Pedro could ever really die, he thought, entering his chambers and pouring himself a glass of rum. Not only was he a vampire, but he was also one of the Fallen Angels. Only his Master, Satan himself, or one of those blasted Goody Two-shoes Archangels could end Pedro's existence.

If Pedro could force Damien to take a life, Satan would reward Pedro with even greater powers. Plus the bonus of everlasting life with Angelina, of course.

At the thought of having her, Pedro grew hard. Reaching down, he released himself from the stricture of his pants and stroked. Imagined burying himself in her warm depths. Drinking of her blood, so full of light and life.

Only an Angel's blood could be so rare and satisfying.

By Christmas morning, Pedro would have Angelina as his own, he vowed. He couldn't imagine a better present to receive.

ANGELINA WAVERED BETWEEN BOUTS of consciousness as Damien gently bathed her and tended to the wounds along her back. Two deep gashes, each nearly six inches long and located high up along her shoulder blades, marred the otherwise smooth perfection of her creamy skin. Odd wounds, made by the slice of a knife or a clean swift slash of a sword, as if cutting off an appendage. The latter made no sense to him considering the position of the injuries.

When he finished cleansing the angry furrows, Damien applied antiseptic and covered the yawning slashes with gauze. He bound the injuries with soft strips of fabric he had torn from an old flannel work shirt.

Cautiously, he rolled Angelina onto her back, but not gently enough. She moaned at the pressure and opened her eyes, gazed up him with a slightly feverish look that made her emerald eyes glitter.

"I'm sorry. I'll try to be more careful," he promised.

Angelina sensed his distress. She gathered her waning strength, wanting to reassure him. Raising her hand, she cradled his cheek, the rasp of his evening beard prickly against her palm. He looked haggard, his skin pale even for a vampire, especially in contrast to the coal-black of his hair. Yet nothing could be more welcome than the sight of his face.

"You're really here," she said, almost unable to fathom

that she had been given the chance for which she had been praying for nearly a year. Not that her visit this time had begun as she had expected.

"I can say the same, Angelina. I hoped you might return to me—"

"And your prayers have been answered," she said, guessing at why the Archangel Raphael had released her to return. Raphael had been grumbling about having to listen to constant caterwauling. She supposed he had been referring to their combined and persistent entreaties for another chance to make things right.

Damien released a harsh laugh and chided her, his handsome features twisted with resentment. "Prayers. Do you think I even believe in God after all that I've seen? All that I've done?"

She smiled sadly, but understood. From the day of his birth, Damien had been destined for nothing but pain and misery. The bastard son of a coldhearted and cruel man, Damien had known little love and much loss. But despite all his errant ways, there was goodness and love within his heart. She had seen it time and time again during his early life and so had her boss, the Archangel Raphael. As the Archangel who possessed the power of healing, Raphael had believed Damien could be cured. It was why she had been sent down nearly a century earlier to become Damien's Guardian Angel.

Because of the strength of Damien's spirit and goodness in spite of the adversity he had faced, Raphael wanted Damien to become one of their Angels, but only if Damien could finally prove himself worthy.

"No matter what you say you believe, my love. It's here in your heart," she said and lowered her hand to rest over the bare skin of his chest. He had taken off his wet and bloodied shirt to tend to her. The skin of his upper body was smooth and had been warmed by the heat from the logs burning in a nearby fireplace.

"You are what's here," he said and covered her hand with his own. His palms were rough from centuries of hard physical labor. Powerful, and yet in bed he was incredibly gentle and giving. Even in her weakened state, desire awoke as she thought of being with him. She didn't want to waste a moment of her time with him.

They had only a very short time to be together, but truth be told, an eternity with Damien would not be enough for her. Even before her visit, she had been growing attracted to him as she had watched his life in preparation for her assignment. Then she had violated the first rule of being a Guardian Angel: never fall in love with your assignment. It was why Raphael had waited nearly a century before sending her back, hoping to quench that emotion so that she could perform the task she had been given.

"Come lie with me," she said, and Damien didn't hesitate, rising to pull off the rest of his wet clothes and then slip into the bed beside her. She shuddered at the chill the dampness his pants had left behind on the skin of his lower body.

"So sorry," he said and transformed, awakening the heat of the vampire to warm his skin and hers.

His silver-gray eyes, which always reminded her of an ocean during a hurricane, bled out to the bright neon blue-green of the vampire. From beneath the fullness of his lips his long canines emerged. She raised her hand and ran her thumb along his lips and those lethal-looking fangs. She had no fear of him because deep in her heart she knew he would not kill.

He'd had several opportunities over the course of his long existence to do so, but each and every time he had held back, seemingly aware that taking a life would forever damn his eternal soul.

As her gaze locked with his, he spoke, the animal growl of the vampire coloring his words. "Do not place me on a pedestal. It's too far a fall."

"You could have killed before, but you didn't. That young boy in the alley who stole your food—"

"Was younger and hungrier than I was. Anyone would have done the same," he parried with his words as quickly as he did with his sword and fists. She had always thought Damien made a better pairing with the warrior Archangel Michael, but it had been Raphael who had taken up Damien's cause.

"Not Ramirez," she argued, certain there was no goodness in the vampire captain.

The paleness of Damien's skin grew even lighter, almost translucent. It made a stark contrast to the pitch-black of his hair, which shimmered with touches of steel-blue from the light of the fire. Softly, he urged, "Do not ruin this moment by speaking of him. All that matters is that we're together now."

"I must speak of him, because…" She hesitated, unsure that Damien would believe her. And she worried that if he did, the temper that had earned him his reputation and his short mortal life would erupt.

"What is it, Angelina? Surely after all that has happened between us you can tell me what troubles you." He cradled her cheek with his rough, but caring hand. The warmth of his transformation seeped into her, driving away some of the chill in her body. Deep within, however, fear and doubt remained, which was not good considering her role in his life. Before she could trust him with more of the truth, she had to master her own emotions. Her own fears, doubts and hopes, which had, in part, been responsible for her failure to save him during her prior two visits.

"I'm tired, Damien. I'd like to rest," she fibbed, hoping that God would forgive her the one little white lie necessary for her to fulfill her celestial obligation.

Understanding filled Damien's gaze and his eyes grew hooded with worry. He pulled the sheets higher, tucking them tight around her the way a parent might lovingly swaddle a child.

"Rest, Angelina," he replied, saying her name in a voice that seemed as if he was convincing himself that she was really there. Then he continued. "Tomorrow is Christmas Eve, and this time I intend on it being a happy one."

CHAPTER THREE

DAMIEN DIDN'T KNOW WHAT woke him, only that there was an undeniable presence in the room. Something powerful and otherwordly that beat against his preternatural senses. He came instantly alert and reached for Angelina protectively, but she was no longer beside him.

He had cared for her during the past few hours, feeding her sips of nourishing broth made from the few limp vegetables and a small chunk of dried beef he'd found in the larder. Only blood provided him true sustenance, but on occasion he would have a guest, usually one of the hungry, traveling laborers. They were trying to find work and something to fill their bellies during the economic depression gripping the country.

The broth had seemed to offer her strength, and he had tended to her wounds, surprised by how quickly she appeared to be healing. Not less than an hour ago the skin on her back had begun knitting over the ugly gashes.

But now she was gone, he thought, sitting up quickly only to find Angelina standing at the window, staring out at the night. She was bathed in the platinum light of the full moon. The beams caressed her and streamed beyond the outline of her body, making her look ethereal. Angelic, he thought fancifully, until she turned, revealing the beauty of her naked body. Then, the only thoughts he had were purely sinful.

"Come to bed, my love," he said, the purr of the vampire tingeing his voice as need slammed into him. His erection tented the light sheet as he became painfully hard. His desire for her had grown exponentially in the year they had been apart.

"I cannot," she replied with outstretched hands, her palms raised to the heavens, almost in supplication. To his surprise, tiny pinpricks of light gathered there and slowly grew in size, illuminating the room with an intense golden glow. When the shimmering light spread along the perimeter of the space, the room changed before his eyes, almost as if he were watching a Saturday matinee movie play on the walls.

The window behind Angelina vanished and the white of the nearby wall became the rough-hewn stucco and dark wood of a familiar sight—the sailor's saloon where he had first met Angelina just over a century earlier.

"What's going on? How is this happening?"

"Twice before I was sent to you, Damien," she answered, her voice filled with strength and an underlying drone that sounded like voices murmuring in prayer. Or maybe a choir singing glorious praise. He couldn't be sure, although he was certain that the origin of the sound was not of this mortal realm.

Before his eyes, the light from her palms spread even farther, overtaking the confines of his bedroom and turning it into that Cuban den of iniquity, replete with sailors from the many ships docked in the port and the women who hoped to ply their wares to them.

Damien recalled the scene vividly, even after so long a time. He had just made a run down from Philadelphia to pick up a load of tobacco and rum. Such wares normally fetched a nice price back in the States, although not as good a price as slave running. The talk against slavery had been growing. It would be only a matter of time before that issue caused bloodshed, Damien had worried during that long-ago visit.

Despite his desire for money and success, Damien had never desired to trade in such misery. He had been a slave of poverty for too long and would not visit such a fate on another human.

But vices such as tobacco and rum had been a different matter, Damien recalled.

He watched the scene unfold before his eyes as people came and went in the vision. Only seconds passed before he heard a familiar voice—Angelina's sweet tones—and then his own gruff and slightly slurred reply. "A pint of rum will do."

Damien was drawn to the sight of the two of them. They were tucked into a far corner of the saloon. He had met Angelina just a few short days into his trip and had been instantly drawn to her.

That attraction had led to many a pleasurable night in her bed. Although Angelina had asked for no coin in return, he had left it nevertheless. He had money to spare and was certain she had need of it. Unlike his miserly father, who had provided nothing for him and his mother, Damien would not do the same to another woman.

"This was our first Christmas Eve, Damien. Remember it well. Remember how it ended," the Angelina of the present said to him as she slowly faded from sight and the vision overwhelmed him, filling every corner of his bedroom with the sights, scents and noises from 1830 Havana.

When Angelina completely disappeared from sight, something powerful slammed into Damien, so intensely that he fell back against the edge of the bed, weakened. Then that force yanked him roughly from where he stood. He felt as if he were flying through the air, his arms and legs flailing for purchase. Then he landed with a jolt on a rough-hewn bench in that Cuban tavern.

"You all right, Captain? You look like you've just seen a ghost," his first mate said from beside him.

His own ghost if any, Damien thought as he collected himself and peered around the room, trying to understand what had occurred. How was it possible that he had returned to 1830 and Havana?

Angelina approached not seconds later, carrying a large tray loaded with beverages and food for those at his table. She looked different from the apparition that had graced his bed just moments before. Sexily voluptuous, but more tired around the eyes.

He hadn't noticed that fatigue during their first encounter over a century ago. All he had seen was a beautiful woman he wanted to be his. A diversion from his loneliness.

Her emerald gaze locked with his as she bent to pass out pints of alcohol and plates filled with fragrant chicken and rice. When she laid his drink before him, her position and the décolletage of her plain white blouse allowed him to see the tidily mended chemise beneath that barely contained the generous globes of her breasts.

A peek of a nipple popping free had him instantly hard as he imagined tasting her. Savoring the sweetness of her body.

She must have noticed where his attention had drifted since she brushed her breast along his arm as she laid the dish of food before him. The smell of her, that familiar aroma of warm sunshine and wildflowers, wafted into his senses, obliterating the foul odors of unwashed bodies, cheap liquor and the untold detritus littering the floor of the sleazy tavern.

When she would have moved away, he tenderly laid a

hand on her arm. Skin smooth as fresh-picked peaches was warm beneath his palm. "We need to talk," he said.

Confusion clouded her eyes before she playfully teased, "Talk, is it? That wasn't what you wanted last night, *mi amor.*"

Damien realized then that this Angelina had no idea about their future or their past. She was a part of the vision, not that it mattered. All that was important was that he be with her. That he show her how much he cared and protect her from harm.

He knew she could not leave her station without making enough money to satisfy the barkeep, who was also the demanding owner of the saloon. Reaching for the bag of coins on his belt, he pulled it off and eased it into her free hand. "Will that be enough for you to go with me right now for a talk?"

She hefted the weight of it in her hands and narrowed her eyes. Shot a quick glance over her shoulder at the barkeep, who watched them intently. "In a rush? Afraid the Devil's got your number?"

Damien had tempted Fate and probably the Devil more than once in his life. With his father denying his existence and abandoning his mother, Damien had been forced to survive in any way he could. Legal or illegal didn't matter. It was too tough to worry about rules when hunger was gnawing a hole in your belly.

Much like desire for Angelina was burning through his gut just now.

"I'm an impatient man," he admitted and a moment of déjà vu flitted over him. It occurred to him then that he was being forced to relive his earliest encounter with Angelina, almost word for word, although why he did not know. Was it some kind of penance for his past actions?

It's a chance for you to prove that you are not the

man you once were, said a voice in his head, a message from the Angelina who was bringing him this view into a Christmas Eve Past.

"Damien? Are you okay?" asked the Angelina of his vision, her eyes narrowed as she considered him.

He shook his head to drive away the conflicting thoughts. Eager to be alone with her, he said, "I'm okay, love. Can we go?"

"Well, I've got another half an hour before break. You'll have to cool your heels until then to *talk,*" she said with a wink and a sly glance down to his lap, where his erection already strained the fabric of his pants.

She rushed away, but not before allowing her generous breasts to slip along his body once again, causing his body to jump in anticipation.

He grabbed his pint of rum and took a long swallow. The cheap alcohol burned his throat while he watched her attend to the other customers. Mindlessly, he shoveled the chicken and rice into his mouth, his hunger elsewhere.

Every now and again she would glance his way and smile knowingly. If she came close to him, she made a point of making contact. Another teasing brush of her breasts or of a womanly hip. The caress of her hand along the nape of his neck. So soft despite her labors.

And her scent. That intoxicating irresistible scent of home, it finally occurred to him. Her perfume brought back memories of the small cottage just outside of Philadelphia where he had lived with his mother before her untimely death.

That recollection quenched his desire somewhat, but as he took another long pull on his drink and Angelina swept by once more, those rounded hips swaying as if she was already riding him, the heat of passion rekindled in his gut and drove away all other thoughts.

When she laid down her tray and approached him, he rushed to her side, impatient desire in control.

She held out her hand and he took it, following her to the small hallway leading to the rooms for hire. But they had gone no farther than a few feet down that hallway when he hauled her to him, needing the feel of all those feminine curves against him. Wanting to bury himself in her then and there.

He backed her into the wall and her eyes widened, dilated with passion. He reached beneath her skirt and trailed his hand up the satiny skin of her leg until he was at her center.

She wore no underwear, he discovered, although he refused to think about how many other men also knew that fact.

He skimmed his hand across the silken curls at her core. Felt the heat and wet of her beneath his fingers as he slipped them along her cleft. When she rocked her hips against his hand and urged him on with a husky moan, he nearly came undone.

"Upstairs, love. Not like this," he said, something he had not said during that long-ago encounter. He didn't want to take her like he would a cheap slut. She meant more to him than that.

No sooner had the thought come to his consciousness when an immense pull erupted in his center, like someone yanking at his soul. He murmured a protest, wanting to remain with Angelina, but to no avail.

Damien once again experienced the rush of flying through the air and falling, endlessly it seemed, before he landed roughly on hard wood again. This time the floor of his bedroom.

He sat naked on the cold floorboards, and in front of his eyes the scene from the saloon continued to play out, showing him what had really happened. Showing him, painfully, the man he had been back then.

Damien hadn't taken Angelina up to a room. He hadn't treated her with care or love.

Something inside of him felt sick as he watched himself thrust into her and heard her anguished cry. Saw the tears slip down her face while he pumped his hips into her without a care to her pleasure or embarrassment. Rutting with her in the hallway, just feet from public view. Treating her like a common whore.

"I didn't know," he offered in explanation, glancing up at the Angelina of the present as she materialized before his eyes and came to stand beside him.

"You didn't care," she replied, sadness stealing the joy from her voice and dulling the life in her verdant gaze.

The scene continued while he sat there, the wooden boards frosty beneath him. The logs in the fireplace had burned to low embers, increasing the chill in the room. The storm raged outside while another tempest swirled within him as he observed the vision of their first Christmas Eve together.

A Christmas Eve Past he'd just as soon forget.

After the past-Damien had finished satisfying himself, he awkwardly stumbled from Angelina and returned to his crew.

Damien finally remembered that he had actually been quite drunk that night as he had been on so many others. Alcohol had helped dull the pain of his loneliness and the anger at his father's disapproval and rejection.

He knew what would come next, and he didn't want to watch as the door crashed open.

CHAPTER FOUR

CAPTAIN PEDRO RAMIREZ STRUTTED into the Cuban tavern like a bantam cock, all show and bluster. He was a short, stout fellow, but that didn't diminish the sense of danger that surrounded him. A loose shirt that might have once been white, but had been yellowed by time, covered his hard, round belly. A thick leather belt surrounded his broad girth and held a long silver knife and a brace of pistols. Also dangling from his belt was a heavy cutlass that banged against his leg as his rolling gait carried him into the room.

Ramirez was followed by quite a few members of his crew. Only now, seeing them through the distance of time and the clarity of the vision, did Damien note the paleness of their skin and the slight demonic glow in their eyes.

The men in the bar gave Ramirez and his crew a wide berth, clearing out of their way with fearful glances.

Ramirez walked right toward the Damien of that Christmas Eve Past, blocking his path back to his table and crew. The captain looked up at Damien from his shorter height, disdain obvious in his gaze.

"Move, boy," he said, the words achingly familiar as was his demeaning look. They were the first words his father had said to him when a young Damien had stepped up to him, wanting to meet the man who had sired and then abandoned him.

Misplaced anger had risen up in Damien at Ramirez's

dismissal. So instead of giving way, Damien pushed right into him, knocking aside the smaller man.

The Damien watching the vision understood well. He'd wished he'd had the nerve to do the same to his dismal excuse for a father.

A hush descended over the room at Damien's action, almost as if everyone in the place was holding their collective breath, knowing what would follow.

Ramirez turned and grabbed hold of Damien's shoulder, growled his request. "Apologize, *mi amigo.*"

Damien moved the other captain's hand off his shoulder like it was a piece of refuse. Leaning down until his nose was almost bumping the other man's face he said, "I'm not your *amigo.*"

A rush of wings sounded in the bar and suddenly there was a body before him. Angelina. Her sharp cry of pain was quite clear now, to the Damien viewing the scene, but back then he hadn't heard it. So full of himself and his own pain and ego, all he had seen was the challenge in Ramirez's gaze as the other man thrust aside the barmaid.

Damien hadn't seen Angelina fall. Hadn't noticed the blood soaking the front of her shirt where Ramirez had stabbed her through the heart with a thin silver blade.

A blade that had been meant for Damien.

But he saw it now and realized that Angelina had sacrificed herself to save his life. He reached out to the image of a dying Angelina, lying just inches before him, but his hand only swept through empty air.

He was so engrossed with the vision of her fighting for life, that for a moment he failed to see the rest of the scene playing out. But then his own pained shout filtered into his consciousness and drew his gaze back to the vision of him wrestling with Ramirez.

The vampire captain grabbed hold of Damien, twisting him until he sank his teeth deep into Damien's neck and fed. Blood ran down the other captain's face, dripped onto his yellowed shirt. Sick slurping sounds escaped him as Ramirez sucked the life from a drunken Damien.

A moment later, Ramirez's crew morphed and descended upon Damien's crew members and the other patrons, attacking and feeding from them while the rest of the crowd in the bar scattered, running for their lives.

With his neck nearly bitten in half, the Damien of the past fell to the ground, dying. What was left of his life-blood spilled out beside Angelina's before his eyes glazed over and he joined Angelina in death.

From the present, his voice quavered with realization. "I didn't know. Didn't see what he was," he explained to his lover as she stood beside him, her hand on his shoulder, trying to offer comfort. Although she seemed to know his inner heart better than he did. Or at least, she knew there was more that he was unwilling to admit.

"Would it have mattered back then? Would you have refrained from challenging him had you known he was a demon?" she countered.

Damien searched his soul, but the answer that came was one he didn't like. He had been so full of pain and pride back then that he had thought little of those around him. Any real or perceived attack to his status or ego would have been met with anger. With violence. If his father thought him the Devil's spawn, he was prepared to prove it with his fists or swords or whatever instrument of violence was nearby.

It was Damien's way of getting back at his father for his rejection, for the disdain he showed Damien each time they met.

But no longer. *I am no longer that man,* he thought.

"Really? Do you think you are different?" Angelina challenged as if reading his mind. Lovingly, she caressed the slope of his shoulder, bent and whispered into his ear, "Be honest with yourself."

"I've changed," he repeated, almost like a child responding to being chastised, but in his heart he understood why she was pressing her case. He was no longer that man, but he was still not a worthy individual. He was a demon who took from others, stealing their lifeblood. Hiding the truth of what he was. Making his livelihood illegally no matter that he fancied himself some kind of Robin Hood by sharing the lucre from his activities.

A hundred years had passed since that long-ago Cuban night, yet his temper still hurt others. More than once since becoming a demon, he had used his powers in fights prompted by men who had sought to challenge him. Men who had thought themselves superior or who had wanted to hurt those for whom Damien cared.

Like Angelina, who he had hurt once again, he thought, acknowledging the guilt that had been with him for nearly a year. Since last Christmas Eve when he had been responsible for her death, for the second time.

With the admission of that responsibility came yet more change in the room around him. The image of their bloodied bodies faded and was replaced by a different scene.

In this vision, the shades and curtains in the room were drawn against the daylight. Bright rays spilled in around the edges, providing enough illumination for him to see that they were in his bedroom, but at another point in time—a scant year ago in his long existence.

Another Christmas Eve that had also ended in tragedy. The sights and sounds from a year ago overwhelmed his senses as a trill of laughter filled the air. The door to the room in the vision flung open.

Angelina tumbled in like a playful puppy, her face alight with joy. The Damien in the vision chased after her, a broad smile on his face as he worked on the buttons of his linen shirt.

Damien knew what would follow and didn't want to see. He didn't want a reminder of all that he had lost. Yet the scene continued, punishing him with its presence.

"Do not show me this, Angelina," he commanded, pushing to his feet and grabbing hold of her arms. He tempered his hold when she breathed a complaint at the force of his grasp.

"Are you afraid, Damien? Do you fear what you might learn about the man that you are?"

Do you fear what you might feel? came her voice in his head, challenging him to face not only the past, but his own heart.

Maybe I haven't changed, Damien thought, accepting her challenge. Allowing himself to leave her and return to that moment in the past to face his demons. As had happened before, he experienced a wild glide through the air until he slammed into the body of the Damien in the vision.

He stumbled back from Angelina as he came alert to everything in the room. His senses registered the smell of wood smoke from the fire burning brightly in the grate. The cheery warmth of it was in direct contrast to the slight chill coming from the edges of the curtains drawn against the bright winter sun.

"We don't have long," Angelina said, reaching for the buttons on his shirt, but he brushed away her hands. If some God somewhere had decided that this was the only time he would have with her, he would not rush.

"Then let us not waste this moment," he replied, lifting his hand and dragging his fingers along the smooth skin in the enticing V of her pale lavender blouse. The hue accentuated the color of her eyes, making them appear an even more striking green. He repeatedly ran his thumb up and down the silkiness of her skin and watched the emerald color darken in passion.

"Please, Damien. I only have an hour for lunch," she complained, although the playful tone of her voice was hard to miss.

He relented and, with a slight tug, undid the bow holding the butterfly blouse closed. As the fabric draped open, it exposed more of the cleavage between her generous breasts. Dipping one finger beneath the fabric, he traced the full swells above the lace cups of her bra and smiled as her nipples puckered beneath his caress. The hard points were noticeably visible through her brassiere and the gauzy cotton of the blouse.

He shifted his hand to stroke his thumb across the peaked tip and she sighed her pleasure.

He met her gaze then, different and yet the same. That exotic tilt at the edge of her eyes was not as severe as before and her skin was a trifle lighter in color. Her pupils widened when he took the hard tip of her breast between his thumb and forefinger, rotating it gently.

Her emerald eyes were brighter this time, not as tired-looking. Her face had a little more fullness, and a becoming and healthy blush blossomed on her smooth skin at his caress. This Angelina was full of life, maybe slightly younger.

Still incredibly beautiful. Alluring, he thought as he bent his head to the crook of her neck and inhaled deeply.

Summer and flowers. Home, he thought again before kissing that spot. He nuzzled her neck with his nose, moving upward to rub it along the shell of her ear while he cupped her breasts.

"You are so lovely. So innocent," he whispered and she swayed toward him, resting her hands against his chest.

"Touch me," he urged, needing to feel the softness of her hands on him. Wanting to feel her warmth, he quickly parted the flowing fabric of her blouse, exposing more of her flesh.

She grew reticent then, pulling the gaping fabric closed to hide her breasts beneath the flimsy bra she wore. He recalled then what he had not known at the time.

This Angelina had been a virgin the first and only time he had taken her.

During all of their earlier encounters over the week before this Christmas Eve, marvelous intense moments, they had not progressed to the point where today seemed to be leading.

To the bed just a few feet away.

"I will be gentle," he promised and unlike the Damien of the past, he meant it. She was too precious to hurt. Too special to treat without care.

She locked her gaze with his and murmured, "I trust you."

He wanted to tell her not to trust. Not to believe in him because he could offer only pain and no future. He was a vampire, and she was mortal. He was painfully reminded of that fact as he laid his hands over hers and urged them from their grip on her blouse.

She splayed her hands on his chest, and he rubbed his hands over hers. Shifted them to his shirt where she hesitantly undid the buttons. She let the fabric drift open to reveal the defined ridges of his chest and abdomen.

"Touch me," he said, inviting her to take the lead in their lovemaking.

She shot him a half glance where hesitation and desire battled. Desire quickly won out.

She edged her hands beneath the smooth and expensive linen of his shirt. The proceeds of his rum-running allowed him many fine things. Things he wanted to share with her, only she was too proud to take charity.

"You're cold," she said, after placing her hands on the swell of his pectorals.

The vampire's chill, he thought, and released a bit of the demon to heat up his skin.

"I was out on the water until you arrived," he lied, not wanting to reveal to her what he was. Afraid that if he did so, she would leave him. She had eased so much of his loneliness that he couldn't bear the thought of her not being in his life. But he also hated that their time together was tainted by his lie.

Can love truly exist if it's based on lies? The Angelina he was coming to understand was the voice of his conscience intruded into his thoughts.

It is *love,* he shot back, not wanting to lose a minute of the vision and the happiness he had once had.

He inched his fingers beneath the thin cotton of her blouse and ran the back of his hand along the smooth skin at her waist. "But you're nice and warm," he said, trying to divert this Angelina's attention from the nervousness she might be feeling.

Leisurely, he shifted his hand upward until he was just beneath her breasts. Not wanting to spook her, he looked at her and softly asked, "May I touch you?"

CHAPTER FIVE

ANGELINA WORRIED HER bottom lip with perfect white teeth and nodded.

He eased the shirt off her shoulders, reached around and undid her bra. Slipping his hands beneath the straps, he slowly pulled it away until she was bared to his gaze. She made a motion to once again cover herself, but he murmured a protest and raised his hand the final distance to cup her breast. Its lush fullness filled his hand. Stroking his thumb along her peaked nipple, he pulled a soft sigh of pleasure from her.

"There is much more of that to come, my love," he vowed, slipping his other hand upward to cradle her other breast. He gently rotated and tweaked her nipples until she mewled her delight and leaned her body along his. She reached down and hesitantly explored the hard ridge beneath the fine fabric of his pants.

He growled his own sharp delight at her innocent touch and bent to nuzzle the sensitive skin along the underside of her jaw. Tugged gently on her earlobe with his teeth and whispered, "Do you want more?"

Her answer came in the awkward rush of her fingers undoing the buttons on his pants and parting the soft wool to free his long, hard shaft. He sucked in a breath and pleaded, "I want to feel your skin against mine."

His little virgin surprised him then, quickly moving her hand beneath the cotton to grasp his erection. She stroked her hand up and down, exploring his smooth length until he was almost shaking.

"May I make love to you?" he said, aware of her inexperience and wanting there to be no tears of shame this time. He would not hurt her for all the world.

"You may," she said, a playful note in her voice as she took a step back toward his bed. When her knees hit the edge, she sat down and leaned on her elbows, offering him a dangerous view of her upper torso. So beautiful, he thought and bent to take hold of her skirt.

As his hands came into contact with the cheap gray fabric, it tore slightly beneath his impatient hands.

He restrained his need, and slowly inched up her skirts to reveal the long shapely length of her legs beneath the woolen socks she wore against the winter chill. With care, he slipped off her low-heeled shoes and rolled down her socks to reveal her lovely legs. Strong and yet totally feminine, and with that thought came a moment of guilt as he remembered their first encounter a century earlier. He hadn't taken the time to appreciate her beauty. To pleasure her and let her know how much he valued the gift she was bestowing upon him.

This time had been different from that first fateful Christmas Eve. He had been patient with her, inviting her to take each step in their lovemaking, the consciousness of the present Damien recalled before he lost himself to reliving the past.

He took her skirts up along with the passage of his hand. Revealing the soft cotton panties she wore.

"May I?" he asked again, conscious of her virginity and wishing to remove any fear on her part.

Her shy smile was the only answer he needed.

He grasped the thin cotton, vowing that one day he would replace it with silk and satin. Leisurely pulling off her panties, he planted a series of kisses on the sensitive inside of her ankle, then at the crook where her calf met her knee, eliciting a tiny giggle from her which dragged a smile to his lips. An unhurried brush of his mouth along the inside of her thigh made her muscles quiver.

As he neared her core, his vamp senses immediately picked up the scent of her feminine arousal, musky and clean.

He nuzzled the soft thatch of ebony curls with his nose, drawing a shaky breath from her. He smiled and glanced down as he parted her curls with his fingers to reveal the glistening nub at her center and the flushed nether lips along her cleft.

"Beautiful," he murmured before lowering his head for that first intimate kiss.

She arched her hips with the contact and gasped in surprise before a rise of heat and damp confirmed her desire for him.

He nearly came then, overwhelmed by emotion and the expectation of what would come next.

His hands shook as if he was the virgin, and maybe he was. He had never made love to a woman he cared about before.

He kissed her over and over, sucking and biting at the nub between her legs. He used his fingers to stroke and caress her until she was shaking beneath him. On the edge and pleading with him, she dipped her hand down and threaded her fingers through his hair.

Sucking in a deep breath perfumed with her need, he rose and positioned himself at her center. The tip of him poised near her moist warmth.

She lay before him, her lush breasts exposed. The nipples now a dark coral, flush with her desire.

He bent and kissed the tip of one breast.

Angelina called out his name and held his head to her. He could wait no longer.

In one slow stroke he entered her tightness until the fragile barrier provided resistance. He experienced the tension in her body as he pressed forward.

He skimmed one hand across her cheek as he promised, "The hurt will fade."

"I trust you," she repeated again, worrying her bottom lip with uncertainty.

He nodded and grasped her hips, the cotton of her skirt laundry-soft and care-worn beneath his hands. The drape of her skirts hid their union, but he wanted to see. Needed to see.

Lifting the skirts high and bundling them at her waist, he watched as he withdrew with care, mindful of her state. A mistake, he realized, as the faint scent of blood mixed with that of their loving and pulled at the demon.

He gritted his teeth and closed his eyes, fighting the vampire who wanted a taste of that virgin's desire.

The demon he hated because releasing it brought pain and hurt.

"Damien? Is something wrong?"

He shook his head, but then her hand slipped up over his chest, directly above his heart. "I love you, Damien. Do not shut me out."

Gritting his teeth, because the pain in his jaw warned him that the vampire was about to emerge, he met her gaze with his.

Her eyes widened with surprise as they took in the growing neon in his gaze. He could feel his humanity losing out to the demon.

"What…what's happening?" she asked, but there was no fear or uncertainty in her voice, which surprised him.

"I'm not what you think I am," he replied, the low growl of the demon threaded through his voice.

Her easy smile calmed him as did the tender caress of her hand at the spot over his heart. "I think you are a good person." She stroked her hand over his heart again and continued. "I *know* your heart is true."

He groaned then, with joy and pain. He had not been a good man and as a demon he had done things that sickened him. Despite all that, she still believed in him.

Emotion rose up in him, nearly choking him and breaking the control he had been exerting. A sharp burst of pain came as his fangs exploded, erupting beyond his top lip.

He expected her to scream. To rip her body from his and run away. But instead, she offered up another smile, a determined one this time.

Raising her other hand, she cupped his jaw and traced the line of his lips and fangs. Explored them with a mix of fascination and love.

"You are not afraid?" he asked, narrowing his eyes as he considered her reaction.

"I've always sensed you were different, and no, I am not afraid. I love you," she replied, her answer clear and without doubt.

Inside him came a freedom and lightness of being he had not experienced in too long. Not since his mother had anyone given him love so unequivocally and so freely. As much as he feared that he did not deserve such love, because of the man he had been and the demon he had become, he would not cast such a gift aside.

"I think I love you, too," Damien answered, his heart filled with joy at the admission.

No sooner had the words left him than he experienced

a vicious jerk at his center. Panic replaced the happiness he had been feeling on that year-ago Christmas Eve.

He was leaving her again. Leaving the vision filled with their joy and love.

"No," he shouted, but in his mind Angelina's voice came instead, both soothing and punishing at the same time.

Maybe one lesson learned. I think. But not another.

Damien was painfully conscious of what would happen next.

CHAPTER SIX

WIND RACED PAST HIM as he once again flew from his body and departed the vision he had been reliving. Long moments idled while a whirlwind of images raced by.

His abrupt landing on the floor before the Angelina of the present rattled his teeth and painfully jarred his bones. But Damien had only a moment to recover before the walls of his bedroom transformed once more, becoming the calm waters off the Jersey Shore. He recognized the precise moment in time and that less than a dozen hours had passed since his lunchtime tryst with Angelina.

A schooner was sailing parallel to the beachfront during a dark moonless night that hid its passage.

Ramirez's ship—although Damien hadn't known it at the time.

Damien had been given the details for the rum pickup and the money to make the purchase. As always, he had set off down the river inlet to meet the ship, collect the liquor and return it to shore for distribution. He made similar trips once or twice a week, managing to avoid the Coast Guard and others intent on stopping the flow of alcohol to the many clandestine bars and speakeasies that had sprung up during Prohibition.

After motoring his skiff up to the Cuban rumrunner, Damien had been shocked to see a familiar crew manning the schooner. A familiar crew with an infamous captain.

Although the transfer of the kegs had gone smoothly,

vampire strength making the movement of so many loads go quickly, Damien had understood that this would not be the last time he would see Ramirez. There was too much bad blood between them for the other captain not to take advantage of their chance encounter.

After loading the skiff and paying Ramirez, Damien had snuck up the river inlet to the scattered sandbars where the locals and the Newark bosses would come ashore for their deliveries. Damien kept one keg for the owner of the small tavern where Angelina worked. Her boss was expecting Damien to hand deliver that rum when he came in for a bite of food later that night.

But Damien had errands to run before that delivery. First, he had to quench his hunger. He secured the keg in his skiff before returning to the small dock adjacent to the tavern. When he came ashore, luck was on his side as one of the local fishermen stumbled from the building, clearly having had a nip too much of the bootleg liquor supplied to the tavern's clientele.

Damien rushed up to the man, eased an arm around him and helped him to a keg of nails sitting on the dock. The man plopped down, too drunk to continue home. He murmured his thanks, causing a momentary pang of guilt in Damien, but one that couldn't quench his need to feed. The burst of vamp power he had used to help load the skiff had drained him. If Ramirez showed up tonight, he had to be at full strength.

And then there was Angelina. He had lost his control over the demon earlier because he had not fed in some time. He did not want to lose control again when they met later. It was Christmas Eve after all and he wanted to celebrate it with her. As a human—not as the demon he despised.

Bending toward the man, he held his breath to avoid

the smell of cheap rum, cabbage and a body that had not seen a bar of soap for some time. Transforming, Damien sank his fangs into the man's neck. The rush of blood brought a surge of power and painful desire. In another life he might have slaked that need on the next unsuspecting female that wandered by, but no longer.

He was in love with Angelina and her faith in him was far stronger than such base demon desire.

When the man moaned and slumped against him, nearly boneless from liquor and the loss of blood, Damien reared back. If he kept feeding he would kill the man. He had never done so in the century since he had become immortal and he would not kill tonight on such a Holy Night.

Sated, he paused to draw in a few bracing breaths of sea-kissed air and drive back the demon. After lowering the man to rest comfortably against the keg of nails, he rushed from behind the tavern to the main street in the tiny fishing village. Quickly, he finished his errands, stopping by the general store and paying off not only his accounts, but some of the debt owed by his housekeeper, dock hands and Angelina. They were too proud to take the money outright, but had yet to suspect why their credit was still good at the store.

I did not know, came Angelina's heartfelt words in his head.

I did not want you to know, he silently replied and buried his head against his knees, unwilling to watch the scenes from the past any longer.

As their story unfolded on the walls of his bedroom, Angelina walked to his side and knelt behind him. She wrapped her arms around his body as the vision played on around them. Angelina understood this was meant to be his punishment: to relive her death yet again.

But the fact that he could not escape the visions did not mean that she could not comfort him, much as he had comforted her during her last moments on Earth.

The images around them blurred and spun until they arrived at the small tavern where she had worked during her last mortal visit.

Damien entered, a happy smile on his face, which broadened even further when he caught sight of her.

Angelina recalled how her heart had fluttered in her chest with his arrival. He was so handsome with his dark hair and silver-gray eyes. His body was lean and well-muscled from his many days at sea and his life as a vampire had not changed it much. If anything, his immortality had preserved his physical beauty, but Angelina's role was to safeguard something much more important: his soul.

She had failed that first time a century ago when she had first been assigned to protect Damien. She had not perceived just how great a threat Ramirez could be. She had been too inexperienced a Guardian Angel, having no other experience on which to rely during that first assignment.

Nothing about Damien was easy, especially as she had found herself falling in love with him from the moment she'd first viewed his past life, a method Guardian Angels used to understand their charges.

She had been a little better prepared during this, her second visitation. The one that was now playing before her eyes and his, and yet she had still not understood what had been required of both her and Damien.

In the vision swirling around them, she saw their happiness and her heart swelled with the joy of it. It made her hope that this time—the third and very rare opportunity with which she had been gifted—would be the lucky one.

At a Christmas Eve so close to the present it could

not really be called the past, Damien strode toward her, a sexy smile on his lips and the promise of so much more in his glittering gaze. As Angelina's heart sped up, she suddenly experienced a strange sensation at her core. The draw was like the one she felt when coming down from Heaven to visit the mortal plain, but not quite the same. The feeling intensified and suddenly everything around her whirled, becoming a dizzying panorama until the images jarred to an abrupt halt.

She jerked back as Damien took another step toward her, his eyes gleaming with passion and joy. A small dimple peeked from the corner of his mouth as he headed straight to one of her tables, much as he had a year earlier.

Angelina unexpectedly realized that she, too, was reliving that fateful night.

Did you think Damien was the only one who had something to learn? came the voice of the Archangel Raphael in her head.

But before she could respond, the Angelina in the vision took control, forcing her into action as Damien sat down at one of the rough oak tables along with several of the town's fishermen, sailors and laborers who frequented the tavern. She hurried to the bar and ladled up a bowl of the day's chowder made from a mix of clams and fish fresh from the docks to feed him. She brought the chowder over to him along with a big hunk of bread she had baked that afternoon. Although vampires had no need of food, she now knew that Damien regularly ate with his human friends as a way to be part of their world.

Beside his plate she also placed a pint of rum-laced apple cider that was more rum than cider. The local police officers turned a blind eye to such activities, choosing to crack down on the more blatant speakeasies in the up-scale parts of town.

The police left the common folk alone, seeming to understand they needed a nip to ease the chill of the sea and soothe muscles made sore by hard labor. Not to mention the value of a small diversion from the weariness of the Depression, where work, money and food were sometimes hard to find.

As she served him, Angelina made a point of grazing her breast along his arm. Her nipple beaded instantly from that simple contact and when he shot her a slumberous half glance that promised so much more, her sex throbbed and dampened in anticipation. Their encounter earlier that day had left her wanting him.

Angels were not meant to love humans, much less demons, the Archangel Raphael warned, offering her yet another reason why she had been thrust into reexperiencing the past. But despite Raphael's warning, the Angelina of that Christmas Eve smiled at Damien and did as she had a year earlier.

She leaned down and whispered in her lover's ear, "It is a Holy Night, you know. The Devil may take you for such wicked thoughts."

Damien chuckled, wrapping his arm around her and teasing back, "The Devil can have me if it means being in your arms later."

The Devil must have heard them for he chose that moment to interrupt their happiness.

CHAPTER SEVEN

THE THICK OAK DOOR of the tavern flew open and rebounded against the wall as Ramirez, his first mate and one of his sailors entered. The vampire crewmen flanked their captain's back as he strutted into the tavern. His waddling gait and aggressive demeanor were painfully familiar.

Aware that danger approached, Damien patted her side, handed her his mug and said, "Why don't you get me another drink?"

Since his mug was still nearly full, she understood he just wanted her out of the way. Because her role here was not to intrude, as she had last time, a fact the Archangels had reminded her of repeatedly before allowing her to return, she stepped away, hoping that this time Damien would make the right choice.

She walked to the bar and, from the corner of her eye, kept a distant vigil.

Damien turned his back to Ramirez and hunched over his bowl of chowder, clearly attempting to pay no heed to the other vampire. He picked up his spoon and began to eat, ignoring his foe until Ramirez walked right up beside him.

The other men at the table, sensing that there would be trouble, grabbed their plates and mugs and moved away.

"You cheated me, *amigo*," Ramirez said, spreading his legs and jamming his hands on his hips. The action brought his hands dangerously close to the weapons on his belt.

"First, I'm not your *amigo.* Second, I paid you what was agreed upon," Damien said and then scooped up another spoonful of the chowder. He never once looked at the vampire captain, but instead of appeasing Ramirez it only seemed to incense him.

The vampire captain reached down and with a swing of his arm, sent the plates and cups in front of Damien flying.

Damien finally looked up at the man and his two friends. She prayed for him to act carefully. Prayed for him to appease the other man rather than incite further violence.

Disappointment sank in as Damien replied, "You'll not get another dime from me."

I didn't have the money to return, Angelina heard the Damien of the present mutter and finally understood. He had paid every last cent of what he had made to the grocery store owner.

"Have you forgotten already, *mi amigo?* I never take no for an answer." Ramirez leaned close, his pale and pockmarked face barely an inch from Damien's.

"I guess there's a first time for everything," Damien replied, the slow rise of anger apparent in his voice.

"Son of a bitch," Ramirez growled and grabbed hold of the collar of Damien's woolen peacoat.

Angelina understood Damien's burst of pain and anger at the mention of his sainted mother. Much like hate for his father had driven him a century ago, now love for his mother and her memory caused Damien's violence to erupt.

Before Ramirez could do anything else, Damien was on him, battling the smaller man to get free of his hold.

Throwing punch after punch, which finally caused the vampire captain to release him. But instead of stepping away as she hoped, Damien launched himself at Ramirez, tackling him to the ground and pounding his face, overwhelming the other vampire.

Seeing that their captain had lost the upper hand, Ramirez's two goons jumped into the fray and so did some of the other men in the bar. They knew Damien well, and he had helped them on more than one occasion. But Angelina worried that the men were no match for Ramirez and his vampire crew.

She was not mistaken. One local man after another was flung around the room while Ramirez and Damien continued to fight. The damage to the locals only seemed to cause more violence as the remaining sailors and fishermen joined the fight. The very air grew electric, charged with aggression and hate.

But even with dozens of men engaged in the brawl, they failed to overcome Ramirez and his men, who seemed to delight in the escalation of the violence. While Damien and Ramirez wrestled and beat each other, blood pouring from their mouths and noses, Ramirez's men decimated the town folk, gouging eyes and slashing razor-sharp nails across the other men as the crewmen watched their captain's back.

Angelina rushed forward, urging the men she knew away from the quartet fighting in the center of the bar. They had families who needed them and could ill afford to lose a breadwinner. She laid a calming hand on one man after the next, imparting peace to them, urging them away from the fray. Eventually, she'd made her way to Ramirez's vampire crewmen.

They were large, imposing creatures filled with such malevolence that she could feel it beat against her. But she tried to reach them anyway, hoping for peace before Damien and Ramirez killed one another.

"Please let me pass. There has been enough blood shed tonight," she urged the vampires.

The one crewman threw his head back and laughed, almost braying like a jackass, but to her surprise the second vampire gave ground. He stepped away, giving her enough space to move toward Damien and Ramirez.

She was no more than a step from them when Ramirez wildly swung his arm around and walloped the middle of her chest.

A sharp gasp escaped her. The distressed sound pierced the violence, bringing a halt to the fight.

Damien's eyes went wide and he was quickly at her side as her knees weakened and became rubbery. Only then did the pain register.

As he slowly lowered her to the ground, she looked down and saw the hilt of the knife protruding from her body. Felt the warmth drain from all her extremities, leaving behind cold and weakness.

You should not have interfered, Raphael's voice boomed, chastising her again, much as he had upon her return to Heaven after the failure of her first mission.

I was wrong to do so, she admitted, and this time she finally understood that by her actions she had denied Damien the opportunity to save his soul.

With that understanding came a dense feeling in her center that gathered into a heavy ball and burst from her. It dragged her forward, sending her on a wild ride and dropping her back into the present. Her heart raced as she found herself beside Damien again.

He raised his face and the anguish there had darkened his eyes almost to black. She tightened her hold on him and together they watched the remainder of the vision play out.

Damien lowered a mortally wounded Angelina to the ground and cradled her in his arms.

"No, Angelina. Please don't die," Damien whispered. His blood and tears fell on her face as she struggled for breath. Each inhale more labored and less forceful. Life failed her until darkness claimed her.

Darkness likewise swept away the images in the room, leaving her and Damien bathed only in the moonlight streaming through the windows of his bedroom.

Damien was still huddled on the ground with her embracing him. Their bodies shook from the emotions they had been forced to reexperience. From the lessons they'd both had to learn.

But then something seemed to course through Damien. He shuddered and rose, taking hold of her hand to urge her upward. His resolute, determined gaze met hers.

"You've shown me the past and the present. What of the future?" he asked, gripping her hand tightly, almost as if fearing what she would show him.

"I do not know the future, Damien. Only you can decide what it will be."

His generous lips thinned into a tight line. His silver-blue gaze grew hard, like polished stone. "I will not risk your life again. I will not face Ramirez."

Her gut twisted, the pain so great she pressed her free hand to her middle as if she had been struck.

"I'm not sure that's possible," she said, fearing what she would tell him next.

He searched her features, seeking some clue to what she meant, and then shook his head when he could not. "I don't understand. Are we fated to meet again? Is that the punishment for the life I've led? To suffer the hell of losing you over and over?"

Sadly, she knew this was the last Christmas Eve they would share. "If you do not learn your lesson, I must leave and never return."

He laughed harshly and dropped her hand. He laid his arms across his chest defensively and stalked away from her, to the window, where he stood for long moments, peering out at the storm, clearly deep in thought.

Finally, he faced her, the lines of his face looking gaunt beneath the silvering of the moonlight. "And if I learn my lesson? What then?"

She walked back to him, laid a hand on his shoulder, willing peace into his soul. "My task is to guide you to the path of what is right. If I succeed, I move on. If I fail…"

She didn't really know what would happen if she failed. She supposed she'd go to Heaven, but just not as a Guardian Angel. It had never occurred to her that she might go elsewhere.…

"You must confront Ramirez," she said, dreading what might happen if the two men came together once more, but understanding that it was fated. It was an unavoidable battle in the war for Damien's soul.

"Why? What is so important that I would risk my immortal soul and yours for that piece of slime?" he argued.

Angelina girded herself, drawing in a shaky breath, preparing herself for what she would ask of him.

"Ramirez took my wings and I must get them back."

CHAPTER EIGHT

DAMIEN WAS PUZZLED, unable to understand why this visit of hers was so radically different. Why had he not noticed that she was not human during their earlier encounters? Why hadn't her inhumanity occurred to him, given her reappearance in his life?

"The first two times you came to me…you didn't have wings."

She dipped her head to confirm his observations. "Not when I came to see you, but when I first arrived in the mortal realm I did. To hide our presence here on Earth while we're on a mission, our wings disappear almost as soon as we land."

"Then what happened this time? What changed?" Damien asked, narrowing his eyes as he searched her features for any sign that she was different from the Angelina he had met in his two other lifetimes.

"When I came back to Earth this time Ramirez was there, waiting. It was almost as if he knew I was returning."

Understanding dawned as he recalled the injuries he had tended earlier in the night. "Those wounds on your back…"

"Before I could become fully human, his men grabbed me and Ramirez sliced off my wings."

Damien shook his head and then dragged a hand through his hair in frustration. Some had said Ramirez had made a pact with the Devil. Maybe it was true. Maybe that's how he had known where to be so that he could ambush Angelina.

But regardless of how Ramirez had captured her wings, Damien intended to help her retrieve them. He reached out, tenderly wrapping her in his arms. Bending his head, he rested his forehead against hers. "Why does he want your wings?"

"They are the key to my immortal soul. If I do not get them back soon—"

"You go to Hell? Never. No just God would allow someone as good as you to go to Hell," he said, digging his hands into the thick masses of her dark hair. Cradling her head gently, he tried to reassure her.

Angelina worried her lower lip, and the glint of her tears shimmered in the moonlight. "I do not know what will happen if I don't get them back. All I know is that as long as he has them I am bound to this mortal plane."

"Which is a good thing, right? That means you can stay with me." He massaged her scalp with his hands in an effort to ease her obvious distress.

"I wish I could stay, Damien. But that is not why I was sent here. I'm supposed to help you see the right path so you can save your soul…remember?" She looked up at him, the tears subsiding and determination taking up residence on her face.

Damien laughed harshly and shook his head. "You forget that I'm not worth saving, my love."

Angelina knew he wanted to believe that. Had convinced himself of it, maybe as a way to deal with his father's rejection and his mother's loss. But she had seen his actions as he helped others, as had the Archangel Raphael. It was why Damien had been chosen for salvation.

And he had grown during her past two visits. He had become capable of love. But she also understood that he could not fully love another until he was ready to love himself.

"You only think you're not good enough. You've hidden your real self so that you won't be hurt again."

He pushed away from her and stalked to the window. He repeatedly dragged his hands through his hair in frustration, as if wanting to pull it out. When he turned he was in his vampire form, eyes blazing and long deadly canines exposed.

"I'm a demon, remember. Evil," he argued and stalked back toward her, the rumble of the animal in his voice.

Angelina stood her ground, tilting her chin up at a defiant angle. Showing no fear of what he was. "Demon or human doesn't change the true nature of your soul. Of who you really are inside."

"And who am I?" he said, continuing with his defiance.

"A good soul. One who will make the right choice this time," she urged and ran her hand across the sandpapery beard on his cheek.

"And if I do? What then? You go back to Heaven?"

"If I have my wings, I can return to Heaven," she confirmed with a curt dip of her head.

Damien morphed back to his human form, processing all that she had said.

Without her wings she was doomed to remain in this mortal realm, but at the risk of her soul. But to get her wings back he would have to confront Ramirez yet again. And if he did so, would they play out the same scene they had played out twice before?

Not if he had any role in it. This time it would be different. Even if it meant losing Angelina again once her angelic mission was over, he would do it to save her soul. He would do it to be the kind of man she believed he could be.

"We will make things right. Together," he urged, truly convinced that with all that he had learned he would make the right choices this time.

A brave smile came to her lips, although tears did finally slip from her lids and down her face. "Together," she whispered.

He stroked his thumbs across her cheeks and pulled her close, offering solace with his embrace. But they had too long been denied the pleasure of being together and comfort soon gave way to desire.

Angelina could feel the passion rising in his body, from the very obvious jut of his erection along her belly to the tension filling his arms and shoulders. He was restraining himself for her, yet another indication of his growing measure as a man.

But if this was to be their final time together, the last thing she wanted was restraint. And although she knew the Archangel Raphael might be angry, she could not deny her love for Damien no matter the price to be paid in Heaven for such a transgression.

Easing away from him slightly, she raised her hand and laid it flush along the center of his chest. Beneath her palm came the faintest hint of a heartbeat. A vampire heartbeat, not that it mattered to her. It was a good heart. One that knew how to love.

She shifted her hand over to cup the swell of his pectoral muscle and lazily ran her thumb over his hard masculine nipple. A tiny shudder crossed his body and spoke of the pleasure that her simple action brought him.

Glancing up at him while she continued with her caress, she said, "Will you touch me like that?"

His low guttural groan stoked desire within her, which burst into flame as he cupped her breasts and gently fingered her tight nipples. His actions dragged a sharp gasp from her.

"Have I hurt you?" he asked, worry evident in the deep furrow marring his brow.

She offered him a smile, reached up and brushed back the errant lock of ebony hair that had spilled forward when he gazed down at her. "No, my love. It's just that I'd forgotten how wonderful it feels to have you touch me."

"Sweet Lord," burst from his lips, and he swept into action. Bending, he lifted her into his arms and strode the short distance to his bed, where he gently laid her on the silken comforter, mindful of her earlier injuries.

Before she could do a thing, he had slipped between her legs as they draped over the edge of the bed. His erection was poised at her center, creating a pool of heat and wetness. She waited for his entry, but he smiled and cupped her breasts again.

"I can feel your need. Down there," he said, his voice a low tone that vibrated through her body. That made her shudder as he moved his erection along her swollen lips, but didn't enter.

"Damien," she said, half plea, half question.

"I want to pleasure you," he replied and bent, trailing a line of kisses along the edge of her mouth and jaw until he was at the shell of her ear.

"Only you," he whispered before kissing her just behind the ear.

He continued tweaking the sensitive tips of her breasts. Each little pinch and tug sent a burst of need between her legs.

Then he began a slow descent down the edge of her

collarbone. Butterfly-light kisses, which had her grasping his shoulders and urging him closer, until he finally closed his mouth on the peak of her breast.

Angelina arched off the bed at the heat of that kiss. She threaded her hands through the silk of his hair and held him to her, lost in the sensations he was creating with his mouth and hands.

Damien nearly came at the way she cried out his name, but held back, wanting her to experience every pleasure, every bit of joy he was capable of giving her. Over and over he suckled her breasts, licking and tugging at the sweet caramel tips. Alternating his hands and mouth from one breast to the other until she was shaking beneath him and bumping her hips upward in a plea for more.

He chuckled then and raised his head, smiling at her abandon. "If all Angels are as tempting as you, why would any fool choose the Devil?"

She returned his smile, but it had a bittersweet tinge, as did her words. "Because the Devil fools those who think desire means anything without love."

As he had been fooled, but no longer, Damien realized. From the vision of that Christmas Past in Cuba to the one of a very painful Christmas Present, he had come to appreciate the difference. Which was why he would not waste the opportunity to let her know his heart this Christmas Eve.

"I love you, Angelina. Whatever happens tomorrow, please remember that," he said. He knew that no matter what he did, she would leave him again. Because of that, he wanted this to be as special as possible between them.

She must have seen his distress. She stroked her hand over his hair and said, "If I could stay with you forever, I would."

"I know, my love." He dropped a kiss directly over her

heart. Then he laid a line of kisses down her center until he was poised at the first hint of lush ebony curls.

He eased his hands to the juncture of thigh and hip, stroking the smooth skin there. About to shift and urge her legs open, she made that movement on her own, parting her thighs wide.

Her nether lips were flush with the rush of passion and he stroked the back of one hand along that sensitive cleft. She raised herself against him and murmured a plea.

"Make love to me, Damien."

He smiled. "In time, Angelina. I would not rush this for all the world."

Tenderly, he caressed her again, teasing his fingers around where she most wanted him to touch. He moved his other hand down so that he could part her curls and expose the swollen and responsive nub at her center. He bent then, placing his lips there in a provocative kiss.

She moaned and lifted her hips. Dragged her fingers into the thick locks of his hair to urge him on.

He licked and sucked at the nub until she was almost writhing on the bed, her body shaking. The aroma of her desire sharp in his nose. The taste of her passion alive on his lips as he moved downward, continuing to caress that sensitive tip with his fingers while he sought to bring her yet more pleasure.

He kissed and laved her lips until he could slip his tongue into her center, mimicking the way he would shortly love her.

A climax slammed through her then and he nearly came himself as her body quaked beneath his mouth.

She uttered his name in a long, heartfelt cry and he could wait no longer.

He rose to his feet and ran his hands along her thighs, holding her steady as he positioned himself at her entrance. She watched him, her dark emerald eyes nearly black with her passion. A very visible aura of blue light, like a halo, limning her body as she rested on his silken comforter.

As the tip of him probed and then slipped in just a bit, her gaze dropped down to their joining. Then she rose on one elbow, reached for him, her thumb riding along the top of his erection. It made him quiver and his heart ached with that tender caress.

Slowly, he pressed forward, ever so conscious of his size and her body. Of the warmth of her encircling him as she welcomed each inch of him. Of the wetness of her, so slick.

Once he was home, buried deep within her, Angelina lay back down and wrapped her legs around his hips. "Please don't move. I love the feel of you inside me."

If he died again right then, held in her embrace, nothing could be better. Except moving in her. Feeling her heat and wetness caressing him.

But he held back, her pleasure being foremost. Her happiness meaning the world to the man he had become.

He was shaking, his body damp with sweat as he battled for control, when she offered yet another temptation. As he watched, she raised her hands and cupped her breasts, running her fingers along their tips, which caused a jump of her muscles all along his length.

He groaned and closed his eyes, afraid of losing control, but her voice came in soft command.

"Open your eyes, love. Watch me."

He couldn't disobey.

CHAPTER NINE

ENTRANCED, HE FOLLOWED the graceful movement of her hands at her breasts. The way she grasped the turgid peaks of her nipples, flushed with desire. Rotated them, each twist generating a pulse that echoed through her body and his until he was almost panting with need.

She seemed to sense he was on the edge. She relented, asking, "Will you kiss me?"

Damien needed no further invitation, but surprised her, dipping his head to kiss the sensitive tip of each nipple. His actions tripped another climax, sending a wave throughout her body. She arched up and deepened his penetration, her muscles milking his erection with one swell after another as her satisfaction peaked and ebbed.

She tightened her legs around his waist, reaching up and encircling his back. Then she pulled away, nearly letting him slip out of her before she once again drew him in, moaning her pleasure.

That low, almost animal sound was his undoing.

With his own hoarse shout, he joined her in the release, spilling his seed within her. Savoring the final undulations of her climax before he dropped down on her, covering her body with his.

Angelina pulled him close and took a long breath to steady herself. How she wished the night would never end, but there was no escaping tomorrow.

And no avoiding the fact that no matter what happened, this might be their last time together.

Damien must have sensed her sadness. He braced one hand beside her and raised himself up.

"Why the tears?" he asked and bent to kiss away the drops on her cheeks.

"Tomorrow…" she began, but couldn't finish. Yet he knew.

"Tomorrow is promised to no one. Isn't that the saying?" He dipped his head to brush his lips across hers.

"I wish there was some promise I could make, but I don't know what the future holds in store," she acknowledged.

He lifted himself from her, his silver-gray eyes turbulent like the ocean outside. The tone of his voice was somber as he said, "Promise me you'll love me no matter what."

She knew what he wanted: unconditional love. In a way, she had given him that for over a century, although he had not known it. If it hadn't been for Ramirez catching her off guard, Damien might be clueless about her role in his life. About the love she had shown him each time the question of saving his soul arose before the Angels.

And, as she had done each time, she reaffirmed what was in her heart. What couldn't be denied.

"I love you, Damien. No matter what Fate decides for us, I will love you forever."

Overwhelmed it seemed, all he could do was grunt his acceptance and take her into his arms. They held each other tightly for long moments until he shifted them beneath the covers and into the center of the bed. Tucking her close and wrapping his arms around her, he said in a husky voice, "Rest. We'll talk more in the morning."

But rest was impossible for either of them.

Angelina's thoughts were filled with fear at what would once again happen with Ramirez. Whether this time Damien would make the right choices. But even if he did, there was still the issue of her wings. Each time that fatigue dragged her eyes closed, images of violence and death jerked her awake as she imagined how Damien would have to secure their return.

Damien could not sleep, either, his mind reliving each and every encounter with Ramirez. Contemplating what it would take to defeat the deadly vampire who was not only physically powerful despite his rotund and small stature, but also a seasoned warrior. Over and over Damien imagined the captain's moves. How a feint to the left or right could have changed the outcome of their two prior encounters.

During one such imaginary fight he jumped, so powerfully that Angelina turned in his arms to see what was the matter.

"Are you all right?" she asked and laid her hand along his cheek.

Damien forced a smile and covered her hand with his. "Just trying to prepare myself for Ramirez."

"You plan to fight him again?" she asked, the tone of her voice flat.

Because he did not want to worry her more, he said, "I will do what I must."

She nodded and then tracked her thumb across his lips. "How can I help?"

Stay away, he thought, but knew she would not leave him to face Ramirez on his own. There was one thing she could do, however loath as he was to ask it.

As her gaze met his, though, she seemed to understand.

"Are you strong enough or do you need to feed?"

"I have not fed from anything living in some time," he admitted and raised his hand to stroke it gently along the delicate slope of her shoulder.

"Will it hurt?" she asked, sounding so innocent his heart ached, but if he was to save her from eternal damnation, he needed to be fortified.

"Not so much," he admitted, then quickly added, "I can make it pleasurable, as well."

The first hint of a smile relieved the seriousness of her features. "Like you did before?"

He chuckled and ran his thumb along the straight line of her collarbone. With each pass he inched his thumb lower until he was caressing the swell of her breasts. They tightened in anticipation, and he lifted his gaze back up to hers.

"Better than before," he promised, moving the final short distance to caress the tight tip of her breast. Dipping his head, he nipped and sucked at the other breast until she threaded her hands through his hair and held him to her.

Inside him came the rush of desire and, as it usually did, the clamor of the vampire to be released. He had restrained the beast when he was with her, but this time he set it free.

The animal within him shook with the joy of liberation, but he reined it in, wanting to make sure he gave Angelina the pleasure that might bring forgetfulness of the beast's bite.

With the sharp edge of his fangs, he traced the puckered tip of her breasts, earning a surprised gasp from her. More gently, he took the tip into his mouth, suckling her until she was digging her fingers into his shoulders.

The sensation was familiar and yet foreign, Angelina thought. With each gentle pull, she experienced the scrape of his fangs along sensitized skin. At one particularly rough tug that created both pleasure and pain, she cried out and arched her back, bringing herself flush along his body.

He raised his head. His silver-gray gaze had bled out to the neon-blue of the vampire and long canines extended beyond the fullness of his lips. He hesitated a moment, then trailed a line of kisses down her center to the apex of her legs, where he parted her and sucked at her core.

She opened her legs wide, offering herself to him. He continued his sensual kiss at her center while easing one finger and then another into her, preparing her for his possession once more.

Angelina closed her eyes against the pleasure he was bringing her. Surely this was Heaven and anywhere without him—Hell. She threaded her fingers through the silk of his hair and held him close, savoring the sensations he was creating. As one sharp tug at her nether lips had her shaking, she lifted her hips up, asking him for more.

He chuckled and the sound reverberated against her center, dragging a moan from her. "Do not tease me so, Damien," she pleaded, feeling empty inside without him.

He slowly shifted upward until his body covered hers. It was warm with the heat of the vampire. His eyes blazing with light and those long, wickedly lethal fangs bright in the dim light of early morning.

"It seems only fair since you tempt me beyond reason, Angelina," he said, guiding himself to her center where, with a slight move, he slipped the tip of his erection into her.

She moaned and arched her hips, taking him in a little deeper, but he held back.

"Why do you hesitate?" she asked, puzzled by his restraint.

A bittersweet smile tempered the harsh look of his lips with their deadly fangs.

"I do not wish for this to end too quickly. For Heaven to slip through my fingers," he readily admitted.

She could not argue with him. Today brought no promise for their future and because of that, she did not rush him, but instead took the moment to run her hands up and down the hard muscles of his arms. She inched her hands inward to cup and explore his chest and the ridges of his midsection.

He sucked in a rough breath then, his body beginning to quiver.

"Take me," she pleaded, her own body waiting for his full possession. Waiting for the bite that would feed his demon body the way their loving was nourishing their souls.

At her plea, he complied, easing in the final inches to fill her. Drawing a long, satisfied breath from her as the powerful length and width of him drove away the emptiness in both her body and her soul.

He lowered himself onto her and bent his head, alternating a series of kisses and love bites along the line of her collarbone until he was at the crook of her neck. He nuzzled that area, the sensation almost ticklish until the sharp, undeniable teeth of the demon scraped her skin.

She shuddered, fear and need battling one another.

Softly, he whispered, "Forgive me, my love."

Pain burst from the spot on her neck as he bit down and she experienced the pull of his mouth, drawing in sustenance. Soon, however, desire snaked through her body and pleasure obliterated all other sensation.

Damien fed from her. Nothing he had tasted had ever been as glorious or as potent.

Angel's blood. So clean and vital. So beautiful, he

thought, as he sucked hard, feeding from her. Feeling himself growing stronger with each pull of his mouth. Feeling her respond to the desire the vampire's bite created as she lifted herself against him and mewled with pleasure.

He wanted her to be satisfied. He needed this time, if it was meant to be their last, to be perfect.

He reached between their bodies and cradled her breast. Found the turgid tip and caressed it, her soft cry of contentment urging him on.

Slowly, he moved, shifting his hips to pull himself in and out of her, the long, slow movements creating delicious friction. So much so that he cried out against her neck and broke from his feeding.

Shaking his head, he drove away the vampire who wanted yet more blood from her. He was not that demon, he told himself, mustering the control to morph back to his human form and savor these moments with her.

Moments which might be their last together.

He braced his arms on either side of her as he rocked his hips, urging her to climax.

She gazed up at him, her dark eyes locked on his as he loved her. He rolled onto his back and let her straddle him, deepening his penetration.

She gasped at that sudden move and the joining that it wrought, but the surprise was short-lived as she began to ride him. Drawing out her own pleasure with the roll of her hips.

He cupped her breasts, squeezing and playing with her nipples. Earning her soft cries of pleasure as she closed her eyes and tossed her head back. She arched into him until her body exploded with her climax, the waves of it washing across him. Squeezing and caressing his erection deep within her until he, too, came with a rough shout.

But even then he did not leave her, using his immense strength to sit up and encircle her hips with his arms, keeping her joined to him.

"I wish I could keep you here for always," he said, kissing the side of her face and then lower, over the site of his bite that was already healed, but still sensitive.

Angelina shivered at that and wrapped her arms around his shoulders, likewise loath to leave him. Although she knew she would. That was the only thing of which she was certain.

Tomorrow they would be apart.

He must have sensed the finality of the moment, also. It was as if God himself understood it, as well, for suddenly there came a rough pounding on Damien's front door.

Ramirez clearly was too impatient to wait for them to come to him.

CHAPTER TEN

WITH THE KIND OF SPEED only a vampire could manage, Damien dressed and armed himself with a knife and a revolver.

Angelina's heart sank as she sat on the edge of the bed, watching him prepare for battle. She gazed up at him as he paused by her side and tenderly cupped her chin.

"Do not worry. I will get your wings back. Stay here," he commanded and before she could offer her goodbyes, he was gone.

Sadness twisted her gut at the thought of being without him, but that had always been the only certain outcome. Her role here in this mortal realm was to guide him to the right path. It was not to walk beside him on that journey.

Hurrying from the bed, she grabbed a shirt from Damien's closet and slipped it on. Because of his size, the shirt hung down to midthigh, covering most of her body. Barefoot, she raced down the stairs, the soft pad of her feet imperceptible against the noise of the men clomping in from outside and the scrape of something heavy being dragged along the wooden floor.

The storm still raged beyond the walls of the building, darkening the morning sky. That false night had made it possible for Ramirez and his men to invade their peace. The wind howled and blew snow into the hallway before one of Ramirez's vampire crewmen shouldered the door shut and strode into a nearby room at the front of the house.

She hurried to the room's entrance and peered inside. Fear gripped her heart as she realized that Damien was at an immense disadvantage. Not only was Ramirez there, but also two other large and powerfully built vampires who were minding the large wood-and-leather trunk at their feet.

Damien shot her a glowering look when he realized she had disobeyed him. "I told you to stay upstairs."

"Why should she miss all the fun, *amigo?*" Ramirez said with a sly smile and a gentlemanly bow made ungainly by his large belly.

Damien gritted his teeth, controlling his anger. The hot-tempered youth he had once been had already cost him too much. As much as the demon within wanted a taste of blood for the harm done to Angelina, Damien would not release the beast. Being with Angelina, tasting her goodness of spirit and body, had imbued him with the renewed sense of the humanity she claimed had always been in his heart.

He could not squander that precious gift, especially not on a day like today. This Christmas Eve would be different, even if at the end of this confrontation Angelina would be forced to leave him. He loved her enough to let her successfully complete her mission here on Earth and return to Heaven. Maybe in time, some God somewhere might allow them to meet again in another existence.

"Mi amigo," Damien began with what he hoped was a good-humored smile. "We both know what you want. But I will not give you the fight you desire until you return Angelina's wings."

Ramirez chuckled loudly, displaying a bright gold tooth engraved with a skull. A new addition since their last encounter. As the vampire realized it had caught Damien's attention, he said, "Do you like? It seems appropriate considering that I am a master of death. Especially your little friend's demise."

"The Devil himself would approve," Damien replied calmly, trying to placate the other vampire in the hopes of securing Angelina's wings without bloodshed.

Ramirez laughed even more briskly, but then narrowed his eyes to consider Damien. "Do I sense a change? Is it possible that you've actually grown wiser?"

"Wiser and stronger, Pedro. But I guess you will find that out as soon as you return Angelina's wings," Damien challenged, aware that he was walking a tightrope to gain his objective.

Ramirez jammed his hands on his hips and the action drew attention to the long knife and pistols tucked into his belt. He stood there for what seemed like an eternity, contemplating Damien and his demand.

Then Ramirez moved so swiftly, Damien had little time to react.

He stepped in front of Angelina just as the point of Ramirez's pistol tipped upward and he fired.

Searing pain erupted in Damien's side, but he held his ground and did not engage. "Worried I might best you this time?" he taunted, each word coming on a short breath due to the agony in his side. It would not last long as his vampire body was already at work, expelling the bullet and sealing its path into his body.

In response to Damien's gibe, a dull flush worked across the other vampire's face and low chatter rose from his crewmen.

Ramirez pulled out his long thin knife and the blade glinted even in the subdued light in the room. He tossed the blade back and forth between his hands before jabbing it toward Damien.

Damien ducked backward, but the tip grazed his midsection, opening a thin line across his abdomen. Even though the cut was not deep, it burned brutally.

"Silver? You must be worried, *mi amigo*. Did you promise the Devil something you're afraid you cannot deliver?" Damien parried and dodged another swipe of the blade, all the time keeping Angelina behind him.

"I promised him your soul and I intend to deliver." Once again Ramirez slashed at him, catching Damien across his bicep. Fire erupted along his arm, but he held his anger.

"I will not fight you until Angelina has her wings and without a fight…"

There would be no killing. No sin to damn him eternally. Damien understood that now. Despite the fact that Ramirez had taken his life and the demon was a part of him, Damien's soul was apparently still up for grabs.

Ramirez lowered his weapon, seeming to realize that if he was going to pay the Devil his due, he would have to do as Damien had asked. With a reluctant jerk of his hand in the direction of his men, he commanded, "Give her the sea chest."

Angelina stood just behind Damien, her hands tightly clasped. Her brow furrowed with worry and sadness as her verdant gaze met his.

The vampires muscled the immense wooden sea chest before her, raking deep gouges in the wood of the floor. When it sat at her feet, one of the men threw open the lid.

Blinding light, so pure it drove Damien and Ramirez's two men away, burst from the snowy-white wings crammed into the container.

Angelina reached down and stroked the feathers, some of which stuck out at odd angles from being mishandled. With another delicate brush of her hands, the wings seemed to come alive, the feathers fluttering slowly before another intense burst of light had all the vampires in the room shielding their eyes against the glare.

The sound of wings beating filled the air along with a heavenly choir of song before the light abruptly died down.

Angelina now stood before him in glorious splendor. Her body naked and her shimmering wings of white outstretched. Then, with a shake of her shoulders, she tucked the wings tight against her body. Her dark gaze settled on him and instead of doubt and worry, there was nothing but conviction there as the wings deliberately disappeared from view.

She believed in him, he realized.

Angelina reached up and cradled his cheek, her skin softer than it had ever been. Warmer, driving away the pain of his wounds. Loving, without restraint or limit. Inside him came an uplifting lightness in his soul, a priceless gift that fought against the darkness into which Ramirez wanted to drag him. A darkness in which the vampire would be content to live, but he was not that demon. He never had been that monster despite the physical change that Ramirez had wrought on him.

Empowered by that knowledge, Damien faced the other vampire, arms spread in surrender. Inviting the violence that could no longer touch his soul. "Come, Pedro. Do your worst, but know that you will not win this Holy Night."

Ramirez seemed startled by the summons, but didn't refuse it. He struck out at Damien with the knife and sliced a deep furrow from shoulder to rib, but Damien didn't move. He just bit his lip against the pain and prepared himself to endure another blow.

Ramirez honored his unspoken request, slashing out at Damien, this time with a swipe from rib to rib. Damien grunted in distress and bent slightly, but then straightened and once again outstretched his arms. Blood flowed from every wound, the metallic smell scenting the air and exciting the nearby vampire crewmen. Their eyes glowed more brightly as they picked up the odor and licked their lips, ready for a taste.

But Damien glanced at them and issued a growl and a warning. "This is between the two of us."

The crewmen held back, cowed by Damien's resolve and by the snarl of their captain, warning them to stay out of the fray.

"Will you not fight, boy? Are you afraid of me like you were of your father?" Ramirez taunted, but Damien held his ground, no longer that frightened and angry young man.

Damien's peace only seemed to enrage Ramirez. The vampire captain thrust forward and the silver dagger pierced deeply into Damien's gut.

As Ramirez ripped out the blade, blood spurted from the wound and soaked Damien's already bloodstained shirt. Within him the traces of silver burned, weakening him, but he kept his position in front of Angelina, offering his protection.

Time and time again Ramirez struck. Each blow took a little more of Damien's life, but he held fast, somehow staying on his feet. Somehow protecting Angelina until she was pleading for him to act.

"You cannot do this, my love. Defend yourself before it's too late," she cried, but Damien ignored her pleas. As long as he did not engage, there would not be a repeat of the Christmas Past and Present that Angelina had shown him.

Dark circles grew ever more present in his gaze and he swayed, close to falling.

"Coward," Ramirez growled and grabbed hold of Damien's arm, trying to pull him away from Angelina, but Damien dug deep within himself and held his ground, shielding his beloved.

Angered beyond reason and clearly aware of the possibility that he would fail to get what he wanted, Ramirez reared back with his knife and rushed toward Damien. Ramirez obviously planned to reach the one thing that might goad Damien to act: Angelina.

Damien realized his foe's intent and blocked Ramirez's path, absorbing the full impact.

The force of the blow was so powerful that Ramirez's knife cleaved bone, heart and spine until the hilt became buried against the wall of Damien's chest.

Both men stared down at the weapon, which Ramirez still held, but then the vampire captain released the hilt and backpedaled away, seemingly stunned by Damien's sacrifice, aware that it meant he had lost the battle.

The silver in the weapon seared Damien. His heart, pumping futilely against the damage, sent miniscule bits of the poisonous metal throughout his body. It was a wound he would not survive with the silver contaminating his system so quickly.

Damien huffed in surprise as the pain of the injury slowly faded and the chill of death arrived. Almost in slow motion his knees gave way.

Angelina's arms immediately encircled him, gently lowering him to the ground. She supported him in her arms and tried to draw the knife from his chest, but only partially succeeded since it was buried so deep.

"Do...not...fret," he said, awkwardly patting her hand, movement growing more difficult with each passing second.

"I do not want to lose you," she cried, tears running

down her face and spilling onto his, their warmth a vivid contrast to the cold seizing his body.

"I love you," he said, wanting her to know that he understood this time. That the power of their love had saved her and him. The right choice, painful as it was, had kept him from killing Ramirez and losing his immortal soul.

She bent her head to his and kissed him. "I will love you forever," she vowed and shifted her face to drop a kiss on his cheek, across his temple.

From the corner of his eye, Damien saw Ramirez grab a larger sword from one of his men. Wild-eyed at his defeat, the vampire captain rushed toward them, raising the sword high above his head, determined to do more harm.

Damien reached deep and collected the last of his waning strength. He grabbed the handle of the knife and ripped it from his chest. With his last ounce of power, he flung it in Ramirez's direction.

As if some unseen hand guided the knife, it bit true, high up and deep in the vampire captain's shoulder.

Ramirez screamed and dropped his sword as the silver burned his body. Aware of the risk if the dagger stayed for too long, he yanked the knife out quickly and began to advance again, his intent clear.

Ramirez wanted Angelina's wings so he could keep her in this realm. So she would be his captive.

"Save yourself," Damien said, feebly pushing at her to leave his side.

Angelina sensed the threat, but it took all her willpower to release Damien and rise up. Inside her, righteous anger ignited at the last futile beats of Damien's heart and his body went limp at her feet.

She stretched out her wings to a spectacular and frightening span. Her body began to glow brightly with the heat of her fury, driving back Ramirez and his two men.

They had to shield their eyes against the brilliance of her power and the furious flap of her wings.

She had never felt such strength and realized then that Damien's sacrifice had fulfilled her mission as his Guardian Angel and moved her to another level. But the pain in her heart sought justice.

She wanted to lash out at the vampires and seek vengeance, but she had no desire to become an Avenging Angel. Her only wish was to be reunited with Damien.

As that thought formed in her mind, a low drone filled the space of the room and was soon followed by the sound of dozens of rushing wings. So powerful was the clamor that it pummeled her body, making her tuck her wings tight around herself protectively. As she did so, a brilliant light suffused her, and the room, forcing her to shield her eyes against its strength.

The screams came a heartbeat later, loud and fearful.

Angelina peeked from behind the shelter of one wing. Vicious flames rose up from the ground and engulfed Ramirez and his two crewmen. Skin and meat fell from their bodies and became ash even before the gore hit the floor. The cries of the vampires continued until they were nothing more than skeletons. Then they disappeared from sight as the flames and light completed their gruesome task, obliterating all traces of the three demons.

The low drone rose up higher with the disappearance of the flames. Now she recognized the voices of the Herald Angels, singing brightly. Their clear, strong notes entered deep into her soul and offered unexpected hope with their joyous chorus. Their song provided her the strength to battle back the anger and pain that might have consumed her and led her on a path to the Devil.

From within that gleeful sound boomed a powerful voice. Raphael, she thought, as his words filled her head and heart, trying to heal her of the anger threatening to consume her soul.

Believe in the power of love.

She thought of Damien, a good man who had persevered even when trapped in a demon's body. She thought of his sacrifice and his love even as he lay dying in her arms.

I believe, she confirmed to Raphael, driving the rage out of herself.

The song of the Herald Angels grew even more powerful with her admission as did the beating of their feathered appendages against her body. The heavenly wings thrashed wildly, almost painfully. They lifted her up, high off the ground, before suddenly releasing her.

Angelina felt herself falling and reached out for purchase, but there was nothing in the blinding light surrounding her. Her plummet continued, but no fear entered her as she repeated what she knew to be true. As she repeated Raphael's words.

Believe in the power of love.

The fall continued for long seconds until she landed hard on the ground. Dazed from the impact, which had driven the air from her body, it took her a second to register that she was back in Damien's parlor room.

Ramirez and his men were gone, but the trunk and a thin layer of ash remained on the marred wooden floor, giving evidence of what had transpired. Damien lay sprawled a few feet away, his life's blood forming a large pool on the floor beneath him. Too much blood, she thought, but then his hand moved. So slight was the motion that for a second she thought she was imagining it. Then he moved his hand again.

A second later a soft groan came from him and he rolled onto his back, revealing the torn and bloodied front of his shirt, marked with what looked like burns from embers.

Angelina rushed to his side and slipped her hands beneath his shoulders, cradling him close. His body was warm. Humanly warm.

His eyelids flickered open and then snapped wide as he saw her. He reached up and cradled her cheek, seemingly to make sure she was not a dream.

She smiled. "I'm really here, Damien."

A deep dimple appeared at the right side of his mouth and his eyes glimmered like a sun-silvered sea. But then concern slipped into his features along with puzzlement.

"Ramirez?" he asked and sat up a little more, wincing with pain as he did so.

"Gone to Hell along with his men." The vision of that was something she would not quickly forget.

Damien laid his hand on the center of his chest, directly above where Ramirez had driven his blade deep. He grimaced as if the spot was still sore and looked down at the cut in his shirt. He opened it to peer down at the skin beneath.

No wound. Not even a scar, Angelina realized. But then another surprise greeted them.

"I feel different," he said and tried to rise. Weakness made him falter until Angelina slipped beneath his shoulder and helped him to his feet.

Together they walked to a nearby mirror and stood before it. Their dual images stared back, confirming what she had suspected with her first touch of his warm body.

"I'm human again," Damien said and rubbed a hand along his cheek, sensing mortal heat. Moving his hand quickly back to the spot over his heart where the strong pulse of life had replaced the tepid thrum of the vampire.

"Why?" he asked, facing her. Taking her hands into

his and noticing for the first time that she no longer had her wings.

"And you? Are you still my Angel?"

"Always, my love. But I hope you won't mind that we share this life together before Heaven calls for us," she replied, a radiant smile on her face. She sensed the difference in herself, as well.

Damien was not the only human on this Christmas Eve.

Damien's heart raced with the reality of the miracle that had taken place. After so many Christmas Eves of pain and misery, the gift of happiness was now theirs. A gift made possible by selfless sacrifice and love.

He had learned the lesson and made the right choice after all.

With a playful shake of her hand, he said, "Let us share our love this day."

"And night," she replied with a sexy grin while a fresh blush of color swept over her cheeks.

"Still my naughty Angel, I see."

"Forever and always," she replied and tugged on his hand to lead him back to his bedroom.

She walked ahead of him to his bed and sat on its edge, her hand outstretched with impatient welcome.

He ripped away the torn remnants of his bloodied shirt and quickly shimmied out of his shoes and pants. Blood beat through his body, the pulse throbbing in his ears, an unusual sound and sensation after so much time in his undead state.

When he stood before her, staring down at her beauty, emotion nearly stole his breath as he realized she was his. That they would share this life together until Heaven called to them again.

"I love you," he said and the words had never meant as

much as they did at that moment. In his head and heart came a glorious sound, almost as if the Herald Angels in the heavens were singing with joy.

"I love you, too," she said and took hold of his hand, guiding him closer.

Her words and gentle touch filled his senses, making everything around him more alive with her love.

There was no rush this time as they committed to each other. No despair that this would be the last time. They had received the greatest of gifts this Christmas Eve and as he covered her body with his and entered her, he finally understood.

Believe in the power of love and all of Heaven will be yours.

* * * * *

ALL I WANT FOR CHRISTMAS

To M & J—
thank you for the best anniversary present ever!

CHAPTER ONE

"DECK THE FREAKIN' halls."

The freezing Seattle cold made Eagan McHale's words come out in short puffs of steam. With no one within listening range, he added a chorus of curse words just for the heck of it. He wasn't a happy man and saw no reason to pretend otherwise. Even his fangs ached from the cold air.

When he ran out of obscenities, he started listing all the things he hated: his boss for forcing him to do this job on his own, the cold for making him miserable, and the twinkling Christmas lights just because. And, oh yeah, he hated anyone who would prey on young teenagers. Lately, several young men in this area of Seattle had been reported missing, and no one knew how many of the runaways had also disappeared.

He hated that, too.

Down the street a moth-eaten Santa rang his brass bell for all he was worth. Eagan took perverse pleasure in the obnoxious sound it made. Bells were supposed to chime; this one clunked. It suited his mood, so he dropped a twenty in the old elf's bucket and kept walking.

The next turn brought him back to where he'd begun. For what seemed like the hundredth time in the past three nights, he paused to stare at the late-night diner across the street. Originally, it had drawn his attention because it looked way too warm and cozy, two things he usually avoided. Red-checkered tablecloths and lace curtains made his skin crawl, but tonight he'd put up with them if it meant he could get warm.

The place certainly drew an odd mix of people. Some were holiday shoppers. Others probably had trouble scraping together enough change to buy a cup of regular coffee much less the lattes advertised in the diner window.

There were even a few nonhumans mixed in the bunch. As usual the regular folks were blissfully unaware that some of their neighbors drank blood for dinner or sprouted fur and fangs come the full of the moon.

Right now the real object of his interest was standing at the counter and smiling at a pair of teenagers who'd just strutted into the diner as if they owned the place. Eagan recognized trouble when he saw it and automatically reached for the gun stuck in the waistband of his jeans. At the first sign of violence, he'd charge across the street to save the day even if it blew his cover. The lieutenant was already mad at him; one more transgression wouldn't make much of a difference.

But in a matter of seconds, the diner's owner had the two punks sitting at the counter with big sloppy grins on their faces with two hot drinks and pie in front of them. Problem solved. Amazing. He would've bet on the pair being armed and after some fast cash.

He didn't yet know the owner's name, only that she had a smile for every customer who walked through the door. As if sensing his gaze, she glanced in his direction. He swore he could feel her warmth all the way across to where he stood shivering in the cold.

Tamping down his brief adrenaline rush, Eagan considered his options. Maybe he should've accepted the flask his two-natured partner, Duncan, had offered him before leaving the precinct house. A stiff shot of straight whiskey would taste good about now, a bit of antifreeze for his veins.

He could make another lap around the block and hope that would warm up his blood while he hunted for any sign of his target's presence in the area. Or he could simply call it a night.

He glanced across the street again. Okay, so there was another option. Without even realizing he'd made a decision, he stepped off the curb and headed straight for the diner door.

DARN IT, THAT GUY HAD CAUGHT her staring! Della Breit's hand shot up to check her hair. Stupid, she knew. Nothing controlled her unruly curls, especially when she was working. Lipstick might have helped, but there was no time to slip out of sight long enough to apply some without being obvious about it.

She wished she'd worn something a little fancier than one of her holiday T-shirts. Tonight's version was festooned with giggling snowmen dancing around a Christmas tree.

"Hey, Della! More coffee?"

She forced her attention away from the man outside and back to the one sitting in the corner booth. Old Harry usually only stopped in for a hot cup of coffee and a bowl of soup, all he could afford on his small pension. Tonight, though, with the temperature outside unusually cold for Seattle, she'd insisted he stay longer and eat a full meal before heading back to his apartment.

Harry hated any hint of charity. If he insisted, she'd let him work off the difference in price crushing boxes and tossing them in the recycle bin out back. With his arthritis, she hated to let him do even that much, but she understood pride.

The bell over the door chimed, playing a quick chorus of sleigh bells. She refilled Harry's decaf before turning to greet the newcomer. When she realized who it was, she almost dropped the carafe on the floor. Biting back a curse, she pasted on a bright smile as she turned to face the hard-eyed stranger who'd been standing across the street.

"Hi! Pick any spot and I'll bring you a menu and a cup of coffee."

He didn't say a word, responding only with a quick nod before heading over to the table next to the front window, which afforded him a clear view of the diner as well as the street outside. Somehow she doubted his choice was random.

He also kept on his long, leather duster as he stretched his legs out under the table with a grimace. His hand massaged his lower right thigh, kneading the thick muscle as if it were cramping.

She caught herself flexing her fingers and imagining what it would feel to slide her own hand over that tight denim. As if sensing her gaze, he slowly turned to glare at her from across the room. His eyebrows drew down low over his icy-blue eyes making it clear that her interest wasn't appreciated.

Della, get your head back in the game.

Embarrassed at getting caught watching him again, she broke off the connection and focused instead on snagging a menu while she waited for the fresh pot of coffee to finish brewing. When it was done, she took an indirect route toward the table by the window, stopping to top off a few other cups along the way.

When she finally reached his table, she toned her smile

down a notch, aiming instead for efficient and business-like. She held out the menu and filled his cup and tried to think of something to say.

"Cream and sugar are already on the table."

Like he couldn't see that for himself. What was it about this guy that had her so badly rattled?

"I'll be back to take your order in a couple of minutes."

He waved the menu away. "No need. All I want is coffee. I've already fed."

What an odd way to put it.

"Fine. Let me know if you change your mind or maybe want some dessert. The pie is homemade and the muffins are fresh out of the oven."

She walked away, fighting the urge to look back. When she returned to her usual spot behind the counter, he was sipping his coffee and staring out the window. Even in profile, he was striking-looking although it was obvious his nose had been broken on at least one occasion.

She bet that it wasn't a sports injury, either, although she had no idea why she thought that. Something about the guy just screamed loner, and the image of him being a team player just wouldn't come into focus.

A movement over near the register caught her eye, dragging her attention back to those two teenagers who'd come in earlier. Great. One had his hand in the tip jar. For her own part, she didn't care, but her staff depended on that money to help make ends meet.

"Gentlemen, do you need change for a dollar?"

The kid froze and then slowly withdrew his hand from the jar still clutching a handful of bills. Darn it, she thought the free coffee and pie had convinced the two not to cause trouble. So much for playing nice.

"I'm sorry, but put that money back and leave." Della

kept her voice even, injecting a note of quiet authority in it.

It didn't work. One of the kids sneered and dipped his hand back in the jar. Fine, if it meant that they'd just leave, but she knew better. If she blinked now, they'd be back again for more.

"I said put the money back and leave, boys. I'd rather not call the police." Like they'd bother to respond to a petty theft at this hour of the night.

Meanwhile, his buddy joined the conversation, his hand sliding into the pocket of his jacket. "That's not happening. While we're at it, we want what you've got in the register, too. Put it in the jar now, and we'll leave all peaceable like."

Did he actually have a weapon or did he just want her to think so? She couldn't take the chance, not with a roomful of customers. As soon as she backed up a step, the boys knew they'd won. She opened the register.

They both stood up, ready to grab the jar and run. "Smart woman. You don't want to tangle with us."

"And you two don't want to tangle with me."

Della was so intent on keeping the confrontation from escalating, she didn't notice someone else had joined the party.

Duster guy grabbed both of the boys and shoved them up against the wall, his hands wrapped around their throats and squeezing just hard enough to make it difficult for them to breathe.

His voice was deep, his words devoid of any emotion and all the more effective for it. "Now, put the money back and apologize to the lady, and we'll call it even."

He let the one loose who'd raided the tip jar.

The kid started to say something, but one look at his much-scarier opponent had him nodding like a bobblehead doll. When he dropped the cash back in the jar, her rescuer released the second one. He made a show of straightening the kid's jacket and then brushing some imaginary dust off his shoulder.

"Apologize," he repeated.

Their heads both swiveled in Della's direction. "Sorry, ma'am. We was only kidding around."

She accepted both the apology and the lie. They weren't sorry; they were scared. Fine. Anything to get them out of her diner. Before they made it to the door, the man had one more thing to say.

"And boys, cause the lady any more problems, and we'll dance, just the three of us."

They both swallowed hard and fought to be the first one out the door. She watched to make sure they kept going. When they were out of sight, she turned around, intending to thank her hero. He was already back at his table doing the crossword puzzle someone had left behind and acting as if nothing had even happened.

Okay, she got it. The man didn't want her gratitude or a fuss made over what he'd done. That didn't make him any less of a hero in her eyes. She'd honor his desire for privacy, but maybe he'd at least accept a refill on his coffee instead.

CHAPTER TWO

ALL RIGHT, that was stupidity to the nth degree, Eagan thought. So much for blending in. There was no way that woman or any of her regulars would forget him anytime soon.

Especially the lady herself—Della, according to her name tag. Even before those two punks got caught ripping off the tip jar, she'd been way too interested in him. Now there was no way Eagan could continue to patrol this area without her noticing him. He'd have to come up with some excuse to hang around that held more weight than just a craving for hot coffee.

Hell, under other circumstances he might have even taken her up on what those big brown eyes were offering. Just the thought of what she could serve up with that generous mouth was enough to have his cock sitting up and begging.

Yeah, right. Who was he fooling? Even if he wasn't an undercover cop, he was a vampire. Somehow he doubted she'd be willing to add fresh blood to the list of daily specials.

No, far better that sweet, innocent Della remain happily unaware of the supernaturals whose world occasionally bumped up against hers. He looked up from the crossword puzzle that he had no real interest in. Della was chatting with the wolf bitch seated in the corner booth when she leaned over to look at something the redhead was showing her. Damn, the way those faded jeans cupped that sweet ass should be outlawed. The wolf caught his scent, her eyes briefly flashing gold and angry. Clearly she did not like him paying attention to her friend's lush attributes. He considered flashing his fangs at her, but restrained himself—barely. There was no use in antagonizing the local pack, especially in front of the unsuspecting humans. He tipped his head to ac-knowledge the warning but lifted his upper lip to briefly reveal the tip of his fangs.

Her eyes sparked gold again. Message received. He turned his attention back to the crossword puzzle. Four across, three letters. Santa's helper. He rolled his eyes. Was he the only one who was already tired of the tin-sel and twinkle lights? Evidently. He neatly filled in the boxes with *e-l-f* and moved on.

He was reaching for his coffee when he finally spot-ted some action across the street. A pair of males in black hoodies were double-timing it down the sidewalk with a smaller guy between them. There was no indication he was there under duress, but he appeared to be purely human. His companions definitely weren't.

Even if it turned out to be nothing, it was time to go anyway. Eagan tossed back the last of his coffee before heading up to the register to pay his bill. However, when he reached inside his coat for his wallet, it wasn't there.

What the hell? Had one of those punks lifted it when Eagan had them pinned against the wall? No, he would've noticed. He closed his eyes and thought back to when he'd last seen it. For sure he'd had it with him earlier when he'd bought coffee on his way to the precinct.

One look down at his well-worn jeans and faded sweatshirt gave him the answer. He'd changed into street clothes before going on the prowl. No doubt his wallet was in his leather bomber jacket, the one he didn't wear while on the job. He muttered a curse and checked to see how much change he had: two quarters and four pennies.

"Is there a problem?"

Eagan looked up from the motley collection of coins and lint he'd pulled out of his pocket. "I left my wallet in my other jacket, ma'am."

And how lame did that sound? Della's dark eyes were sympathetic, as if finding a customer was a bit short on money was a common occurrence.

"Considering what you did earlier, the coffee is on the house. And it's Della, not ma'am." Her smile was gentle when she dropped her voice and said, "If being short on funds is why you didn't eat anything, I'd be glad to spot you a hot meal."

"I'm not hungry, but I appreciate your offer."

Not unless she was talking about a quick hit off that pulsing artery at the side of her neck, the only kind of meal he was interested in at the moment. Even then, he'd want to be someplace a whole lot more private and with a lot fewer clothes on.

Still, he needed to maintain his current persona of a down-on-his-luck day laborer. "I'll drop by with the money for the coffee tomorrow night after I get paid."

The perfect excuse to return and not even a lie.

"Really, it's okay. You don't have to, mister."

She emphasized that last word, obviously hinting for something else to call him. He surprised himself by answering her unspoken question with his real name.

"It's Eagan, and yeah, I do." Then he dropped the change in the tip jar and walked out into the night.

"Happy holidays!" she called after him.

He pretended not to hear.

Outside, Eagan shoved his hands in his pockets and

stalked off down the street. There was nothing happy about the holidays, not for him and not for the local teenagers being lured into a web of deceit and death. Several bodies had been found, mutilated and drained of blood. There'd been no solid leads so far, only rumors and hints that there was someone new on the scene. Based on the nature of the attacks, that someone wasn't human. No one wanted that truth to make the evening news, and it was Eagan's job to make sure that didn't happen by putting a stop to the deaths and taking out the bastard behind them.

He fought down the wave of rage that threatened his control. No one deserved to suffer and die the way those kids had. There would be a reckoning and the guilty would be dealt with. He just wished that would be the end of it, but there was always another killer waiting in the wings. He should know. He'd spent decades hunting down predators and eliminating them. Always the same dance of death, one that played on and on.

Eagan waited until he was at the far end of the block before crossing over to the other corner in case Della was watching where he was going. The last thing he needed was for her to poke that cute little nose in his business. He stopped to taste the night air, hoping to pick up the trail left by those two supers and their human companion.

Nothing.

They had to have gone to ground somewhere close by. He studied the area in all directions. No hint of any movement anywhere. All he could do was circle the block again and hope he got lucky. If not, he'd call it a night and try again tomorrow.

DELLA BUSSED THE LAST FEW tables herself. One of her usual helpers hadn't shown up for work and hadn't called. She'd learned long ago not to let herself worry too much about that sort of thing, but she couldn't seem to help herself when it came to Daniel Cortez. Hopefully he'd check in before she turned the lights off.

Daniel's home situation was complicated, thanks to an absentee father and a mother who often took extra jobs cleaning offices to make ends meet. When that happened, Daniel stayed home to watch over his younger siblings. With that thought in mind, she packed up some of the leftovers from the daily special so she could send them home with him in the event he came by.

She looked outside, telling herself it was Daniel she was looking for even though she knew better. Not seeing anyone out there, she turned off the neon Open sign but left the twin Christmas wreaths in the front windows plugged in, liking their soft glow in the night. Her last few customers started for the door. On her way out, Lupe stopped to talk.

"You watch out for him, Della. He's trouble."

At first Della thought her friend was talking about Daniel, but then Lupe glanced toward the table by the front window. Oh, Eagan, not Daniel. Well, tell her something she didn't know.

"That was his first time here. Considering how embarrassed he was about not being able to pay for his coffee, I doubt I'll see him again anytime soon."

Lupe stepped closer. "But he promised to come back with the money, didn't he? He wants something. A man like him has no reason to be hanging around a place like this."

How had Lupe heard him when she'd been all the way over in a far corner? The place had been pretty crowded, not to mention the Christmas music playing over the intercom.

Della wiped down the counter. "I told him not to bother, that it was on the house. But why do you say that? Do you know him?"

The older woman shook her head. "I just know his type. The world would be better off without them."

The vehemence in her friend's voice shocked her. Lupe rarely had anything bad to say about anyone. Who did she mean by "them"? Tall men? Ones who wore dusters?

She tossed her washcloth back in the sink. "Look, all I can say is that I was glad to have him here. I still can't believe those boys tried to rob me after I gave them pie and coffee. And right before Christmas, too!"

Her friend frowned. "I keep telling you that you're a soft touch for every hard luck story in this town. You need to be more careful, especially when it comes to a man like him."

Lupe gave the empty table another pointed look. "Trust me on this, Della. A lot more careful."

Then she was gone. Della started to lock the door but realized the diner wasn't completely empty yet. Old Harry had evidently dozed off. She went over to shake his shoulder.

"Harry, it's time for you to go now."

He sat up and blinked at her. "Sorry, Della. Didn't mean to fall asleep."

"That's all right, Harry. Let me fix you something hot to drink on your walk home."

"If it's no trouble." He stood up and shuffled off to the restroom.

While she waited for the milk to heat, there was a knock on the front door. Good, it was Daniel. He pushed back the hood of his sweatshirt and flashed her a guilty smile as he pointed at the lock on the door. She hurried to let him in.

"Sorry I didn't get a chance to call, Della." He shifted from one foot to the other in that high-energy way he had. "Hope it wasn't too busy."

"We did fine, Daniel. Don't worry about it. Did your mom have to work?"

His eyes shifted to focus somewhere over her right shoulder. "Uh, yeah. It was a last-minute thing."

Although he'd never openly lied to her before, she was pretty sure he just had. Maybe he was embarrassed for having blown off his shift to hang with his buddies. At least he'd taken the time to come let her know he was all right. She opened the cooler to retrieve the care package she'd prepared for him.

"You'd better get back home so your mom doesn't worry, Daniel. I put this together for you. Tonight's special was meat loaf, and I made too much."

It was one of Daniel's favorites. Besides, he'd long ago learned not to argue with her about it. Even if he didn't want to accept charity for himself, he'd never deny his siblings a hot meal.

"The Christmas cookies are for your brothers and sister, but the piece of pie is for you. I made blueberry today."

For the first time since he'd come in out of the cold, Daniel's smile was genuine. "That won't make it all the way home with me."

She grinned back at him. "I figured that, so I stuck in a plastic fork."

When she opened the door to let him out, she spotted someone standing in the shadows across the street. She started to grab Daniel's arm and drag him back inside. Even in Seattle, predators roamed the streets looking for vulnerable prey. But as if sensing her concern, the man stepped into the light of the streetlamp long enough for her to recognize him. Eagan.

She released Daniel's arm. "Go straight home. Promise?"

The teenager shrugged his shoulders. "I will, Della. See you tomorrow."

She latched the door again, still staring at the shadows across the street. What was Eagan doing out there at this time of night?

"Is my drink ready?"

Della jumped. Darn it, she'd forgotten all about Harry. "It will be in just a second."

On impulse, she filled two cups and added extra whipped cream. "Harry, do me a favor. This one is for you. The other is for my friend Eagan standing across the street. Will you take it to him?"

"Sure thing, Della."

As soon as he walked out the door, she turned off the lights and scurried upstairs to her small apartment over the diner. She headed straight for her bedroom and the only window that overlooked the street below.

Harry looked dwarfed standing next to Eagan as he offered him the extra cup of hot chocolate. She really hoped Eagan didn't refuse the drink. It would only confuse Harry—and maybe hurt her feelings.

But no, he accepted the cup and even patted Harry on the shoulder before the older man shuffled on down the sidewalk toward home. Meanwhile, Eagan took a long sip from the cup, the whole time staring straight up at her window.

Did he know she was watching him? It wasn't as if he knew where she lived, and she hadn't turned on any lights in the apartment. He shouldn't be able to see her at all, but she suspected he saw her all too clearly.

When she raised her hand in a tentative wave, he held the cup up as if toasting her before fading back into the shadows. Turning away from the window, she felt as if she'd just brushed up against something powerful and potentially dangerous.

She shivered. Maybe she'd soak in the tub before curling up under the covers in her flannel gown and wool socks. Not a very sexy image, but then it had been a long, long time since she'd last had someone to warm her bed.

For sure Eagan was a far cry from her usual choice in men, but there was just something about the guy that made her want to learn more about him. As she slipped into her old claw-foot tub filled with hot water and lavender bath salts, she pictured him in her mind.

He had a rough look about him, as if life had left him a bit battered but definitely not broken. A woman could get lost in those intense ice-blue eyes. Did he ever smile? She'd like to see that. Her fingers flexed, imagining the sleek muscle under that T-shirt and those faded jeans. What had he done to his leg that left it aching? So many questions with no answers.

There was also a kind of strength in him that was impossible to miss. Even though he wore his solitude as comfortably as he did that scuffed leather duster, he hadn't hesitated to come to her aid and he'd been kind to old Harry out there. Yes, Eagan was quite the puzzle, one she had no business wanting to solve.

CHAPTER THREE

EAGAN SAVORED THE hot drink as he walked down the street. Damn that woman anyway. He didn't want to feel grateful for the small bit of warmth, but he did. It didn't help that the rich scent had him thinking of Della's dark chocolate eyes staring down at him from above the diner.

She hadn't thought he'd notice her, but with his night vision she might as well have been standing in a spotlight. Had she been worried that he'd refuse her gift or that he'd abuse her friend Harry?

The old man had actually warned Eagan that it was impossible to derail Della once she got it in her head to do something nice for a person. Also, if it bothered him, he could always work off the debt doing odd jobs for her. Harry himself broke up boxes for her when she'd let him.

Yeah, Eagan had been right about Della being a chronic do-gooder. He supposed the world needed people like her.

He sure as hell didn't.

Of course, since he hadn't been able to pay for his coffee, she now had him pegged as another person who needed a helping hand. Yeah, well, he had better uses for her hands than making him a cup of hot chocolate. He smiled, revealing his fangs at the thought of explaining what that would entail. Her fair skin might blush all rosy, but he was willing to bet there'd be a healthy dose of desire mixed with curiosity in those expressive eyes.

Not happening, though.

He'd been born vampire, but it was possible to share his longevity and strength with a human mate through periodic blood exchanges. The V gene was dominant, so any offspring would be vampire like him. Night dwellers. Blood drinkers destined to dwell in the shadows in a life filled with secrets. They could consume human food, but it was human blood they needed to thrive.

As he walked, he entertained himself by toying with the image of Della in his bed. It was all too easy to picture her there with that sweet face surrounded by a halo of dark curls, the taste of those lush lips, and the hot spice of her blood on his tongue.

He drank the last of the hot chocolate and tossed the cup in a handy trash can. Time to move on. The streets remained quiet with no sign of those three youngsters he was looking for. The sun would start peeking over the Cascades to the east in a couple of hours. He'd stop at the special ops office in the local precinct to see if there'd been any new reports of missing teenagers.

Then home to bed, alone as usual.

"Hey, McHale, haul your ass in here."

Eagan winced. He'd hoped to sneak in to check on a few things, and then escape without being seen. Obviously that wasn't going to happen. He tossed his coat on the back of his chair and headed for Lt. Hughes's office.

"Close the door."

That was the boss's token effort at offering privacy, not that it worked when the man only had two volumes—loud and even louder. Couple that with the fact that everyone who worked for him was a supernatural of one sort or another, and the door did little to muffle the particulars of any conversation.

Even so, Eagan appreciated the gesture. He sat down and waited for the ass-chewing to begin.

"So, did you spot anything out there tonight?" Hughes peered at him over his reading glasses. "And don't bother lying. I know you went out patrolling on your own."

Eagan shrugged. "I saw two supers walking with a young human but lost their trail. They had to have gone to ground somewhere in that same eight-block area where other kids have been reported missing."

His boss looked incredulous. "They outran you even with a human slowing them down?"

"Not exactly, but there was no indication the human was under any duress." He mentally crossed his fingers the lieutenant wouldn't ask any more questions.

Hughes leaned back in his chair. "You were supposed to be taking it easy for a few more days until that fractured leg heals. However, I'm not your nursemaid. If you're going to patrol anyway, I'll put you back on active duty, but take it easy."

Okay, Hughes was being a little too nice.

Eagan stretched his legs out, trying to ease the bone-deep ache in the right one. "What's happened now?"

"Another parent called in saying that some vampire wannabes were hassling her son, offering him money for blood. She thinks they're involved in some kind of cult or street gang." He shoved a file across the desk. "Here are the details."

Eagan skimmed the report. "I take it that you're not buying the whole wannabe part. You think these are the real thing out looking for trouble."

His boss frowned. "Seriously, I don't know, but that would explain what happened to the other victims. Either way, we need to find out. I've marked all the complaints on this map."

Hughes held out the paper. "You can keep this copy."

Eagan leaned forward to take it. One glance had him wanting to swear. "Damn it, they're all in the same area where I saw those kids tonight. I'll check it out again."

His boss pinched his nose as if fighting a headache. "Do that. My only concern is that if you hang around too much without a good reason for being there, they'll move their operation somewhere else in the city. Then we'll be back at square one. Any suggestions?"

The image of the diner flashed in Eagan's mind. If Della thought he was really down on his luck, maybe she'd let him work off a few free meals. Inwardly, he cringed over the idea. He'd hate to abuse Della's hospitality by lying to her even for a good cause, but he would. The safety of those kids had to come first.

"Yeah, there's a diner right smack in the middle of that area. Maybe I can do some odd jobs for the owner. That would give me an in with the locals and give me an excuse to be in the area for hours at a time."

For the first time his boss's expression lightened up. "What about the owner? Any chance he's involved?"

Eagan's job had taught him to expect the worst of most people, but his gut was telling him that Della was on the level. He shook his head.

"It's run by a woman, and I'm betting she's one of the good guys."

Hughes's eyes immediately narrowed in suspicion. "Tell me she's old and ugly."

Eagan grinned. "I would, boss, but I try not to lie to you any more than I absolutely have to. She's pretty enough, but she's also human. I steer clear of that kind of complication, especially on the job."

At least up until now.

Hughes stared at the report for a few seconds but finally nodded. "Okay, let's do it. Let me know how the diner thing works out. If you need a break, I can always send in one of the other guys to keep watch for a night."

Yeah, like Eagan was going to let that bunch of horn dogs anywhere near Della. "I'll be fine."

"Good. Now go get some rest. Keep me posted."

Eagan was up and heading for the door, happy to escape before Hughes remembered Eagan had disobeyed his orders to stay off the street in the first place. As soon as his hand landed on the doorknob, his boss called his name.

"One more thing, Eagan."

He braced himself. "Yes, sir?"

"Next time I tell you to take some time off, do it or we'll have issues."

There were very few people strong enough to strike fear in a vampire with even just a hint of a threat, but Hughes had that ability in spades. No one was quite sure what category of supernatural he fell in. But whatever he was, the man carried some serious firepower.

"Yes, sir. It's just that—"

Hughes cut him off. "Yeah, I know. It's because it involves kids. I get that. I have the same problem. Now get out. One of us has work to do."

Eagan walked out. The sun was rising in the east, meaning he needed to haul ass home and get horizontal before the day sleep claimed him right out in the middle of the squad room. The last vampire that had happened to hadn't fared well at the hands of their jokester coworkers. Eagan smiled at the memory but hurried his steps all the same.

"Is something wrong?"

The question was accompanied by a tug on Della's

sleeve. She dragged her eyes back from staring at the door to look around the diner. From the exasperation underlying Lupe's question and the concerned looks on several other faces, it was clear Della's mind had wandered afar long enough to worry her friends.

"No, nothing's wrong. I was just considering where I want to put the rest of the Christmas decorations."

To give some truth to her claim, she looked up toward the ceiling. "Even with the ladder, I'm not tall enough to hang the lights up around there."

"I'm taller. Maybe I could do it."

That offer came from Harry, but she was already shaking her head. He might have another whole inch over her in height, but there was no way she was going to let him up on a ladder. Not at his age. Before she could come up with a better solution, the sleigh bells over the doorway chimed.

She drew a breath, ready to greet her new customer, but then let it all out on a sigh when she recognized the new arrival. Eagan was back.

She'd been distracted all day, hoping he'd show up.

Somehow she'd suspected that if Eagan did return, he'd do so after dark. He'd looked too at home in the shadows across the street for it to be anything other than second nature for him.

He frowned and looked around the diner, making her aware that she wasn't the only one staring. "Hi, take a seat and I'll bring you a menu."

At least he didn't argue. He immediately parked himself at the same table as he'd chosen last night. Considering there were half a dozen others available, it confirmed her earlier impression that it was a deliberate choice on his part. Why? Because it was familiar since he'd sat there the previous night or because of the view it offered of the diner as well as the street outside?

Ignoring Lupe's disapproving glare, she grabbed the coffeepot and a menu before heading over to Eagan's table. She normally had a steady hand when carrying hot liquids, but right now her pulse was racing hard enough to send ripples sloshing through the carafe. What a stupid reaction. It wasn't as if she didn't get handsome men in the diner on a regular basis, especially during the lunch crowd when men from the local high-rise office buildings came in.

There was just something different about Eagan.

"Coffee?"

He nodded and pushed the empty cup closer to the edge of the table. "Thanks."

At least he didn't wave off the menu this time, even if he did just toss it down on the table. "I'll check back with you in a few minutes."

Della took her time, making her rounds with the coffee and stopping to talk to a few friends before finally making her way back to Eagan. The menu was still right where he'd left it on the table. While she wasn't surprised, the real question was why.

Maybe the best way to find out was to come at the problem from a different angle. She dropped her voice, hoping to keep the conversation private.

"Eagan, would you mind if I asked a favor?"

He looked up from his coffee, his eyebrows riding low over his eyes in clear suspicion.

"You can ask."

Which translated that he wouldn't necessarily agree to it. Fine, she got that.

"I made the mistake of mentioning I wanted to string Christmas lights all around the room along the ceiling.

It's been done before, so the hooks are all up there. The problem is that I can't reach the hooks myself, and Harry wants to put them up for me."

Eagan glanced in Harry's direction. "And?"

"I was thinking if you did it for me in exchange for dinner and dessert, Harry wouldn't get his feelings hurt."

"Or his hip broken from falling off the ladder?"

She smiled big-time. "Exactly. So do we have a deal?"

He nodded. "I already ate, but some of your pie would taste good. Let's do the lights first."

"When you're done, let me know whether you like blueberry or chocolate cream pie better."

The corners of his eyes crinkled even though the smile didn't reach that stern mouth. "Maybe if I do a really good job, I could have a little of both."

When he stood up, he staggered a bit as if his leg wouldn't support him. She automatically reached to steady him. He jerked his arm out of reach, and one look at those angry blue eyes made her rethink anything she was about to say. He'd hang the lights even if it killed him, and they both knew it. There was no use in arguing the point.

Any more than there was denying that there was something unmistakably powerful about Eagan.

CHAPTER FOUR

As it was, Harry insisted on showing Eagan where Della kept the ladder in the basement and carrying the plastic crate of Christmas lights up the stairs himself. The older man was puffing pretty hard by the time they reached the front table. Eagan kept a close eye on him to make sure he wasn't overdoing it until Harry plunked the crate down and sat on the extra chair.

As soon as Harry was settled, Della was there with two hot chocolates with thick mounds of whipped cream floating on top. Eagan suspected it was an excuse to check on her friend without appearing to hover.

She popped the lid on the crate and peeked inside. "I checked all the bulbs last week, so they should be good to go."

Della smelled like cinnamon and vanilla, two of Eagan's favorite scents. The heady combination had him hungering for something far more personal than a cup of hot chocolate as a reward.

It was a fight to keep his fangs from showing. "Don't worry, we'll take care of it. If I've got any questions, I'll ask."

She accepted the dismissal with good grace and walked away. Meanwhile, Eagan waited until Harry had finished his drink before setting the ladder up in the front corner. Somehow Eagan figured he'd acquired a self-appointed assistant for the duration. The old man obviously needed to feel useful. It was that or else he was trying to stay between Eagan and Della, which wouldn't surprise him. For sure the wolf bitch wasn't happy to have him hanging around the diner, either.

Too bad, although he sure couldn't fault her instincts. She clearly didn't trust his reasons for being there. What were her lupine senses telling her that had her fur all ruffled? As far as he knew, he'd never laid eyes on the woman before last night, so it couldn't be anything he'd done. Most likely it was just the usual prejudice some shifters had against vampires.

As long as she didn't try to interfere with him insinuating himself into Della's diner crowd, Lupe could hate him all she wanted to. But for Della's sake, he'd do what he could to maintain the peace.

He finished the last of his hot chocolate. "Ready to get started?"

Harry nodded and set his own cup down. "Let's do it." With his preternatural strength and speed, Eagan could've hung the lights in a fraction of the time, but he needed to pass for human. After dragging the whole ordeal out as long as he could, Eagan finally stepped down off the ladder and waved Della over to join them. Given how small the diner was, she didn't have far to come.

He held out the plug from the extension cord. "Thought you'd want to do the honors."

"Wait a minute!"

Della rushed to the other side of the diner. "Everybody freeze. I'm going to turn the lights off for a second."

The few people left in the diner did as she asked. Since most were already seated, it didn't take long for them all to get settled. She flipped the switch that turned off the overhead lights and then wended her way back through the tables to where Eagan stood waiting for her.

She moved through the darkness with far more assurance than most humans would have. Even he was impressed.

He wasn't sure how much the others could see, but her smile positively glowed as she coasted to a stop beside him. The warmth of her body seeped across those last few inches, her pulse racing and calling to his vampire hunger. It didn't help that when she reached for the extension cord, her fingers brushed across his, the brief connection setting off a jolt of white-hot blood hunger.

From the way she jerked her hand back, she'd felt it, too. Good. He didn't want to be the only one suffering here. But considering their audience, this definitely wasn't the time or place to explore the possibilities. Especially considering she was both human and innocent. He'd lived too long, had seen too much, to deserve a woman who looked at the world through such gentle eyes and smiled at a soul-weary vampire as if he were still capable of being someone's hero.

He cupped her hand with his and placed the plug in it. "Here. Let's see how it looks."

She curled her fingers around the cord and knelt down to plug in the lights. In an instant, the room went from shadowed to shimmering. Even a hard case like him had to admit the glow of the lights softened all the harsh lines of chrome and plastic, bathing the whole room with an appealing warmth.

Just as its owner did each time she smiled.

Della gave Harry a hug with a quick kiss on the cheek. "Thanks, Harry. Dinner is on me tomorrow!"

Her friend beamed at her. "Ordinarily I'd refuse, considering how little I really did, but only a fool would turn down your pot roast."

What kind of man was jealous of an old man getting

a hug and free meal? Evidently Eagan's kind, because that's exactly how he was feeling right now.

Della turned her bright eyes in his direction. "Same deal. Pie tonight as promised, but how does dinner tomorrow night sound?"

Damn it, his job demanded he accept the invitation, but his conscience argued he didn't deserve it. He hated being here under false pretenses and only pretending to be part of the family of friends Della had gathered around her.

"Like the man said, only a fool would pass up anything you offered."

Okay, that came out wrong.

Della's eyes widened in surprise as someone in the background sniffed in disapproval. He knew without looking it was the wolf bitch again.

To cover the awkward silence, he blurted, "Is there anything else you need hung up around here while I've got the ladder out?"

Della nodded slowly. "Yes, I have a few more decorations I'd like to put up before I do the tree."

When she didn't move, he tried to rustle up a reassuring smile. "Want to tell me where they are?"

Della hit her fingertips against her forehead and shook her head. "Well, duh, that would help, wouldn't it? They're upstairs in my apartment. Blue crate in the corner of my living room."

She tossed him a set of keys. "You want the one with the red tag."

He snagged the key ring out of the air and headed for the staircase at the back of the kitchen before he changed his mind and bolted out the front door. Was she crazy? Letting a man she'd only met twice in her apartment.

Hell, she thought he was flat broke. How did she know he wouldn't steal something while he was up there?

The answer was easy: she didn't. Either she had nothing worth taking or else she had her picture next to the word naive in the dictionary.

Upstairs he took a deep breath and turned the key. Out of habit rather than necessity he turned on the kitchen light. The bright overhead light allowed him to see everything in exquisite detail.

The apartment looked just like its owner: warm, soft and inviting with the occasional touch of whimsy. A row of gargoyles decorated the top of a cluttered bookshelf. Each one sported a tiny Santa hat in honor of the season. He was surprised they weren't wearing T-shirts to match the one she had on. It was similar in style to the one she'd worn yesterday, although today's version had a reindeer with a nose that blinked on and off. Normally he'd find it irritating. On her, it was cute.

Odd that he'd think so. He wasn't quite sure why he was so drawn to her. Maybe because in her own way she offered a haven to those who needed one, and he liked that about her. It was obvious that many of her customers lingered in the diner far longer than eating a meal required. She looked out for them, and they returned the favor. More than one had given him a considering look, wondering about his interest in their friend. Smart of them.

The crate was right where she'd said it would be. Before carrying it downstairs, though, he wanted to take a quick peek out of her front window to see if anything was happening on the street below.

He pushed the door open, hoping he was heading into a guest room. No such luck. This was definitely Della's bedroom, her most private space, and here he was clomping through uninvited. He passed by the big brass bed, firmly ignoring the interesting possibilities that sprang to mind. Especially the ones involving those silk scarves hanging on the mirror and the brass railings on her bed.

Looking out the window, he studied the sidewalk below. The streetlights had been on for hours already since the sun set by about four o'clock this time of year. It was late enough that most of the commuters were long gone, leaving only a few people out walking the street. Most looked like shoppers on their way home.

Nothing out of the ordinary. He was about to walk away when a movement at the far end of the block caught his attention. It was those same three kids he'd seen the previous night. He froze, knowing if he was right about the two taller ones being his kind the slightest motion might draw their attention to where he stood.

A few seconds later they passed under the overhang, and he could see the two vampires continue on and heard the bells chiming downstairs. Whoever the kid was, he was now in the diner. Eagan hurried back to the living room to grab the crate. This could be the first break in the case.

Della was waiting for him at the bottom of the steps looking a bit puzzled. "Did you have trouble finding it?"

Damn, he realized he'd been gone too long. "Not at all. I got a phone call I had to take."

And of course she accepted the excuse without question. As an undercover cop, he was used to lying to everybody. It never bothered him, figuring the end justified the means. So why did he feel like such a creep for lying to this one woman?

He thrust the crate at her. "Show me what you want where."

Fearing he'd sounded like a jerk, he added, "Please."

Della headed toward the front of the diner to unload the crate. As she unpacked the crate, she carefully touched each item, treating each one as if it were precious and made of gold instead of plastic and paint. When she was done, she handed them out to her friends, letting them decide where each Santa, reindeer, and snowman would look best.

When they were all busy, she handed Eagan another pair of wreaths made of jingle bells and bows to hang. He took down a pair of pictures and replaced them with the wreaths. When that was done, she asked him to set a dancing Santa on a high shelf out of the reach of small children. He could only be grateful for that much. After setting it off twice, he was ready to heave it against the wall.

When everything had been dispersed, Della walked through the room, touching a decoration here, patting a friend on the shoulder there and straightening one of the wreaths just a hair. Finally, when she'd made the rounds, she turned back to Eagan with a huge grin.

"It's perfect!"

But her smile quickly disappeared. "I take that back. I forgot something. I bought it to hang in the center of the room."

Eagan dragged the ladder into the middle of the room while she disappeared into the kitchen, where he could hear her muttering under her breath.

Finally, she hooted in triumph. "Found it!"

She came back into the main room holding a ball of what looked like herbs tied together with a bow. She handed it up to him on the ladder. He slipped the loop over the hook and started down the ladder. Before he could collapse it to take it back downstairs, Harry spoke up.

"Wait a minute, young fellow! You and Della are

standing under the mistletoe. Don't tell me you're foolish enough not to take advantage of that! When I was your
age, we relished such moments. 'Tis the season after all."

Eagan wasn't sure which he was having a harder time
processing: being called *young fellow* by a man who had
to be decades younger than he was or that he was going
to have to kiss Della in front of everybody. There was no
way to avoid it without hurting her feelings and alienat-
ing most of her friends.

As far as the lady herself, she'd backed up half a step.
He suspected she was about to chastise Harry for putting
both of them in such an awkward position. He could let
her go ahead, shifting the attention back to the old man.

But maybe this was the one opportunity he'd ever have
to find out if Della tasted every bit as sweet as she looked.
Evidently his curiosity was running hotter than his common sense because he held out his hand with a wink and
waited for the lady to take the dare.

CHAPTER FIVE

DELLA FOCUSED ON Eagan's hand for several seconds before she could work up enough courage to look him in the eye. To make matters worse, her friends were chanting "Kiss him! Kiss him!"

It didn't help that last night she'd dreamed about what it would be like to be held in those powerful arms and how that straight slash of a mouth would feel. Well, now was her one chance to find out if her subconscious had come close to the reality.

Placing her hand in Eagan's somehow carried more weight than it should have. The palm-to-palm connection between them sparked and sizzled. When had the room gotten so hot? Eagan tugged her closer, wrapping her in his embrace firmly enough to say he meant it, gently enough not to leave her feeling trapped.

"Shall we dazzle them?"

The teasing note in his whispered question gave her the courage to nod. When his lips settled over hers, the rest of the world faded away, leaving just the two of them standing there amidst the twinkling lights and Christmas music. If anyone had asked her at that moment what she wanted from Santa, she would've said nothing more than this amazing gift from a man she hardly knew.

He teased her with a soft nibble of her lower lip before getting down to business. Okay, it was time for her to join in the fun. She circled his neck with her hands and leaned in close. When he smiled against her mouth, she grew more adventurous and touched her tongue to his lips.

It was as if she'd touched a match to tinder. His tongue swept in and conquered her mouth, staking a claim, making her wish they were someplace a lot more private. This couldn't go on much longer. She knew it. Hopefully he knew it, too. But for the duration, she was determined to enjoy every second.

"Ahem!"

Someone nearby cleared her throat and then did it again. No doubt Lupe. Eagan broke off the kiss long enough to glare at the woman before picking up right where he'd left off. But then he gentled the kiss, slowly banking the fire, leaving only a few softly glowing embers when he stepped back at last.

"I guess we showed them," Eagan said for the benefit of their audience. Then leaned close enough to whisper near her ear, "And us."

Her face was as red as her T-shirt when she bowed to acknowledge everybody's applause. Rather than look Eagan in the eye, she kept her attention focused on the others in the room. "Okay, then, I guess it's time to break out the eggnog!"

Everyone applauded again and retreated to their tables while she made a beeline for the kitchen. The eggnog was only an excuse to give herself a few seconds to catch her breath. Leaning her forehead against the cool stainless steel of the fridge, she waited for her pulse to slow down to normal.

That man should come with a warning sign pinned to his shirt. If his casual kiss was that potent, how overwhelming would it be if he'd really meant it?

And darned if she didn't want to find out.

"Della, are you all right?"

Darn it, she'd forgotten all about Daniel coming in to work. She straightened up and opened the refrigerator. "I'm fine. Just a bit of a headache."

"Did you take something for it?"

"Not yet, but I will if it gets worse. How about you? How was school today?"

"Okay I guess."

He started scrubbing one of her baking pans with renewed gusto, a clear sign he didn't want her to pursue that line of questioning any further. Too bad. He might have a mother, but the woman was overworked and had three other kids to worry about. As Daniel's employer, Della claimed the right to do some nagging of her own.

"Why did you blow off school?"

His shoulders sagged, but he didn't respond, telling her she'd been right on target. It would be one thing if this was the first time he'd skipped, but it wasn't. She knew for a fact he'd been spotted hanging around the neighborhood during school hours at least twice in the past month.

She started pouring cups of eggnog. "Is something going on that I can help you with?"

"I'm handling it."

He rinsed the pan and reached for the next one. Odd that he still had on his hoodie despite the heat in the kitchen. She couldn't very well demand he take it off, but it bothered her even if she couldn't quite figure out why.

"When you finish with those, you can call it quits for the night if you'd like. I'll run the dishwasher one last time when everyone is gone."

She picked up the tray. "I'm going to close up early tonight. It's been slow all evening, and I'm tired."

Not really, since Eagan's kiss had left her feeling buzzed, but it was the only excuse she could think of on short notice to give the boy a break.

That he didn't argue indicated just how tired he really was. "If you're sure."

"I am, but promise me you'll go straight home and get some sleep."

"Will do. I've got homework, but that won't take long."

She'd done all she could to help without talking to Daniel's mom. He wouldn't appreciate her going behind his back, but she would if that's what it took to get him back on track. Crossing her fingers that it wouldn't come to that, she headed back out to the dining room.

Eagan was nowhere in sight, a good thing. Harry was still looking pretty proud of himself, but Lupe clearly wasn't happy. Too bad. It was just a kiss. Well, not *just*, but it wasn't as if it was going to happen again.

At best she suspected Eagan might be up for a brief fling, but she wouldn't risk her heart on a man who wouldn't stick around. She was looking for a man who would build a life and a family with her. Since her mother's death ten years ago, Della had been alone. Her friends here at the diner helped fill in the gap, but it wasn't the same as having a man who loved her and would give her children. Unfortunately, Eagan wore his solitude like a second skin.

Not even all of her favorite Christmas decorations could make that thought any cheerier. Rather than dwell on it, she started handing out the eggnog.

EAGAN SKIPPED THE EGGNOG, preferring to use the time to check out the human hanging out in Della's kitchen. He'd heard pots banging around and the sound of running water. It wasn't much of a leap to realize the kid was her dishwasher.

Eagan shifted the ladder to his other side as an excuse to pause in the doorway. The teenager appeared to be about sixteen, seventeen tops. Odd that he was wearing his sweatshirt zipped up and the hood cinched down close to his face.

He wasn't cold, not with the way he just swiped a rivulet of sweat off his forehead with his sleeve. He was hiding something under that fleece, and Eagan had a good suspicion about what it might be. He'd bet anything the kid was sporting fang marks either on his neck or his wrists or both.

The kid didn't reek of leftover fear, which meant he'd been a willing donor. Maybe that was a plus, but Eagan couldn't see how. The question was why? Money, if Eagan were to hazard a guess, but that didn't exonerate the vampire feeding off someone Daniel's age. Cautious vampires survived by moving in the shadows and making sure their blood sources didn't remember being bitten. They also didn't leave marks behind. The chemistry of their saliva should ensure puncture wounds faded within minutes.

Only the very young and the stupid left obvious evidence behind. The young might be forgiven and taken under an older vampire's wing until they mastered both their hunger and their survival skills. The stupid were ruthlessly culled from the herd for the benefit of everyone. Now that Eagan knew this boy had been used as a traveling buffet line, he'd hunt down those two vamps and see whether they warranted a tutor or an executioner.

The kid finally noticed him standing there. Lots of resentment in that gaze and then a flare of awareness. Shit, had he been made? Eagan set the ladder down, ready to shut the kid up by fair means or foul if he tried to sound the alarm.

But instead of screaming, the kid shoved his hands in the pockets of his sweatshirt and glared at Eagan. "What are you staring at?"

Not much. Eagan forced a small smile. "Sorry, I didn't mean to startle you. I've got a bum leg, and climbing up and down to hang lights for Della has the muscle cramping. I was giving it a rest before carrying the ladder back down to the basement."

That much was true, not that he would've admitted as much in front of Della. "My name's Eagan."

The kid actually grinned. "I'm Daniel, and better you than me with the whole light thing. I figured I'd end up doing that for her."

Okay, maybe he wasn't such a pain in the ass. "Yeah, well, it was me or Harry."

Daniel raised his eyebrows. "Seriously? I don't believe Della was going to let him."

"No, she wasn't. That's why she asked me."

He shouldered the ladder again. "Nice meeting you. I'd better get back to work. She promised me pie if I did a good job."

Daniel wiped down the counter and tossed the towel in a bin in the far corner. "Her blueberry is my favorite, but they're all good."

He headed out of the kitchen. "See you around."

Eagan waited until he was out of sight to take several deep breaths to draw Daniel's scent deep into his lungs. With luck, he'd be able to track the boy's trail back to the place the vampires were using as a feedlot. Once he located it, he'd call the lieutenant and request some backup to keep an eye on the place.

For now, he'd haul the ladder back to the basement.

After that, he'd claim his reward. Too bad it wouldn't be another kiss. As good as Della's pie was reputed to be, he seriously doubted it could possibly taste as sweet as Della herself did.

Just the thought of how well she'd fit in his arms, how right she'd felt there, had him rock hard and hungry. No human woman had ever had such a powerful effect on him. In fact, no woman ever. He didn't like it, not one bit. She was human, and an innocent. His job was to protect people like Della, not to seduce her and risk drawing her into the darkness of his world.

Damn it, he wanted to heave the stupid ladder down the steps, grab his coat and get the hell out of the diner. He was there to investigate a case and find the rogue vampires who were threatening the secret existence of all supernaturals, not to hang Christmas lights and mistletoe.

If these guys weren't stopped, and soon, more teenagers would disappear or die, and the merely human would learn that their worst nightmares lived right next door. He needed to get his head back in the game. His first solid lead had just walked out the front door, and instead of tracking Daniel, all Eagan could think about was kissing Della again. His senses were overloaded with the memory of how she looked, her scent and how she tasted.

His imagination shifted into hyperdrive. He suspected her blood would leave him both sated and jazzed for days. The only way to find out for sure would be to strip them both down and get skin-to-skin in a tangle of arms and legs in that brass bed right upstairs from where he now stood. Whoa, boy, that painted one hell of an image. One he couldn't afford to hold on to right now. In fact, not ever. He needed to leave before he lost it altogether. He jumped the length of the steps, wincing only slightly when his leg reminded him that it still wasn't happy with him. Ignoring the twinge, he hung the ladder up on the wall and headed back upstairs.

He really hated the thought of missing out on that pie. Besides, it would hurt Della's feelings if he refused payment for services rendered. Rather than think about why that bothered him so much, he walked out into the diner, pretending to be on his phone. He hung up as soon as Della spotted him.

"Sorry, I got another call and have to leave. Any chance I could get that pie to go?"

She nodded. "Will you be able to come for dinner tomorrow night?"

Lies upon lies. "I'm not sure, but I'll try."

As he yanked his coat back on, he cursed himself for a fool. Why had he said that? Stupid question when he already knew the answer. It was because he'd kissed her. She wasn't the kind of woman who gave herself up to a moment like that easily or often. He knew next to nothing about her, but he knew that much.

He'd kissed Della as if it meant something. If he simply disappeared now, it would hurt her. What had started off as a joke had turned into something far more serious and not just for her. Yet another reason to exit from Della's life with as much grace as he could muster.

"Here's the pie. It's blueberry."

"Thank you." He stared down at the container. "Your employee Daniel said it was his favorite."

"If you come back tomorrow, you can try the chocolate so you have something to compare it to." Her eyes twinkled when she added, "Of course, then there's also peach and the banana cream, not to mention I also make a mean Dutch apple pie. Gee, Eagan, think how much you've been missing out on all this time."

"That's just mean, woman." He opened the door, still oddly reluctantly to step out into the darkness.

Della surprised him by raising up to press a quick kiss to his cheek. "Not mean, just truthful. Now go. My electric bill is bad enough without trying to heat the streets of Seattle, too."

He did as she said, walking away without looking back. Her kiss was meant as a small gesture between friends but still somehow packed a powerful punch. All he knew was that if it was really cold outside, he didn't notice.

Two hours later the pie was gone and the kiss-induced warmth had dissipated, leaving Eagan cold and empty. Hungry, too, but not for pie. He wanted blood, warm and straight from the source. Della's vein, to be specific.

Most often he fed from blood packs at the precinct. They kept a steady supply on hand for the nights the vampires on the force didn't have time to hunt for themselves. A hungry vampire was more likely to lose control in the midst of a crisis. No one wanted that. It had happened before, and it wasn't a pretty picture.

Just for grins, Eagan swung by the diner one last time. The lights were out, upstairs and down. He stopped briefly before moving on. He'd followed Daniel's scent all the way to an apartment a few blocks away. After watching to make sure the kid stayed in for the night, he'd circled the area looking for the two young vamps. He hadn't really expected to find them. If they'd fed from Daniel, they were probably done hunting for the night.

Time to head back to the office and report in. He hoped Lt. Hughes would assign someone to keep an eye on Daniel whenever Eagan couldn't. After that, he'd chug down a couple of packs of blood and seek out his own bed.

For the first time since starting this case, it felt like he'd made progress. Not enough, but at least now they had the identity of one of the teenagers involved. With luck, Daniel was the first link in the chain that would lead them right to those behind the attacks.

EAGAN HAD SPENT the past twenty-four hours trying without success to find another lead in the case, one that would allow him to put some distance between him and Della. There were so many reasons he needed to stay away from her, but he was still tempted to accept her dinner invitation.

He remained convinced that blowing her off, even knowing it would hurt her feelings, was the right thing to do for both of them.

Soon, maybe in just a few days, he'd be but a faint memory. Someone she might think of briefly when she took down the Christmas lights and mistletoe.

He hated knowing that.

Now that they knew that Daniel was involved, he'd convinced his lieutenant that Eagan no longer needed to use the diner for cover. Since they knew where the kid lived, they could keep an eye on Daniel whenever he wasn't in school or working. He suspected his boss knew he wasn't being completely forthcoming on why, but Hughes had let it slide. Eagan had walked out of his office determined to spend the night alone, once again an outsider looking in.

Instead, here he was standing in the alley across the street again, his feet leaden and reluctant to move. In or out? Which was it going to be?

Out.

He caught himself rubbing his chest as if his heart hurt. How stupid was that? It didn't help that twice he'd seen Della standing at the door and peering up and down the street. Was she looking for him or someone else? No way to know and the answer didn't matter. It wouldn't change anything.

Restless and edgy, he headed back down the alley to the next block. With luck he'd eventually cross paths with someone he could take out his bad mood on.

Fangs down and predatory senses running hot, he was ready to hunt.

CHAPTER SIX

THE PAST THREE DAYS had been long, hard and hurtful. Even decorating the small tree she'd bought for the front window hadn't improved Della's mood. Normally, unwrapping the ornaments she'd collected over the years had her smiling as she sang along with the Christmas music playing on the radio. Right now it felt like just one more thing on her long to-do list before turning in for the night.

It was bad enough that Eagan had been a no-show for the past three nights, but then she'd gotten in an argument over him with Lupe. Yeah, maybe she overreacted when her friend noticed that Della had kept the front table available all evening just in case he came. Lupe looked thoroughly disgusted and said flat out that it would be best for all concerned if Eagan never stepped through the front door again.

Yeah, her emotions were a tangled mess right now. The whole thought of never seeing him again hurt a lot more than was justified by their brief acquaintance. If only Lupe would simply say what she had against the man, but she refused. After a brief exchange of words, Della had announced to any and all who were listening that regardless of Eagan's reasons for not returning, he was still welcome anytime.

To make matters worse, right after Lupe left, Della had a run-in with Daniel over something equally stupid—his sweatshirt. The kitchen had been steaming hot, but he'd kept it on even though he'd been sweating like crazy. When she'd asked him about it, he'd exploded. Even though she'd tried to apologize, he'd continued to slam pots and pans around loudly enough to bother her customers.

In the end, she'd sent him home. Her only worry was that when he'd walked out of the door, he'd headed in the opposite direction of his family's apartment. At least he'd called her an hour later to apologize. She'd heard his brothers playing in the background, so he'd been calling from home. A few of the knots in her stomach had loosened, but not all of them. There was something going on with her young friend. All she could do was cross her fingers that he got it figured out and soon.

She pulled out the next ornament and smiled. It was a small gargoyle, a funny mix of ugly and cute. Her mother had collected gargoyles for years, and Della had bought her a new one every Christmas. This little guy was the one she'd given her mother their last Christmas together. Every year since he had held a position of honor on her tree, right out front where everyone could see him because nothing screamed Christmas like a guy with an impish smile and fangs. The thought made her giggle.

Earlier, she'd wrapped a few packages to put under the tree for her favorite customers. Over the summer, she had knitted a cap and scarf for Harry and tucked a handmade gift certificate for five dinners inside. She'd bought a small wolf ornament for Lupe, who collected them much as Della did gargoyles. For Daniel, she'd gotten a gift card to one of his favorite clothing stores. The rest of her staff got similar presents. She arranged them around the bottom of the tree and stood back to admire her work.

It looked good. Christmas was only three days away now. She always stayed open on the twenty-fourth for the last-minute shoppers. Christmas Day, too, could also be a lonely day without someone to share it with. She should know. Lacking any family of her own, she'd built one.

Each year more and more people came by. A few stayed the whole time. Others popped in for a few minutes before heading on to their next stop. She kept the menu simple: soup, homemade bread, mulled cider and Christmas cookies. That left her free to play board games and watch favorite holiday movies with her friends. Everyone pitched in to help with the cleanup.

She hung the last few ornaments and lugged the empty boxes back down to the basement. Despite the late hour, she was too restless to go to bed. Maybe she'd bake that last batch of cookies now instead of in the morning. Tomorrow she'd box them up with a bow to hand out as gifts.

Eagan popped into her mind. Despite his continued absence, she wanted him to have something under the tree with his name on it. Just in case.

She crossed the dining room to look outside. For the past few days she'd had the strangest feeling she was being watched. Normally that would creep her out, but this was different. Maybe she was playing mind games with herself, but she had the strangest sense that someone was watching over her.

Feeling foolish, she turned off the lights and headed for the kitchen. Those cookies wouldn't bake themselves. She tied on her apron and turned on the ovens to heat. While they did their thing, she went into the storeroom and half dragged, half carried a new fifty-pound bag of flour out into the kitchen and heaved it up on the counter.

Then she went back to get a package of baker's chocolate. After unwrapping it, she used her chef's knife to chop the dark chocolate into small pieces before dropping them into the top of her double boiler. She added the first batch to the pan and then went back to cutting as she did her best to ignore her aching back and tired feet.

As late as it was, she probably should've waited until tomorrow to start this, but baking always relaxed her. She kept rocking the knife, whittling away at the chocolate. When she had another pile ready, she scooped it up with the back edge of her knife blade.

That's when the trouble started. Her foot slipped causing her to bump the counter with her hip hard enough to send the bag of flour toppling over to collide with her arm. The chocolate flew everywhere while the razor-sharp blade sliced her hand wide-open.

A flood of crimson pooled in the palm of her hand and poured onto the floor. She grabbed a clean towel and stepped over the pile of flour on her way to the dining room. She'd call for help from the phone by the register and unlock the front door so the medics could get in.

She dripped a trail of blood on the floor all the way into the other room. Her head was already woozy as she fumbled with the lock. She needed to sit down. Now. Maybe lying down would be even smarter, but not until she called 911. She'd been using her good hand to hold pressure on the cut. When she let go to dial the phone the blood started gushing again.

Stars and spots danced in her eyes, and the floor came rushing up. Or at least she thought it was, but somehow she never hit bottom. Something had stopped her fall. No, someone. As her world spun, she closed her eyes and whispered a one-word question.

"Who?"

"Della, it's me."

She knew that deep voice. That, combined with the

smell of fine leather, put a name to the man who had swooped her up in his arms and then settled her in a chair near the kitchen. How odd that he'd kneel at her feet.

Her eyes stubbornly refused to cooperate enough for her to see her rescuer clearly. "Eagan, is that you?"

"Yes, damn it, it is. Now relax and let me see your hand. I'm going to lift the towel away to see how badly you're hurt."

She tried to comply but couldn't quit shivering. Eagan muttered a curse and then wrapped her in his coat. As grateful as she was for its warmth, she was worried about ruining it. When she tried to shrug it off her shoulders, he tugged it right back up in place.

"It will get blood all over it."

"It won't be the first time. Now sit still and let me do this."

Eagan hissed when he peeled the towel away from her hand. "Damn, that's deep. Okay, we'll do this the hard way."

He caught her chin in his hand. "Open your eyes and look at me, Della."

Although his voice remained calm, she didn't mistake his request for anything other than a direct order. She stared down into his blue eyes. No, right now they weren't blue at all, but black. "Eagan, your eyes!"

"I know, but don't be scared. I won't hurt you."

That darkness in his gaze was swallowing her whole. She could still hear him talking, but from a long distance away. He smiled at her. Such a sad, sad smile on his handsome face. And when had his teeth gotten so big? Not all of them. Just those two.

He was nodding, so maybe she'd said all that out loud, although she didn't think so.

He kept talking. "Breathe slowly, Della, and everything will be fine. Some of this is going to seem weird, but I'm hoping you won't remember any of it. I swear you can trust me not to hurt you."

She smiled down into those blazing black eyes. "I know that, Eagan."

Then he did the oddest thing. He raised her hand up to his mouth and licked her blood-drenched palm.

MAN OH MAN, HER BLOOD was so damned sweet. Eagan lapped at the open wound, letting the coagulant in his saliva do its job. Already the flow was growing more sluggish. He turned his attention to the rest of her hand, cleansing the surrounding skin so he could make sure there were no other secondary wounds.

She'd sure done one hell of a number on her hand. What was she doing messing with a knife this late at night? She had to be tired after putting in a full day and half the night waiting on her customers.

By the time he got the worst of the blood cleaned away he knew there was no way he was going to be able to block this from her mind. Although the chemicals in his saliva would eventually seal the wound closed, they weren't powerful enough to make the resulting scar fade fast enough to keep her from seeing it.

The other problem was the potential damage to tendons and nerves. Della needed her hand to do her job. Seattle offered some of the best medical care in the world, but the healing properties of his blood would beat a surgeon's best efforts. It wouldn't take much. Just a few drops.

She was already going to freak out over this. He might as well go for broke. Della might hate what he'd done, might hate what he was, but he could live with that if it gave her back full use of her hand.

He covered the wound with the bloody towel to keep her from seeing it closing up on its own accord.

"I'll be right back, Della. You need fluids."

She frowned. "Shouldn't we go to the hospital? I need stitches."

His hold on her mind was already slipping, which meant he needed to get moving. "It's not as bad as you thought, but I'll keep an eye on it. If you need emergency care, I'll see that you get it."

In the kitchen, he rooted through the industrial refrigerator for something that would cover the taste of his blood. The best he could come up with was a bottle of chai tea. He cut into the pad of his thumb and squeezed a few drops of blood into a mug and then added a few more. Better too much than too little. After adding the tea, he gave it a quick stir with his finger and hurried back to Della.

He shoved the mug into her free hand. "Drink this down."

"Bossy."

"I know, but this is the best thing for what ails you."

She dutifully took a sip. Her eyebrows drew together in a frown. "What is this?"

"Chai tea."

"It doesn't taste like any tea I've ever tasted."

"I added my own special blend of ingredients." That was true enough.

After several sips, she smiled. "I like it. You'll have to give me the recipe."

He knelt by her side again. "How about I promise to make it for you anytime you want some?"

She drained it to the last drop. Already her color was improving and her eyes looked more focused. On him. Really seeing him for the first time.

"Your eyes," she whispered, reaching out to touch his cheek. "I wasn't dreaming. They are black."

Her gaze dropped to his mouth. "And your teeth. What happened to them?"

He rocked back on his heels, putting that much room between them. The bleeding had stopped, but the scent still hung heavily in the air, leaving his control shaky.

"It's the blood, Della. It calls to me."

"That makes no sense, Eagan. Why would you say such a thing?"

He stood up. "Because it's true. Sit still while I get you another drink."

And throw the blood-soaked towel outside in the trash and pour bleach on it to kill the scent, which was making it nearly impossible to keep his vampire nature under control. For both their sakes, he also needed to mop up the gruesome trail that stretched across two rooms.

He didn't bother to hide his unnatural speed while cleaning up. He could hear Della moving around. Based on her footsteps, she was in the ladies' room washing her hand.

"What the heck? That's not possible."

While waiting for her to reappear, he refilled her tea, this time without the extra ingredient. He poured a glass for himself, too. A stiff shot of scotch or three would've done him more good, but that wasn't an option right now. He leaned his shoulder against the wall and waited for the inquisition to begin.

CHAPTER SEVEN

DELLA STARED INTO THE mirror over the sink and tried to come to terms with what she was seeing and figure out whatever it was that Eagan was trying not to tell her. Her stomach lurched in fear when she held her freshly washed hand up to the bright light overhead to study her palm. It hadn't changed since the cold water had washed away the last of the dried blood.

A long, jagged line stretched from just under her forefinger down to her wrist. A reddish scar, not an open wound. How was that possible? The scar itself was proof enough that she wasn't dreaming that she'd cut herself badly and bled her way to the front door. That much she remembered. After that the facts became fuzzy. Eagan had appeared out of nowhere to keep her from hitting the floor.

What next? His eyes had gone all weird and so had his teeth. Who had solid black eyes? No one. Who had such long canine teeth? Not Eagan the last time she'd seen him. What had changed?

At first she'd thought he'd leaned in closer to study her wound. But no, he'd licked her hand, over and over again. She closed her eyes as she remembered the soft bobbing motion of his head as the smooth velvet of his tongue had swept across her palm.

What had he said? The blood called to him. Who said something like that?

A soft knock at the door reminded her she wasn't alone.

"Della, please come out or let me come in. We need to talk. I won't hurt you."

She hadn't locked the door, so there was nothing keeping Eagan out. He was waiting for an invitation.

"Come in."

The bathroom wasn't big. Just three stalls and a counter. She watched Eagan's reflection as he eased into the room, moving slowly and obviously unsure of his welcome. When he realized where she was looking, he grinned, briefly revealing those freaky teeth.

He gestured toward the mirror. "That's a myth, by the way."

"What is?"

He edged closer, but managed not to block her access to the door. "That I have no reflection. I also like garlic."

"You're not making any sense, Eagan."

But he was. Horrible, terrifying, but amazing sense. All the pieces shifted and turned until one by one they fell into place. A single word filled her mind, shouting its truth even though common sense and reality said it couldn't be true.

Eagan was already nodding. "The word you're looking for is *vampire*. Believe me, if I could make you forget this night ever happened, I would. My people are gifted with the ability to affect a human's thoughts, but there's no way to deny the scar on your hand."

She stared down at her palm in wonder. "My hand is almost healed."

Holding it out for his inspection, she asked, "How is that possible?"

That same sad smile was back. "My saliva has a coagulant that stopped the bleeding, but my blood has even stronger healing properties. I put a few drops in your tea. By this time tomorrow, that scar will have all but disappeared."

Her lips curled in distaste. "Your blood! Why would you do such a thing!"

Eagan flinched as if she'd hit him. "Because you cut your hand bad enough to cause permanent nerve and tendon damage. I couldn't let that happen, not if I could prevent it. Now, if you're all right, I'll be going."

He stopped in the doorway to pull out a business card and sat it on the counter. "I have no right to ask you to keep this between the two of us, Della, but it would be better for all concerned if you did. Here's my number if you should ever want to talk…or anything."

His eyes faded back to their usual beautiful shade of blue. As the door drifted shut, she reached for the card. She wasn't sure what she expected, but all it said was his name and a phone number. Not much in the way of information. Nothing like Eagan McHale, Vampire. Or Hero. Or Rescuer of Damsels in Distress.

She shoved the card in her pocket, determined to hold on to that much of him. Maybe she should be scared, but she wasn't. Eagan had just taken her whole worldview and shattered it, but he'd also saved her. In her book, that made him a hero in every sense of the world. He'd also had to reveal his secret life to her, trusting Della with his truth before walking away. Why? Because he'd assumed she wouldn't want him to stay.

Silly man.

Tearing out of the bathroom, she ran straight through the diner and out into the cold Seattle night. Where was he? She looked up and down the block. Nothing. She stared at the alley across the street where he'd stood before. "Eagan!"

She strained to listen. All she could hear was the distant traffic on the interstate. "Eagan, come back. Please."

Nothing but silence. She fingered his card in her pocket. At least she had a way to get in touch with him. The only question was if she should try now or wait. Her eyes burned with tears from the shock of everything that had happened combined with a profound sense of loss, as if she'd let something precious slip through her fingers.

Time to go inside. She still had a mess to clean up if she didn't want to answer a lot of awkward questions in the morning. But before she went inside, she froze. That same feeling of being watched was back.

She closed her eyes, afraid to look, and even more afraid that she was imagining things. "Eagan, tell me that it's you."

His voice came from right behind her shoulder. "Are you sure you want it to be?"

Two steps backward was all it took to bump into his solid strength. "Very sure."

He didn't back away, but neither did he embrace her. "I can't change what I am, Della."

"I don't remember asking you to."

When his hands came to rest on her shoulders, she tipped her head back to look up at him. The blue in his eyes was ringed with a circle of black. Striking, but not scary. The tips of those long teeth were a little unnerving. When he realized that she was looking at them, he clamped his lips shut.

That's all it took to have her spinning around to face him. She brushed her fingertips across that stern mouth and followed up the caress with a soft kiss. "Sorry, Eagan, I didn't mean to stare. This is all new to me."

He remained stiff, poised as if to disappear again if she made the wrong move or said the wrong thing. Okay, if he needed her to take charge, she would, starting with trailing her hands up the length of his arms up to encircle his neck. She slowly eased forward, closing the last small gap between them, seeking his warmth.

Rather than rush things, she laid her cheek against the staccato beat of his heart. Had he just pressed a soft kiss to the top of her head? Maybe. She hoped so. She sighed as his arms slowly wrapped around her with a gentle strength that made it clear he wouldn't be letting go anytime soon.

Time to step up the game.

"Kiss me, Eagan."

He looked so darn serious. "You're playing with fire here, Della. There are things you should know before we go any further. About me. What I am and what I do."

She smiled and shook her head. "It's just a kiss, Eagan."

That was a lie, and they both knew it. That didn't mean that she was strong enough to resist temptation, and evidently neither was he.

He tipped his head at just the perfect angle to mate his mouth to hers. She smiled against the gentle pressure, loving the soft feel of his lips. She traced the full curve of his mouth with her tongue. When she felt the tips of his canine teeth, she paused long enough to test their sharpness.

Eagan growled deep in his chest, ramping up their embrace from a slow burn to a total conflagration in only seconds. The fire slid through her veins, through her bones, to pool hot and deep within her. She raised up on her toes, frantic to get closer, demanding he fill the emptiness that had haunted her life for far too long.

A single kiss would never be enough, not when she needed so much more from him. With considerable effort she managed to pull away long enough to say, "Let's go inside."

And if she hadn't made her intentions clear enough, she added, "Take me upstairs, Eagan. Now."

When he hesitated, she caught his hand in hers and tugged him along in her wake. As soon as they were inside with the door locked against the world outside, he pressed her against the wall for another soul-searing kiss. His powerful hands kneaded her bottom as he rocked against her, the rigid proof of his desire for her all too clear—and impressive. Her desire for his touch was unlike anything she'd ever experienced before.

There were too many layers of clothing between them, though, when she was craving skin-to-skin contact. While she loved how Eagan looked in his leather duster, right now she wanted the coat gone. He smiled against her mouth as she jerked it down his arms and let it fall to the floor.

She was that much closer to all that sleek muscle. Next up, his shirt. But as she tugged it free of his jeans, a car drove down the street, its headlights passing over them. Della froze at the reminder that they were standing where anyone could see them. If the two of them were going to follow this encounter to its logical conclusion, the front of the diner was not nearly private enough.

"My bedroom is better suited for this sort of thing."

Eagan rested his forehead against hers, his hands stroking her back. "Only if you're sure, Della. I can stop now. I can't guarantee I'll be able to if we go much further."

Ever the gentleman. She placed the palm of her hand over his heart, glad that she wasn't the only one with a pulse running at the red line. Staring up into his eyes, now more black than blue, she let her hand slide down and down until she cupped him through the heavy denim.

"I want you." She gently squeezed. "I want this."

He caught her wayward hand in his and brought it up to his lips for a soft kiss. "We should talk about what could happen if I take your blood again."

She was in no mood for conversation. Before she could protest, he swept her up against his chest, guiding her legs around his waist.

"But not now. We can talk afterward."

She buried her face next to his neck, drawing his scent deep into her lungs. "Perfect."

And it would be. She just knew it.

CHAPTER EIGHT

NOW THAT HE NO LONGER had to hide his true nature from Della, Eagan didn't hold back, taking the stairs three at a time. At the top, he headed straight for the bedroom and that brass bed that had haunted his thoughts for days. Not to mention his dreams. From the way Della dug her fingers into his shoulders and scrunched her eyes, maybe the speed hadn't been such a good idea. He gave her a quick squeeze, hoping to reassure her.

Thanks to his night vision, he moved easily through the shadowed rooms. He considered the lamp beside the bed, but wasn't sure if she'd want it on. The lights from the small Christmas tree by the window would be enough.

"I'm going to put you down now."

Della nodded and released her death hold on him as he lowered her slowly, waiting to make sure her legs would support her before letting go. He crooked a finger and used it to lift her chin, trying to read her mood without invading the privacy of her thoughts.

"You still up for this?"

To his immense relief, she smiled, a teasing glint in her dark eyes. "As long as you are. If not, I'm betting I can fix that."

She waited to see if he got the joke and looked pleased when he grinned. Damned if he could remember ever laughing with a lover.

"Believe me, I'm definitely up for it."

To prove his point he picked her up by the waist and tossed her down on the mattress and followed her down, making a place for himself between her legs. Her eyes widened as he rocked against her, the slow friction driving both of them a little crazy.

She dragged him down for another of her mind-frying kisses as he worked his hands underneath that great ass of hers. God, he loved its perfect shape and fit. She immediately lifted her legs high around his hips, slowly driving him crazy as she brought her core into direct contact with his erection.

Time to get shed of all these clothes. He rolled to the side and stripped off his shirt. Della followed suit, sending her Santa T-shirt flying through the air to land on the rocker across the room. His pants were a little trickier to deal with, but the jeans along with his boxers closely followed.

When Della stood up on the mattress to shimmy out of her jeans, he was pretty sure his tongue was hanging out. All those luscious curves just for him. When she hooked her fingers in the elastic of her panties he stopped her. There were some jobs a man wanted to take care of himself. He knelt in front of her and ran his hands up the back of her thighs to support her as he nuzzled the soft curve of her belly and then worked his way lower. Her breath caught in her throat as he reached the juncture of her legs, testing and tasting with his tongue.

"Eagan! You can't!"

"Yes, I can."

He wasn't sure if she was protesting or approving, but he loved the huskiness in her voice as she repeated his name a second time. Smiling up at her, he slowly dragged the scrap of blue lace down the length of her legs. She held on to his shoulders to steady herself as she lifted each foot in turn.

This time he cupped the round curves of her backside to hold her still while he used his tongue to slowly tear down the last bit of her control. He was pretty sure her nails were going to leave marks in his skin, but the little nips of pain only added to the intensity of the moment.

He drove her hard, not stopping until her whole body went rigid and then slowly folded down to straddle his thighs as she shuddered in release.

Finally, she lifted her head to smile at him, her eyes at half-mast. "Wow. That was amazing."

He thrust upward, pressing hard against her core. "Glad you liked it, but that was just the appetizer."

"What if I want dessert first?"

Her question was accompanied by a lingering kiss and wandering hands. If she kept that up, it would all be over before the party really got started. He picked her up and laid her back down on the bed, capturing those talented hands with one of his, holding them prisoner over her head.

As he looked his fill at her curvaceous body stretched out for his enjoyment, she blushed. He loved that hint of innocence mixed in with the siren. He nuzzled the lower curve of her breasts, deliberately taking a circuitous route to finally capture her pert nipple with his lips. So sweet. He worked it hard, enjoying the way her entire body undulated on the mattress in response.

"Eagan, you're driving me crazy."

"That's the whole idea," he murmured as he moved on to pay homage to her other breast.

As he learned what she liked and what she craved, her pulse called to him. He vowed not to take her vein. That didn't mean resisting the urge was easy. He pressed a kiss against the pulse point in her wrist, loving the soft throb just under the skin. Even that distant connection with her life's blood ramped up his need for her to a whole new height.

He needed to claim her. Now. With everything he had.

He closed his eyes, knowing they were more black than blue, not wanting to remind Della that her lover was something other than human. Then she opened her arms, her legs, her body to him. Her touch was so welcoming that he had to look, had to watch her pretty face as he took her.

"Hold on, sweetheart. I'll try to go slow. I don't want to hurt you."

They both knew he was talking about far more than just the joining of their bodies. There was a world of womanly understanding in those dark eyes gazing up him. She eased her hand between them, wrapping it around his shaft and guiding him right to where they both wanted him to be. With a series of sharp thrusts, he seated himself firmly in her welcoming heat.

He let out a slow breath, for the moment content to savor the profound connection. But then she stroked her hands down the length of his back to dig her fingernails into his ass, making a few demands of her own.

"Now, Eagan. Fast and hard."

Her demand flipped a switch, sending him right into overdrive. His hips flexed sharply, seating him even more deeply. He withdrew almost completely, only to immediately plunge deeper yet.

And again, over and over, until he was no longer conscious of himself or Della as individuals. There was only pounding sensation and burning desire coupled with a craving to claim her in every way he could as a man— and as a vampire.

Just as she keened out her second release, he buried his face at the juncture of her neck and shoulder. Before he realized what was happening, his fangs pierced her soft skin, and he took a long sweet pull directly from her vein.

Her legs clamped down around his thighs as she rode out her climax with a scream. That combined with the coppery beauty of her blood flooding down his throat was enough to throw Eagan plummeting over the edge with her. With a shout, he retracted his fangs and shuddered in her arms, pouring out his own release deep within her.

When the last wave of triumph crashed over them both, he briefly collapsed in the sanctuary of her arms before rolling onto his back. He tucked Della in at his side although right then he really needed to put some space between them. If he did that, she might interpret it as rejection, and he wouldn't risk hurting her that way.

But as he thought about what he'd just done, his lungs refused to fill with air even as his fangs throbbed with the need for more blood. Her blood. As much as she'd let him take. To stake his claim on Della, to make her his permanently.

What a damn fool he was. His rational mind argued that this was a fling, a momentary escape from a life spent alone hunting in the cold shadows. It had to be.

But the truth was that he'd inadvertently completed the circle of connections that could link his life with Della's in the way vampires did when claiming a mate. In a very short time, he'd tasted her blood while treating her wound, and then she'd taken his blood even if it was without her knowledge. Those two things alone wouldn't have caused her lasting any harm.

But in a moment of weakness, he'd lost control and taken her blood a second time while they'd made love.

All of it within the time frame needed to seal the connection.

The only thing that would save them was if the amount of blood he'd given her had been too small. The hand she had on his chest was the one that had been lacerated. He turned it over.

No cut. No scab. No scar.

Son of a bitch, he'd given her enough of his blood to complete the bond. As a human, she might be able to walk away with little or no effect. Normally, a vampire seeking to take a human mate would continue to feed her small amounts of his blood, slowly building up both her tolerance and her need for it.

But through their newly forged connection, he'd always know where she was and what she was feeling. There would be an empty ache in his chest and his heart that nothing would ever completely assuage. His fault. His problem.

He needed to leave, to put some distance between them so he could get his head around what he'd done.

"Eagan?" His name came out on a yawn. "Is everything all right."

No.

"Yes," he lied as he sat up on the edge of the bed. "I just realized what time it was. I need to get back to my place before dawn."

She rose up to look at him. "So the reflection and garlic are myths, but not the whole sun allergy thing?"

"Yeah, unless you like your vampire well-done."

His clothes were scattered across the room. When he retrieved his boxers and pants, he realized that they'd never gotten around to getting under the covers. She'd be cold as soon as he moved away.

He left the jeans unzipped and started to turn down

the quilt she used as a comforter. "Let me help you get between the sheets."

She smiled up at him. "I've been putting myself to bed for years, Eagan."

Della did so much for everyone around her, and as far as he could tell she asked for very little in return. It seemed important to do this one last insignificant thing for her. He got her tucked in, fighting hard not to crawl right back in beside her. To take her again, further cementing their connection.

He picked up his shirt and shoes before tiptoeing toward the door. Before he made it, she spoke one last time.

"Thank you, Eagan. For my hand, and well, everything."

What could he say to that? Certainly not "anytime," not when he already knew he wouldn't be coming back. He settled for a simple, "You're welcome. Now get some sleep while you can. My blood might have given you a boost, but healing that fast will still have taken a lot out of you."

"Nag," she teased. "See you later."

No, in fact she wouldn't, not if he were careful. He still had a case to solve, but then he'd move on to the next assignment. Maybe he'd even consider a transfer to Portland or even somewhere in California, any place that would keep him too busy to think about what he might have held in his arms only to lose it minutes later.

CHAPTER NINE

THE MORNING CAME WAY TOO EARLY, but somewhere between slumber and awake, it hit Della that she'd left the kitchen a total wreck last night. What had her staff thought about walking into a room splattered with flour and blood? How could she explain it when her hand no longer had even a hint of a scar? She couldn't very well tell them that her lover had magically healed her wound. Heck, she hadn't come to terms with Eagan being a vampire herself.

She bolted upright and charged for the bathroom. A quick shower and clean clothes did little to disguise the effects of a night spent…well, spent the way she'd spent hers.

Flexing her wounded hand, she couldn't detect even the smallest amount of stiffness or pain, all thanks to Eagan and the gift of his trust. She poked and prodded, trying to figure out how she felt about the knowledge that she owed the use of her hand to the ingestion of his blood.

Definitely grateful, even if a bit queasy if she thought about it too much.

She also checked the side of her neck, looking to see if he'd given her a love bite. She had vague memories of a brief pain right before he exploded deep inside her. Nope, no mark, but the memory of how spectacular the sex had been left her smiling. It might have been a long time since she'd last had a man in her bed, but no one else had ever made her feel the way Eagan did.

Which left only one question unanswered: would he disappear from her life as quickly as he'd appeared?

She very much feared the answer was yes. Obviously he'd never meant for her to know the truth about what he was. That she'd want him in her arms and in her bed had clearly come as a shock to the man. She'd been a bit surprised, too, but couldn't regret her decision.

His reluctance to share the secret of his people's existence was understandable. After all, he wasn't just outing himself to her. Who else hid their secret nature right in plain sight? Were there only vampires or did some of the other ancient myths actually walk the streets of Seattle?

Now wasn't the time. She really needed to get downstairs and do damage control on the mess she'd left behind. Explaining the flour was one thing; the blood would definitely be harder.

Bracing herself for the inquisition, she paused at the bottom of the steps for a calming breath. Turning the corner, she stared in amazement. Everyone was calm—well, as calm as a diner kitchen ever was at the height of the breakfast hour.

Skillets sizzled; pots banged; and dishes rattled. Orders were shouted, and the cook was complaining that his assistant wasn't keeping up and where the hell was the dishwasher? All normal. All the usual.

"Good morning!"

Tennessee glowered at her. "Not now, Della. You know how I hate when you're bright and chipper in the morning. Either pitch in or get out of the way. Daniel didn't show up again."

Okay, that was worrisome, but right now she didn't have time to hunt the boy down. He was out of school for the next two weeks, which is why he was scheduled on a morning shift. Daniel always wanted more hours when he had a break from school.

"I'll fill in for him."

She ignored Tenn's glare and gave him a quick pat on the cheek as she passed by. He pretended to hate it, but she didn't miss the way his lips twitched in a brief smile before he could hide it. The man had showed up six months before looking for a job. He had an interesting past; she was sure of it. Maybe even a questionable one, but hiring him had been the smartest thing she'd ever done.

As she tied on an apron, Tenn poured her cup of coffee and plated up a couple of eggs and toast for her. "Eat first. By the way, thanks for cleaning the grill, Della. I meant to do it yesterday, but ran out of time."

She'd done no such thing, but she could guess who had—Eagan. When he'd found the time, she had no idea, but bless him for doing so.

"It was nothing."

Literally. She made quick work of her meal. The two of them worked side by side, falling into a familiar rhythm until the backlog of orders was under control.

During a brief lull, she called Daniel's home number but got no answer. Maybe his mother had taken the kids to her sister's house. She sometimes did that when school was out. A phone call would've been nice, but Daniel was getting more and more unpredictable.

She'd try again later but for now she had paperwork to do. Anything to pass the time to see if Eagan returned at nightfall. The pragmatic part of her was betting not. The man obviously had some serious trust issues. All things considered, perhaps he had good cause.

But this was the season of miracles, so she wouldn't give up hope. Not yet.

When the last bill was paid, she looked around for something else to keep her mind occupied. Cookies. She'd never gotten back to making those chocolate-dipped ones she'd been working on last night. Tenn wouldn't begrudge her a small corner of the kitchen, would he?

Yeah, he would. The man was nothing if not territorial. Too bad. She needed some way to pass the time until sunset, which was still too many hours away.

Tenn gave her a puzzled look when she started pulling out the ingredients for the cookies. He said nothing at all when she encroached on his normal area. Maybe he sensed something was bothering her, but it wasn't like him to poke his nose into her business.

As she rolled out the dough, he cocked a hip against the counter and watched her. "I'm figuring it must be man trouble."

She kept right on working, trying to decide if she'd heard him right. When she looked around to see where she left the cookie cutters, he calmly pointed six inches to the left of where she'd just set down the rolling pin.

"Thanks."

"So, you want to talk about it?"

"Talk about what?"

"Oh, I don't know," he said with a shrug. "Maybe whatever had you up cleaning the kitchen at all hours or whoever put that smile on your face this morning."

Okay, now she was blushing. "Tenn, in the six months I've known you, you've never asked me one personal question. Why start now?"

"Because I've never seen you screw up a recipe like you just did that batch of dough you're working to death. That was cake flour you used, not all-purpose, and you added salt twice."

Seriously? She tasted the dough. Rats, she had. No wonder it was acting strange.

"You could've said something sooner, you big jerk." She scraped it up and tossed it in the trash.

Tenn laughed. "I figured it was therapeutic. Now, what's up?"

She'd never expected a guy who looked more like a biker than a fry cook would double as a therapist. It was the real concern in his caramel-brown eyes that got her talking.

"I'm worried about Daniel. Something is up with him, and he won't let me in."

Tenn's expression turned grim. "You can't save everyone, Della, no matter how hard you try."

"I know, especially if they don't want to be saved." She started measuring out the correct ingredients into the mixer. "And there's Eagan. You haven't met him because he only comes in during the evenings."

Tenn was already nodding. "Must be the one Lupe was complaining about."

"No doubt. She took an immediate dislike to him even though she's never said more than five words to him."

Tenn looked away. "She has her reasons, but it's nothing he's done."

It was pretty clear that was all he was going to say on the subject. Did Lupe's reaction to Eagan have something to do with his vampire nature? If so, how did Lupe recognize what he was? Did she even want to know? Rather than press for answers, Della concentrated on finishing the cookies before the lunchtime rush started.

SLEEP WAS SHORT-LIVED. By midafternoon Eagan was up and pacing the floor of his condo. He swore the clock had quit moving at all. Finally, he couldn't stand being cooped up any longer. He'd be better off working than beating himself up over the events of the previous night.

He headed to the garage. His car had windows which blocked the sun's most lethal wavelengths. If he drove straight to the precinct, he'd be all right since the day was gray and overcast.

At least at the office he'd be able to do something useful. Hell, maybe he'd dazzle his boss by getting caught up on his files. Anything at all to keep from thinking about Della. About how right she'd felt in his arms, how perfectly they'd fit together.

Her easy acceptance of his truth had been a real shocker, but then that's what Della did. She opened her door and her heart to those who didn't quite fit anywhere else. He had no right to take advantage of her generous nature, not when it meant dragging her into the darkness with him.

But damn, he wanted to do exactly that. The thought of coming home to her every morning had him having to adjust the fit of his jeans. God, he had it bad.

The squad room was empty when he got there and so he tackled a stack of papers. An hour later, he finished the last report and tossed it on the pile. Now what? Might as well spread the joy. He picked up the folders and headed for the boss's office. The lieutenant looked up at Eagan's knock on the door and waved him in. His eyes widened at the stack of files in Eagan's hand. He immediately grabbed a newspaper off the corner of his desk and started flipping through it like a madman.

"Okay, what are you looking for?"

Hughes tossed the paper aside. "To see when hell had frozen over. That's when I figured you'd get around to doing those reports. Good thing I don't have a bad heart because the shock could've killed me."

Okay, he'd never known the man actually had a sense of humor. Eagan dropped the pile in the lieutenant's in-basket.

"Is there anything else I can do?"

As soon as he spoke, he wished he could take it all back because his boss went on point. There'd be no escape now.

"Okay, McHale, park it and tell me what's going on. Is there a problem with the case?"

"No, sir. Once the sun goes down, I'll be following up on that kid we've been watching. I checked in with the day crew earlier, but there's been no sign of movement today."

He frowned. "I know school is out for the holidays, but it worries me that no one has seen him all today."

"He has a job. Maybe he's at the diner."

"I'll have someone check there." But not him. He couldn't risk Della catching him spying on her place—or her.

Hughes leaned back in his chair. "Someone? Why not you? I thought you had an in with the owner."

"Yes, sir, but people were paying a bit too much attention to me."

"People or a single person, Eagan?"

He wasn't sure which was more surprising: the sympathy in his boss's voice or his use of Eagan's first name.

"The owner. Della."

"And that's a problem for you?"

"For her. She's human, sir."

He found himself pouring out the whole story, figuring the boss could only kill him once. Instead, Hughes got up to fix them each a cup of coffee laced with the scotch he kept in a locked cabinet. The burn did little to warm the ache in Eagan's gut, but he appreciated the gesture.

"I'd tell you that was a damn stupid thing to do, Eagan,

but you're a good cop because of your desire to protect people. It would've gone against your nature to let that woman suffer when you could fix it, especially when you've obviously got a major thing for her."

Eagan sipped the coffee as an excuse not to say anything. Hughes stared at him for a while. "I'm guessing she showed her gratitude with more than a simple thank you."

Rather than deny it, Eagan confessed the worst of it, ending with, "I lost control and took her blood a second time."

Hughes's eyebrows shot straight up. "Does she understand the significance of that?"

"I didn't tell her." But he'd wanted to. Still did, for that matter.

"Why the hell not?"

"She's human." Like he hadn't already pointed that out.

"So? From what you've told me, she obviously didn't hate what you are."

"No, in fact, I tried to leave right after I healed her hand and told her what I was, but she called me back inside."

Hughes finally sat back down. "Did she kick your ass out of bed when your eyes flashed black or when she saw your fangs?"

"No, sir, she didn't." A fact that still amazed him. "But you know what our lives are like. Always living with secrets. And then there's my job. Some women aren't cut out to be a cop's wife."

"Sounds like a bunch of bullshit excuses, McHale. You're doing this woman and yourself a great disservice by not giving her a chance. She won't appreciate you deciding what she can or can't handle. I'm also guessing that you've never felt like this about a woman, and you're running scared."

Was it true? Was he afraid to risk being hurt if she decided she couldn't accept Eagan's true nature? He thought back to last night and how perfect it had been to connect with Della on so many levels. She'd felt—

Scared? He sat up straighter. Not him. Her. Right now. Della was frightened, the taste of her fear almost overwhelming. He lurched to his feet.

"Eagan, what's wrong?"

"It's Della, sir. She's terrified, and I don't know why. I've got to go."

He was already running for the door, but Hughes kept pace with him. "Don't do anything stupid, McHale. Call for backup if you need it."

"I will."

He meant that, but only if there was time. If someone had laid a hand on Della, there would be hell to pay.

CHAPTER TEN

THE SUN HADN'T SET, but it was dark enough for Eagan to risk running straight for the diner. Seven minutes later he charged through the door, ready to take names and kick ass if that's what it took to find out what was wrong.

The wolf bitch was pacing back and forth just inside the door. When he walked in, her eyes flashed gold and her upper lip curled back over an impressive set of fangs. The rest of the diner was empty except for some guy wearing an apron walking out of the kitchen as he dried his hands on a towel.

Both he and Eagan sized each other up. Great. Another damned shifter, although Eagan was betting Della had no idea that's what he was.

He stared right back, not caring if that riled the guy's alpha nature. "Where is she, wolf? And don't bother telling me it's none of my business."

Lupe got between them. "Tennessee, don't tell him anything. He has no claim on Della."

The male wolf stepped around the female and sniffed the air around Eagan. He immediately nodded as if he'd just confirmed something he already guessed.

"He does have the right, Lupe. He's bonded to her."

Lupe actually growled, her eyes turning feral. "When did that happen? Darn her, I warned Della to stay away from you."

There was no time for this. "Woman, I have no idea

what your issues are with my kind and don't give a damn. Right now Della's in danger, so tell me what you know. If she gets hurt because you held something back, I guarantee you won't like what happens next."

The woman stared at him in disbelief. "She's not in danger. She just went to check on Daniel and take his family her presents for them."

Eagan got right in her face. "Like the man said, bitch, I'm bonded to her. That means I feel what she feels, and I'm telling you that she's terrified. I can track her through the bond, but it would help to know what I'll be walking into."

"If she's in danger, call the police."

He pulled out his badge and shoved in her obstinate face. "Damn it, I am the police. Now talk."

Some of the female's aggression died down. "Right after she left, Daniel called. When I told him that she was heading for his house, he sounded really worried and asked how long ago she'd left. He hung up before I could get more out of him."

Eagan pulled out one of his cards. "Here's my cell phone number. If you hear from her or the kid, call me immediately."

He headed back outside to start hunting. He closed his eyes and breathed deeply of the night air. Before he'd gone two steps, the diner door opened again. It was the male wolf shrugging on a biker jacket.

Eagan did not have time to screw around with Della's friends. "What do you want?"

Tennessee held up his hands and tipped his head to the side, a sign of surrender among his kind. "I know you can feel her through the bond, but it's too new to make finding her all that easy. I thought maybe you could use a second nose. Besides, I'm pretty handy in a fight."

The guy pulled up his sleeve to reveal a familiar tattoo. Eagan asked, "Special Forces?"

"Used to be. Now let's get moving."

As they loped down the street, Eagan prayed they'd get to her in time. If those young vamps sensed the bond between him and Della, they might kill her to end the connection.

The entire downtown area was clogged with last-minute shoppers. Every store and street were festooned with Christmas decorations. He bet Della loved it all.

But this was not the time to get distracted by bright shiny lights and thoughts of making love to Della underneath the mistletoe.

Right now the only Christmas present he wanted was to find Della and make sure she was safe. He struggled to keep his lips closed over his fangs, but it was difficult with all of his protective instincts running hot. Whoever had dared threaten his mate would pay with their blood.

He turned his focus inward, trying to sense if there'd been any change in what she was feeling. She was still scared, but no worse than she had been. He wasn't sure what that meant.

The only good news was that she was close. He could feel her too-rapid pulse and taste her fear on the night air. Tennessee had slowed down, tipping his head back as he turned in a circle to hunt for Della's scent.

"Am I glad to see you, young man. You, too, Tenn."

Eagan was so focused on Della that it took him several seconds to recognize the elderly man headed straight for them. The last thing he need right now was a distraction, even if Harry was one of Della's personal favorites.

"Not now, Harry. We've got a problem we're working on."

The old man caught Eagan's sleeve and refused to

let go. "I know. I just called the diner to summon help and spoke to Lupe. You're looking for Della, and I know where she is."

"Where?"

If Harry noticed Eagan's eyes were the color of obsidian or that Tenn's were gleaming gold, he didn't say anything. Instead, he started shuffling back down the street.

"This way. I saw her and Daniel run into an alley down this way. Two young men followed them in. There was something definitely off about those two. Something about the way they moved. Sorry if I'm not making myself clear."

Actually, he was. The young vamps were in predator mode, moving with the inhuman grace and power of their kind. At their young age, they wouldn't stand a chance against Eagan or even Tennessee, but the two humans were no match for them.

At the next corner, Harry pointed down the cross street. "See that alley? That's where they went. I'll stay here out of the way."

Eagan clapped the older man on the shoulder. "Thanks, Harry. We'll make sure she's safe."

"See that you do, since I'm not up to doing it myself." His voice wavered. "She's like a daughter to me."

Eagan understood a man's need to be useful when it came to protecting those he cared about. He handed Harry his cell phone and flashed his badge. "Hit two on the speed dial and tell my lieutenant where we are. When my backup gets here, point them toward the right alley."

Harry stood taller. "I'll do that. Now get going."

"Tenn, you take this side while I come in from the far end. Hopefully I'll be able to drive them back in your direction before they get to her."

Tennessee nodded. Eagan waited for him to get in position before using his strength and speed to go up over the buildings to the opposite end of the alley to make sure they trapped the young vamps in between them.

Before returning to street level, he closed his eyes briefly, trying to get a clear reading on what Della was feeling. Fear definitely. Worry, most likely for Daniel. And pain.

That did it. The bastards would die. With fangs out, Eagan dropped down two stories back to the ground and took the hunt to the hunters.

DELLA'S CHEST HURT. She wasn't dressed warm enough for the cold, but that wasn't what had her shivering. Daniel wasn't faring much better as the two of them huddled in the corner behind a stack of trash cans. They'd only meant to stop long enough to catch their breath, but their pursuers were closing in.

She and Daniel had tried everything to lose them, but nothing had worked. She'd also lost her pack when she'd first seen them trying to drag Daniel into an abandoned building, so she didn't have her cell phone to call for help. When she'd swung the bag at the closest one's head, it had connected with a satisfying thud. However, Daniel's attacker had latched on to the strap and ripped it out of her hand.

At least it had distracted him long enough for Daniel to get free. He'd grabbed her hand and dragged her back down the street at a dead run. Unfortunately, they were in a section of town where few shops were open, leaving them no easy place to take sanctuary.

They had to get moving again before they were cornered here, where it was unlikely anyone would hear them calling for help. She started to reach for Daniel's hand when she heard Eagan's voice faintly whisper, "Stay where you are, Della. We're on our way."

When she didn't immediately spot Eagan, she whispered, "Where are you?"

Daniel's eyes, already wide with fright, zeroed in on her face. "I'm right here, Della."

She squeezed his hand. "Not you. Eagan. Didn't you hear him say he was coming?"

When Daniel slowly shook his head, she closed her eyes to listen harder. "Eagan?"

When he answered, his words were stronger this time, but felt as if they were brushing against the inside of her head. "We're almost there. Me and your friend Tennessee. Just stay hidden. Those two punks tracking you are between you and us. I'm afraid they'll use you as hostages if we rush them."

Good grief, he was using telepathy! She tried thinking her response. "I think they're like you, Eagan. Well, not like you, but your kind."

His mental sigh was telling. "Yes, they are. Don't worry. They're no match for us, but it's likely to turn ugly. I'm sorry you and your young friend got caught up in this."

Then the connection broke. A rock bounced off the wall behind her followed by a nasty laugh.

"Hey, kid, come out and play. Who knows, maybe we'll let your pretty lady friend live."

Daniel actually started to stand up, but she jerked him back down by her side. "Stay still. Help is coming."

He clearly didn't believe her and struggled to get free. "I got you into this, Della. Let me distract them while you run. You can send help."

Like those two would let him survive that long. "They can't let me live, Daniel. We both know that. And you must not think much of me if you think I'd abandon you now."

He still fought her, panic taking over. "Then we'll both die."

His voice had grown louder, but knowing who was after them meant it didn't matter. They'd probably heard every word they'd said. The two punks couldn't be more than a few feet away now. She braced herself to fight with everything she had.

Then there they were, with their gleaming eyes looking like black holes and their fangs ghostly white against their lower lips. One jabbed the other in the ribs with his elbow.

"Hey, look what I got you for Christmas. Dinner for two! She's even wearing Santa on her shirt."

As the two kept themselves entertained, they failed to notice they were no longer alone in the alley. Eagan stood behind them, looking like an avenging angel. The two young vampires might be dangerous, but they didn't radiate pure death in the way Eagan did.

She should find him every bit as terrifying as they were, if not more so. All she felt was relief.

He latched onto the back of their collars and sent them both flying across the alley to bounce against a brick wall. Planting himself firmly between them and Della, he looked back over his shoulder at her.

"Go that way, and you'll run straight into Tennessee. He'll make sure you get back to the diner safely. Some of my friends will arrive any second. Don't be scared of them. They're the good guys."

"Will you come find me when you've—"

She broke off midsentence, not wanting to think about what was going to happen to the two young vampires who were already back on their feet and attacking.

"Go, Della. Now."

She grabbed Daniel and hauled him down the alley. But before she reached the other end, she stopped long enough to think one last thought.

"Come back to me, Eagan. Don't make me spend Christmas without you."

Then she ran to where Tennessee stood waiting.

CHAPTER ELEVEN

DELLA THOUGHT ABOUT CLOSING the diner early, but it was Christmas Eve and her friends were counting on her. So she'd showered, changed into another Christmas shirt and forced her lips to curve up in a smile she didn't really feel.

No word from Eagan. Not last night and not all day. She kept telling herself that he'd gotten caught up in his case. Odd that she found him being an undercover cop harder to believe than that he was a vampire. By the time she and Daniel had reached Tenn at the end of the alley, half a dozen men all flashing badges and fangs had arrived.

One had stopped long enough to introduce himself as Eagan's boss, Lieutenant Hughes. After making sure that she was all right, he'd warned her that Eagan might be tied up for a while and not to worry, that he'd come around. Then he'd winked at her and headed off down the alley. She wasn't sure exactly what he'd meant.

Someone had driven Daniel home. Later, the teenager had called, all excited. His mother was moving them to a better apartment where she'd be managing the building in return for a salary and free rent. Della suspected Eagan was behind the family's windfall, bless him. On the other hand, after taking a brief statement from her, she hadn't heard another word from the police over what had happened in the alley.

That had been twenty-four hours ago.

Tenn was in the kitchen whistling an off-key rendition of one of her favorite Christmas carols. When he spotted her, he nodded and kept stirring the pot of vegetable soup she'd asked him to make for Christmas Day.

"Have we been busy?"

"Not bad. Enough to keep us from getting bored. Not enough to spoil my good mood."

He studied her. "How about you? Have you recovered from yesterday?"

"Mostly." She ran her hands up and down her arms at the memory. "I never got around to thanking you for coming to rescue us. You have no idea how dangerous those guys were."

"Yeah, actually I do." He set the spoon back down on the counter. "You seem to be handling the fact that your boyfriend is a vampire pretty well. Would it surprise you to learn that your fry cook gets all furry every full moon?"

She swallowed hard as she stared into his eyes, now more gold than caramel-brown. "Uh, all things considered, not all that much. I'm not sure Eagan would appreciate being called my boyfriend, though."

"Then he's an idiot. Now get out of my kitchen. You're in my way."

She ignored the order long enough to give him a quick hug on her way by. "Your secret is safe with me."

He squeezed her back. "I know. And you might try calling him. I'm betting he'll come."

When she pulled out her cell phone, Tenn took it from her. "Not that way. Talk to him the way you did in the alley."

"You could hear us?"

"No, but that's how vampires communicate with their, uh, well, damn. Just try it and see what happens."

She wasn't so sure it was a good idea. One night of hot sex didn't a commitment make, no matter how perfect it had been. Out in the dining room, she looked around for something to do. Harry was at his usual table talking with Lupe.

The old man waved her over. "There you are, young lady! We were getting worried about you. Come sit with us."

Lupe scooted over to make room for her. "I can only stay a minute, then I should get busy."

"I hope you had no lasting effects from last night, Della. Thank goodness that young man of yours and his fellow detectives arrived when they did. I was just telling Lupe how he and Tenn were able to track you. I may have pointed them toward the alley, but I'm convinced they would have found you even without my help."

Then Harry smiled at her. "Vampires and werewolves have such heightened senses, you know. Back in my prime, I would've given them a run for their money, but we fae are at a distinct disadvantage with so much metal around. Most of my abilities have faded away completely."

Was she the only purely human in the room? Evidently, considering Lupe's eyes were the same shade of burnished gold as Tenn's. Her friend merely shrugged.

"I admit I was wrong about your Eagan."

Della accepted two more hugs before moving on to greet the few remaining customers. When they were gone, she'd close up shop. She'd already handed out most of the gifts from under the tree. The remaining ones were for the friends she knew would be back tomorrow for soup and games.

And the one she'd put there for Eagan. She fingered the ribbon on the package. Maybe after she locked up, she'd give him a call. Just friend-to-friend, to make sure he was all right. After all, that's what Christmas was all about: hope, friendship and love.

Her gargoyle ornament caught her attention, his eyes reflecting the twinkle of the lights and his dimpled smile showing off his big teeth to perfection. Like she'd always thought, nothing said Christmas like a smile and a flash of fangs. She just hadn't realized how right on target she'd been for all these years.

For the first time all day, her own smile felt genuine, her heart lighter. Oh, yeah, she was definitely going to make that call.

As much as Eagan had wanted to destroy the two vampires who'd cornered Della and Daniel, he'd restrained himself. They were only little fish in a much-bigger pond. In exchange for their help tracking down the barracuda at the top of the food chain, he'd let them live. Bruised and battered, yeah, but they'd heal. Della would've been proud of him for his forbearance.

It didn't help that no one had ever explained the rules to them, the ones that helped supernaturals survive in the human world. Whoever had turned them had callously sent them out on the streets to entice desperate teenagers with the promise of money for blood. The lieutenant was looking into placing the two with a friend of his to see if they could be redeemed. If not, well, at least they'd been given a second chance. It was up to them to do something with it.

The bottom line was that Eagan had been so caught up in the case, the rest of the night and most of the day had passed by before he'd had a chance to come up for air. Sometime during those long hours, he'd come to the realization that he didn't want to go back to his condo alone.

No, the only place he wanted to be was decorated with checkered tablecloths, lace curtains, and had a dress code that mandated T-shirts with a holiday theme. Thank goodness the stores were still open because he definitely had some last-minute shopping to do.

"MERRY CHRISTMAS and good night! See you all tomorrow!"

Della waited until her friends were all out of sight before she stepped out onto the sidewalk herself. She closed her eyes and opened her thoughts.

"Eagan, please come back."

A pair of warm hands settled on her shoulders. "I'm already here."

Her heart did backflips in her chest. "It's about time."

Eagan slid his arms around her waist and pulled her against the hard planes of his chest. "Sorry, but the case took longer than I expected, and I hadn't done my Christmas shopping yet. I didn't want to be the only one here tomorrow without presents for everyone."

She basked in his warmth along her back. "I wasn't sure you'd come."

"I almost didn't. I have to be honest with you, Della. Living with a vampire is hard enough, but my job only makes it that much worse. When I get tied up in a case, I can be gone for days at a time."

He nuzzled her neck. "But then I realized the only present I wanted for Christmas was you. That is, if you'll have me. Not sure how it happened, but I love you, Della."

She let his truth settle deep inside her. "I love you, too, Eagan. And I don't care how long you're gone as long as you promise to always come back to me."

He gently spun her around to face him and held out a small box. "Wild horses, werewolves and old elves couldn't keep me away. Marry me?"

"Oh, yes." She slipped the ring on her finger and then leaped into his arms. His kiss was everything she'd ever hoped for. More than a little breathless, she retreated a step. "We'd better take this inside."

Then she blinked. "What are you wearing?"

Eagan grinned and held his coat open to give her a better look. It was a black T-shirt. The huge snowman on the front was sporting its own pair of particularly large canine teeth, which glowed in the dark. Underneath it said, The Holidays Are Fangtastic!

Her vampire looked darn cute and so proud of himself. "I'm glad you like it because I got you one just like it. Thought we could be a matched set tomorrow."

"You bet. Now sweep me off my feet! I'm in the mood to do a little private celebrating before the others get here tomorrow."

His eyes flashed black as he tossed her over his shoulder and bounded up the steps.

"I definitely like the way you think, lady, and I can't wait to unwrap the best present I've ever had—you."

* * * * *